ALL FALL DOWN

All Fall Down

— STORIES —

Mary Caponegro

— quasi omnipotent narrators
That course seamlessly & effortlessly
across spatial, temporal & ~~emo~~
psychological terrain But that
Become Bogged down in a present
That is none of those But is emotional

— The weight of the wait, the
heft of the far emotional present

COFFEE HOUSE PRESS

MINNEAPOLIS :: 2009

Coffee House Press books are available to the trade through our primary distributor, Consortium Book Sales & Distribution, www.cbsd.com. For personal orders, catalogs, or other information, write to: Coffee House Press, 79 Thirteenth Avenue NE, Suite 110, Minneapolis, MN 55413.

Coffee House Press is a nonprofit literary publishing house. Support from private foundations, corporate giving programs, government programs, and generous individuals helps make the publication of our books possible. We gratefully acknowledge their support in detail in the back of this book.

Good books are brewing at coffeehousepress.org

LIBRARY OF CONGRESS CATALOGING-IN-PUBLICATION DATA
Library of Congress Cataloging-in-Publication Data

Caponegro, Mary, 1956–
All fall down : stories / Mary Caponegro.
p. cm.
ISBN-13: 978-1-56689-226-1 (alk. paper)
I. Title.
PS3553.A5877A79 2009
813'.54—DC22
2008052723

PRINTED IN THE UNITED STATES

ACKNOWLEDGMENTS
I am grateful to Bard College and Syracuse University for sabbatical time used in creating this collection. I also wish to thank the Lannan Foundation and the American Academy in Rome for space, inspiration, and solicitude. And much gratitude to Dr. Connie Dong for generously sharing her ophthalmological expertise.

The stories "Last Resort Retreat," "Ashes Ashes We All Fall Down," "Junior Achievement," and an excerpt of "The Translator" first appeared in *Conjunctions*.

"A Daughter in Time" appeared in *Bridge* on line. An excerpt of "Ill-Timed" is included in the anthology of writing and Heide Hatry scuptures entitled *Heads and Tales* published by Charta Art Books.

FOR MICHAEL

Last Resort Retreat

As to the majesty of the animal in the road, its beauty, formidable and fragile both, its poignant vulnerability, well, all that is lost in the crudity of her scream, her bark; that's how he hears it anyway, and thinks he'd find the deer less skittish, on a daily basis, than his wife: her ever-fretful, hawking gaze and blaring trumpet vigilance. Poor, nevermore frolicsome deer, maimed-by-him-with-her-as-accessory, when what he would have wished, in all honesty—the honesty of his momentary rage—was to shut her up, for once, for all the love and habituals, to have, through any means, a moment's peace. It's snowing, always snow or rain or fog on this road; to him it's no big deal, but all it takes is one flake, drop, or patch to get her started: the anxiety machine—women and weather, what *is* that about, and wouldn't you know that this would be the road to their theoretical "recovery"; is it symbolic? He suspects so, she too, and as the weekend wears on, they will come to believe, increasingly, that each activity, each event, is both symbolic and contrived.

Left, right, right to the Last Resort Retreat—that's how she memorized it, so keen as she is on infantile mnemonics: yet another item on the list of her compulsive what-we-musn't-forget cosmologies. When they're finally done with all the winding, to the accompaniment of her whining, "Have we gone too far? We might have passed it. Are you sure we're on the right road?"; (he) "Don't *need* to ask directions, no one's here to ask"; (as she) "Don't go so fast, *please*"; (he) "*You* drive, then"; (she) "All right, fine"; (he) "No thanks, I take it back, that's all we need"; and then, of course, the deer, and finally, quite a bit the worse for wear (though obviously not to the deer's degree), they reach the elusive rural road, the final left before they are (theoretically) twice righted by the Last Resort Retreat.

Sometimes she can step outside of it, of them: their dance, their schtick, their trance, whatever new age term their couple chemistry—lately so volatile—deserves. Look at the two of them, she thinks: they could be any couple really, any couple certain when they started up of lifelong passion, at least guaranteed compatibility; were they not uncannily compatible? Had not everyone remarked? But lately everything seemed tentative, they felt certain only occasionally and when certain: of inevitable demise.

What really is the point, she wonders, if he has no interest, no receptivity, not a shred of generosity, about this project, this weekend, this intensive retreat that by the time it's done will feel in its duration as many years as they've been married? Oh, poor dumb dead deer, I'll take your place, she thinks, envying the leaden flesh now nothing but a memory in the rearview mirror, wanting to have the guts, the benighted recklessness, the trusting spontaneity to leap across a road, without vacillation, into oncoming traffic, traffic likely consisting at this moment exclusively of cars whose destination is identical to theirs, a destination far too embarrassing to admit, too compromising to reveal in other than a whisper to anyone other than this poor innocent deceased creature whose last breath will be forever mingled with their memory of the Last Resort Retreat, for which she'd seen a flyer (also something on the internet), nothing more—what were they getting into, he'd complained—no references, no guarantees, already its effect was exacerbation rather than amelioration.

"Come in and let's get started, sign these waivers please."

No, it can't be that these two clowns beckoning with forms and pencils are *in charge?* And what a sorry looking set of "peers"; from day one he'll refer to them as contestants (as if they'd accidentally signed up for some game show the objective of which is consummate humiliation: tune in for *The Old-ly-wed Game!*—not a laugh- but a cry-track); shed their boots, get in the circle, is this kindergarten? "Take you to your cabin later, since you're late." Oh, punitive, is that it? Make them suffer publicly; what if they have to pee? (All those seventies EST anecdotes flood his brain.) She *always* has to: infernal recurring bladder infection—is particularly prone whenever any hint of conjugal connection arises. Her idea, to do this stupid thing, and she's the one that makes them late—for what?

For kitty litter, or was it trash bags, not to mention the unending existential dilemma of what to wear.

"It's a retreat, for chrissake, not a prom. What are you doing in the closet
all this time," he'd yelled up to her, "masturbating?"

"Could you blame me?"

Sometimes she could be a real downer.

Pen and paper are being passed out. Like the first day of school? He
begins to write atop the page: *My summer vacation,* then nudges her to display his mischief. He dares them to solicit a title for his composition: *My
marriage, my time-has-not-been-flying-for-some-time-I-am-not-having-fun
marriage. My whose-idea-was-this-anyway-get-me-out-of-here marriage. My
hell-and-welcome-to-it, etc.* One presumes the rest of the couples to be in
dire straits as well or they wouldn't be subjecting themselves to such compromising tripe. But it turns out all the form-and-pencil-waving morons
want is some pedestrian, why-are-you-here-what-do-you-hope-to-gain sort
of info; oh god, he hates to pay through the nose for such scams: you pay
and you do all the work. And now the first activity.

Groups are being formed. Well, isn't that original? Placed on the left are
all the couples who consider themselves to have healthy, active sex lives. On
the right: those for whom sex is no longer . . . viable. Laughter at the disproportionate size of the groups.

"Do you envy them?" A few heads nodding. "Do you think there is anything in this group that the other group might envy?"

"Yeah, more time," says someone from the left.

"More sleep": another.

Under his breath, <u>Norm</u> volunteers, "More jerking off!"

"Let's ask them," the guy in charge continues.

"Well, yes, I have to say," says a weepy woman from the right group, "I
feel even worse to go from connection on that grand a scale to missing each
other in all other important aspects of our lives, you know?"

The female facilitator, earnest yet imperious, comments, "We might
want to note here that the tendency seems to be so far for men to do the
joking and women, the feeling."

"Yeah, and how do you think *I* feel to have my wife sob every time she
has an orgasm?"—from the trembling voiced woman's formidable looking
husband.

"Now, there'll be no defensiveness in this session. Here are the rules: we
demarcate the space. No attacking, no defending except in the ways we

prescribe, which we will soon provide you, and which, we promise you, will be ample. Isn't that right, Pierre?"

"Yes, that's absolutely right, Elizabeth." (It's like a game show, or a news hour with two chummy hosts.) "Aside from those constraints, there is an honor code. Sign on the dotted line, couples. These contracts bind you to your best intentions. Hug your partner, as wholeheartedly as you can. Now back to small groups."

"Docedo ho ho ho. Hey, when is milk and cookies? Or will it be s'mores?"

"Norm, please behave."

And as if to back him up, a pitcher and plate appear, although the milk is soy and the cookies not nostalgic chocolate chip but something more resembling molten granola.

At the break, they finally get to "check in" to their cabin: rustic, but serviceable (just the sort of place, he thinks, she'd never go if *he* proposed a woodsy "getaway"—but hey, whatever).

"Look, a private bath!" Thank god, a private bath, she thinks, with him so antisocial, not to mention her cystitis. He paces, leans against the wall, surveys the place. In his peripheral vision, he sees his wife hanging up what appears to be her wedding dress, and remembers talk of some absurd "reenactment" on the final day. In the humble cabin, the garment looks like Cinderella's dowry. The tux he'd worn would never fit him now, that's for sure. He stands there, in a kind of stupor, watching her unpack her toiletries.

"Why are you brushing your teeth now?"

And he claims *she* nags. "I guess it's my business if I feel like—"

"Forget it, I can't hear you through the foam."

She takes the toothbrush out. "Who knows, I might just want to kiss somebody!" No sooner has she rinsed and spit than the bell rings; all the cabins start to empty out for round two. "Come on, we can't be late again."

"What'll they do, send us to the principal? Or maybe we'll get lucky and be expelled!"

"Speak for yourself. Tell me something, do you think the facilitators are married?"

"How should I know?"

"I asked you do you *think*, not do you *know*?"

"What, to each other?"

"Duhhh!"

"Well, they could be married . . . separately, outside this circus, and have a . . . professional affiliation. If you can call this bullshit professional. Besides, I think he's gay. You have the key, right?"

"Yeah, I've got it. You think every non-He-Man man is gay."

"He's not the one you want to kiss, I hope?"

"The one I want to kiss would be my husband, *idiot!* Not that he deserves the wish."

"You know, I think I've had enough of this whole thing already, Martha."

"We just got here, Norm. Could you make just a teeny-weeny effort to cooperate?" She strides ahead. He catches up, accomplished almost instantly, his legs by far the longer.

"Yeah, what's in it for me? Just kidding." (Oh, there she goes, all sulky; he really *was* just kidding.)

When they reach the main building, there is on every chair some doughy looking object, like a bolster—can it be . . . a dildo?—some gigantic chunky surrogate because some secret questionnaire revealed she wasn't satisfied? Did anyone ask him if *he* was satisfied? The diameter of a small tree trunk really. So they've come all this way, laid out all this cash, for their enlightened facilitators to say, in effect, give up, you're better off with sex toys than your husband's dick? And is there any solace for said dick? It has, he supposes, to fend for itself.

"This, gentlemen,"—Ms. Cheekbones is making an announcement—"is your partner's throat." (There is a collective gasp from the female portion of the room—and a certain new focus from the male contingent.) "For all intents and purposes. When you feel most frustrated in the course of these five days, you can grasp this special high-density viscoelastic foam and squeeze. The heat of your hands will make it conform."

"And what do *we* get?" says an indignant woman, who had held it like a trophy before its identity metamorphosed, as it were, in her hands. "To bake a cake?"

"In this case, no, you don't . . . create," the puling male facilitator says. "You, ladies, you get to—"

Cheekbones chimes in, "O.K., let's not beat around the bush . . . Castrate."

Once the horror, bemusement, indignation, and I-want-my-money-back protests subside, they allow themselves, one at a time, to be schooled in pseudoviolence. But their novice practice must not take place, they are told, in mixed company. Just as in bathhouses, the clientele is segregated; here, when the women take their oversized plastic bats to do the deed, the men will be sent back to their individual cabins to commence composing their legal defense for the faux murder they are about to commit (or have just committed), and when the men's hands collectively prepare to grip the vessel of breath, there will be a changing of the guard, and the women are to take up their pens and make their husbands history, by each composing as earnestly as circumstances will allow, a eulogy. These randomly gendered writing tasks will themselves then be switched, such that by week's end everyone will be thoroughly murdered and thoroughly mourned. All are assigned the composition of a private "missed list," comprised of all the attributes a husband or wife will miss most in a (hypothetically) permanently absent spouse.

"Now, sit down, each of you, sit down and hear me out. I will tell you something very sad." (Something in those eyes is undeniably hypnotic.) "This is what you do each day through your misunderstandings: think of a dog that grips someone by the throat. Or the expression, to have a man by the balls. What do you feel when you reflect on this?"

"Do you ever get the feeling these two might not be quite . . . legitimate?"

"So, squeeze or slice to your heart's delight, any time of day or night."

"What's this, the ax murderer's anthem?"

"Norm, hush, I can't hear. This is the most important part."

"We provide you these tools and this room to get it out of your system, but after any action with our special props, you are obliged to then sit back and observe your handiwork, and ponder the consequences of your repeated actions. The pondering, in fact, may lead you to emotional areas you have never traversed. This navigation will of course be your responsibility. Any questions?"

"May I ask why you chose these two . . . images?" someone asks.

"If you don't mind," the unctuous male facilitator says, "we'd rather let you answer that yourselves before you leave the Last Resort Retreat."

"Other questions?"

"What's the point of all this?"

"The point, participants, is this: We provide you hypothetical space to go to your emotional limit, and then we provide the means to imagine the worst-case extremes that would result. Think of it as a controlled environment in which you can be out of control. Through these means, we hope to help you achieve catharsis, healing, and ultimately, reunion."

"How many times do you think they've delivered *that* speech?"

Everyone receives another break after the segregated tutorials, to allow them to process all the information and to resume their primary pairings. (Solitary challenges lie ahead, such as a night apart in the solitary confinement cabin complete with barred windows.) On go coats and boots again and out stream couples. "I need a nap," says Norm, and when they enter the cabin, he immediately flings his body like a board across the bed.

"Oh look," says Martha, "chocolates on the pillow! Just like a—"

"Let me guess"—in chorus: "bed and breakfast!" Rolls his eyes. "I'll need more than chocolate to recuperate from this day."

"The day's not over yet." She bends to scoop the foil-wrapped candy from the bed, declaring, "Well, I *never* say no to chocolate."

"You should do a commercial." Women and chocolate, what's *that* about? Like fetal alcoholism, they're born addicted. "The bed's made too. I thought you said you locked the door."

"I said I took the key, I don't remember if I locked it."

"So where do they hide the chambermaids?" Austere Elizabeth in a little black, aproned number: provocative image. Bothers him some. "I don't like the idea of people coming in when we're not here."

"I wouldn't worry about Last Resort robbers. Or privacy either." She peers down and picks one up. "You know what? They're not chocolates, honey. They're condoms."

He opens one eye, squints at the contents of her hand. "What is that— to make us feel diseased?"

"No, they're a backup, I suppose, in case we didn't bring any, knowing we'd be too busy psuedostrangling and castrating each other and so forth. I don't know, maybe they're for all the men whose tubes aren't tied."

"Once our dicks get lopped off, it's a moot point, isn't it?"

"You make it sound like the violence is for real."

"I thought that was the idea: invest fully in the illusion."

"Or maybe it's a prop to help us dump all our bad history and renew our curiosity, to pretend we just met at a bar or something."

"Yeah, or at a marriage retreat."

"You know, you're really a downer sometimes."

"Take that back." He rolls over onto his stomach.

"o.k., you're right, that isn't true, you're really a downer *all* the time."

"I'm a hard-nosed realist, darling, if you haven't figured that out yet."

"Give me another sixteen years and maybe I'll catch on."

"Doesn't sound like you *want* another sixteen years." He buries his head in the pillow; she firmly pries it from its shroud, and pushes his shoulder until he's lying on his side, puts her face beside his.

"Don't do that pouting thing, o.k.? What I *want* is a marriage that doesn't feel like a wake."

"We'll throw a party then. A Sour Sixteen party, what do you say?"

"I say that doesn't deserve a response. Maybe they're *chocolate-covered* condoms."

"Just don't swallow, ha ha; you'd choke and then I wouldn't have the satisfaction of metastrangling you anymore!"

"You know, your jokes are pretty violent on the whole. Do you think *brutal sense of humor* is an accurate description?"

"Twenty-some-odd years ago in college you called it *gutsy and original.*"

And he was right, she had. Everyone had. Her first exposure to his scathing humor was his comedy routine at the Friday night open mike. Everyone said he should take his act on the road. They praised its edge, its originality. Made comparisons to Lenny Bruce, to even Dick Gregory. And she, along with many of her peers, was in awe of the combination of intelligence and audacity that fueled his anti-Nixon rants as well as his critiques of conservatism, materialism, "suburbanism, sexual-uptightism, domestic-nuclear-monogamism, yeasty-no-thinkism," to use his words, his sort of wordplay. An intense guy with big dark eyes, muscular build, and a black T-shirt that he sweated straight through by the time his act was done. She watched him pull it from his body once he was off the stage, somehow entranced, in spite of herself, by the muscles of his bare back. He turned by chance and saw her, no doubt also saw her blush, and on an impulse, smiling, threw it in mock gesture like a bride does her bouquet to all the single girls, but threw it straight to her. She never washed it, never gave it back, not even when, ten years later, he stood beside her as she threw a real bridal bouquet, and never confessed, even after they'd shared countless acts of sex, how many times she had fantasized with that cloth memento between her thighs. (And that was twenty-seven years ago!) Wasn't change a sad thing sometimes? Now his trenchant humor just seemed grating, no longer seductive or unique, certainly not sexy; larger-than-life captivating had turned, like milk gone sour, to just plain annoying. She couldn't pinpoint when. She has no clear idea why. All she wondered then was why, of all the girls he could have taken home that night, and what's more, gone steady with, etc., did he choose her, wholesome Martha, whose only prior boyfriend was Brian, the nerdy bio major—oh, the

She

privilege of having Norman Cohen's attentions (despite the condescending surprise on the part of his admirers)—indeed it made her blush and now she cringes to think of blushing then. And then feels guilty.

"Everything changes."

"Oh, that's profound."

"Subversive at fifty just doesn't cut it, Norm. I hate to tell you; it isn't charming anymore."

"I'm forty-nine, you're forty-seven. And I don't give a shit about charm."

The bell rings again in the main building, to signal the end of break and the resumption of structured activity.

"Who would *ever* have guessed! Be bold and bald then!"

"What? Where did *that* come from?"

"Your head is close to hairless. Go all the way, why don't you? Cut off that stupid ponytail. It's thin and gray!" yuck!

"I'll meet you over there, when you're ready to be civil."

"When *I'm* civil? That's a good one. I'll stay right here."

"I'm gonna te-*ell*: Martha's playing hooky."

"Hooky nothing, gotta write your eulogy."

"All right, suit yourself. I'll bring you back a veggie burger, if you're good."

What really is the point, he wonders, if she has no resilience, no willingness to roll with the punches, no stamina for the long haul? Though she would claim the greater investment in their relationship, she's the one who dwells on every minor infraction—will not let it go. She has demands, oh does she ever have demands, but he has faith. She calls him oblivious but he thinks all the molehills of their differences are made mountainous by her willful histrionics—by her hyperbolic, melodramatic preoccupation with the so-called problematic aspects of their scrutinized-to-death relationship. All she does is carry on, whereas he can overlook occasional peccadilloes on her part; he can, in the other, *positive* sense, *carry on*, from day to day: a working, functional, satisfying, healthy, rather than discussion-saturated, crisis-driven, relationship. Not sure

But it *was* once healthy—living, breathing, satisfying, wasn't it? Their marriage? Until recently? At least initially? Before money woes, miscarriages, stagnancy, silences, intolerances, mutual disillusionments never made explicit, before their marriage landed up against a concrete wall. When their relationship was supple instead of brittle. Nubile. When she looked at him with something besides resignation; was it ever admiration? When she yearned for him. And he for her. When they considered themselves *made for* rather than *stuck with* each other. When their relationship was light instead of laden? Oh, he remembers light, one image of inexpungable light. Moth (the nickname she used to love) was far too nervous on their wedding day to be considered a radiant bride, and never pregnant long enough to be radiant in that traditional maternal way, but oh, was she luminous the day that declared to him their physical compatibility. It was July. First visit after the school year had ended. First opportunity to be spared negotiating dorm rooms and roommates, etc. Her parents' private cabana on the shore. They had been dodging waves in the Atlantic Ocean that sultry, humid day. Between the waves, he lifted her into his arms and carried her, making like King Kong and leaving footprints in the dark, wet sand, then spontaneously took her hand and ran back to the cabin, to the cramped outdoor stall where they showered off the sand, and peeled off each other's clammy suits: her blue and green tie-dyed bikini—he still remembers how it looked, how she looked *in* it, despite her ever-self-conscious "I'm too chunky/dumpy/hippy/ busty" bullshit.

"None of the above," he always said, and says. "Stand corrected, zaftig goddess; you, babe, are my brick house." And he knows there is some feature of her physical being, some pheromonal andrenalin that made possible the spontaneous lifting of her short but buxom 5'-3" body while the gulls flew above them. Can't even now remember how, on an impulse, he managed to hoist her all the way up to his shoulders. Her buttocks in his hands, her breasts falling softly over his head, as he made himself her pedestal, holding her more intimately than if she were his infant, his pooch or kitty, his doll or trophy; and if that power to be both her possessor and protector was an incredible turn-on, if so, then so what? It was to *her*, too, he was sure, even if she never said; he felt her ecstasy as he made her still more buoyant than the ocean could. When they had showered off the sand, he wouldn't let her wash what was inside: "I'll do it for you," with his tongue, and he can still taste how the ocean's salt and her juices melded into something tangy: tart and sweet together, and he never felt so capable. She said, "You'll hurt your back." "I won't," he said, "I'm Superman." But somehow he'd turned into Bozo.

And why not be true to that destiny, he thinks, fatalistically.

In an unobtrusive manner, between sessions, Monsieur Pierre and Madame Elizabeth take orders for the evening meal, gliding down the aisles where everyone is dutifully getting "in touch with" the symbolic foam shapes that lie under their hands, as if each were fashioning clay on a potter's wheel, intuitively calibrating pressure to yield form and create contour. "Vegetarian or venison, vegetarian or venison," like a stewardess making rounds up and down every aisle, he thinks. Chicken or beef. Coffee, tea, me. He sees her for a moment in stockings, short navy-blue skirt and tucked-in shirt, maybe mock blowing into an inflatable vest—he's never seen a stewardess that tall, though—but then she's once again in the long, flared gypsy skirt and blouse, a flowing figure intoning veggie or venison, veggie or venison.

Martha, having kept her distance, feels suddenly famished, and makes her way over to the main building, noticing for the first time how its spacious white interior echoes the landscape. One could be peaceful here. Then she hears commotion, and peers into the auditorium to see food flying everywhere. Veggie burgers are being thrown like frisbees and someone has organized a subversive volleyball game with the phallus-necks as surrogates for a ball. Someone even got hold of a badminton racquet, it looks like. Someone who couldn't resist the lure of a metaliteral shuttlecock. She has a feeling of foreboding, and as her eye moves center stage, she sees her husband, undoubtedly the instigator of all this, Norm, the court jester, with two of the dense foam cylinders affixed to his head (lord knows how he made them stick), prancing about like a mascot at halftime, with his potbelly wobbling, mimicking a Mouseketeer, distorting the lyrics in his typical, infantile, improvisatory fashion (spelling out his own private anthem), "Forever let us hold our dickheads high!" but by the time he's gotten to the refrain: M-I-D / D-L-E / MIDDLE A-G-E," she is on her way out with head down, too mortified to stick around. Unfortunately, someone recognizes her affiliation, corners her before she can escape.

"Your husband is a riot. How refreshing to find someone with a sense of humor to offset all this piety."

"If you say so." Martha hopes her burning cheeks are somehow not discernible.

"Tell me, though, how did he manage to make those velcro patches stick to his head?"

"Things stick better to skin than hair!" Finally she makes her exit and races for the cabin.

Who really gives a shit, she thinks, if he's alive or dead, for all the good it's done to have a living, breathing spouse beside her day and night, the contrast of their early married years to these last few, like day to night, as gasping passion cedes, inevitably, to snoring. All those marital clichés that she, that they, resisted, felt irrelevant to *their* relationship, *their* future: who knew or cared then whose better half was who to whom; but now, no doubt about it: two worse halves don't make a whole. Martha and Norm, once a single entity, are a mere sum of parts that no longer cohere, or did they ever? Too remote to imagine a past existing before anger, during fervor, in the thick of incalculable ardor; yet she remembers the sensation of glorious abandon, when sheer certainty (hormonally, emotionally, etceterally) dictated *this*, good woman, is *the one*, and seize the day, this is, *at last*, the one, and who knows if there'll ever be another? And she was in her twenties then! It all comes down to this, she thinks: I'm fucking fed up with this nurtureless environment. But what sort of eulogy is that? Try it as a letter maybe. *Dear Norm, you're dead, you ain't no good to me no more.* Even she can see how sophomoric *that* sounds. (Bogus blues song, he would say.) Oh fuck it, try it later.

In the castration cubicle, she tries to put more oomph into her swing, with Pierre's coaching. His calm solicitousness is like a salve. He seems incapable of irritation as he patiently explains, then demonstrates, then asks her permission to hold her arms as she holds the bat. She senses he's athletic underneath his elegant appearance. A bat girl (doubling as waitress and chambermaid, no doubt), retrieves the fallen phalluses and reattaches them to the velcro bullseye centered on the wall. When Martha's broken a sweat, she starts to get into the literal swing of it, but once Pierre moves on to coach the woman in the next cubicle, instead of being exhilarated by the exercise, it makes her feel fatigued and depressed. Maybe it's her turn for a nap. But then she has to confront Norm. She's got a better plan. She won't even let on that she saw him.

"How's the writing going?"

"Fine. I got A in argumentative/persuasive writing, remember?"

"Yeah, I helped you write those papers, if you recall."

"You couldn't have; it was sophomore year; you weren't there yet."

"No, that was expository writing."

"What, did you memorize my transcript?"

"You showed me the papers, remember? They impressed me. Except for the grammar."

"Whatever. So how'd you do on the chopping block?"

"In the end I couldn't kill you, I just ripped your dick off a bunch of times and wished you dead."

"Good job."

"I'm not even tall enough to kill you."

"That's logical."

"You know, I never liked that word."

"*Tall?*"

"No."

"Oh, *kill?*"

"No, *dick*. The word *dick.*"

"That's true, you never did. *What is the sound of one dick ripping?*"

"Is that a Zen C-o-h-e-n?"

"Pretty clever. But who can concentrate around here? To tell you the truth, I'm a long way from done, I feel ambivalent about the whole exercise, and I would do much better after a few Zs. Do you hear them moaning next door? It's like being trapped in a bad porno, but on the other side of the screen! I just want a nap, this whole retreat is way too organized. Jesus, what a racket."

"Take it easy."

"If this is their idea of audio-visual aids, we could have gone to a no-tell motel instead—saved a lot of trouble and money. Hey, have you got a quarter?"

"You need to make a phone call *now?*"

"No, I want to see if there's a slot somewhere on this bed to put a coin in—to make it vibrate. Good grief, why don't they cut it out?" he yells, shaking the bed violently with his arms, then attacking the wall.

"Norm, *you* cut it out, stop banging on the wall, we'll be in even more debt if we have to pay for damages. Besides, we're supposed to hear them, remember? It's supposed to inspire us!"

"Oh, I get it, no sex *and* no sleep—great therapy they dole out here. And what's that . . . stink?"

"I think it's some passion aromatherapy."

"You have to be . . . tell me you're kidding."

"You're the one in charge of kidding, darling, I'm dead serious."

"Well, seriously, then, *darling,* can you remind me why we're here?"

"Because we're fucking *desperate,* Norm, in case you forgot. Because our marriage has cancer!"

"Desperate fucking for the fucking desperate, is that it then? Spanish fly might have been more to the point. Tomorrow, maybe they'll have us switch sheets—roll around in their come: a sort of new age wetsuit! Day 1) Rip off his dick; Day 2) Squirm in their sperm; Day 3) Dust off those vows.

"You're gross. And I have to say, even some *desperate* fucking I could go for."

"What, you didn't see the banner over the altar as you walked down the aisle arm in arm with your father, sixteen years ago? *Abandon sex, all ye who enter here!*"

"I guess I was never one to see what's right in front of me."

"Hey, if you're really horny, though, I guess that deer isn't going anywhere."

"You know that's *really* gross. That's insulting on so many levels I can't even begin . . ."

"Well, look, it has its advantages. No HIV risk. Only Lyme disease."

"Try Norm disease, or maybe *Ab*norm disease?"

"You should consider doing stand-up comedy."

"You should consider your words before you blurt them out. Not only was that crude, it was cruel—don't you get it?—to me, to that . . . creature."

"Look, it wasn't directed at you personally."

"At me *im*personally, I suppose."

"Look, I'll aim it at myself, my male self, will that cheer you up? I'll even sing for you. *Do a doe, a female deer*—wait a second, O.K., I got it—*with a drop of golden spunk.* See, I'm not offended, I'm amused."

"You're *sick* is what you are! You killed it, don't you understand? How can you?"

"*I* killed it? You're the one who screamed and made me swerve."

"You're the one who stopped relating sexually!"

"You know, if you had a church, it would be named Perpetual Queen of the Non Sequitur. And could you spare me the jargon; they've brainwashed you already! What are you trying to say?"

"Don't fuck *with* me, *fuck me,* that's what I'm trying to say! Is that plain enough?"

"Oh, that's plain all right, that's plenty plain." He shoves his feet, first left then right, into his boots and slams the cabin door. She opens it to call out after him.

"Look, Norm, Harrison Ford can do something outrageous like staple his hat to his head and be dashing as Indiana Jones, but don't you see, with your cockheaded crazy-glue antics, you're just making an ass of yourself?"

(Standing in the snow, he looks, for a priceless moment, sheepish, realizing that putting himself on display meant that his wife could see him too.)

"I thought you would see me as what's-his-face, Bottom, in *A Midsummer Night's Dream.*"

"Don't give yourself airs. I hate to tell you, just being onstage doesn't automatically make it Shakespeare."

"Actually, now that's it's all out in the open, do you have any skin cream in that cosmetics bag? Peeling that glue off really wrecked my skin."

"Find it yourself!" She flings the nylon travel case to him. "You know, Norm, it would have been a lot easier to take the thirty seconds to stick those deer-warning thingies on the bumper of the car than to put those dense rubbery cones on the flesh of your fat head! But you couldn't be bothered to do the more sensible thing that might have spared a creature's life."

"Moth, I told you, those whistles don't do—"

"Don't call me that when I'm mad at you. And I'm not finished yelling at you, if you don't mind. You had to take on the ludicrous, I-must-be-at-all-times-the-center-of-attention challenge instead! Why'd you even bother to remove them? You should have left your donkey ears on for the trial!"

He'd forgotten the trial! The biggest event! And of course, he'll be first, right on top of Elizabeth's shit list after the food fight. He'll be grilled like venison shish kebab. And no more time to refine his defense speech.

"Sit up front to give me moral support, O.K.?"

"At my *own* murder trial? Are you out of your mind?"

On go boots and jacket only to remove them in the so-called courtroom. He takes with him the folded piece of paper on which he has written only this: *I don't know which is worse, the guilt or the loneliness.*

Yup, he's up first, and no surprise. He's dead meat. Somehow the gravity of even an ersatz jury is sobering, makes the thing less rinky-dink than he anticipated. Not to mention the aristocratic Elizabeth of the cheekbones, now standing over him in judgment, in judge's *robes*, no less. Hey, happy Halloween. Can you believe it? Where's the powdered wig?

"Where were you on the night of the fourteenth, right? Isn't that the script?" Ha ha.

"No, Norman, the question is not so simple or technical. The question is, why did you murder your wife?"—and something in that schoolmarmy-ish sobriety makes him feel instantly like a criminal, persuades him he's some O. J. sans athletic prowess, and in the middle of rambling that his wife was so uptight and didn't give him space and she was always in his face and didn't acknowledge his efforts or appreciate his attentiveness or attend to *his* pride (as if through mist he sees his wife's hand rise repeatedly, her mouth form syllables), or value his masculinity (such as it was), or be willing to look at *her* flaws for a change, just as diversion from her broken-record list of grievances, he starts, in spite of himself, to bawl—how mortifying—she's a witch, he thinks, her Honor, the Honorable New Age Queen of Mending Hearts is a sorceress. Eliciting emotion through coercion.

"I must tell you, Norman, you are not making the strongest case for yourself." Those big, gray, rheumy eyes, loomy with pseudowisdom, or could it be genuine compassion? Did they drug him, for god's sake? Downers laced into the vegan *dejeuner*? Pathetic successor of the sublime hash brownies of his youth, enough of which would never fail to make for a relaxed and happy roll in the preconjugal hay, hey, wasn't that eons ago?— and for that matter, wasn't that the very eon in which, in a bliss not derived from any form of cannabis, under no influence but that of Venus, they listened to the ocean pounding in their ears, and she said, "I'm so ready for you now," and he said, "No, you're coming *this* way," and his memory is a vivid wash of clitoris and tongue, wave and foam, and her irrepressible high-tide joy that seemed to him to detonate the very ocean. Could Brian, the bio major dweeb, have provided that? Could any frat boy on campus have offered her that? Would they ever again visit that particular paradise? How long since they'd done, or felt anything like that? He weeps even more now, for the beauty of the memory, for the sorrow of its status *as* memory. For the hardship he continues to inflict on his wife. He's overwhelmed, he's ashamed of his ways, of his tears.

Martha—who only now he realizes throughout his testimony was shouting, "I object!"—comes to greet him open-armed, console him, so proud of his bravery in exposing a vulnerability she seems to cherish, for he suspects misguided and likely self-serving reasons. Defensive, over-whelmed, confused, he evades her embrace, goes a.w.o.l., stalks away from the podium to clear his head, hears *her* crying. A sound he knows too well, especially lately, lately in this case comprising the last six, twelve, or twenty months—a sound you become inured to and learn, wearily, begrudgingly, guiltily, to tune out like a lawnmower, buzz saw, or trash truck, though it's probably more, in spirit, like a blaring alarm clock—attend to this, attend to this, wake up and do something or you will be too late, don't just push the snooze button—a sound, in any case, that makes you sad and angry at the same time, a sound you can't stand, a sound intrinsically incriminating, a sound you know if you let it in will overwhelm you. So what do you do? You do the obvious self-preservational thing and tune it right out! And here for the first time in maybe five years, *he* produces tears; nonetheless, *she* steals the show, it's got to be *her* show even though she does on autopilot what for him is cataclysmic, wrenching, devastating, never-show-his-face-again emasculating. He'll need a retreat from his retreat, like a vacation from vacation, ha ha ha, and no doubt there are, at this very moment, classes somewhere for healing those stressed-out from healing. Overhauls for the overhealed. They put a mickey in his drink, he thinks: a new age *sissy*-mickey, that's the ticket, some concealed crybaby pills.

He's reeling; she who sits in judgment over him can see it; he can see her see him reeling, see right through him, through his schtick, his hype, his fright. This all-seeing queen lifts her viscoelastic gavel, which for all its foam-rubbery give makes a thud of such authority it startles him, as she demands, "Is your grief, sir, for your murdered wife, or for your own frustration?"

Well, aren't we suddenly specific? Where's that all-embracing-new-age tuna meld now? My grief is for my wife, my life, my wrong-place-at-the-wrong-time-permanently-out-of-commission deer, my dearly departed virility, my annihilated spontaneity, my definitively-do-not-resuscitate marriage—how would *I* know what I'm grieving for *exactly?* How would *I* know why I feel like shit? I thought I was paying *you* for answers! For the last sixteen years—not to mention the more casually committed decade before— I was trying my damnedest only now to find out none of it counts; I'm supposed to try harder despite the fact that it's definitely too late. But all he can manage to articulate is the much cruder, "Take that rented tux and shove it up your—"

"You're in contempt of court!" (Of cunt, more like it.) Oh, give me a break, how far will they take this charade? He stalks out of the auditorium, finds her in the corridor, tries to reason with her, tries to embrace her, now *she's* resistant. He retreats, disconsolate, to the cabin; the only thing he has energy for is a nap. He notices a letter on the rustic desk—a Dear John note, no doubt. Yup, sure enough, "Dear Norm," it starts, but now he understands it's what she wrote down for the eulogy:

Dear Norm,

Fuck you, you wouldn't fuck me anymore (you should appreciate the bluntness), or was it I who wouldn't you? Who knows who won't fuck whom at this point, at this juncture. Is it over? At the point of dissolution, who can see clearly anymore? Dear Norm, I want you back, but I'm so pissed, I want you dead (oh right, you are dead), I wish I were dead myself: a spent, still body, me, because only over it will I admit I have a

*stake in this relationship, this knot we tied so tightly, and now it pinches
everywhere, and who could care less who is pinching whom. Dear Norm,
I want you back, but in the old way, irretrievable. I grieve for what can't
be retrieved, I grieve for my capacity to love you, Norm, I grieve for my
memory of the delight of harboring you inside me, dear Norm, my stupid spouse, I'm stuck with you, I took your fucking name, I was insane
in my romantic girlish glee—if only I had at least hyphenated it, but that
seemed too precious, too trendy, cumbersome, awkward, too multisyl-
labic, your stupid name, first worse than last; the irony so fucking patent!
You're the furthest thing from norm-al, Norm. You know, I never wrote
a eulogy before. But I should have for the deer; poor creature, my scream
killed you. I'm a cartoon of that fucking Edvard Munch on every wall
and even once a huge inflated doll thereof, more or less a mouth with legs.
I shoved our marriage in my mouth, and now I spit it out. I scream and
everything in earshot dies. O deer, your carcass is our gutted fucking. This
is a eulogy for me, I think. I need to pee.*

Isn't a eulogy supposed to have a certain dignity? He wants a chance, at
least, to edit the thing. He wants to respond to it, but he can't quite get himself together. And he weeps again, with his head on the desk, because it also
moves him. Undoes him, really. He wants someone to slap him, as someone
inevitably would do the hysterical leading lady in old movies. Maybe he can
go out and find a snow bank to weep in, then freeze to death—his carcass a
warning on the path like the poor, there-but-for-fortune ex-trekkers lining Mt.
Everest. But if he plans to do that, he should at least be able to pass for a snow-
man, shouldn't he? He wouldn't want to frighten any children passing by. He
rises and rummages through Martha's cosmetics bag and finds a cuticle scissors
with which he unceremoniously shears off the offending ponytail and surrounding hair; his head, but for a thin hedge level with his ears, now nearly
nothing but skin. Shorn is newborn in a sense, isn't it, he thinks, getting his
messed-up self into fleece jacket and cap and out the door. Just what he wants:
bracing. He needs something to brace him. Almost instantly, it seems, his eye-
lashes are coated with tiny icicles. Fresh snow has fallen, continues to fall. He
walks in a trance. If he were to fall asleep here for years like Rip Van Winkle,
the whole field could be his beard and his bed; he deserves no better bed than
its frozen expanse, like a while-you-were-out index of obliviousness. You need
to open your eyes, Mr. Winkle. Visibility is not terribly high with the snow
blowing sort of . . . sideways. There are drifts. He turns back, and sees her.

She in her wedding dress—surreal, all billowy; the expression *like a vision* never seemed so literal or less clichéd. But something's distorted, ambiguous, like she's too big or too small, displaced. He sees his wife larger-than-life, but he knows she can't be any taller than normal—walking over the snow-covered field, with her stupid down jacket all puffy on top and the giant, bustling satin-and-lace layered skirt puffy below. She looks lost, uncertain, absurd, but determined, overdressed, to be sure. As she approaches, he sees the even dumber earmuffs clamped over the wedding veil, whose train, with the dress, swish over the snow, making a broad, delicate trail that is shallower than the corrugated imprint made by the soles of her L. L. Bean boots. Every fiber of her costume and her person fascinates him, but in an almost grotesque way. White deer make a ring around her, walk beside her, as if her protectors. The trail of bootprints and pawprints and veil-trail read out as if abstract musical phrases. And in his ears is "their song" from the Beatles' *White Album,* the song he would ceaselessly croon to her in their first years together. Is he dreaming, tripping? Are they white-coated creatures, or are their coats coated in snow? He never believed that legend of the ostensibly albino deer from the fenced-in army depot site, some controversy about radiation vs. natural mutation, but maybe it's true after all. One who'd supposedly leapt into an acquaintance's living room. But in this crazy region with its classical place names, this ideal spot for new age healing extravaganzas, why couldn't it be true: wild turkeys smashing like tornadoes into bathrooms and inadvertently attacking girls in the shower, white deer breaking though picture windows? Hey, why not? What is that anyway, a plea for domestication? Or a refusal to be kept in one's circumscribed "savage" place; an insistence on shattering the illusion of civilization. That might make good comic material. He'd be on stage now, on the road, if she hadn't preferred, years ago, to create a domestic life. Or he thought she had preferred that. Thought she said she'd preferred for the long term to have that. She lifts the front of the huge skirt as she steps, left, right, left, and apart from the clunky orange boots, all the rest of her lower half seems to merge with the snow, as if she were poured onto it. Suddenly he feels it an urgent issue, whether the deer surrounding her are snow-covered deer or intrinsically white, but in either case it seems as if they emerged from her billowing skirt, as if she'd given birth to them, one by one, and they accompany her as her attendants as well as her goslings. "I found a pen," she seems to be shouting—is it something she wants him to sign? "No, silly girl," he shouts back, "the vows are spoken, not written. Why wear a gown just to write something down?" What is she calling out now? Did she hear him? Is that really a pen in her mittened hand? "Hold it out," he commands. He bets that she would eagerly hold out her hand if McCartney were singing instructions instead of Norm Cohen. But instead she yells, "I let them out." After which he insists, "Moth, stop shouting; we need to declare in unison"—then as if on a Broadway stage instead of a snow-covered field, he bursts into song: *that you and me*—he does not sound the least bit like Paul—*were meant to be*—Norm's falsetto sounds screechy and ludicrous—*for each other.* The lyrics, even through this compromised presentation, make Norm cry anew, with nostalgia, and then with distress. What if the pen was to sign their divorce papers? What if she'd been saying, "I found a pen. I'm getting out"? Of their rut, of their bond, their ball-and-chain conjugal bond. Martha, my fear. "I found a pen; I let them out." owwww owww; something hurts. The syllable expands over the ocean of snow. Or is it woooww, like the cartoon of a pothead at a party, stupid with bliss, the whole universe is singing (unless it is crying, moaning, in pain). Which is it Norm, which? The deer too (wait, aren't deer silent creatures?) would seem to be entreating or enjoining him: *take the voooowwws, Norm. Take the voooows. You ooowwwe us that.* All she needs is a shepherd's staff. Martha had a little faun, and it was pure as snow, and everywhere that Martha went—*Do a doe, a female deer, with a drop of golden*—it shames him now, the *Sound of Music* gag, against this more ecstatic, authentic music of the universe. Could this be what they meant by music of the spheres? It seems to keep echoing, the sound, the syllable, mutating. They couldn't be saying *chihuahua!* They do not resemble chihuahuas at all. They are deer, and by no stretch of the imagination ordinary deer. *(Take the vows—you owe us—take the vows—you owe us.)* They are definitively deer. His cheeks and ears are red with cold. His head feels colder without his token hair, but the silver lining is that the cold anesthetizes his two head wounds. The bullet only grazed me, Officer. You see, the trouble is, I ripped my dick, her neck, off my thick, yet ultimately fragile, head. My head deserves the cradle of this snow bank, wouldn't you agree. If an ostrich can put its head in the sand, Martha, my deer—my deer, that's it—can't a man put his head in the snow? The damp is penetrating his no-longer waterproof boots to his toes. Norman stands on his head and waves his legs, trying to air-dry his feet, then tumbles over. He makes snow angels all in a row. He stands up, soaked through. He is reaching his hand across the field, calling her name, hoping she will see or hear, and he feels as if he were indeed Rip Van Winkle, awakening to a strange, new world.

Ashes Ashes We All Fall Down

Every night, Carter sleeps beside a woman not his wife and feels both virtuous and guilty; virtuous, because the woman not his wife is not a mistress either but his mother, to whose side he cleaves in part to spare his wife, and guilty, because despite the cumulative nights of sacrifice, he cannot save his mother, for whose sake he nevertheless continues to deprive his wife—his wife who has her own legitimate needs but who because of these merciless circumstances receives only the dregs of his attention and energy. How can he, how can the cosmos, justify it? How has all this come to pass? How has Carter come to find himself at age thirty-six in the house in which he grew up, on the far side of a hospital bed with broken crank, with his wife asleep, at least at rest (he hopes) upstairs in the twin bed that once was his, and will in years to come be their child's, and which will soon be insufficient to accommodate her? Furthermore, how can Carter possibly be sufficiently husband and sufficiently son to a wife who is with child, to a mother who is near death: this cruel irony of timing to which he has become injured and, in his more philosophical moments, considers ineluctable. And if by some perverse coincidence the day of birth and death should coincide? He would have to choose to be cursed by the living or by the dead: by his wife, who asks so little, almost too little of him, but who will no doubt consider it her obligation at some point to disclose to their child the anguished story of a father who made a reservation for his offspring's birth but stood him or her up—or by his mother, who after all blessed him with life, and disclosed to him reluctantly, gradually, in response to his importunate inquiries, the story of the complications of that event: his birth, which she in some sense nearly missed herself!

Or perhaps this curse, thinks Carter, is not a property of the future but of the past, more disconcerting still, a property transcending time, intrinsic to his nature. Perhaps curse and Carter go together, like failing and falling, like loving and losing, like causing, by means of some subtle, mysterious yet insidious mechanism situated elusively between a sin of commission and a sin of omission, an accident to befall the very ones one wants least in the world to be afflicted, one's daughter or mother or wife. But perhaps Carter is letting his imagination get carried away with him. It is not the first time he has entertained such a notion, and far from the last. How is a man to occupy his mind in such a state—when time is measured by a pendulum that doubles as a magic wand—correction: as a metal wand that travels over Carter's mother's sagging breast, and then his wife's distended belly, in search of likely (in the former) or less likely (in the latter) complications, supplemented by the purpose of not second-guessing sex?

It is easy enough to be carried away in these circumstances: surrounded, rather sandwiched, by beloved but bloated female bodies—in fact, the sense of a woman as robust, independent, and sexual is already like some ancient myth (I'm sleeping with two women, jokes Carter to himself, and I'm not getting any!)—riddled with anxiety, anticipation, inadequacy, fatigue, awakened every hour, seemingly on the hour, to fetch or soothe or fuss and increasingly to engage in absurd exchanges that perpetuate this, he feels lately, largely losing battle between good will and futility.

Which takes today the form of lozenges. The triviality of it astounds him, and yet does not mitigate the violence of his feeling. Innocent cardboard box of innocent lemon drops. She wants one. He refuses. She begs him. He will not relent. Why can't Carter be as stubborn as the cosmos—as frugal, as intractable, as niggardly with what is his to give? Meting out bizarre exchanges, substitutions, symmetries? Eye for an eye, tooth for a tooth. His child will, he presumes, he hopes, have two eyes, two hands, ten toes, and in accordance with the laws of nature, now grows, right on schedule, in its mother's womb, with heart and liver protruding since the second month, as his wife's midsection swells, and as his mother's tumor burgeons in distorted mimicry.

As cruel as that would Carter now appear to any uninitiated observer: one without a history, one who *hadn't* observed her nearly choke already several times. How can he responsibly let her suck them lying down? Nor can she easily sit up, so obviously he must forbid those ostensibly innocent lemon discs, not even candies technically—and yet for her, refreshment, stimulation, her only sensual opportunity; he must deny her, he has denied his dying mother not just a stupid candy but Capital *S* Sensation! She may partake neither of sweet nor sour. How she must resent his parroting, "It's for your own good." (As he resents—despite his best intentions—her every-minute-on-the-minute request for what she knows he must continue to refuse her.) "Don't you get it? Don't you get it, Mom? It isn't safe." A cough drop as luxury, how pathetic. And how strange on the eve, as it were, of being a father, he endures, in fact creates, this role reversal, knows he should instead be playful, resort to their shared idioms, euphemisms, coded intimacies of old. "Cat got your tongue?" she used to say to him affectionately, whenever he was shy in front of others; later, he to her, when one of her episodes commenced, or passed, to signal, "Mommy shouldn't be ashamed of this," though Carter was afraid—their banter much more tender than what passes, later, between Carter and his daughter, when she's older, when she's fresh. "Now don't be sassy, Missy." "Name's not missy, CAR-TER." It's a stage, they'll assure each other, he and Andrea, as Emily drags them through the terrible twos, fours, sixes, eights, and even tens and twelves, for heaven's sake. "A daughter shouldn't call her father Carter, Missy." "Name's not Missy, sissy!" "That's enough. Upstairs. Go to your room."

They strike a bargain. Suck to a timer. He borrows the kitchen gadget whose tick and ding he so resents, yet has deigned to use when concocting meals of her choosing in homage to some Platonic idea of appetite. (He'd always get it wrong, it seemed, the timing or the recipes, and on those rare occasions he'd succeed, it seemed both Andrea and his mother couldn't surmount their respective nauseas. Then if the next time he brought home meager takeout, assuming meager hunger, one might say, "Today's a good day, I have quite an appetite," or, "No, I haven't been nauseous since the first trimester, honey.") But today is not, by anybody's reckoning, a good day. Today requires strategy. And Carter has devised one. If she will be willing to surrender it, the lemon drop, at thirty seconds (approximately the time she can sustain sitting?) then she can wet her whistle in increments. "O.K., Mom?" Carter pleads. "Is that all right with you, Mom? How about a deal?"

Easier said than done, and the saying was chore enough, worn down as Carter is by now, and how much more his mother must be, he thinks, on last legs, with precious little ambulation, dependent on her son who is not by nature the sort to make the grand gesture, would not, for example, be likely to carry wife over threshold on honeymoon, can barely manage lugging the TV back and forth from her (once his) room upstairs to his mother's bedroom ("Wee Willy Winky," Carter sometimes has the irresistible urge to sing in stupid voice, "runs through the town, upstairs, downstairs . . .") and means to buy a second TV just as soon as he gets a moment). Where is a man to find that ever-elusive moment between ferrying her to bathroom, to dining room, to automobile, to hospital, barely time to catnap, until the set is reduced to the fewest props: the portapotty, basin, tray and bell, wife's intercom and shared TV? By then the chemo-lite, as he refers to it, is her sole outing (complete with festive milkshake after), or if she is in a whimsical (read *reckless*) mood, corned beef on rye. "Oh Carter, you didn't!" when he tells his wife, who even if she wanted has no option to indulge in pickles and ice cream or the like brought home by faithful unencumbered hubby. Nobody eats corned beef on rye after chemo! Not even *your* mother. Chemo my ass. Chemo-on-rye. For which if he would build a ramp the carrying would be obviated; a wheelchair could do all the work transporting, but that, feels Carter, would be cheating. For does not she who carried him nine months deserve the cradle of his arms? Does not his name imply a beast of burden? Cart her. What he was born to do but didn't know till now. He'd carry her up a mountain if he had to—and he wants to—huffing, puffing, granted, but he'd gladly climb—though no doubt once atop the summit only to run into God-of-Abraham, who'd say, "Now Carter, by the way, today I bid you sacrifice your only mother for your at-the-moment only child. O.K. with you, pal?"

Carried him for nine but now has only six to live—the cliché of it: six months to live—like some made-for-TV movie—he flew in just in time, yes, right on cue to hear the news from a compassionate oncologist who nonetheless the moment she perceived his tears seemed put off. Carter has a theory that regardless of how much women claim they want more sensitive, more vulnerable men, more demonstrative men, if male tears shed themselves in public it's as if an angel farted. Indeed, he felt as if he smelled when she proceeded to outline the kinds of chemotherapy or radiation they might try, the risks, the gains . . . "at this point." Surely he could offer six months to his dying mother, who gave him several exclusively while she turned inward from the world, attending only to his nurture—even if they were the most important six months of his marriage, the development of his first and likely only child, even if it necessitated sacrificing his wife's ease and joy—his wife who did not have an easy road to—or through—pregnancy. She had to "lie in," as they called it. One of the obstetricians in her group apparently said, "We mustn't rock the boat, must not upset the apple cart"—that vessel, in each case, the uterus, he presumes. "Don't have to snag the bag," the same (wouldn't you know he'd be the one on call?) will later say when she comes in, with amniotic sac already ruptured, just in time. She will attempt to explain to Carter later the sensation of the episiotomy: "They think it's all one pain, you're in agony anyway, why not slice? But there are nerves in there, they should only know—a separate, distinct sear." (Thank god they're spared the circumcision decision with the daughter. From the sonogram forward he feels relieved.)

Ding. But not the timer this time—the doorbell. "Give me the lozenge, Mom. Come on." Who could it be? A rare event the doorbell ringing here. Oh god, he hopes it's not the priest. (She couldn't have called by herself, could she?) No. "I've got to get the door, Mom, and I can't have you in here alone with that lozenge. Please, Mom." He is reluctant but not squeamish when he inserts his (after washing) hand, reminded of dear old Sloopy who when ill could only be persuaded (read *coerced*) to take a pill the way the vet suggested, clamping closed her jaws until she had no option but to swallow, and of how no pill would save her when she raided the Easter basket—or was it Christmas stocking—of its foil-wrapped chocolate candy, foil intact. His basket he had left unguarded downstairs. He had killed her. (Easter— always honored by his mother because Jesus from the dead was like a woman from a coma. "Should have named me Lazarus, for chrissake," he once said in irritation, then regretted.)

It rings again. Goddamn that bell. They'll wake poor Andrea. "Mom, be reasonable, I've got to answer that." How easy it is to slide his hand—a man should not be so familiar with his mother's mouth; is it unseemly? But hadn't he stood sentry half his life, grasping a wadded handkerchief, ready to place between her teeth at each incipient seizure? Hadn't he won over teacher after teacher by appearing first and every other day of school, not especially well-groomed and yet seeming so due to the neatly folded hanky perpetually in his pocket, the talisman as pragmatic as symbolic, whose true significance he did not to any one of them reveal? It could happen to anyone. He dreaded it when she had them, and yet he prayed to the very God his mother urged him to believe in that he be present when they did occur—to be her little helper, to protect her. (The least he could do, considering their origin—mingled, after all, with his.) From his youngest years he'd memorized the drill. Check for no constriction, no obstruction. That instruction conspicuously absent, noticed

Carter, from both primary and secondary school curricula. For years he was afraid to kiss a girl the sexy way for fear of choking her; no other boy he knew had any such concerns. Some worried later to be swallowed up or scraped by teeth, but no vagina dentata fear in Carter, nor stereotypical one-track male mind; his one track was the trachea, and the desperate wish to keep that passageway open for breath. Only to his wife could he confide this fear—his wife, who, instead of laughing, seemed so tender, understanding, and relieved. "I knew you weren't a lousy kisser." Forgave his tongue's tentativity. How could such a man begin to be equipped to tell a son the facts of life? Hence Carter's joy, call it relief, when through the marvels of technology, he learns he is to be a daughter's father, not a son's.

"Now spit it out, Mom. You promised me." And finally she does. He grabs a tissue as he races to the door but not in time to prevent a third chime. "O.K., O.K., I'm here," and there before his eyes is Andy—no, Jerry—is it Becker? Who could forget that jaw? But nearly bald already? After a moment of confusion he recognizes the fraternity brother with whom he used to get a ride up to school after vacations from how many years ago, and just the kind of guy to ring a doorbell relentlessly. "Carter, man. How's it going?"

"Well, that's a long story, I'm afraid. What can I do for you, Jerry? Still live here in town?" And Jerry stands explaining that he never really left and that's just fine, and he commutes to work, stays in the city overnight two days a week sometimes three and doesn't mind at all, but his mom told him Carter's mom was sick and he thought he'd stop by to see if Carter needed anything and does he?

Does he ever, Carter thinks but doesn't say, and finally, against his better judgment, takes Jerry down to the cluttered finished basement where they occasionally had a beer together in the old days and takes a break, thinking it might be good for everyone concerned and hell, why not go get a beer for both of them? Just sit and shoot the shit with someone neither wife nor mother, someone neutral, talk about some stupid subject hopefully irrelevant to sickness, health or birth or death. But Jerry asks again how Carter is, and doesn't even smile when Carter, desperate, says, "It's like this, Jerry. Since we're old fraternity brothers, I can trust you, right? I'm sleeping with two women and I'm not getting any!" Jerry definitely does not take his cue and join him in uproarious pre-inebriated laughter. He looks instead uncomfortable, then looks Carter in the eye and asks, "So what kind of cancer is it, buddy?"

"What kind of cancer *isn't* it, you mean, by now?" he wants to shout at Jerry, perhaps does raise his voice, perhaps screams only in his head: "In all its metastatic splendor, taking dominion over every fucking organ, every tissue, every cell." When he confesses his reaction to his wife, he feels chastened. "It's a reasonable question, Carter, really—different cancers behave differently, after all." And she should know, far better than he, being officially "pre"-cancerous before her surgery. Dysplasia. A pity, such a lovely word. Dysplasia Annabella Carcinoma—there's a name to give one's daughter. Would the beauty justify the stigma? Certainly apposite, in this case. He vividly recalls Andrea's anecdote about the ob-gyn intern, sweating and fumbling as he tried to guide his speculum to perform the pelvic exam on/in an interior no longer as intact. She found it funny, in a way. Almost. He does admire her equilibrium. Besides, she told him, all she cared about was his conclusion: what they'd cut away would not preclude her having children. But Carter, far less reasonable than his better half, is agitated—from the doorbell, from the cough drops, from the day after day in the landscape of someone else's disease, sandwiched as he is between his post-precancerous pre-postpartum wife and his postcancerous pre-posthumous mother—buffering and ferrying and shepherding from hospital bed at home to hospital proper, from pre-op to post-op to "hear the heartbeat, honey, can you feel the kick?" while life kicks him again and again and again in the balls, as God the referee counts theatrically from one to ten. Seven, eight, nine, oh shit, he's up again, there's Carter for another round. Dizzy, staggering, but on his feet, Wee Willy Winky, headless chicken, well-intentioned idiot!

What difference does it make in the end what kind his mother's cancer is or was? Do people offering condolences after car crashes inquire, "And was she killed then by an SUV? A Pontiac? A Ford?" Only the brilliant steel-trap-minded Scandinavian technicians racing to the scene would ask such questions, do their calculations, draw conclusions, make suggestions. But for the *next* guy, not for *that* poor slob. He's dead already. Better luck next time, you six-feet-under fool, with *next* year's model, *next* year's air-bagged, all-wheeled coffin, *next* year's chemo, on the cusp of *next* year's surrogate incurable horror to replace whatever medical research just resolved. For the greater good, for the greater good at least of those who could afford the most solid crashworthy car, the most seamless surgical procedure, the most durable immuno-friendly genes. Maybe just a bunch of curious blood-thirsty Swedes in need of titillation? Not an engineer in the lot! Who gives a fuck what kind of cancer? Carter doesn't (hates the shared letters of his name—also caretaker, though, he realizes), hates his own propensity to perseverate on such decorative esoterics as aural associations and slippery semantics? In times when sex is lacking in his life, supposes he indulges all the more in mental masturbation. To distract himself from counting down and balancing the equation of his daughter's forming organs, limbs against his mother's wasting same.

Meanwhile God-of-Abraham looks down from cloud-surrounded-mountain, holding up fingers, keeping tabs, correcting Carter's math: "eye = eye, tooth = tooth. Shave off intestine, send to fetus," crosses off another number on his godly calendar. But in the short space between prodrome and seizure and longer space between seizure and prodrome, how is a boy to occupy his mind if not with mystical hooey, desperate nonsense, superstition? Certainly not with the equivalent of the calculations of Swedish engineers who certainly were not there to prevent the accident that put his mother in a coma that made the better part of *his* (that is, hers with him) pregnancy more than literally lying-in, and set the stage for later seizures (never right at the times of stress but after, he recalls) that were the formative landmarks of his life! (His life now measured by the six months of his mother's time on earth, the same interval until his child's debut into the very world from which his mother, day by day, recedes.) His life engendered by the miracle (so called) of *his* evolving consciousness inside the body of a woman who had temporarily surrendered such.

All of which inspired—for good or ill—his wife to think that *all* is possible, no obstacle too great in pregnancy, that romanticized, miraculous mother-nature vision with which Carter feels *all* too familiar, and so even after the trauma of one lying-in affair whose punctuation equaled nearly not arriving, she will, approximately two years later say, "Let's try again, let's do it one more time, no matter what the risk, I'll be too old soon." And he will guardedly assent, and she will readily conceive and will enjoy this time a smooth and virtually unimpeded nine months. Not a single complication. Carter will be thrilled to bring three-year-old Emily to meet her brand-new baby sister, finds his perfect parking space on level three, what luck, the same floor as maternity, and goes to take the flowers from the trunk and suddenly she isn't there. Emily isn't there. "Emmy. EMMY. Where are you, darling? This isn't hide-and-seek, sweetheart. Please answer Daddy." Stern now: *"Emily."* Looks in the car and under, repeats procedure, then looks in and under all the cars parked beside them. "EMILY!" He's panicking. How can he visit Andrea now? How could some sicko child-snatcher be so swift and crafty as to lie in wait outside the hospital's maternity ward? Has malevolence become so customized as that? In this marvelous burgeoning-with-progress, this tumescent-with-terrificness twenty-first century? And then her distant voice: "Daddy, I'm bad." What, is he hearing things now? Hearing voices? Coming from below, it seems? Alice down the rabbit hole? And he peers down the gap that is the absent portion of the garage floor's right angle to the wall and sees her standing there. "Emily, how in the world?" A cat landing on its feet? Thank god. "Wait, I'm coming, darling. Stay right there." He races down the stairs. "Daddy, I'm bad." Daughter, I'm worse. I'm cursed, and by extension so are you. Accidents await me to happen. All my life. He can't tell Andrea. Doesn't. "Not a word to Mommy, o.k.?" (What, should he try to sue the hospital, the contractor who built the booby-trapped garage?) Until at home that evening poor dear little thing starts vomiting violently. And he thinks, did I ruin her in those crucial several hours of assuming all's well that seems? Back to the hospital: cat scans and e-grams and all *is* eventually well, but Andrea spends the night hobbling back and forth between emergency and maternity in the interstices of their newborn's feedings. And assuring Carter all is well, who had intended to be reassuring *her*. (He fashions analogies for his own private standardized test: Labor is to pregnancy as plane . . . When the trip there is smooth you know the return is bound to be hell. No such thing as a free . . .) No repercussions, admits Carter, though he never rests assured, never takes his eyes off her from that point on. For years his vigilance will envelop her, as if his eyes could cushion her every action, every gesture, until he realizes, he's been duped again. She was a decoy.   True

"I guess I better be going," says Andy/Jerry/Becker. "You've got so much to take care of," after Carter's outburst. "Sorry if I upset you, buddy." And Carter will feel rotten about losing it like that, and make it up to him much later, after Jerry has his own kid, a kid who won't enjoy the vigilance that Carter offers Emily and who will be blessedly oblivious to danger, with the advantage of a father who possesses utter equanimity and seems genuinely unperturbed by any incident, while Carter knows no haven but anxiety. He envies Jerry's joking manner when his son, then later, daughter, bumps his or her head and he, instead of panicking, says, "There goes Harvard." Hugs the kid, dries tears, says soothing words, and carries on. There goes Harvard—no big deal, imagine that. The guy's a card, that Jerry.

"Yeah, hey, sorry, Jerry. Got to check on my mom. Listen, thanks for coming." Sees him up and out and hurries to the bedroom where he sees his mother clutching something in each hand—is that a mirror in her left, where did she get that, didn't get it from the dresser, did she? Didn't get up out of bed while he—yes, she's about to put the lozenge in her mouth again;

he's just in time, "I told you, Mom, *no cough drops.*" And suddenly over-come with irritation, takes the box and throws it at the wall. It makes a pathetic sound between a thud and a splat—and lemon hail pours down in lieu of afternoon sunlight. Seeing that she still clutches a single lozenge, he starts wrestling it away from her, she, pleading for its custody. He feels both foolish and driven—chagrined and indignant. Touched that she must have thought that to watch herself sucking would be a way to duplicate his vigi-lance. "Don't exert yourself please, Mama. Give it to me, would you please?" "I need to ask you something, honey." "I told you, Mom, don't ask again. It's for your own—" "No I need . . ." She's breathing weakly—what is he, crazy? Wrestling with his dying mother, exerting *her* . . . "To ask you some-thing else." Suddenly he comes to sense, relents, releases her hand, so she in turn can unfist the translucent disc, bring her palm up to her face, let down the mirror, look him in the eye and say, "Tell me the truth, please, Carter." What is she about to ask? (The man on the phone, with the accent—ask-ing about the accident, expressing concern; Carter never told—so many years ago. A touch of the proscriptive in his manner even then?) "Am I this yellow?" And he realizes all at once what the mirror was for—that her mis-sion was not one of oral gratification this time, but a layman's—woman's—a lying-in laywoman's homespun diagnostic tool to see how jaundiced she'd become, the damn cancer having spread now to the liver, good as over, six months having shrunk to five four three two—no one even pretending they could save her, just assuage her pain, sustain some strength at best, and yes, how better than with chemo-lite? Embellished placebo lets you go through all the motions without many side effects and without *any* lasting good result: drive in, hook up your i.v., get your hopes up, get up, go home, all for what? To pass the time in counting down from six to five to four to three to two to . . .

Won that round, o.k. And how? By bullying his poor, defenseless, dear-est, dying mother. What is his problem? A control freak? Is that what he's become? Straightjacketing experience? His own, his unborn child's, his mother's, his wife's? Has he no trust in life? No faith? "No priest! Please god, no priest," he yells when she, intuiting the end is near, requests commun-ion. "I hate to tell you, Mom, that host is no more salubrious than a lemon drop." This Christian nonsense all began because of his birth, because she regained consciousness for that event—not a death- but a birth-bed con-version in this case. Because she, like Sleeping Beauty, awoke to bear a healthy, two-eyed, ten-toed baby boy who became, eventually, a man of some intelligence, of perhaps greater than average sensitivity, not particularly good-looking admittedly, but a certain kind of ladies' man, no womanizer, but with a certain sensibility that appealed to certain women, always faithful to his wife, with the exception of this call-it-metaphysical transgression, this inadvertent infidelity, divided loyalty, sleeping nightly by his dying mother so he won't disturb his wife's sleep. But consequently cannot pay attention as he should to all the needs of either woman. Sometimes pays attention to the wrong things, sometimes stubborn, even obstinate—doesn't build a ramp so almost drops his mother carrying her to the car, doesn't hire a nurse or contact hospice since he feels he should provide all care, gets worn out, run down, and compromises pregnant wife's and dying mother's immunity through exposure to his own germs. "O ye of little faith, of little sense, of little luck," bellows the mountain-topping, cloud-surrounded voice, "you'll see the pattern in the lives of those who fail to pay attention. And by the way, say three Hail Marys, two Our Fathers, take two lemon lozenges and call me in the morning—that is, if you're still alive."

Carter, in his middle age, will feel schooled, brutally, in the nuances of paying attention. He will, in retrospect, conclude that he paid attention to the wrong things: to the wrong child, to the first and not the second, with whom he foolishly assumed he could be more relaxed, knowing by then the ropes. Because the first looked with disgust as he hovered over soccer practice, and as he subsequently expressed dismay that field hockey should demand a girl to wield a stick as well as run, two activities that should be mutually exclusive, for heaven's sake—the sight of that entangled nest of ball and sticks and feet enough to make him vomit. She laughed at him and said, "That's the game, Sillydaddy" (his nickname based upon a squishy product in a plastic egg, because he once complained that he was putty in her hands), and in later years, "The point of playing, it's exciting, Dad, I like that." (No more Daddy-I'm-bad—now it's Daddy-you're-dumb.) Fortunately the second less fearless, less adventurous (less fresh as well—at least thus far), content to find adventure in the simple things: wading pool and sandbox and ring around the rosy, swing behind which he could stand and push, meting out velocity, in pocketful of posies, innocuous pink bicycle with training wheels, which when removed at the appropriate time should present no obstacle—first a little tentative, of course, he'll stand beside her balancing, providing her support until she balances intuitively, "No, Daddy, let me do it now, alone," then giddy with it up and down the street as he applauds each triumphant return.

"Last time, O.K., sweetheart?" "O.K., Daddy. This is my masterpiece!" (Where did she learn the word? Not from her sister, who he knows already salts vocabulary with vulgar words.) She's off in a blur of pink handlebars and purple jacket. Her favorite color this month. Swaying ponytail. And suddenly the pink and purple blur flops sideways. "Corey? Sweetheart?" Déjà vu is disconcerting, Carter finds. Any minute tears, no doubt, but he will dry them. It's not Formula One racing after all; it isn't snowboarding, jet-skiing, sky-jumping, only an innocent pink bicycle sans training wheels on an insipid suburban sidewalk, the same upon which Carter learned to ride—"Corey, Daddy's coming." Daddy's running, Daddy can't run fast enough to offer consolation for the skinned knee or loose tooth, maybe bumped head to boot, at worst, dislocated elbow. "Corey, darling"—why is she not getting up? I'm coming, sweetpea. Why is she not opening her eyes? (Show me those lovely blue-gray eyes.) Innocuous concuss innocuous concuss innocuous pink bicycle should harbor no relation to insidious concussion, nor to headaches whose severity increases exponentially in later years, all encoded in a black spot on a bright screen, four minutes unconscious, four minutes of lost, irreplaceable cells, cat got your scan, eye for an eye and a brain for a brain. Yes, there goes Harvard, there goes Barnard, there goes Stanford and Haverford, U.B. and U.C. and SUNY and CUNY and Payless Community College as well—there goes health and happiness, here comes hell. And sure enough, here comes Carter to inhabit it, right on cue, feels right at home in tragedy. For *causality;* read *enemy.* His life a perpetual prodrome to emotional seizure. How can life be whole again, he wonders. Often wonders. Ashes, ashes—for *hospice* read *hubris*—we all fall . . .

Her back hurts. Will he rub it for her? "Of course I will." A Tylenol to ease the pain? What, is she kidding? One placebo good as any other, he supposes. Her shaking hand can hardly hold the cup. "Of course you're not that yellow, Mama, meant to tell you yesterday, last week, last month, last—tell me though, now you tell *me* the truth, am I this callow? Please forgive me." Feels tears welling up. Blinks them back. Hands on her sallow skin, all tenderness to soothe her wasting flesh, then both doze for who knows how long. Carter, groggy after what seems this time more than fitful catnapped sleep, observes her parted lips, coated with that whitish film, her skin cool. Holds her hand in his to warm it. Squeezes. "Cat got your nap?" Whispers it again. Then Andrea has come, as in a dream, to help him ascertain if this cold body's chill reads temperature of death. How did she get here? Knows she shouldn't use the stairs alone, in her condition. All in white and huge she stands before him, nudges him to wakefulness. At what point, Andrea, he wants to ask, does sleep concede to death? And at what point does death yield grief? When, exactly when, does grief commence in earnest? And what is its configuration: mountain, ocean, column, vector, black hole? A revolutionary universe with its own laws, its own specific gravity? A world without end, amen? Here they are now, both his charges, both his life's loves in the same room. He is momentarily whole. Ever-shrinking Willy Winky need no longer run: upstairs, downstairs. "Carter, Carter, please get up, we have to go, we have to go right now, my water broke." And then a dam inside him bursts to marry hers, and he can't hold it back.

Ill-Timed

Paula deems the waiting room sad. It lacks charm. It lacks character. It lacks tchotchkes. How can one have confidence in a doctor whose office seems the professional equivalent of a commuter apartment? Judging from the lack of amenities, the guy could barely swing the rent. Who could be inspired to heal between these dingy, barely decorated walls? The only source of color is the tower of magazine spines radiating, even to Paula's weak eyes, that unmistakable *National Geographic* gold.

Like a zombie, Paula finds herself drawn to the tower of yellow, as if it truly were gold, infused with magic; a segmented spire housing Frodo's magic ring. (Just imagine, she thinks: I could be the world's first albino hobbit!) She enjoys a private session of mirth within the cheerless ambience; she wants to burst into the doctor/patient inner sanctum to report her joke to Alex, who would also laugh, who would say, hey, that's a good one, P. At least the old Alex would laugh, perhaps laugh and then scold, as she habitually did at even the faintest whiff of Paula's self-deprecation. The new Alex seldom had the impulse or the energy—and was most likely too preoccupied—to laugh.

Inside, a skinny man with graying hair and wire-rimmed glasses scrutinizes his new patient from across the room, squinting and pacing like a painter sizing up a model for the most auspicious vantage. His gaze could only be called penetrating; it is certainly intimidating. His eyes bear down on her skin, bore into her body, exhibiting a different male gaze than Alex is used to—an investment in her body entirely clinical. She finds herself surprisingly

MARY CAPONEGRO *43* ALL FALL DOWN

defenseless before this man who wants a diagnosis, not a fuck. Silent for over five minutes, he then presents a barrage of questions: from trivial to profound with seemingly no hierarchy, questions that she answers as if her life depended on it. And in her mind, it essentially does, for no conventional diagnostic tool has yet managed to yield an answer. So bore away, she speaks through her own warm, deep brown eyes to his impenetrable steely ones; bore in, bear down, and bear fruit, as no breed of x-ray has yet done.

Paula, in the waiting room, surveys the stack of *National Geographics,* plucks issues more or less at random, browses. One proves far more relevant than she could have imagined; its centerfold a staggering shot of rock climbers' makeshift accommodations. Even as recently as several months ago, in a relationship now just shy of its first anniversary, Paula would have earmarked that photo for one of her daily valentines to Alex: intrepid rock climbers, with elaborate dangling appendages and miles of rope, inching their way up a vertiginous cliff face. And depicted on the opposite page were the gravity-defying temporary dwellings in which they apparently spent the night, their tents pitched into the side of the mountain; sleeping vertically, with literally no ground beneath their feet, sleeping, as it were, on air. Yes, even six months ago she'd have said to her then still-new lover, look, that's *your* clan, or drawn a little diagram in ink over the photo with an arrow leading from Alex's name to the most precarious tent, then drawn a large outline of a heart encircling it. *My heroine. My Superwoman.* She would have done the uncharacteristically *unci-* tizen-like gesture of tearing the page out of the magazine, depriving future browsing waiting-room patients of the awe of that image, just to surprise her lover with that cute little thinking-of-you gesture, hidden under a pillow or taped to the bathroom mirror—a spontaneous valentine. But today she only stares at it bemused, as one might view an image connected to an ancestral past. Besides, it practically gives her vertigo to look at it, since street level in Boulder—all five thousand feet of it—is plenty high for Paula, whose myopia et cetera transforms *every* object into a distant mountain.

"So what did he say?"

"In God's time, not your time."

"Come again?"

"In God's time, not your time."

"What does my time have to do—?"

"No, *my* time, he said to *me,* quote, in God's time, not your time, end quote."

"For two-hundred-something dollars, that's the prescription! You're kidding me, right?"

"No, I'm serious. Can you calm down?"

"What is this, fundamentalist homeopathy? Two species of hokum fused? Is that *all* he said?"

"No, of course not, he said lots of things, but that was more or less the conclusion."

"So there's no medicine to take or anything?"

"Well yes, these." Alex holds out a tiny manila envelope, and Paula pinches its sides to peer in.

"These are . . . these are some kind of candy, for heaven's sake."

"No, it's not candy. Sugar is what's on the outside, what you see, but apparently there's something else in there you *can't* see that will help me. Over time."

"Over God's time, you mean?"

"Yes, I suppose. Can you call that cab now, I'm really tired."   *Tired*

"You're always tired."

The original philosophy behind the nightly videos was to help Alex regain the strength and confidence that the filmed image of herself displayed—to reconnect with physical achievement. But to Paula's consternation, instead of galvanizing Alex, they exacerbate despair, take her further from any prospect of robust reality. In fact, from Alex's perspective, it seems a dream that she could ever have been weightless, or adventurous. Was it truly she who floated through a porous sky, active enough to embrace passivity, relinquishing the right to lead as she danced with gravity? What could be more expansive than the air's embrace? What greater surrender was there than the bold act of free-falling, feeling one's muscles instinctively tensing to compensate for limitlessness? What greater exhilaration?—especially if Paula could be clinging to her as they floated.

For Alex, one of the more subjective aspects of skydiving's allure was the symbolism inherent in the stages of its training: at first the novice was virtually glued to the instructor, as dependent as a baby kangaroo was inside its mother's pouch: the necessary prerequisite to autonomy. When through this apprenticeship-slash-symbiosis, she achieved a skill level adequate for solo falling, she became independent and finally certified to be the mother of another baby kangaroo, whom she of course had designated to be Paula. And in these fantasies of Alex's, mother was transformed to lover when the clinging was no longer mentoring, nor craven desperation, but a compound exhilaration. She and Paula would be sexually coupled, their tongues commingled as they plunged, kissing deeply in the endless vulva of the sky—thus the sensation of controlled surrender to both lover and a mythic mother: time stopped by eros. This was the clichéd fantasy of making love while flying taken to its most extreme instantiation. For Paula, on the other hand, being up above the clouds seemed not only physically but emotionally precarious. She thinks of recent tabloid headlines: *Astronauts in parking lots with mace, Austrian balloonists in a jealous rage.* Sky plus love apparently made woman pathologically lightheaded.

Alex puts her head on the desk and gauges five, *just five minutes,* then I'll surface, fortified and rested; but when she lifts her sluggish head the inch or so required to glimpse the watch strapped to her wrist, its face now as close to her gazing eye as a monocle would be, she sees that five has dilated to ten, fifteen—could it be twenty-five whole minutes since she succumbed, once again, to inertia. Dozens of sleek, dark braids cascade, like delicate woven strands; these weavings mask the slender but unbending semaphores that lie upon the small, white face whose perimeter is festooned with numerals.

Where is the crane, she silently asks the window, to help lift this boulder? After such high-powered education, would that it were knowledge that made for such a heavy head.

Alex's head: inert like some oversized paperweight plopped haphazardly on a desk, heavy as bronze or brass but in fact comprised of stubborn bone and whatever useless jelly housed therein that strains to fashion thought and will of increasingly feeble signals. Although maybe it's a tad more elegant than that, maybe a Brancusi-sculpted paperweight, a beautifully shaped if currently useless skull; in fact, perhaps a regal one. Didn't a former love declare her head to be as elegant as Nefertiti's? He'd been her longest love because he'd noticed something other than the portions of her body most conspicuously female; the "hey, you got great tits, great ass, great tummy, great calves—and unlike most chicks, great abs!" had become predictable, even undesirable: men and their stock perceptions, stock articulations. No doubt that was why when Leroy said, not you *give*, but you've *got* great head, well, she was startled to attention—five years worth of it. In fact she scarcely gave another man a glance; her glances thereafter tending to be reserved for women. Those five years went by without blinking, it seemed, but now five minutes possess the elasticity, or perhaps stagnancy, of eternity—some entity, in any case, irrelevant to ticking time.

Time in Alexandra's mind has formed itself as gray-brown sludge, and she is trying to step free of it; meanwhile, the uncharitable watch hands are not reaching forth to pull her to safety, but rather covering their face in an indifferent see-no-evil stance, while tacitly instructing her to do the same—to hide her shame each time a passing acquaintance, stewing in a braised nostalgia, croons, "My, how you've changed; how could such a gorgeous, vivacious—do tell me, now, Alexandra, how did you manage to let yourself . . . go?" Oh the shame of it, the shock of it, that she who previously could leave no minute unfilled, who seemed to set a record every second, could tackle twenty tasks before breakfast, was now reduced to mopey mantras like, "I'll gather my strength," or "Five minutes rest and then I'll be up to the task." But by that time, who could remember which task it was anyway?

So many tasks: so little strength, Alex has posted on her door, or rather, Paula has posted on Alex's door.

"O.K., Paula, I believe you that this sign was meant to cheer me up, but it actually reinforces everything I need *not* to think about, O.K.?"

"Would you rather have something completely humorless? How about a cryptic, optimistic fortune-cookie slogan? Or better still, something generically upbeat in a new age kind of way, off the back of one of your zillion herbal tea boxes? In fact, we can raid Celestial Seasoning's stash, since they're virtually next door."

"Yeah, something upbeat like *abandon hope, all ye who enter here?*"

"Ask them if they'll change their name to Infernal Seasonings when we take that free tour of their plant."

Rising from her chair seems to take as much preparation as parachuting, perhaps more, given that Alex has always had the tendency to act instinctively, the riskier the better, the more challenging the less procrastination. A much different sort of risk than those of recent vintage, such as pricing, behind Paula's back, a number of remote-control La-Z-Boy chairs. (She had once dubbed them the cushy equivalent of an ejector seat.) Alex has investigated this not only online but in person at FlatIron Crossing, on a surreptitious expedition—which cost her a great deal in energy. She watched attentively as several salesmen demonstrated the salient features that made

47

this chair unique in all the world, and concluded that their product lived up to the clever brand name that transformed derogatory into commodity. (Her mother would undoubtedly endorse the notion of a La-Z-Girl chair custom made for Alex.) Nonetheless, the daughter who much of her life had scorned automobiles and elevators and escalators now found herself enchanted by the remote control back and seat-tilting mechanism, never having imagined that she of all people would come to intersect a demographic of sedentary middle-class senior citizens.

Alex, in a life both recent and yet irretrievably past, has often fallen voluntarily from heaven through glorious blue and cumulus, now only to find herself parachuting through viscid, grayish-brown hell, each Dantean circle thereof. The plunge contained none of skydiving's exhilaration, but all of the tedium; it was the equivalent of driving to the airfield and suiting up on the off chance that the weather would be suitable, frequently only to have to start from scratch again the next time, driving, suiting, gearing up, then huddling in the plane. What this new falling lacked was the thrill of the grand finale: the grabbing on and actually jumping out and down into open sky, and the pièce-de-résistance moment of truth, opening the chute.

"George Bush Senior did it at seventy-five, for god's sake," she'd goaded Paula. She'd made her come along for Alex's thirtieth birthday, yes, practically coerced her with her zealousness—for which she feels a touch of remorse now. "Is that your idea of an inducement? That Bush's father did it?" was Paula's initial response, but eventually Alex changed tactics and lured her with the sensual dimension of the experience. That birthday wasn't all that long ago, and yet she is a different body now. It's all she can manage to rise from a chair or to lift up her head from her desk. Every hard-won millimeter is like fifty meters of Olympic pool with an exhausting Australian crawl or ten miles of uphill mountain biking or three consecutive running marathons. Oh, why bother to make comparisons? Suffering is not a metaphor.

Now if life were a Tour de France bike race, and she the cancer-ridden champion, Alex feels she could have something formidable and white-whalishly huge to conquer, something tangibly tragic—like a mountain insisting you vanish or vanquish it. She could pace herself heroically against a universal, validated, AMA-approved enemy.

Paula, meanwhile, inverse of athletic, is perplexed by sporting's capricious specificity, contentious with the sequence of activities that constitute an Ironman triathlon, for instance. Why, she asks, should there be 112 miles of cycling, 26.3 miles of running, 2.4 miles of swimming?

"Who comes up with that? They seem such arbitrary measures."

"Who comes up with anything?"

"Gee, that's informative. Glad to have an expert in the family! Come on, you know, like water boils at 112 degrees; light travels at 186,000 miles per second. Is there some science behind these equivalences? Calibrated energy expenditures for different activities or some such?"

"Suddenly you're Little Miss Statistic! And anyway, it's not like there aren't modified versions of those measures. For less ambitious athletes. Or beginners. Whatever."

She still refuses to indulge her lover; she will not be sympathetic to Alex's asinine coveting of cancer. Thus she turns crabby, sarcastic.

"Go for it," Paula goads. "You always wanted to compete on a man's terms. I bet if you try hard enough to get testicular cancer, you'll set a precedent. Declare it unconstitutional that women are left out of the running."

"Correction: not Little Miss Statistic, Little Miss Sarcastic."

"And don't forget you can exploit all of these doping scandals. You might even end up champion by default. If all the steroid-driven athletes end up disqualified, you'll be the only one left who didn't cheat, because you were too weak even to compete! You said homeopathic remedies are undetectable in the bloodstream, right?"

"That's correct."

"Perfect then. Can't you hear the broadcast now? Those silly athletes tried to enhance performance with testosterone, and Alexandra Davis showed them their mistake; she did it all with sugar pills. The tortoise, ladies and gentlemen, wins the race!"

"Paula's Paradox, is that it?"

Better then, to dwell within the realm of sensation. Today, Alex will concentrate on skydiving; if she can't bring her body to the sky, she'll instead bring the sky to her mind. She'll describe the exhilaration in every possible permutation, to whomever will listen, i.e., Paula. "In freefall, you surrender to gravity until the parachute offers resistance, which is a form of assistance; it's like a condom that slows you down so you don't have cosmic premature ejaculation."

"You mean premature annihilation," Paula says, when Alex offers this— to her absurd—analogy, feeling in this moment that her lover lacks appropriate perspective—needs a corrective to this romanticized interpretation. "You're ignoring that statistical minority of parachutes that don't open! The broken condom, if you will. And those are just the obvious predictable perils. Don't forget that Austrian or German woman who knocked off her lover's lover!" The argument was futile anyway. The sport of skydiving, in Paula's eyes (granted, not as sharply focused as her lover's) is essentially the celestial equivalent of a kid holding his nose and springing off a diving board into a massive wad of blue. She says as much. But this is not a useful metaphor for Alex, because from her point of view, she has become precisely that kid, she has plunged in and never surfaced, as if in diving she acquired a ball and chain around her ankle; as if, in fact, her leaden head and dangling body, once nearly weightless in space, has itself become a ball and rattling chain.

Even so, water is life giving, nurturing, healing. Therefore Alex enfolds herself within the warm, now-filled tub, letting it envelop her as if she were a baby in amnio, unable yet to survive on her own. She feels as if she could stay forever in this warmth. A full nine months, at least. Every so often she reaches forward to rotate the hot water tap until perfect temperature is reestablished. She begins to feel as if she were a tea bag and the tub a cup, the tap a boiling kettle's spout, and only after no more heat is forthcoming does she remember that Paula was about to do the dishes when she started.

It is unlike Alex to be inefficient. For example, she was once exclusively a shower person. But everything she now is is unlike her: at least unlike the her she once was. (This is the most mystifying aspect of it all, Alex finds, that she has, in spite of herself, gradually become her own unlikeness: a fully inverted person.) Therefore it seems philosophically untenable to acknowledge boundaries, to move from one activity to the next, for how can one discern or fashion closure if experience itself is utterly unstable?

Alex has thus found ideological support for her failure to eject herself from this eventually only lukewarm womb, soon to grow uninvitingly cold. Not until her toffee skin is puckered and saturated does she emerge to wrap herself lethargically in a towel. The step that once communicated morning briskness now is mournful, listless.

"You were in there for almost an hour. And you didn't even wash your hair. What were you doing? Did you hear me?"

Alex is not about to tell Paula that she was doing healing visualizations: picturing a parachute, mentally opening it as if it were a jasmine pearl in hot water, or a rose from the Tea House garden where she had drunk the very tea the jasmine pearl produced, or a dandelion blooming in space; then when it reverted to a dandelion again, she would concentrate on the delicate filaments, each fragile one, steeling them against the wind, fortifying them with her determination such that no one could blow, that no one could blow . . .

If she were to share this with Paula, she knows the response will be, "How big a check did you write to get that exercise?" Along with the coda, if she were in a particularly snippy mood, "Or did they teach you that at Harvard?"

"Did you hear me?"

"Yes, I heard, Paula. I don't know why I stayed in so long. I'm waiting for change, I suppose."

"What, did you put a dollar bill in the soap dish? I don't want to miss it when the faucet spews out four quarters."

"You're a scream."

"Hit the jackpot and didn't even have to go to Vegas. So much for *filthy* lucre!"

"Are you finished?"

"Am *I* finished? Is the hot water finished?"

"Look, I'm sorry for hogging the hot water, but apparently you're not for being a prick."

"I can't be a prick, I'm a clit, remember? And a lesbian-in-training to boot."

"Your training wheels should have come off six months ago. And I'm trying to explain something I don't quite get myself. It's not easy."

"So what *has* been easy lately? Name one thing."

"Pissing you off."

"Touché."

At first the sensation of being with a woman was strange for Paula. Lesbian friends had described an experience predicated upon familiarity. They had said it was like touching yourself, untutored, natural, and yet this is not a useful reference, because Alex, for Paula, is anything but familiar; she is exotic beyond assimilation, her difference the quintessential attracted opposite. Alex equals Cinderella after transformation, and Paula is her ashed-blonde, soot-smeared precursor. (But then, almost anyone, appearance-wise, cannot help but be other to Paula.) Alex was not alone in waiting for change, for after processing the attentions of several lovers of less than flattering motivation: out-of-charity Matt, on-a-dare Trevor, and out-of-curiosity Jason, Paula had become increasingly adept at touching herself!

In their initial weeks together, she felt transformed by mere proximity, as if vicariously through their connected breath, Paula could endow herself with Alex-energy, Alex-competence, Alex-beauty. Yes, that was the original formula: Paula of hermetic beauty fused with Alex of ineluctable beauty. But somehow without warning, it reconstituted itself as Paula, witness to the precipitous, inexplicable decline of the seemingly super-endowed Alex, who on sculpted legs could once run like a gazelle, a match for any mountain lion. Why, just the sight of those calves, those thighs, those gluteal lobes could make men hard as they jogged in her dust at Chautauqua, and made Paula herself, precisely eleven months ago, experience an internal sensation markedly contrastive to the sauna's dry heat as she, seated below, perused their creamy curvature before her eyes. What more perfect vantage could there be for the myopic, astigmatic captive audience, as the voluptuous mouth high above those sculpted calves uttered playfully the equally creamy invitation, "Would you like to be on top?"

And that was how it started.

Neither can believe their love has logged nearly a year.

In Alex and Paula's private universe, time is not measured against the prelude to and aftermath of Christian resurrection. For them, BC—supplemented by a third letter, F—became the acronym for Before Chronic Fatigue, and those initials were capacious enough to accommodate an infinite storehouse of nostalgia. And from that line forward, infinite regret.

Two women: one statuesque, voluptuous, stunning really; the other also tall, but not as shapely, somehow even more commanding. This second woman's stunningness is almost literal, her skin much lighter than the first one's flawless café-au-lait complexion. She is almost preternaturally light.

She suggests a Nordic blizzard sky compared to the other's burnished aura.

For Alex one might offer the following descriptors: tawny, toffee, golden honey, mocha. Paula thinks and speaks of her in just such terms. But for her own self, Paula claims that nouns are more forthcoming—whiteout, laser-printer paper, desert sand.

"I love the color of your skin: it's warm and tawny, glowy."

"And I love *yours*, O land of the midnight sun."

"More like midnight fluorescent bulb!"

"Oh, cut it out already. Bask in your uniqueness. In fact, I have an idea: let's take a little excursion that will help you get a new perspective."

Two women, mesmerizing to the naked eye of bystanders, strolling arm in arm in downtown Boulder, saunter through the elegant arcaded streets, placing synchronized feet over red brick. They pass under green awnings, peering into the windows of antique shops, bookstores, cafés, boutiques. An emporium of vintage clothing and accessories lures them in, or rather, Alex sees it and lures Paula in. Then both succumb.

"One of the best things about a lesbian lifestyle is you always have someone to shop with, don't you think, P.?"

"Isn't that a tad superficial for an Ivy League thinker? Aren't you reinforcing every gender stereotype?"

"Well, of course silly, I don't mean *best* in any substantive respect. But if we're racking up the day-to-day fringe benefits, I certainly prefer an enthusiastic partner-in-crime to some macho martyr humoring me, pacing back and forth, looking at his watch while clearly feeling awkward and bored. As if some sexy garment in the bedroom could materialize out of thin air, without a shopping process."

"Alexandra Davis, raising shopping consciousness around the globe." At that point, such sarcastic comments were considered playful, and intended so, and always tempered by a compliment: "You know that looking at his watch was just to count the minutes until he could get you back home into bed and have you to himself."

And then some coded shorthand reference, such as "strictly missionary," would make them both dissolve in laughter, regardless of who might be watching.

"Far be it from me, my sweet, to denigrate the sport of shopping: the only one a klutz like me has a prayer of participating in, and besides, it's only when we're window shopping that you remember to adjust your pace to a mere mortal's. On non-shopping expeditions, I can barely keep up with you."

"I'm working on that, P. It's hard for me to keep my energy in check."

They load their arms with long, satin evening gowns and feather boas, urging each other to try this or that item, fingering fabric, vintage everything, fake-fur stoles and elbow-length gloves, pillbox hats with netted brims and tear-shaped, pearl-headed pins, not to mention velvet capes and satin slips.

The boutique's name? Couldn't you guess? The Whole Nine Yards. And the two take up the giddy spirit of compulsiveness. They find themselves the sole occupants of the large communal dressing room. Conveniently, no salesgirl sits dispensing numbered plastic chits to keep a tally of the items taken in. Thus they have the liberty to use it as a private theater, strutting, preening, observing every gesture of each other in the mirror. "I think this silky peach material is so sensual, I could come just putting it on." "That's too tight," Paula says to Alex as she sucks in her breath while enduring the fastening of a corset. "It's supposed to be tight, that's the nature of a corset," Alex scolds playfully, as she continues to pull the unfileted satin fabric taut across the other's bust, spanning from burgeoning cleavage to navel, guiding each tiny hook into its respective metal eye. "But it's uncomfortable." "Think of it as a pair of strong hands cupping your breasts." "There's a difference between cupping and strangling." "It makes your nipples erect." "It will probably give me a rash. Or a stroke." "I'll do the stroking," Alex says, and transfers her fastening hands down below the other's waist. "Alex, we're in a public place." "Public makes it even hotter. Let that get you even wetter." "I guess I should have known better than to take my black pearl onto perilous, decadent Pearl Street, where so many sensual, bourgeois distractions reside."

And so on and so forth, as the clock ticks toward dusk, when in homage to surfeit, and further—i.e., deferred—foreplay, they put some articles on hold, and go out for tea with the intention of returning, invigorated, for a second round. There is apparently no limit to how many items can be held, or for how long, despite store policy. No salesgirl ever failed to fall for Alexandra's charms. To see her in their wares was worth extending hours, worth bending rules.

"Tell Oprah next time she goes purse shopping in London to bring you along. You're as good as 'open sesame'!"

The two skip down the street, arms linked, the mountain ever at their side, rejecting numerous closer opportunities for refreshment so as to press on toward Thirteenth Street and Alex's beloved Dushanbe Tea House.

"Fine by me; I've never been to London—though my parents seem to think I should have played Wimbledon a few times by now. In fact, given that I'm all of thirty, they'd expect at least a Serena Williams Australian Open comeback on the resume by now."

"I know what you mean. Sometimes parents can go overboard with confidence."

"Not exactly confidence in this case, more like arrogance. Do it best or don't bother—that kind of attitude."

"But that works out fine, since everything you do you do the best."

"Thanks, sweets, but first of all you're biased, and secondly, it's a bit more complicated than that."

"Well, I'm still listening. Or would you rather wait until we're at the Tea House?"

"No, I can walk and talk no problem: one of the fringe benefits of training!"

"So talk then!"

"O.K., I'm formulating here, give me a second!" Alex takes a deep breath. "I think that since it was assumed I could win Wimbledon if I bothered, it therefore followed that winning a Widowmaker was a pretty asinine goal. The only thing that ever made a sport legitimate in their eyes was to do it world-class and competitive. And televised."

"Well, rest assured, I don't need you to win at Wimbledon. But don't make me the widow either, O.K.?"

"You have my word."

"It's kind of surreal having this fancy shopping mall right at the border of a mountain park. A little Disneyesque."

"No more surreal than a mall off some highway between industrial sites, à la your home state."

"Excuse me. *Our* home state. You can take the girl out of Jersey, but you can't take—"

"O.K. then, our home state. But you'll get used to those juxtapositions, believe me. In fact, why don't we take a five-mile hike right now instead of getting tea before we make our purchases? Twilight is magical up there."

"Number one: you know I couldn't possibly keep up with you. Number two: I'm nervous about those mountain lions, especially after you told me about that poor boy who got killed by one. Number three: I'd trip in the dark coming down; you'd have to carry me into the dressing room."

"That could be romantic: carrying the bride over the threshold."

"Let's plan a more sedate excursion instead. How about tomorrow we take that free tour of Celestial Seasonings."

"How can I take that tour, sweet P.? It's like a New Yorker going to the Empire State Building or the Statue of Liberty. It's something tourists do."

"You told me secretly you always wanted to. Besides which, tea as local symbol doesn't quite hold up to 'huddled masses yearning to breathe free.'

Furthermore, as we established a few moments ago, you're not exactly a native yourself."

"True enough. Just a transplant like the rest of Boulder."

"You're not kidding. Everyone around here seems to come from somewhere else. That little knickknack shop right there, in fact; the owner told me she was from the East Coast."

"I see you've been collecting data."

"And I need to collect a little more right now. Sit with me on this bench a minute; you walk so fast!" Alex reluctantly complies after her lover physically restrains her, one's hands cupping the other's hips, maneuvering her toward the nearest bench. "Time for a little Southwest yuppie people-watching."

"They look the same as any other day. More likely they'll be checking us out."

"But really, Alex, aren't you ever bothered by the lack of diversity? It seems awfully white here."

"I thought you said that you were awfully white, P."

"Touché, A."

"I just can't win, it seems. Most of my life I get told I look too white, I talk too white. My siblings all resented me because I was the lightest of the litter. Then on a whim I move out West and presto change-o, I'm the blackest chick in Boulder!"

"Whereas *my* siblings were just relieved that it was me instead of them that drew the gene-pool joker from the deck."

"In my case, love, it was the ace, as far as they perceived it. And aces make envy. And envy is nasty. And that's why it's nice to go West, young woman, far from home, and leave the roots to rot."

"That's some strong image. Rotting roots. I better make sure to repot you carefully." She pats her lover's bottom tenderly, as if it were a mound of fertile soil, unfazed by ogling passersby. "Hey, look at that amazing bedroom. What a fancy furniture store! Can I repot you in that king-sized bed?"

"If you repot yourself right next to me."

"Deal! So your parents never visited you since you moved here?"

"Not so far, no, and probably best to keep it that way."

"Maybe they could come for Thanksgiving, though; I could meet them."

"Thanksgiving of 2020 maybe."

"Or we could fly to Jersey for whatchamacallit, Kwanzaa."

"You go for Kwanzaa. I'll stay here. And it's a bit more dignified without the whatchamacallit prefix, O.K.?"

"No need to be defensive."

"I won't if you don't trivialize."

"We're not about to have our first fight, are we?"

"I hope not, because I had some sexy plans for our return to The Whole Nine Yards. So let's get off this bench and to the whatchamacallit *choihona*—or for the layman—tea house."

"Yes, ma'am!"

"Who has the Jade Spring?"

Alex points to herself with an eager, slender finger, nearly intoxicated by the aroma of her very favorite green tea. The waiter sets down one pot from his tray and deftly pours into an elegant glass cup.

"The Boulder Tangerine's for me; I'm feeling fruity."

"Now behave, Paula," Alex threatens, behind a sly smile.

"I think they should bring out the samovar from the glass case just for you."

"And the Tajik crown and wedding dress while they're at it."

"But if we had a wedding, you'd have to tell your folks."

"That's incentive for a rain check!"

"The thing I still don't get, Alex, is why the champion risk-taker never even tried to tell her parents she prefers women. You went to a high-powered, elite college, proved yourself, were obviously exposed to all kinds of sophisticated new ideas; you'd think they might be open to discussing different views. Broadening their own horizons. I'm just worried that one of these days they'll get suspicious and then the shit will hit the fan."

"The fan's already shitfaced, I'm afraid, my dear. I've been in the doghouse ever since I betrayed my gilded B.A. and went with matter over mind."

"You mean with body?"

"Exactly."

"This delectable body? You hardly needed a degree to make a living. They're lucky you're not modeling or doing porn. Sports are pretty wholesome in comparison, I'd say. What's their problem?"

"Their problem—which in their view is *my* problem—is that they both slaved so that I could have choices, and then I made the one they never imagined—I chose not to use my intellectual advantage for intellectual—exclusively intellectual—purposes."

"How is the tea today?"

"Sublime, as always."

"Care for anything else then, ladies?"

"Just the check, thanks. Anyway, where was I? Their idea of options consisted of politics, law, academia, medicine, finance, possibly social work. Maybe think tanks, NGOs. But decidedly not freelance promiscuous athleticism."

"But you're so multifaceted; there's no athletic activity you don't excel at. Or haven't taught. You even led that blind guy on a mountain-climbing expedition. Obviously destiny: preparation for me!"

"You're nowhere near legally blind, my dear, and even if you were, it wouldn't have to be an obstacle. Look at Sabriye Tenberken, for instance—she's trekked across the globe despite the fact that she's been blind since she was twelve."

"No doubt even to Tajikastan, is that what you're about to tell me? Why not invite her here for tea and inspiration? She'll hop right over. Maybe she can fly, too!"

"She's in Tibet right now, teaching blind kids."

"Geez, all this heroism, altruism; where do people get the energy?"

"There's some truth to that old saying, right? The more you do . . ."

"I know, I know—I'm lazy, though. I think I'll just keep following my fearless, gorgeous leader. That blind man had no idea what he was missing; mountain vistas were the least of it!"

"Thanks, P. Believe me, his eyes didn't turn that exquisite mauve."

"Thanks, A. You're very sweet. Back to your parents though, my point is you've had plenty of responsibilities."

"Irrelevant from their perspective. A career in *recreation* is an insult to an Ivy League education, they say. Emulating the worst of the WASPs. Conspicuous indolence."

"Kind of like languishing away the day trying on vintage clothing?" Paula is thoroughly smitten and smiling, leg more exposed here at the bar than if it were under one of the wrought iron tables, nevertheless shamelessly rubbing her lover's, surrounded by Edenic vegetal arabesques and in sight of seven mythic women cast in bronze, all gracefully bearing water vessels atop their heads.

"I call that conspicuous romance, not indolence!"

"The more conspicuous the better, knowing my gorgeous exhibitionist—which I presume in your folks' eyes would be an even more egregious sin? Dare not speak its name, etc.?"

"So you're beginning to see why I didn't push the lesbian disclosure. After I took so much flak getting into the kayak, how could I risk coming out of the closet?"

"I see, I see, the blind girl said—No really, Alex, I do. I hear you. But as long as you're stuck in the closet anyway, you might as well fill it with clothes, right? And if we don't get back before she closes up, you'll be getting some more flak—this time from that adoring salesgirl. Even your charms might turn into a pumpkin by midnight."

So back they go: Paula and her Alexandra, or Alexandra and her Paula, invigorated with sufficient antioxidants, just as they had planned, for their second round.

"Are we allowed to take all this in here?"

"No one's coming after us, are they?"

"I could never wear something like this in public."

"Sure you could."

"You mean *you* could. Only a gorgeous, tall, svelte, stacked—"

"Whoa, whoa, let's get some perspective here. Your body's got its own charisma."

"Yeah, ironing board charisma—I'm so steamy!"

"That would be the iron, not the board, I believe."

"See, told ya!"

"Did you notice that beauty was supposed to be diverse in the twenty-first century, including unconventional notions thereof? Remember all that hoopla over Chloe Sevigny in her first flick?"

"Easy for you to say, since meanwhile conventional beauty never goes out of style."

"Black beauty in this culture has not exactly been a convention except in the form of a little white girl's horse."

"Who needs to get with the twenty-first century? Don't cry bigotry to me; there's not a single man or woman on the planet who would find you less than gorgeous."

"And so I'm set for life, is that it? Being designated beauty queen, ripe for objectifying, provides perfect fulfillment?"

"Well, is it so far-fetched, for someone who just told me only hours ago that she bases sexual preference on the better shopping partner?"

"You're a stitch—speaking of which, check out the stitching on this little number."

Through their banter, they keep gazing at themselves and each other in the mirror, zipping, buttoning, adjusting the other's straps and hems and shimmying into tight skirts and diaphanous silk dresses cut on the bias. Paula, to the naked eye—because her own eyes require extreme proximity to the object being viewed—at times appears a child who wondrously assumes her own reflection is another self.

"Being cut on the bias does nothing for me, it's biased toward curves— it makes the most of curves!"

"For god's sake, you're not a eunuch! Stop trying to tone down your difference. Play it up, be outrageous. Go for broke; you're gorgeous! You have breasts, you have buttocks; your curves are just . . . subtle." She takes the cigarette holder from the counter between two fingers, purses lips to make an ersatz blow, and Paula mimics her pucker for pucker and closes in for a playful, barely-making-contact kiss.

"Don't blow smoke in my face."

"Then how about we trade smoke in your face for tongue in your mouth?" Alex insinuates boldly the aforementioned organ. Upon retracting it, she says in husky, Dietrichesque voice, "A little artificial respiration to repair that nasty, corset-induced"—a tongue-induced caesura is inserted for suspense, the sentence then resumed—"cardiac infarction." From this point on, imaginary smoke rings repeatedly morph into tongue.

"I could get a heart attack this way, since your kisses take my breath away."

"I'd call that big-time progress, Miss Official Lesbian in Training."

"And a big-time heart attack too, once we add the anxiety of the sales-girl coming in to check up on us."

Then, with the ceremony of a groom lifting his beloved's bridal veil for the sanctioned kiss, she raises Paula's voluminous taffeta skirt, kneels at her feet, presses her lips reverently against her satin crotch, and exhales warm moist breath.

With long inhalations between phrases, Paula voices breathily her last concern: "Given that most stores don't allow returns of bathing suits and underwear, I'd say we're closing in . . . on a 'you broke it, you bought it' scenario here."

"Or, you blowed it, you bought it!"

"You came in it, you go in it?"

"Nice one, P."

"Are you sure this is O.K.?"

"Does it feel O.K.?"

"It feels"—and Paula lies back, at last relaxes so as to prepare for an exalted tension—"exquisite."

Paula remembers now the giddy fervor of that intimacy, materialist frivolity turned steamy sensuality. That was the beginning. That was month number one. Or was it two? But it seems a thousand years ago. Some past life securely, irretrievably, in the BCF archival zone. An archive laden with long walks and protracted kisses, constant motion and surprises, unexpected but exciting gestures, every minute an adventure.

In contrast, now, excursions are not frivolous, no levity is forthcoming. The remote control feels like a block of stone in Alex's hand; feels as if it must be made, just like her sculpted head, of lead; how great an effort is required to reach and lift and press, then press again—almost as great, it seems, as the effort of rising, and then raising hand to change the channel manually. And even so, she will not bother Paula to come to the doctor's office with her tomorrow. She will take the bus, she will be independent. Somehow she will find the energy, and save Paula's assistance for the out-of-town, more challenging appointments. She will not let this relationship become a live-in care arrangement. Once in a while when Paula least expects it, she will—although in ways less thrilling than before—surprise her lover. Even surprise herself—for she returns from her next appointment winded but intact.

"So what did he say? Jesus, you're practically hyperventilating. Lie down."

Alex reclines, stretches herself the full length of the couch, still breathing irregularly.

"Well . . ." She pauses until her breathing is controlled. "He said it could be stress, it could be Rocky Mountain spotted fever, it could be fibromyalgia . . ."

"Do you want some Evian?" Paula races to the kitchen and returns to Alex, who nods, extends her arm, receives the bottle, sips. Paula sees the Evian as some distended version of a baby's bottle, around which Paula would do well to maintain her grip—its neck a kind of nipple that stood in for Paula's own. She should be holding Alex to her breast, Alex who needed mothering and more. And yet, she was no mother, Paula. She barely managed lover. She forced herself to concentrate on Alex's breathless report.

"It could be lupus, it could be some other nebulous autoimmune condition, it could be psychosomatic, it could be none of the above."

"Wait a minute. This is the internist? That's what the real doctor told you?"

"Afraid so."

"So that's it? Total ambiguity? Nothing more that can be done?"

"Well, something can. Tests can be done, for what it's worth. Lots of tests. Blood work. And I have to see a neurologist."

"Didn't I always tell you you should have your head examined?"

That evening, Alex gathers—in imagination—all her idle climbing equipment: ropes and harnesses, locking carabiners, superclip and daisy chains, extended range cams, and uses them—not to belay and rappel—but simply to scale the mountainous stairs, placing each slippered foot onto each wooden platform as if it were snow-covered rock, or as if the glossy wood veneer were actually a coating of ice. She must keep thrusting her Cryo ice ax, with what little strength she can muster, to gain purchase, one riser at a time—she who had never for a minute feared a Pamela-Pack-like forearm injury or the prospect of Tod Skinner's fatal tragedy, she who had wished to follow in the footsteps of Kit DesLauriers, freeskiing champion who climbed and skied six thousand feet—and in a mere three weeks—from seven summits of the Himalayas. The banister is beside the point, since Alex is practically crawling—thus skiing back down would be out of the question—but if she can just make it up the stairs, she'll surely reach the summit—not in this case the exotic Hillary Step or the Lhotse Face or even the familiar Flagstaff Mountain, but her very own blissfully horizontal bed! The default goal of her activities has mutated from being vertical at any cost—the higher up the better—to being horizontal as consistently as possible. She has adopted Kit's mountaineering mantra: "like your life depends on it" and adapted it to her own absurdly mundane circumstances. The expression "to climb into bed" has never been taken quite so literally.

Paula tries to steer clear of Alex's household adventures, for both their sakes, unless she's needed. Whenever Alex mounts the stairs, she goes into another room to seek distraction, but her mind does not stray far. She wonders if her recent tendency to see wheelchairs everywhere is some kind of psychosomatic visual phenomenon—the way when Alex almost bought a Subaru—in the BCF time zone of course—it seemed that every other vehicle on the highway was an Outback or a Forrester. Of course, what use is that analogy, given that neither woman now is of any use behind a wheel, the first because of lethargy and inability to focus, the second because of vision that defies the correction of corrective lenses.

While Alex naps, Paula catches herself gazing in the mirror, finding little favor with the image of herself, an image that in the old days was consistently enhanced by Alexandra's verbal, tactile hermeneutics. Her pale unstable eyes, her hair, her lips, her ears, her nose, the disappearing color of her skin, none can stand up to Paula's self-directed disapproval. Without her consultant behind her to transform the image, she is nakedly critical, mournful. The beauty that Alex had over time persuaded her she possessed reverts feature by feature to unattractiveness. She asks this homely-at-best visage in the mirror what has become of the glory days; the heady, carefree, early love days. I'll tell you what happened, says Paula theatrically to the twinned recipient of her own rhetorical question: those lust-driven, luck-laden, head-over-heels days have dwindled, dried up, and possibly died. Then she hears Alex calling her: is there a visitor, who in the world is she talking to now?

More and more often, Alex feels a kinship with Joe Simpson, the abandoned mountain climber of *Into the Void:* broken and hobbled; slouching toward base camp, making his miraculous return down the mountain only to find an ignorant, well-intentioned, highly unskilled helpmeet, i.e., Paula. Once severed from the symbiotic Simon Yates, Joe Simpson had been stunningly resourceful. Surviving against all odds, he had employed counting and singing to keep himself breathing, to keep from surrendering sanity. Alex yearns to be that creative, in service of her considerably less majesterial mission. The mountain is her mind. Or is it body? Her conflated body/mind. Early on, during the glory days, Alex had rented the documentary from Blockbuster to initiate Paula into the excitement of the climb, but these months later, it continues to provide a reference she had not intended. They have often asked each other, on the worst days, "Would you cut the rope?"—each understanding that they have to answer honestly, completely honestly, to this high-stakes hypothetical question; which has in turn spawned ancillary questions, such as, "Who would you prefer to be: the dangler or the danglee?" The verbal back and forth at best is philosophical; at worst, claims Alex, tautological, the latter evidenced in Paula's latest answer, "That depends if *you* would cut the rope."

One man's tautology is another man's common sense, says she who often stubbornly insists on having the last word.

Paula favors creativity as well. She prefers it to order. For example, she would rather institute eccentric decorating schemes than organize or do the house-cleaning. But once in a great while she gets a spurt of energy and tries to be responsible: sorts through the mail, tidies things up, does dishes, even vacuums. Last night, she spent several hours assigning Alex's myriad equipment into designated Rubbermaid bins that she had purchased on sale and brought back via bus, two at a time—bins labeled for climbing vs. hiking vs. skiing vs. cycling vs. camping, etc. She'd seen the scheme in *Outside* magazine and gotten inspired, then made an executive decision that each sport be consigned to long-term storage, given Alex's situation. The one that had been labeled BEER in *Outside* she substituted with the label TEA, assuming it could accommodate the overflow from the burgeoning kitchen cabinets. She is proud of her handiwork, decidedly more practical than her usual artistic ventures, but prouder still that she will carry on in honor of this surrogate adrenaline, and finally address the bills and such that are piled high on the living room table, amid abundant information about various charity triathalon events. Alex, as usual, is supine on the sofa with a blanket over her.

"Hey, I wasn't sure if you wanted to renew your subscription to *Rock Climber*."

"What do you think?"

"Maybe reading about climbing might be a good substitute until you can actually do it again."

"Nah. Just let it expire."

"That obviously goes for *Rock and Ice,* then, too. *Adventure?*

"Ditto."

"*Harper's?*"

"Let me sleep on it."

"*Outside?*"

"Maybe we should keep that one for you, since you were so inspired by it to organize, even though you never asked me if it was O.K."

"Ask if it was O.K. to keep living in total chaos? Right. How about *Ebony,* then? I'm on a roll here."

"Let me think about it."

"What, too upbeat?"

"Something like that."

"Maybe soon you can subscribe to just plain *Bony?*"

"Good one, P."

"Someone should start a magazine for albino women."

"And call it what? *Bino? Biny?*"

"How about . . . *Alabaster?*"

"That's great, actually. That's quite clever. Why don't you do that? Really, P. It's a good idea."

"Think I've got my hands full right now."

"Deep down, you don't think you or your compatriots deserve a magazine, that's the problem."

"Never too tired to play the shrink, eh?"

"I deserve a turn occasionally, don't I? And isn't there a grain of truth in what I'm saying?"

"I guess. There might be, but the whole idea is ludicrous."

"Why is that?"

"Because it would just end up stigmatizing albino people even more, and all the non-albino normal people would be repulsed by it."

"Why do you assume that?"

"Because I've lived on the planet thirty years in my skin, that's why. Oh, and by the way, as long as I'm disposing of these subscription renewal notices, why don't we decide how to handle that bill from the homeopath. Apparently Blue Cross won't cover it, since he's not an MD."

"I'll just have to wait until next month, when I can pay it. I doubt he can afford a collection agency."

"Or would you like me to write on the back of the bill that we'll pay up in God's time?"

"Touché, P."

In general, the décor of Alex's apartment is considerably more homespun in the nearly a year that Paula has cohabited with her. The elegant austere black-and-white photographs, the breathtaking landscapes, the paintings and wall hangings, the posters from the Museum of Contemporary Art and the Harvard diploma (framed by Alex's parents) have been almost occluded by the brightly colored daily valentines and ancillary homemade artifacts, some of which in recent months have veered from sentimental to sententious. Most recently, for instance, Paula has hung from Alex's door a homemade calendar consisting of repeating rows of newly christened weekdays: a substitution for the *Women of Climbing* calendar that had hung there before. At first the columns read like gibberish, inelegant and cryptic. Across the top edge of the poster board reads *Acuday, Chiroday, Homeoday, Neuroday, Reikiday, Shiatsuday.* Pronouncing softly to herself, Alex finally catches on but does not laugh. Then Paula appears behind her.

"Do you like it? It's the official New Age Body Calendar!"

"Well, you cheated, putting in neurology, if the premise is avoiding the conventional."

"Poetic license. Tokenism. Whatever. You know, these body workers really have it made. They cop a feel and you get charged for it."

"You are *really* paranoid. Paula Ann Paranoid!"

"I'm working on the illustrations too—*Acuday* sports a different kind of pinup girl, you might say. You'll be the model for her, naturally. We can patent it and market it to pay off the medical bills."

"Did you realize you left out the seventh day?"

"Yeah, that was deliberate too. The seventh day is cranial-sacred—just for rest. A.k.a. God's private time."

"But tomorrow is cranial-secular, remember? You promised to go with me to the neurologist."

"Fear not, dark damsel in distress. I've already set the alarm. But for the rest of the evening, I'm going back to cleaning this place up before I lose my motivation."

Paula finds this waiting room comparatively—in fact, surprisingly—upbeat. If not downright jolly.

Having left her bioptics at home and thus hindered in reading, she is relieved to have distraction in the waiting room—lest she be tempted to do something reckless, heartless, such as abandoning her lover in favor of the shuttle to the Denver International Airport, though of course she would be courteous enough to leave this information with the receptionist, so that Alex wouldn't be completely stumped as well as shocked when she emerged from her appointment with the neurologist.

A white female caretaker is in the process of occupying her black male charge by placing a starched white handkerchief atop his head; letting it dangle daintily in front of his face, then, in an exaggerated gesture, snatching it away, repeatedly, just as one might do to amuse a child. A second woman, also white, perhaps the first's companion, stands beside them. How genuine seems the two women's amusement; how delighted seems the man they seek to entertain; how jolly they all seem. But how uncomfortable Paula feels in the jolly ward, in fact, jolly jealous of the fun they appear to be having—despite the disability that renders the man simple and chair-bound. What in the end is the difference, Paula asks herself, between a mental and a physical impairment, if a wheelchair is the vehicle for each? Whatever is wrong with this gentleman, he at least isn't too tired to smile, to laugh. Thank you for smiling, she wants to tell him—I don't get enough of that at home. And it is nice to have someone else be the spectacle for a change! She wants to thank him for that too. For once *she* doesn't steal the show.

Paula amuses herself by imagining the hanky as a renegade item from a magician's bag of tricks. The kind that is placed over a ball and then lifted, the ball having meanwhile inexplicably disappeared. What if the jolly ladies found that suddenly under the hanky there was no more head: the most delicate decapitation ever, not by blade but by veil—a convenient way to solve a neurological problem!

See no evil. Hear no evil. Speak no evil. Think no evil. Off with his defective head!

Meanwhile, inside the inner sanctum, the neurologist is unimpressed with Alex's explanation; "feeling fuzzy" does not facilitate a diagnosis. He suggests she furnish him with greater specificity. How can she convey that her head feels filled with outer space? Or is it more like styrofoam peanuts? The doctor does not understand the term *spacy*. Could she be more concrete? "You know, *spacy*" (realizing she is only repeating louder, at best re-inflecting, as if trying to communicate an English word to a non-native speaker): not focused, not locked-in, like a wobbly office chair with the casters loose, like a lamp with its bulb not completely screwed in, dizzy, a little off kilter. *Ditzy,* she suspects the neurologist wishes to substitute: not *dizzy,* but *ditzy.* Alex strains to come up with a better metaphor. It's as if thinking were hearing through water, or seeing through scrim—but not impressionistic, pretty-picture beauty, Doctor, something murky, muddy, far from lovely: something bog-like. A body immured in a bog, Doctor, surely you've heard of a bog?

He seems to take notes skeptically, proclaims her situation unremarkable, but nonetheless prescribes an MRI. Just to be sure, to rule out tumor. Rule out several diagnoses, in fact. If she insists, they'll even do a spinal tap. Alex will not insist. She does not care to be tapped; she feels thoroughly tapped out, in fact.

While the pricey specialist is proving useless, Paula continues to watch the ludicrous, yet somehow charming, inexplicably endearing game between the private nurse and her docile charge, the white cloth draped over the man's brown cheek, then snatched away by the agile white hand, the second woman seeming to provide moral support and additional mirth. So thoroughly distracted is Paula in fact that she doesn't notice Alex has come back out to the waiting room and stands beside her.

"Paula, it's over, I'm done. We can go."

"I'm deeply spectating this game of hanky-head," Paula, standing, whispers into Alex's ear.

"What are you talking about now?"

Paula rises reluctantly and they walk side by side to the elevator. "Never mind; guess it's a you-had-to-be-there kind of thing. So what did he say?"

"He said lots of things that don't add up to much, but the conclusion is I ought to have an MRI."

"Didn't I always tell you you should have your head examined?"

"You already used that joke. Maybe *you* should have your head examined!"

"Touché, madame, touché. Why don't we do them side by side?"

Paula hasn't any idea how relevant her flippant comment is. Nor how potent for her lover, who is currently preoccupied with specialized concerns regarding camaraderie: that skydiving, skating, and flying can transpire in tandem, but most medical technology cannot accommodate the embodiment of moral support. This is the failure of feminist—no, humanist—gestures in medicine, Alex decides: that you can be accompanied into the examining room by a same-sex pal at Pap smear time, or give birth surrounded by a roomful of invited guests, or have the local hospital host a colonoscopy party, and yet an MRI is explicitly *not* designed as a bicycle built for two. (No doubt useful—albeit inadvertent—preparation, she supposes, for entering the vacuum known as death.) The radiologist will read the lineaments of Alex's brain, but she herself, unmentored, can decipher her suddenly transparent psyche. She hadn't bargained for the buy-one-get-one-free fringe benefit of medical technology—for how perfectly the three-quarter-hour claustrophobic aloneness would rhyme with the emotional texture of her thus-far inscrutable illness. Experience—who would have guessed?—was just the vestibule to metaphor.

These are the perks of illness, aren't they? Growing pains that leave you maimed, excruciating revelations, ninety-mile-an-hour psychic crashes euphemistically referred to as epiphanies. She prefers regressing into memory, into the vestibule of Whole Foods, where, side by side, she and her love find themselves as pumped up with adrenaline as when they were about to climb or parachute or ski. (At least for Alex, athletic metaphors worked best to characterize that excitement.) Paula, she recalls, was charmed by the design of the environmentally resourceful cart: a handheld basket that could mutate into wheeled cart with one maneuver. She'd always opt for wheels while Alex, muscle-woman, favored carrying. In either case, they'd roam the amply stocked aisles, overwhelmed with options, giddy with health, bringing erotic charge to every aspect of this mundane process: looking, smelling, touching, choosing, whether vegetable or animal or mineral. For instance, in prepared foods, they'd request a taste and feed it to each other as if ice cream on a spoon. And if it happened to be cranberry-walnut bread day at the bakery, they would grab several of the warm loaves fresh from the oven, hoarding uninhibitedly, breathing in the yeasty sweetness, noses right up against the crust, and gorge, side by side, high on the surfeit of opulent salubriousness—yes, a veritable orgy of salubriousness. Claiming the corner booth in the dining area, they'd tear off chunks with their hands in a new age Neanderthal fashion and commence feeding it to each other like wedding cake, unabashedly making a scene.

"This could be someone's wedding cake, right?"

"Well, carrot cake was big back in the nineties, but cranberry-walnut wedding bread is still ahead of the curve, I'd say. A custom whose time is not yet come."

"If you keep feeding me these warm sweet morsels, my time might yet come—so to speak."

"Hmmmm. Keep feeding me incentive and I'll keep feeding you from my hand."

"Besides, our wedding cake has to be chocolate and vanilla, right? Don't you remember? Blatant symbolism? Our racial statement instigating global harmony and freaking out your mother!"

But as Alex, solo, present tense, lies rigid in her metal tube, the absence of eros is palpable. Assaulted by an unanticipated cacophony—thus unable to meditate—Alex's consciousness constructs a surround-sound, magnetically resonant waking-dream. Every conceivable version of sport is stationed around her, representing in miniature everything at which she once excelled, now turned on her, dangerously out of control. Acoustic chaos assaults her in the private cylindrical stadium. The repertoire is exhaustive: table tennis, hand-hockey, pinball, etc., but the tables and courts and such are stationed upside down as well as right side up, curving when necessary to conform to the specific contours of her confinement. The miniature balls: tennis, ping-pong, golf, pin, racquet, not to mention hockey pucks and such, are whizzing around at considerable speed, very vigorously, upside down, as she lies on her back, inert, with buzzers going off, nearly deafened by the din of collective thwacks from balls and flippers. In her "altered state," she cringes lest she be hit because she has no visor or helmet, no elbow or shin guards, no goggles, not any protection whatsoever. She's battered and buffeted, mentally, by the anticipation. It's like a model village of mini-games, a thriving metropolis of demi-activity hurtled at mega-decibels en masse against her lethargy. She feels as if she's been thrust into a racquetball court, not as a racquet-bearing player but a horizontal floater with neither projectile nor net as defense against the murderous, relentless thwack. She wants to curl up, become fetal, to shield her body with her own embrace, not lie like a pole in a space capsule, in this metal body-condom, this alienating stationary elevator.

When later she tries to explain it to Paula, the latter jokes that Alex must have been like the actress in *Fantastic Voyage,* but after seeing how disturbed her lover is, she changes tune, gets serious, invokes Freud's *Interpretation of Dreams:* the famous illustration in which the urge to pee is progressively aggrandized into a puddle, a pool, a pond, a sea: a body vast enough to accommodate a sailing ship. According to Paula's analogy, Alex's anxiety somehow absorbed the magnet's aleatory music and transformed it into yet more threatening forms.

"But can it really be analogous since I wasn't asleep, and since peeing is something internal while the ping-ping MRI sounds were external?"

"You're awfully picky, after all my hard analysis. You must have gone to Harvard. Look A., what do you say we get something to eat? I'm starving. We can go to your beloved Dushanbe place. I read somewhere that westworld.com voted it the most romantic restaurant in Colorado."

"Then maybe we should save it for our anniversary. Until all these medical expenses get sorted out, I think we shouldn't splurge on fancy food. But I could always use a cup of tea."

And so it is agreed that they will take the SuperShuttle out of Denver and get off at the stop nearest downtown, to recuperate luxuriously amid the decorative Tajik splendor of the Boulder Dushanbe Tea House. But after purchasing tickets and boarding the bus, trying to ignore an altercation between the driver and a female passenger protesting the fact that seat belts seem to be installed for only every other seat, Paula, impatient, begins to question her exhausted lover.

"Do you feel up to answering questions?"

"I'll give it a try."

"So what exactly happens at a consultation with a homeopathist?"

"Homeopath." Alex hasn't the energy to mask her disappointment.

"Whatever."

"Look, I've just this moment come out of a nearly psychedelic technological out-of-body experience and you're asking me for a blow-by-blow account of something much less scintillating . . ."

"Use any other term than *blow*, o.k.?"

"Sure, fine—a minute by minute *account* of an essentially tedious and now week-old clinical exchange."

"Look, no one I talked to before ever cited an MRI as a life-changing experience. And I thought we already discussed it."

Their argument is interrupted by the distressed passenger explaining yet again that she wishes to sit with her husband, directly next to her husband, so they can converse.

"Is that so much to ask? Do you think that's too much to ask," she buttonholes Paula, who feels as always cursed by her conspicuousness.

A University of Colorado student steps in to mediate, more the opportunist than the altruist, suspects Paula, who guesses he intends to impress Alex, him moving ever closer so as to imbibe the aura of her once robust, now fragile, somehow still magnetic beauty. Paula wants to tug his yellow ponytail and whisper in his ear, young man, suppress your gallantry, your hard-on too, for things are not what they appear!

"Do you care about my feelings? At all?"

"I guess if I didn't I wouldn't have been sitting in yet another waiting room for at least an hour, during the course of which I found myself trying to pass the time by trying to imagine exactly how a homeopath makes a diagnosis."

For minutes, many minutes, Alex tunes out Paula; tries instead to focus on the mountain's lineaments, to let the Rockies be her meditation, her fixed point, a visualization that just happens to be actual. And what more logical fixed point could one have? At least one member of the range is there in the background wherever you go, both standing out and blending in, providing a painted backdrop for the charming awnings and tile sidewalks and come-hither-all-ye-Southwest-yuppies shop windows. At times, from afar, it appears so tantalizingly real, you could touch it from here, and then out of the blue it says simultaneously, you can't have me, come and get me, good luck, sucker, I'm your white whale, made of shale. A perverse combination of *come hither* and *noli mi tangere*. Or in the vernacular, *you go, girl* plus *no way, José.* ——— *don't touch me*

In her past life she had many times physically mastered the mountain; but now she has to climb *through* it with exclusively her mind, and would, she thinks, succeed, were not that scowl of Paula's formidable in much the same way. When they reach the mall at Flatiron Crossing, she finally surrenders.

"O.K., we'll go through the process, step by step. What do you want to know?"

"Do you lie on an examining table with a paper gown and all that?"

"I didn't lie. I sat. On a chair."

"With your clothes off?"

"On."

"That's it? He didn't even examine you? All that time?"

"He examined verbally. Kind of like you are now—cross-examining."

"I'm not cross-examining. I'm just curious. You said that if I stayed in Boulder, you'd be my new age education mentor, remember? And I stayed! You owe me. Besides, I want to make sure you're not wasting your money and time."

"Don't be disingenuous. You're already sure that I am and you know it. And isn't it *your* time, not mine, that you're *really* concerned about?"

"Don't forget God's time. God forbid we waste that! Look, who knows? Maybe I'll go to a homeopath someday. Help me prepare."

"You're full of shit." The student looks protective on Alex's behalf; Paula knows already he would not give her the benefit of the doubt, even if Alex hurled insults, or even blows, upon her.

"No, really, is it basically like an interview?"

"All I can tell you is I answered questions. They required thought. The thought, as I recall, was rather tiring."

"Like whether-you-believe-in-God kinds of questions?"

"No."

"In reincarnation?"

"No."

"What sorts of questions?"

"Less grand, less existential. He wanted to know my preferences."

"O.K., I'm starting to get the picture. The sixty-four-million-dollar question: do you sleep with men or women? Two hundred bucks for a placebo with a come-on at no extra charge."

The student is eavesdropping without any subterfuge now.

"Chill out already! One hundred percent *wrong*. He didn't even go there. They were much more mundane preferences he was asking about—billions of them."

"Could you give me an example?"

"What are you, the Gestapo? The only one that sticks in my mind is, do you like chocolate better than cheese?"

"What has that got to do with anything? It seems completely arbitrary!"

"You'll really have to ask the doctor that question."

"The doctor! The doctor! The quackster, you mean. The guy never spent a day in medical school. Or divinity school, for that matter. Next time we'll cut out the middleman and go straight to the preacher—it's cheaper! God's time, my ass. What if someone is indifferent, what if they like chocolate and cheese absolutely equally?"

"Maybe there's a type for that too: indifference or indecisiveness."

"So he asked billions of questions, and that's all you can recall."

"My short-term memory is pretty shaky lately, you, healthy one, may remember! It wasn't yesterday. And as I mentioned before, I'm tired, and you're tiring me more with every question you ask."

"You'll have to forgive your companion for craving a little diversion now and then."

"You know, I liked when you were stupid-funny. That was one of the things I liked best about you—you were corny, silly, funny. But the brittle edge is not becoming. Lose the edge, o.k.?"

"Why should I let you control my personality? I've got my wish list too, you know."

"Because you've gone from corny to crabby."

"And you've from horny to snappy!"

"Touché already. o.k. I stand corrected. Let's try to curb our irritation, shall we? Back to practical matters for a minute. What do you want for dinner tonight?"

"How about corn on the crab?"

"How about we go out to the Tea House?"

"We're already going to the Tea House—she who needs her head examined!"

"I mean for dinner, not just tea."

"As reward for what? Since just a little while ago you said we couldn't afford eating there."

"For getting through the day."

"And what about our resolve to be frugal?"

"Oh, fuck it."

"What—going? Or being frugal?"

"The latter, the latter."

There is surely something otherworldly, or at least unearthly, about the interior design of the Dunshabe Tea House, with its highly elaborate, intricate mandala-like patterns and rich turquoise hues, letting Alex lose herself in imagery of sky or ocean. She tilts back her head as if on a marionette string to better take in the sumptuously designed coffered ceiling with which no cloud formation could compete, an ornately sculpted sky held up with cedar columns.

"I just love that Tajik wedding dress."

"The crown is even better; I can see it on your regal head."

"A crown of thorns might be more apropos at this point. We'd need two anyway—two crowns, two gowns."

"But there's just one in the display case, and it's only logical that it go to the beauty queen."

"You still think I'm a candidate for the eighth beauty, eh, after all this?"

"It's perfect; as a statue you wouldn't have to expend any energy."

"Yeah, I would. They draw water, remember? That's what those dishes on the head are: water vessels."

"I'd hold your dish for you. And add a dish of plov to go."

"Could you be serious? I thought you hated plov."

"Well, it could never compare to this delicious chicken dish with pomegranate sauce with the name only you can pronounce. But listen, here's a news item; I take back my suspicion about that quackster coming on to you. It isn't logical."

"Will wonders never cease?"

"I figured out if homeopathy is based on that premise of like curing like, then same sex couples must be just what the doctor ordered, right?"

"Whatever you say, P."

"I guess I'm a homeo-sexual now. Dyke cures dyke."

"Homosexuality, perhaps you've noticed, is no longer considered a disease. Hence it needs no curing."

"Well, excuuuuuuse me! But one more question, Alex, really truly, not a joke here, if homeopathy is based on everyone having a type, and if you're as different as you claim to be from what you were before, i.e., the you I met approximately a year ago, how can any homeopathic doctor know what type you truly are and thus what remedy to give you?"

Alex parts her lips presumably to form a response to Paula's utterly sincere question, but then closes them again, looking quite perplexed. Suddenly she starts to weep, her tears a complementary motif within the vast turquoise embrace, amid repeating shapes of decorative vegetal arabesques, of medallions and lozenges, grapes and pomegranates, of butterflies and barley chains, partridges and peacocks, of mihrab trees of life and stylized roses.

"I came here in good faith, believing in the Tajik mayor's motto, *When friends sit and talk in a tea house, fatigue disappears.* Why is it, Paula, that after a few minutes conversation with you, I always want to change it to, *Abandon hope all ye who enter here?*"

"Brett, we'll take that check now, if you can."

All her life, Alexandra craved testing her limits: the height of exertion, the edge of survival, the threat of extinction. When life was a workout, she felt most alive; that's what she thrived on. If her heart rate wasn't elevated, she wasn't engaged. But when getting out of bed tests one's limits, then all bets are off; all boundaries redrawn. Limits no longer resemble some beautiful Boulder vista, increasingly seductive as you near it. When climbing into bed equals climbing a mountain, the actual mountain loses its lure, becomes oppressive; it's the view from which you turn your head in modesty, in shame, in disgust, as you might from the person in a lighted window who has temporarily forgotten that the act of undressing, from a viewer's perspective, is spectacle—some big bared breast or cock you can't abide taunting you. The mountain's a tease, Alex screams, from her bed, in her head; the mountain makes me rage, makes me retch; demolish it; nature's such a fucking exhibitionist! She wants to cover it as if a corpse, at least dress it in a permanent cloud to deflect its brazen phallic or mammaen majesty.

And instead of consolation, she has Paula's crackpot theories to refute, a new one every week, it seems. "Maybe getting sick is your psyche's social conscience. Maybe it's a way of having a white girl serve you, turning the historical tables. Consciously or unconsciously, you chose the world's whitest woman as a scapegoat for all white oppression. Symbolic logic, so to speak."

"Are you for real? Symbolic nonsense is more like it. And get out of that climbing harness, for heaven's sake; it's not a costume."

"I'm just grasping at straws, I guess."

"I'll say, given being my slave was entirely your suggestion! You offered it as atonement for your inexcusable behavior, remember?"

"Look, you know it's not easy for me to grovel. I know I can be too persistent. I'm annoying, I admit it; I'm a broken record sometimes, and the truth is I feel really crummy that I made you cry in your beloved Tea House."

"You really truly do?"

Paula's head bowed in remorse is her reply.

"But by all means then, let's put your theory to the test, absurd as it is. Sickness has nothing to do with it, and probably social conscience is just as irrelevant, but go ahead, be my slave. You owe me!"

"Yes, mistress!"

"All right, your first task is to revise that crazy calendar you made. Ditch the new age therapeutics theme, tear down my photo, change it to a slave-wage theme, and get the camera. We're going to snap Paula in seven different postures of servitude, got it?"

Paula immediately arranges herself accordingly. "It's a kind of a thrill being ordered around by you, actually. It's been so long since you've been your royal self. And I wasn't trying to upset you, honestly. It's just the way I figure things out. I have to keep picking at a problem till I solve it. That's how it is for those of us mere mortals who aren't Ivy Leaguers."

"Don't start that defensive, idiotic, didn't-go-to-Harvard bullshit while you're apologizing even!"

"O.K., O.K. Case closed, end of discussion. I'll be your silent slave, I promise. I'll do anything you want, the whole week."

And thus a calendar of drudgery is formed of Paula's daily tasks.

But just when Paula's seventh day is coming to a close, and rest seems sweetly imminent, she receives her most challenging, if most familiar, duty.

"Since we've essentially set our clocks to God's time, courtesy of homeopathy, I figure on the seventh day, *He* got to rest, so I should too."

Alex offers no reaction: neither smile nor roll of eyes.

"Alex, why do you look so glum—was playing master that empowering? You're miserable to give it up?"

"No, silly. I've had my fill of mastering. It's just that while you were out at the post office, my mother called."

"What words of wisdom did she offer this time?"

"She asked me how I was, and I decided to take a risk. I answered honestly for a change."

"Oh boy! I better sit down." Paula puts the packages on the kitchen counter and joins her lover.

"So how exactly did you put it?"

"I said I was tired and depressed and that I couldn't tell whether the depression made me tired or the fatigue made me depressed."

"To which she replied . . . ?"

"She didn't say anything for a while and then she just launched into me."

"Came in for the kill, is that it? O.K., let's have it."

"Mind you, this is more or less verbatim: 'What self-respecting woman wastes her time with foolishness like this? You surround yourself with white folk, Alexandra, now it's seeping in, you've gotten brain-bleached. No black woman's got the luxury to be this lazy.'"

Mrs. Davis's impoverished maternal instincts never failed to galvanize Paula on Alex's behalf. "What kind of bull is that? The real-men-don't-eat - quiche school of thought? Real black women don't get depressed? Wow, that's harsh! And more than a little hypocritical, given that they sent you to ever-so-slightly-white Harvard! And she should only know how white your surroundings have been these past months! Cuz if you're bleached, then what am I? I'm off the charts! I'm practically radioactive!"

"It's the only active I've got, girl!"

"Geez, parents are always one extreme or the other. Where's that happy medium?"

"Believe me, I wouldn't mind a violent pendulum swing right now."

"I understand, A.; for once I don't envy you. But there's that grass-is-always-greener aspect. For instance, my mom always said, you can be anything you want, honey. But it was so patently untrue that I resented her optimism, since I could barely see the blackboard or catch a ball—and out on the playground when the teacher couldn't hear, all the other kids kept saying 'trick or treat' when I'd walk by. The only thing the boys wanted from me was to get me in a dark room—and not to feel me up either—just to see my eyes light up."

"I can't quite blame them. Those eyes are amazing."

"Thanks, A. But I would have felt more normal if they had wanted to touch me too."

The poignancy of this admission is not lost on Alex. "If I'd been there,

I would have led the way, and every boy would have lined up behind me to experience his private version of my fingers' ecstasy."

Paula squeezes Alex's hand appreciatively. "They would have lined up, yeah, but not to touch me—to watch you, the sexpot-special, just like the joggers at Chautauqua do. Didn't you ever wonder why those high-powered hunks never passed you? You're fast, sure, but they're no slouches either. They were taking in the view—and I don't mean geology."

"Says you."

"Says me and every other citizen of Boulder. They were all certifiably mesmerized by your delectable verso!"

"Verso my ass."

"My point exactly."

"Remember that discussion about objectification we had a while back?"

"Hey, that's history!"

"Listen, Paula, sexpot-specials are a dime a dozen, don't you understand? How could any child who manifested something as mystical-sounding as transillumination not feel special?"

"Gee, I don't know, must have been those million mocking voices shrieking in my ear each time I walked past!"

"Don't be droll."

"But anyway, the point was how parental attitudes affect one's being in the world, right?"

"Well, I suppose you could be right. When all is said and done I guess it's no worse to have an obstacle for a parent than a cheerleader."

"Know what else my mother said when I was little?"

"Tell me."

"It's just your self-consciousness that makes you think they're looking at you funny, honey."

"At least she didn't go so far as to say albinism was all in your mind."

"Yeah, but I wouldn't mind having an inconspicuous . . . condition for a change."

"So everyone could say, you're fine, you don't look sick, what's wrong with you? Believe me, inconspicuous is *vastly* overrated."

"Look, I know you're discouraged at this whopper lifestyle change, Alex, and it sucks that your mom's so insensitive to that, but maybe change isn't the end of the world either. Even though you can't do what you used to—I mean obviously you can't make much use of your international mountain guide certification and all that, but you could still get a job. You know, some sedentary, low impact . . . desk job, like most poor slobs do. Who wouldn't hire an Ivy League grad, and a sexpot to boot? We're going to need to get jobs real soon, both of us."

"Oh yeah, black *and* handicapped! *Lights, camera, affirmative action.*"

"Hey, that's a good idea. I'm sure any director would snatch up an actress as gorgeous as you, even if all the action had to be inherently slow motion. He could take a thousand still shots and stitch them together."

"I think *you* should be the actress; you're actually the more dramatic member of this couple."

"Oh yeah, great albino roles have set the precedent for me, right? That kook who tagged along with Jim Carrey in *Me, Myself & Irene.*" Paula does an imitation with her bioptics.

"Paula, cut that out, don't make yourself into some cartoon."

"Or how about that horror movie that had Halle Berry in it?"

"She played an albino? Really?"

"I cannot tell a lie. She kind of looks like you, you know."

"All light-skinned black women look alike, is that it?" Paula rolls her eyes. "On the other hand, last week you said I looked like Lokelani McMichael. Which at least is vocationally closer!"

"Ironman women of the world unite!" Paula wags her hips, then lifts an Evian bottle in each hand as if barbells, feigning strain. "She's beautiful is all I meant; both of them are. Don't get insulted by a compliment."

"How can I stay insulted when you're such a ham? And actually, I do kind of like the idea of me playing you."

"Well, that makes two of us—the most ego boosting I'll enjoy in my great white lifetime."

"That's the sad part—but whatever it takes to uncloud your vision in the self-image realm. One of these days my campaign will succeed."

Paula, after nearly a year in the Mountain State, finds herself positioned rather differently than she'd imagined. Unlike her married-with-children acquaintances, who were constantly ferrying their kids to soccer or girl scouts or play dates, Paula was instead ferrying her lover to acupuncture, massage, chiropractic, homeopathic, biofeedback, cranial-sacral, what-have-you—despite the fact that when they'd met, Alex had been the very person *coaching* kids' soccer or teaching private windsurfing lessons or leading a Pilates class or running a marathon or organizing a women's climbing clinic or serving as a mountain guide. Who could believe that the weakened woman lying on the bodywork table du jour was actually the temporal twin of the marathon-running lover who got bored with what men expected her to do acrobatically in bed, just to show off. She'd show off for her own satisfaction, she'd said. Not for anyone else's applause—or erection.

Like a child demanding a bedtime story, Paula often asked to hear, again, how Alex rendered such men's fantasies impotent.

"Hey, what was that line you gave that guy who requested more athletic sex?"

"'I'm strictly missionary'; I thought you had that memorized."

"You know I do; we joke about it all the time. I mean the line that came right before that."

"Oh, I think it was something like, 'You were expecting maybe jumping jacks between the acts?'"

"I wish I could have seen his face."

"He was a bit stunned, as I recall."

"Lesbian sex is much more supple, isn't it—much more nuanced?"

"You're preaching to the choir—but I'll second your conclusion."

"Cunnilingus is almost like a form of meditation, don't you think?"

"That's a little far-fetched, sweet P. But maybe you could start a special program at Naropa University—the Masters in Contemplative Orality!"

"Can't I be poetic too once in a while? Even though I didn't go to Harvard?"

"If you invoke my alma mater one more time—"

But Paula won't be interrupted. "Six months ago you would have said that was profound! Insight into the spirituality of sexuality!"

"Don't get all defensive. And believe me, most poetic people likely have it beaten out of them at Harvard."

"Corporal punishment in the Ivy League; there's a headline."

"I mean spiritually, dummy. Beaten spiritually. You'd likely find more nurture at our local Boulder institutions."

"All the more reason you need to check out that Naropa place yourself. Maybe you'd find nurture in your own back yard. Seems you're already working for their admissions department anyway!"

But Alex is too busy, too bollixed to empty her mind, busy sorting out so much debris already there, trying, for example, to incorporate the lessons from last weekend's healing retreat, which she half-heartedly attended. The facilitator emphasized pragmatic ways to readjust, to scale back goals, to modify ambition across the board. Alex dutifully bisected the dull yellow sheet of legal paper, made *before* and *after* columns; in the left-hand one wrote *swimming English Channel,* in the right hand one, wrote *channel-surfing.* "Sense of humor anyway," the facilitator said, and was it Alex's imagination, or Paula's internalized projection, that the woman's smile transformed itself from pitying to lascivious?

Alex used to be on everybody's lips, not promiscuously, but verbally: the woman who consistently won this or that marathon, triathlon, the woman who was always higher up than you were on the mountain, fastest on the track along the creek, and who they wished would just stand still a minute for their viewing pleasure, because the woman was a looker, Jesus, nature broke the mold when it produced such stunning beauty. And really smart too, someone said, but she was on the move too much to stop and chat to show off her alleged intellect. What a catch, but who could ever catch her, moving at the speed of light, it seemed. But overnight she'd turned into a hothouse flower.

Now it's, *Alexandra who?* You know, the chick with the braids, with the bod, she's the Jill-of-all-trades when it comes to athletics—or was, until recently. She's the one who could outrun the elevator seven flights, not down but *up,* or jog over to meet you for coffee, arriving before you—even if you drove! Yeah, that one, with her head in her hands. That one, walking as slowly as a senior citizen on the verge of double knee-replacement. Go figure! Moved to Boulder so she could pedal a mountain bike up the Rockies three times a week, and soar with bald eagles at Chautauqua. Unafraid of mountain lions; she always scoffed, *I can outrun them.* One could only be in awe of the hubris, the chutzpah, the confidence, the enthusiasm of the survival queen, because if survival was the province of the fittest, there wasn't any question Alexandra would survive, moreover, thrive. In fact Paula early on had planned—only half in jest—to send her lover's name, cv, and photo to the notorious reality show, because of her amazing skills and looks, and how could they not choose her, after all? She was an obvious contestant and the likely grand prize winner. Who could vote her off an island? Except maybe out of jealousy.

But this summer Alex does not thrive, barely survives, feels like Darwinian detritus. At the weekend farmers' market on Fourteenth Street—everything too loud, too hot—she feels assaulted by the crowd, the sounds, the smells. Paula tries to make an outing of it—goes from stall to stall collecting delicacies for her invalid beloved.

"Here's a dumpling for my darling. Five for a dollar, in fact!"

"That's five too many for me, I'm afraid, Paula." Just the aroma makes Alex nauseous. "I need to find a place to sit. It's just too crowded. Not to mention hot and humid."

"Don't be stupid, Alex. It's dry heat, remember? You're not in New Jersey, you're in Colorado, as you're often reminding me."

"I don't care where I am; it's bothering me."

"The sun bothers me too, probably lots more than you, but I have the sense to slather myself in sunscreen and have a big, wide brim protecting me."

"You mean that dorky sun visor you always wear out here."

"You said it was adorable six months ago."

"On its own it's almost cute, but it's the combination with those senior citizen wrap-arounds."

"Look, Boulder sun isn't exactly ideal for me. I came to visit, remember? It wasn't circled on my places-to-live wish list. Albino eyes are sensitive to sun, remember?"

"Yes, in fact I do. It's not just the sun for me, though. I can smell the smoke from the forest fires."

"It bothers everyone. Not just you. Try to deal with it."

"I mean, I can't stand it. And I can't stand period. I can't be outside right now."

"Look, nobody likes it. Everybody's throat hurts from it, you're experiencing a perfectly normal response! There's nothing remarkable here. You're not special."

But none of the revelers and shoppers seem the least bit afflicted as far as Alex could see. They continue to eat, drink, and be merry.

"But Paula, I can't breathe. I mean, it really feels like I can hardly breathe."

"Don't forget to factor in the altitude."

"I'm used to the altitude. I've lived here for years! It isn't normal to have trouble breathing. Let's go back home."

"Look, you can't walk, you can't eat, you can't breathe, at this rate you'll be dead before you know it. Then you won't have to worry about it anymore."

"Thanks for the support. Guess I'll head back on my own."

"No, hang on. You know I was kidding. I'll go with you." She puts her arm around her feeble lover and leads her to the nearby garden. "But I want to give you some aromatherapy with those gorgeous Tea House roses before we head back to the ole infirmary. Come on, we'll start with your favorite:

Mr. Abraham Darby. And here's your friend Dart's Dash—and Louise Odier and Gourmet Popcorn."

Alex does as commanded, imbibes the perfume of each flower, tries to lose herself within their whorls.

"And last but not least, take a big deep breath of Robusta!"

Alex crouches down beside her lover for the grand finale, but somehow finds Robusta's redness almost painful. Its brightness makes her wince. She realizes even this involuntary resistance is perceived by Paula, and immediately processed into insult. They separate.

Sitting on the garden bench, Paula conducts her customary problem-solving, out loud. "You know how they say that illnesses lie dormant waiting for their opportunity in someone's body? Maybe this was something brewing in you all along. Maybe you weren't tired of men but just plain tired. Maybe you wanted to make love to women because it's less exertion."

"Less exertion than what—than strictly missionary? One day I'll put a strapping Title IX lawsuit to your cockamamie theories."

"No pun intended, right? Cock-amamie."

"I get it, Paula. Besides which, making you come, I must say, my dear, takes lots of stamina."

"What do you mean? I'm highly sensitive, right? Responsive to the slightest touch. You're the one who said I was born to be a lesbian because my body was so polymorphously perverse."

"Yes, I did call you responsive, but there's a difference between responsiveness and full-fledged orgasm—factoring in the cumulative expenditure of energy required to make you come! An hour solid, usually. No wonder you consider it a form of meditation!"

"I didn't realize you were clocking it! Sorry to take up your precious time. I never knew my clitoris was so tedious!" Several teenagers giggle audibly on the sidelines, and a couple wheeling a stroller through the garden offer a dual censorious stare.

"Oh Paula, please don't be defensive. And this isn't quite the subject for the wholesome Boulder farmers' market, is it?"

"Oh, well excuse me, Miss Propriety. Not too long ago you were Miss Who Cares What People Think. Miss No Place Not Eroticized. I'm starting to see how selective your conspicuousness campaign is. When it glorifies you, it's cool, but when it's not aggrandizing, then it's contraband. I can't remember the last time we had sex anyway."

"Look, I'd cut the rope, you hear me? Today I'd cut the rope!"

"Well, that makes two of us, believe me! Where's that knife?"

"I don't want you to take me home—I'll go alone even if I fall down every block, even if I have to crawl. I would happily climb down from any mountain solo even though I'm weaker, just to have some peace."

"Have all the peace you want—with my blessing. That way maybe I'll finally get some. Your being sick is *such* a picnic for me, did you notice? Good riddance."

"Ditto!"

And even though it's excruciating for each of them, Paula watches Alex make her way on sea legs down the street, and will not—no matter what— run after her.

If you had asked Paula what she thought she was getting into when she took up with Alex, she might have said something like this: Why, sure, I'd like to be on top! On top of the world, on top of the clouds, and strong by osmosis, ensconced in the best and most versatile hands. The fact is, she had entertained visions of romantic windsurfing lessons, with her lover sturdy behind her, giving ballast, sensually melded with her as the wind embraced them both. This duplicated Alex's own skydiving scenario: a sexuality of symbiosis. Any such activity, in Paula's fantasy, was followed by long, deep massages in which Alex's strong, graceful hands would intuit her body's every hidden cache of tension and skillfully craft release. By simply climbing on top, she would in essence acquire a live-in personal trainer.

At least, she figured, she'd probably learn how to pronounce Pi-la-tes properly! Every time she turned, she would find Alex nudging her calf or thigh into the proper yoga position or perfecting her stroke for the x–meter crawl, measuring her muscle mass, supplying an affectionate pinch here and there to boost her heart rate and with occasional time-out sessions of oral sex to break the tedium.

She imagined entrusting her head to her lover's hands, as the latter meticulously plaited every one of Paula's limp blonde strands, magically transforming them into sleek, exotic braids. Meanwhile, through the rigors of tandem exercise, Paula's thighs would become firm and her waist contract and her abs steelify and her (as she perceived it) towering body become proportional instead of merely vertical; she would become graceful as well as invincible. Moreover, her eye-hand coordination would instantly improve; she'd excel overnight in all athletic ventures. Paula, in short, would learn all the tricks of the trade without ever having to turn them. All gain, no pain. Ha ha.

And what did Alex imagine, as she gazed upon the Rockies, which had she not climbed them, might seem like some permanent stage setting?

She had regarded the mountain as her mother, her surrogate mother, embracing, providing a solid foundation—but that was already a past life, her climbing days. She held up two mountains, it seemed: that of Paula's idealized projections alongside her mother's unscalable contempt, the latter which was paradoxically assuaged by the former. She still remembers—cherishes—how her adoring Paula comforted her when she reluctantly revealed her mother's parting words before the big move West.

"'Enjoy your athletic excursion in Colorado, Alexandra. However, there's a reason that absurd sport is called *white* water rafting. How many black people get into a boat and risk drowning for thrills? You make a mockery of the middle passage!'"

"She said that with a straight face?"

"Her face is never crooked, trust me."

"And did you say, thanks, Mom, glad that's cleared up, and by the way, you make a mockery of motherhood!"

"Touché, P. Maybe I *will* bring you home for Kwanzaa after all. First I'll have to talk them into celebrating it."

But even then such gestures of support could inexplicably, almost instantaneously, become contentious. And she knows Paula hasn't always necessarily been the one to blame.

"I don't know why they wouldn't. It must be comforting to have a heritage to celebrate."

"You've got a heritage too, my dear, you've got the classic WASP roots everybody lusts for."

"Fat lot of good it does me! Privilege is only skin-deep, right?"

"Can you get past the slogans? What are you getting at here?"

"I don't know. It's hard to explain, but the prejudice against you has a focus—you can organize around it—you know, foster solidarity. If some asshole says, 'Go back to Africa,' you can say, 'I've been, I'm proud, fuck you'—whatever. But where can I go back to if somebody disses me? I can't hightail it to Hermansky Pudlak."

"Where's that again?"

"Inside my cells is where it is! The gene—the gene that made me bleached!"

"You're so kooky sometimes."

"Kooky schmooky. I'm a minority's minority. I mean, no one's gonna designate a section in a bookstore for Albino Lit. And even if they did, they'd call it something cutesy like Ghostwriters."

"So would you like to have a Holocaust or a slavery-ridden history to earn that Barnes & Noble shelf?"

"O.K., touché, A. But you know somewhere I've got a point."

And in a sense she does know—knows that Paula has experienced more isolation being an extreme instead of in-between, as Alex is—in terms of color scheme, in terms of what a populace finds palatable on their skin-tone-du-jour palette. But Paula thinks that beauty is some automatic *open sesame* to every situation, every interaction. She can't hear the strident chorus over thirty years that bellows all the reasons she, Alex, is lacking—perhaps precisely due to so-called *passing,* which from certain social perspectives equals *failing,* equals *not* being accepted despite superficial yeses: *because you're black, because you're not quite . . . white, because you're not black "enough," because you're too beautiful, because you're too fine for a black girl, because you talk white, because you're essentially white, because you're goddamn lazy, because you're over-ambitious, because you're not really . . . black, because you're almost . . . white.* Those voices deafen unless psychic earplugs are employed.

The chorus—not a Greek one either—seeks ablation if not subjugation, even depredation—pounding through her ears and massing deep into her core. The voices had mortgaged her skin, and now that they are bored, they insidiously commuted that mass into a force that wasted muscle, sinew, ligament. If Paula stretched her theories some, Alex guesses she could conjure a label that would equate Alex's inertia with these voices' incessant, ever-more-raucous cacophony. In fact, it would be comforting if she would do so, if Paula could for once come up with a theory both compassionate and accurate, instead of just eccentric. Instead of censorious. For as far as Alex is concerned, she has thus far in her life surmounted at least seven summits of bigotry, in addition to the jealousy of others, not to mention failure, great discomfort from sprained ligaments, pinched nerves and broken bones, etc., but none of them can hold a candle to this mother of all fatigues.

"I come bearing gifts," Paula announces at the threshold of the apartment. "A peace offering." She ventures farther in, then kneels and prostrates herself, hoping her display aligns with Alex's line of sight. Filling the living

86

room with her voice, she continues: "I apologize for being such a schmuck. I apologize for telling you the jig was up. It was inexcusably insensitive of me. When you're sick, you need support, not sarcasm. You *are* going to get better, I promise. We're going to get you better together." Then softer, intimately, squatting closer to the couch, "I brought my beautiful black pearl a five-ounce bag of dragon jasmine pearls, straight from the Dushanbe Tea House—they're your favorite kind, right?"

"Oh . . ." Alex is speechless, her anger melts before this unexpected gesture. "Oh, that's so sweet, Paula. Gee, that's . . . Thank you. The thing is, I can't drink it until an hour after the pills. I . . . I really shouldn't even smell it."

"Pearls after pills. Pearls before swine. Is this the Eucharist or what?"

"Nothing mystical, just caution against chemical interaction."

"But it's special good-for-you green tea, healthy *and* exotic tea! Antioxygen or whatever they call it."

"*Antioxidants* is what you mean. I think you were confusing it with *anaerobic.*"

"Look, little jasmine balls that unfurl as you watch—like sea monkeys!"

"Actually, I'm technically not supposed to have any stimulants at all."

"So does that mean listening to jazz in The Boulderado lobby on our anniversary is out too? And that even in the special honeymoon suite we talked about reserving, there won't be any chance of sex?"

"No silly, not *stimulus, stimulants*—stimulants as in substances, like caffeine. Or toothpaste, for that matter."

"Further eroding all kissing incentive—thank you again, homeopathy!"

"Paula, don't get pissed off. I can brush my teeth, don't worry; I just have to wait an hour."

"See, it *is* the Eucharist after all. But thank goodness you're allowed to go hear jazz, because every once in a while I need an infusion of something more visceral than your Wyndam Hill collection, and whatever floats from NPR on *Hearts of Space* and *Echoes.* You've gotten so addicted to that shit."

"I find it soothing."

"Chicken soup for the ears, is that it? Or should I say *seitan? Tofurkey?*"

"I think of it as spiritual."

"Yeah, spiritual muzak."

"o.k., Paula. You're entitled to your view. Don't piss on mine, though. I don't have so much consolation these days. Next time leave your peace offerings outside; I swear, these days your vibe makes everything antagonistic."

So Paula kicks herself for fucking up again, and vows to leave Alex unassailed for three whole days, to let her rest in perfect peace, only disturbing her on Thursday for their weekly shopping expedition, and only then if she feels up to it, which Alex claims she does—hadn't they once likened Boulder grocery shopping to one giant serotonin boost?—and thus the tentatively hopeful heroines hike the half-block to the bus stop, board the bus with fingers crossed.

Boulder's premier grocery store can cheer up almost anyone who cares for food. In fact, even a vegan would find beef enticing at Whole Foods, not to mention poultry, pork, and seafood. Never mind the produce; that's a given. It's not just the certified no-hormone, no-antibiotic avowals. There is something aesthetic—even painterly—à la Flemish nature morte—about the seductive array of robust red and shimmering bright pink next to a more muted palette of pale pink and white—the pristine bed of ice in a gleaming display case that houses the opulent spread of succulent flesh. All of it fresh that day, fresh kill, prime cut, guaranteed to be optimal quality. Thus appointed, grocery shopping can become a kind of therapy in itself: *nutratherapy,* Paula and Alex have dubbed it—even more fulfilling than consuming food, the perfect simulacrum. When they're hungry or depressed, when they're in crisis, they inevitably go grocery shopping, so the sheer volume of organic bounty can soothe all sense of deprivation. Even securing a shopping cart spikes the adrenaline.

"Here's a good ad, Alex, what do you think? *There ain't nothing half-baked at Whole Foods.*"

"Go see the manager, P., and maybe he'll give you a quarter for that one." Seeing her lover's insulted demeanor, she nudges her contritely. "O.K., I'm sorry, a dollar. No, ten dollars! In fact, skip the middleman; here's a ten. You know I'm still a sucker for your corny jokes." Maybe this expedition will be pleasant after all, thinks Paula, then thinks Alex; maybe grocery shopping will be bonding and exciting even, just like old times.

They cruise the aisles. Once animal and vegetable have been accounted for, the abundance of the mineral presides: organic toiletries and sundries, second- and third-tier delectables: life's lower orders, so to speak. Even items that weren't *ever* living seem to shimmer with vitality in these alluring aisles.

The bergamot known better for its aromatic tea a few aisles down is here infused into a foaming hand and body wash. The household cleaning agents, once chemical repositories, achieve their squeaky clean results via citrus; it seems that laundering can be not only phosphate free but redolent of lavender. The mouthwash that was historically the province of carcinogens now derives from Dead Sea salts and algae. Thus something nearly primeval seems to lure to the domain of oral hygiene these two women, each nostalgic for the shelter of the other's mouth.

"Wait, we're not done with this aisle yet. I need to get some toothpaste without mint."

"What's wrong with mint?"

"I read that it might interfere with the homeopathic remedy."

"Too much zip, is that it? Might speed up God's time? Besides, I thought you couldn't brush your teeth period."

"You know, P., I like our being kids in a candy shop and all, but sometimes talking with you is like talking with some annoying child—one riff and that's it, you're off—you beat it into the ground."

"I'm like a child? I'm the caretaker, for god's sake; you're like the helpless child!"

"Well, maybe we both need to grow up. In fact I've been thinking a lot lately, and I realized that if we had our own child, we might be forced to become real adults."

"You can't be serious."

"I'm dead serious. Parenting would provide structure, motivation."

"Alex, this isn't a roundabout way of trying to tell me that sleazy homeopathist lent you his sperm, is it?"

"How can I ever convince my darling live-in psychopath that I didn't spend my two-hour consultation screwing the homeopath?"

"By saying you didn't, for starters."

"I didn't. I didn't. I didn't. I told you a million times."

"Swear you didn't."

"Bring me a Bible."

"One of the only things probably not for sale here at Whole Foods."

"O.K., scratch the Bible. Let's try logic. If we had had sex, that bill should be his to pay, not mine! You saw that bill with your own eyes."

"Good point. It could be a decoy though."

"This conversation is a decoy—you're running interference and you know it."

"And you're running period—just like old times. Slow down, we skipped your favorite aisle. Maybe we should fight more often; it stimulates your constipated circulation."

"Paula, all I'm doing is expressing a natural, universal desire. Otherwise there wouldn't be a baby products aisle in every grocery store, like the one we just passed."

"Aisle schmaisle. Don't be a fool, Alex. You're expressing a desperate, compulsive . . . caprice! You never learned how to sit still, and now that you finally have to, you've come up with the most generic female way to make passivity *seem* active. You're not even strong enough to go through a pregnancy."

"Maybe it would energize me."

"Maybe it would wear you out. In fact, it might be the last straw for your already overstressed system."

"You could carry then."

"What am I, a shopping bag?" Paula raises and then slams the basket down in approximate demonstration of metaphor. Alex flinches at the loud snap of plastic against the cart. Other shoppers turn and stare, then raise their eyebrows at each other, shrug, and carry on. "I'm already schlepping you to every medical and pseudo-medical office in tarnation!"

"Vessel is the classic term, I believe."

"Great, you're volunteering me now to assist you in your deluded, and may I say, labor-intensive, healing fantasies. I thought lesbianism was a refuge from—wait a minute, let me get this right—that insane procreation compulsion hetero couples have. That's a quote, by the way—I get to quote you too, you know. And, oh for the record, heterosexuals at least get to *have* sex on the way to procreation!"

"Announce my inadequacies through the loudspeaker, why don't you? Attention shoppers: Alexandra Davis can't get it up! And by the way, organic milk and hormone-free cage-free eggs on sale today."

"'Up' is not exactly what 'it' gets anyway, is it? You sound like some defensive middle-aged guy."

"I'm just saying we're in public and that was out of line."

"And I'm saying you're *out-of-mind.*"

"On the contrary. My mind is lucid. It's my *body* I'm out of."

"On the contrary, you're stuck *in* your body."

"Oh, you are *so* wise. I should pay *you* for a diagnosis."

"You know, you're paying everyone else, you might as well."

Now Alex is the one to lift the basket by its handles with intent to hurl, at least to make a racket.

"Could you ladies take it outside?"

Alex and Paula snap out of the intensity of their private argument to notice a muscular, middle-aged, most likely hetero, man with a shaved head, tattooed neck, and single gold earring, peering down through a pair of reading glasses to scrutinize the myriad labels before him.

"I'm trying to concentrate on the teas here. It's supposed to be a serene atmosphere." He gestures indignantly yet reverently toward the fortress of elegant, colorful boxes and tins.

"Serene is right; it's practically an altar," Paula says, in no mood to humor anybody.

But the panoply of tea offerings distracts her temporarily from annoyance, and mesmerizes Alex, and all three, as if under a spell, worship briefly, in concert, at the altar of *Camellia sinensis*.

Before them stand assembled every assorted herbal tisane juxtaposed with every variation of black, white, and green. Paula plucks her own bioptics from her purse and puts them on, intending to mimic her bald, tattooed adversary, but finds herself absorbed in what she reads. She starts to read out loud.

Alex, still insulted at what she deems a deeply unfair characterization of her by her lover, is ignoring her, and the bald man clearly wishes he could too. But Paula is characteristically persistent. "Hey, Alex, look, this says white teas are the best of all for you—even more antioxidants."

Alex is astounded that Paula can be so oblivious. How can she indulge herself in superficial banter after calling Alex a hypochondriac?

"Whitey comes in late and wins the race, well, isn't that familiar?"

"Don't start with that! You sound just like your mother!"

"You've never even heard her voice. You've never met her."

"Maybe for Kwanzaa. Besides, no fear, black's still the queen of tea, no matter what red, white, and green come up with. This aisle is proof that The Republic of Tea is apparently a democracy."

"Some matters aren't for joking, Paula. You're trivializing bigotry."

As if to reinforce Alex's censoriousness, the man announces threateningly, "I'm asking you one more time," turning to glare at Paula. But then he takes a closer look and focuses on Alex, interrupts himself:

"Hey, haven't I seen you jogging at Chautauqua?"

"Not lately. She's been . . . on sabbatical. Just like God."

Alex rolls her eyes.

"Can't she speak for herself?"

"Didn't you notice, she's a deaf-mute?"

"The blind leading the deaf-mute, is that it?" Alex whispers censoriously.

The bald man keeps glaring, but Paula is exceedingly well-versed in being stared at, whether in hostility or curiosity.

"I didn't, but I get the picture that you're her interpreter."

"And what picture should I get from you, sir?" Paula projects a brazen, unapologetic hostility.

"Oh, let's just say the picture of your average, defensive, middle-aged guy."

"He must have heard us arguing before," Alex whispers.

"So what?" says Paula. "Big deal," turns back to him. "Yes, you might say I'm her interpreter, as well as her protector. And her lover, in case you had any ideas."

Paula steps forward aggressively, lined up now with the organic herbal teas, just past the range of greens. The bald man won't be cowed, will not step back, which gives Paula the opportunity to see him in greater detail.

"Not quite sure what you're trying to protect your lover from, though."

"Well, for starters, from all the men who are habitually hitting on her. And believe me, that's the least of it."

"And who'll protect her from you, since it seems to me you were about to hit her, without the *on.*"

"How dare you imply . . . ?" Paula's emphatic but somewhat clumsy arm gesture dislodges several tea boxes, which Alex bends to retrieve.

"But if asking a question equals hitting on, I'd say that's within my constitutional rights, whereas last time I checked, disturbing the peace was still a misdemeanor."

"O.K., guys," says Alex, putting up her arms as if she were an umpire, "disturbance—of whatever variety—officially over." Alex tugs her lover away, grocery cart and all, determined to avoid an even bigger scene.

"Thanks a lot for emasculating me."

"Oh Paula, really now."

"Suddenly you're the pacifist, eh? But what about your precious tea—your highest priority!"

"We'll go back later, when he's gone, and when you've simmered down."

Paula doesn't ultimately resist. They make haste through the poultry, the seafood, the cheeses, allowing themselves to linger over Stilton and Gruyère, Jarlsberg, St. Aubin, and Brie.

"Do you think it's safe?"

"Well, he's not coming after us, at least."

Paula hovers over the olive bar, holding one of the transparent plastic containers as if it were a ouija board's planchette, reverently receiving signals from the Kalamata and Catalan medley, then the antipasto mix. "You want some marinated mushrooms?"

"How about the hot peppers?"

"That a girl. Spicy, zippy, just like your BCF palette. You know, Alex, I think you're starting to get some of your old pep back. I ought to stage an altercation every time we shop. But not with that creep. Did you see his face when you dragged me away?"

"I was a bit preoccupied."

"I could have sworn you winked at him, though."

"Are you kidding?"

"I saw you do something funny with your eyes."

"You saw me blink—the lights are bright in here. They're bothering me."

"The lights are soft in here. A lot softer than the merciless Colorado sun. I should know. I'm the one with eye issues, remember?"

"Pardon me for muscling in on your territory."

"I've had quite enough muscle for today, thank you. That guy was like a new age Schwarzenegger. But the best was that intellectual affectation—the glasses."

"They were for reading, dummy. You of all people should be sympathetic to vision issues."

"You know, you're always scolding me for insufficient sympathy."

"Maybe I feel the need for greater sympathy from you. Meanwhile, load up on those olives; so there's plenty for the both of us."

"Last time you said you couldn't stand the strong taste—or the salt. Or the something."

"I could go for something strong right now."

"I hope that isn't some veiled reference to Mr. Nouveau Muscleman."

"Of course it isn't. He's not even my type, and besides thanks to you we're all officially enemies."

"With olives like these, who needs martinis?"

"I'm glad you're so lighthearted given we almost got arrested back there."

"Arrested! For what? I didn't think sodomy laws applied to lesbians. Oh, you mean our instigating of the Southwest chapter of the Boston Tea Party. Hey, since when are you squeamish about making a scene? Miss Live It Up. Miss Who Cares That We're in Public, We Can Get It On, No Problem."

"It was embarrassing, that's all."

"Don't be so worried about what people think." Paula catches herself. "Role reversal, eh? You used to be the one to say that, right?"

"I used to say a lot of things."

"I know, believe me. For example, you used to say, don't bother with the cart, I want the exercise of carrying the basket. In fact, even two baskets, better balanced. Nowadays—except for that brief spurt of energy today in aisle three, you can't even push the cart! How much strength does it take to push a cart on wheels? An almost *empty* cart! Your muscles are obviously atrophying. Aren't you concerned?"

"No, I'm completely indifferent! That's why I've been seeking out *quote* every pseudo-medical practice in tarnation! Jesus, what do you think? Don't mistake lack of energy for apathy. Blah doesn't necessarily imply blasé, O.K.?"

"O.K., O.K., whatever you say. Here, give me the goddamn cart." She wrests the handle from her lover's grasp, more roughly than intended. "I'll wheel it all the way home if you want. And pay attention. Maybe if you watch me your muscle memory will begin to return. You know what they say—it's like riding a bicycle."

Paula walks briskly and obliviously through the checkout lines and past the electronic eye that greeted them approximately an hour ago, and Alex, zombie-like, behind her. But this time the eye grows a mouth and the mouth shouts, and before you can say *chronic fatigue*, Alex and Paula are surrounded by the store security.

"You had to joke about getting arrested before."

"I was being serious, you were joking. And the manager, you may recall, was being droll when he said they're an innovative store but they don't have checkouts in the parking lot."

"Don't try to change the subject. You were the one who brought it up; you're the one who tempted fate, and now look."

"Paula, you're talking nonsense. Get a grip."

"I am getting a grip, I think, on lots of things, finally. On our relationship for starters. This out-of-the-blue baby mania is illuminating. Maybe that's all you ever wanted me for anyhow—a womb-for-hire with an exotic twist. Target the weirdo, you figured—she'll be so flattered she'll lay an egg!"

"Just remember your nickname, Paula Ann Paranoid!"

"At least it's not Pollyanna—that's reserved for you!—the fool who thinks she'll be magically restored through the universal principle of maternity:

endowed with all the necessary energy to coddle and coo and dote and fuss; a hormonal jump start whose jolt will somehow galvanize those enervated cells. But face facts, Alex, you don't even have the energy to kiss!"

"Kissing takes a special kind of . . . motivation; kissing takes focus. It takes feeling good. You've gotta feel good to want to make someone else feel good, right? Common sense. Logic, whatever. You have to love what you are sharing." (A female security officer passes by, appraising them, raising her eyebrows as if to say, *well, well, what have we here?*)

"All it takes is opening your mouth! You manage it for yawning about every five minutes. You manage it to take those worthless sugar pills. In fact, if you'd go to a few less doctors you wouldn't have to stick out your tongue and say *ah* so much and there might be a little oral action left over for me."

"Gee, that's quite an about-face for the partner who initially asked, 'Could we hold off on tongues for now? Touching is fine, but I've got to work up to the idea of kissing a woman, get used to it gradually.'" Each is oblivious to the pacing of the same security guard, now unabashedly eavesdropping for professional or personal reasons.

"Look, you're opening your mouth right now to complain; see how natural it is."

"Who's complaining? Me? I'm always trying not to impose on you even though I can barely get out of bed! You're the one complaining, like I'm doing it on purpose. Like I enjoy being helpless. Like I enjoy being berated by you any better than by my mother. You guys should get together."

"Yeah, maybe for the holidays. I'll put on some festive mood music first: *I'm dream-ing of a white Kwanzaa.*"

"One of these days, the wrong person will overhear and you'll be off to PC Prison."

"We'll be lucky not to go to real-life prison, do you understand? We're fucked. So at least I'll get to meet your parents when they come to bail you out. And they'll blame me. They'll look at me and say, for this we paid for Harvard!"

"Paid half, paid *half!* I had a fucking scholarship—and worked too; can you get that straight? Meanwhile, you're being, as usual, histrionic. This is a routine shoplifting issue and a misunderstanding at that. I'm sure it will all be cleared up."

A male security guard now stands beside his female coworker; he makes a move to interrupt or clarify, but his partner puts her finger to her lips and shakes her head.

"Don't puncture my fantasy; I'm not finished. When your mother starts bitching, I can distract her by offering her a special invitation to my family's house. How about a pitch like this? Mrs. Davis, I wouldn't dream of disrupting family tradition by inserting my whiter-than-white presence, but won't you join me in inaugurating my own personal holiday?"

"I think I see where this is going."

"I'm celebrating Blondzaa!"

"Will you shut up?"

Someone from behind an office door calls, "Practice what you preach, o.k., lady? Both of you, shut up!"

Obligingly—at last—they whisper. "I thought that that would cheer you up, and you tell me to shut up! That's just the kind of joke you used to love!"

"Used to this, used to that. I've spent my whole life trying to be invincible, you might have noticed. This is no picnic for me either."

"And I spent my life trying to be invisible—it seemed a logical step since I was already a ghost. And hanging out with you I've become exponentially conspicuous."

"Could you quit this hostile joking around for just a minute?"

"If you stop threatening to have children."

"Look, I'm desperate here. Try to hear me, I need something to anchor my life."

"Just call me chopped liver. Guess I'm insubstantial. Guess I don't count. I just steer the boat."

"Call the cab, to be precise."

"Call the cops, you mean! We may not have to worry about transportation if we get locked up! No holistic healing opportunities behind bars either. And don't you dare get on my case because I can't drive. My vision problems aren't psychosomatic—I've got the genes to prove it!"

"What is this, a fucking contest? Who is more pathetic; who deserves more pity?"

"Can you stop being so hypersensitive—and selfish? It's not always about you, o.k.? I can't take this anymore."

Alex offers no verbal response, but when Paula looks into her eyes, she sees how overwhelmed she is. She grasps her hand and squeezes it.

"Look, you're even less invincible crying—could you please stop crying? You'll feel even shittier after. Crying always gives you a headache. I'm not claiming being banned from Whole Foods is indisputably tragic. I'm just being practical, because I hate to tell you, but I think there's a reporter and a photographer coming this way."

"Thank goodness you did all that community service teaching disadvantaged kids to hike and swim and sail and ski. For once being notorious is an advantage!"

"Thank goodness that cop's kid was one of them, you mean, because I'm not at all sure it was common knowledge."

"The poster was still on the community board; I saw it. But I think even without a kid, that cop would have been won over; I saw how he looked at you. He and his partner would have been only too happy to search you."

"Like that movie *Crash,* right? Don't start with that, P. I can't take it now."

"I meant it as a compliment."

"That's inexcusably naïve, P. You must see that by now. I mean, think of the reality, think of that movie at least, the scene where she's searched: it's objectification plus humiliation plus subjugation. Even that same-skinned couple had a whopper fight over it."

"Well, I'm gonna pass on the daily fight, for once, A., and opt to tuck you in with your eye pillow instead, because I think we need a time-out here. We've just been through quite an adventure."

"That's for sure. I must admit, I've never been escorted home in a police car before."

"Best not to make a habit of it."

After the Whole Foods debacle, Paula is pissed whenever she thinks of the procreative status that's been thrust at her without warning—the last straw in the series of indignities that have unmoored her fantasies. Instead of glorious adventures and amenities, she is a glorified gal Friday, a reluctant Clara Barton. Instead of being pummeled by skilled hands or by majestic waves, she's got a sore back from doing laundry, changing sweat-soaked sheets, scrubbing the bathtub, storing equipment in Rubbermaid bins, carrying out the trash and recyclables, and heroically lifting the spring water tank onto its pediment, even though Alex has decided that Evian's minerals better suit her own chemical constitution and thus now rarely employs the in-house device for which they nonetheless continue to pay a monthly fee. She feels as if she were a slave, even though her voluntary penance was completed weeks ago. She feels as if Alex were pregnant and she her attendant—one of those pregnancies in which the woman is on bed rest the entire nine months—especially since today Paula has straightened, mopped, and vacuumed, then done several errands Alex couldn't manage, the last of which she's just returned from.

"By the way," calls Paula from the doorway, "I picked up your dry cleaning for you—walked it all the way home holding it like some stupid banner so it wouldn't wrinkle." Alex doesn't answer. Paula calls her name, investigates the living room, and finally ventures up the stairs to find her other in the bedroom.

"Hey, did you hear me? Here's that dry-cleaning." Paula hangs it in the closet and regards the figure languishing on the bed. "Alex, it's three in the afternoon. Isn't it a bit early to be in your nightgown?"

"Did you leave it out to air?"

"What is this, the nineteenth century?"

"I don't think there were dry-cleaners in the eighteen hundreds."

"If you clean it, it doesn't need to air, right? The chemicals aired it for you, get it? Plus, I walked it home; isn't that air enough? Plus, it was sitting there in storage for a few months, longer than they're obliged to keep it for you if you forget to claim it."

"I mean the chemicals, you have to air *them;* I can't handle the smell of the chemicals."

"Can't handle this, can't stand that—no sun, no smells, no sex. Can't even kiss—"

"Let's not repeat the farmers' market and Whole Foods episodes, O.K., Paula?"

"Hey, third time's the charm, right? O.K., O.K., I don't want to upset you or make you feel more helpless, but look at the irony: You're not even going out. Why do you need to dry-clean anything? You never get out of your nightgown!"

"For your information, I wear this nightie so much because you gave it to me and it's beautiful."

"The first two hundred washings maybe it was beautiful. And don't kid yourself that you're wearing it for sentimental reasons. You wear it because you gave up on your body."

"Paula, that isn't fair. Being naked and sick is pathetic, that's all. Can't you understand I feel vulnerable?"

"Should we sew a scarlet v onto the fraying nightie to remind me of the fact? As if I could forget it for a minute. When I see you in that threadbare getup every single day, all I can think of is 'barefoot and pregnant.'"

"I'm not barefoot; I have slippers on."

"Very funny. Is that a backhanded way of saying that you *are* pregnant?"

"It's not backhanded anything. I just need to tell you something."

"Dear god, you did it with the homeopath!"

"Dear god, shut *up* with that already; you're absurd! I can't conceive right now—"

"You can't con—What?"

"Because my period stopped."

"Wait a minute. Really?"

"Yup."

"I can't believe I hadn't noticed."

"I can't believe it either. I mean, I thought you had and then I realized . . . in Whole Foods . . . that . . . "

"It's a couple of decades premature for menopause, isn't it?"

"Right you are. Garden-variety amenorrhea."

"Geez." Paula stands in bemusement, processing this news. "But it's a blessing, in way. I say amen to amenorrhea."

"Can you curb your enthusiasm? Aren't you concerned at all about my body?"

"Alex, look, it's obvious. Your body's out of whack from losing weight and from stress. The clock just needs to be reset, that's all. Internally reset— it should happen naturally. And I don't mean through getting pregnant either! Thank goodness it's not possible right now. God bless the minute hand of the biological clock!"

Paula does a little dance, exuberant and awkward, such as Alex would usually find endearing in its silliness, but finds in this moment annoying and willfully oblivious.

"It *is* possible, if you're game. Haven't you been paying attention?"

The dance abruptly ends and she stands rigid. "Unfortunately, yes, very closely. You've designated me queen bee by default."

"Queen bees do nothing but breed, right? We're talking one single time here!"

"Come on, Alex, try to see it from my side for once. Here I thought I was going to have a live-in personal trainer, and instead I have a live-in personal invalid, plus I'm forced to be a fucking lab rat, getting artificially inseminated to make designer interracial babies! As if these are genes I feel thrilled to pass on!"

"I didn't realize how opportunistic our involvement was for you! Personal trainer, huh? More important, though, I thought you told me it would be fluky to get two albino genes, that it almost never happens."

"See what you've done—reinforcing the assumption that I was destined to be compared to a little white mouse all my life! Maybe some of those homeopathic sugar pills can induce pregnancy. Why don't you try that first? In case you'd forgotten, I am one of those rare female specimens who isn't obsessively attuned to my biological clock!"

"Maybe that urge was on the funky gene!"

"That 'funky' gene has a name, Alex. I mastered Kwanzaa and Choihona and a ton of African American heritage–related terms, so you can damn well dignify my difference with its scientific name: Hermansky Pudlak! Memorizing one lousy condition shouldn't be beyond a Harvard graduate's grasp."

"That's not your customary rhetoric. But you're absolutely right, Paula; I apologize. I'll be more aware. Although your own derogatory comments regarding albinism set a poor example, may I say."

"You *may say* whatever you like, Professor Davis, but that's a pretty left-handed apology, isn't it? Blaming the victim?"

"I'm not blaming, I'm just trying to explain here that having children is also within this Harvard graduate's grasp, for chrissake."

"And what about *my* grasp? Maybe being in charge of one life is already enough. I don't *want* kids! Not now anyway. If I wanted a kid, I'd hire a man and do it the standard, old-fashioned way."

"Classic vessel."

"Strictly missionary."

Paula has been staring at a long green box labeled in Chinese characters. Underneath the characters, a chicken gazes blankly at the viewer.

"Speaking of vessels, what the hell is this anyway?"

"I don't know; the acupunturist gave it to me. It's supposed to make my period come back."

"Sticking you with pins wasn't sufficient?" Paula opens up the box and removes one of the three black balls nestled inside it.

"Who knows what's in this shit? Mad cow, mad chick—antibiotic- and pesticide-laced Chinese chicken? What if they have avian flu? Ever think of that? Some healing progress that would be! What if you get avian flu from these black balls full of mystery ingredients?"

"You're one mad chick yourself, sweetie pie."

"Not me. I'm just an ugly duckling."

"By all means, continue to indulge in negative self-image."

"I think you're the winner of the negative self-image contest lately. Not to mention the depression prize."

"I see where this is going, Paula. Rage turned inward yields depression. Blah blah blah. Tell me something new already."

"If you tell *me,* something *not* new age."

"Look, say all you want against alternative medicine, but until you try it, you're not qualified to offer an opinion."

"Since when does an opinion need a resume? What happened to free speech? Are we in China now or what?"

"And this," says the Chinese master, as she sails the infinitesimally slender needle into the top of Paula's cranium, "is for your *thinking too much!*"

As the needle penetrates, something shifts within her energy field, and she feels almost as if her molecules were realigned. For the first time since Alex's crisis began, Paula feels some of the skeins of her own tension unraveling. But she dares not surrender completely lest she be, even momentarily, complicit with all this hooey, lest she begin to feel that she herself is in need of some healing wholeness—she wants no truck with the self-pity from which she has steered away her whole life. It's shameful enough to be an enabler, just along for the ride. But how can anyone relax with that obnoxious ticker, more appropriate for timing soft-boiled eggs than human beings commanded to relax while being pricked with needles.

"I can't believe you've conned me into participating in these treatments *with* you, instead of just accompanying for moral support."

"Well, it's less boring than waiting, isn't it? You got all out of whack at the homeopath's."

"*I* was? *I* got out of whack? The *place* is whacked, the whole practice is whacked. A place with bilge-colored walls and no knickknacks and a guy basing a diagnosis on what's your favorite color is one-hundred-percent certifiably whacked."

"Not what's your favorite color, would you rather eat chocolate or cheese. Don't trivialize."

"Whatever." Paula watches an unusual-looking insect traverse the table inches from her pierced limb. She tries to lift her leg and feels profound discomfort, like a modest zap from a low-voltage stun gun.

"I just got stung by something."

"No, you didn't; it's just the needles. You forgot they were there."

"But there's a beetle walking across the table."

"Hmmm?"

"I said there's a beetle. Where's that doctor?"

"Calm down, will you? You saw the beetle, felt the needle, see? It's displacement; it's guilt by association, get it? It was a pseudo-sting."

"But it's not clean."

"They're disposable, use-once, throwaway needles, P. Pre-sterilized."

"No, the office, it's got vermin."

"Vermin-schmermin. It's a humble office. That's why the rates are reasonable."

"Sounds familiar. Can't we try a glamorous office for a change?"

"Try to remember, we're here for the expertise, not the décor."

"There's an ad slogan if I ever heard one. Alexandra Davis says, I come for the expertise, not the décor! Since when do they have to be mutually exclusive? Can't a worthwhile practice have a fancy office?"

"Sure, but you might be paying for style over substance. Big-shot doctors like to show off."

"Wait, I know the second verse for your ad: I come for the expertise, not the décor. When asked, 'you like cheese?' I say . . . hmmm . . . chocolate more."

"Albino poetess of Albion, versifying is not meditative, we're trying to mellow out here."

"I have to compete with the Chinese poetess."

"Who's that?"

"Our hostess, the needle-meister. Don't you remember that quote: something like 'Liver, spleen, kidneys: all one meat.'"

"Shhhhhh! She's just a room away. Besides, she meant where they meet, as in a mundane intersection; m-e-e-t, not a-t. The pathway at which they intersect."

"Rather than a cosmic butcher shop."

"I'm disappointed. I thought maybe administering all those Chinese herbs was doing something trippy. Trust you to find a visionary acupuncturist."

"Maybe there's a fine line between visionary and lost in translation, but I can almost guarantee you this is an instance of the latter. Although no question, acupuncture is a visionary way of seeing mind and body."

"We're some vision right now. Look at us. We look like twin pincushions. Or porcupines with irregular balding patterns."

Alex sees the accuracy of Paula's image, as each lies with slender spikes sticking out of various sites on their anatomy.

"Don't make me laugh, it hurts."

"Just close your eyes. Relax, try to feel your energy getting realigned."

"O.K., I'm trying."

"For instance, my mantra as I lie here is energy/mobility/fertility."

"Check, please! Fertility is not a mantra I endorse for you. Besides, it sounds like some advertising slogan. What about the acupuncturist's assessment? What does Dr. Wang say?"

"She says, stick out your tongue."

"That's what the regular doctor says; I thought non-Western medicine practitioners were more original."

"Well, she actually says, 'Let me see your tongue.' And if you don't pipe down, she'll probably say, 'You two better separate if you can't keep quiet,' as if we were in grade school. Do you want that humiliation? On top of our Whole Foods debacle?"

"No, but can't you just tell me her prognosis? A synopsis?"

"Acupuncture is holistic, don't forget."

"Yeah, yeah, I remember. But can't you remember what she prescribes?"

"Well, I have to take these giant herb pills after I eat—ten each meal?"

"So you have your tiny sugar pills and your monster herb pills. Like eating one-hundred-year-old duck or quail eggs will magically induce your period. And they say allopathic doctors are pill-pushers and cutters! Why are they called allopathic again?"

"You remember *like cures like* is the homeopathic principle, right? You were joking about it just the other day. And allopathic is essentially *un*-like cures like."

"Aloe-pathic? Vera-pathic. Psycho-pathic!"

"Alex, keep your voice down, really!"

When Dr. Wang appears a minute later, Paula fears she has in fact again disturbed the peace and is about to be both scolded and evicted, but the authoritative woman simply says, 'I take them out now,' and proceeds to pluck each slender needle from their respective flesh, one after the other, in swift and deft succession.

"It looks like she's weeding," Paula whispers to her lover.

"Hush, Paula."

The doctor proceeds to instruct each of them on how they should conduct their activities and diet between now and the next session, but Paula sees that Dr. Wang is no fool. She undoubtedly intuits there won't be a second time for Paula. Heaven knows how many sessions Alex has racked up already, few if any covered by insurance. They settle payment with the receptionist, acquire their herbal goodie bags, and imbibe again the clarity of mountain air.

"I feel like I've been on a charging unit."

"Well then, make sure not to put your finger in a socket."

"Or in a dike, right? Ha ha."

"I'll have to start calling you Dutchboy."

"Hey, it wasn't just me on the charging unit; you just had your needle-nosed tune-up in there, you're supposed to be all energized; you should be racing me home."

"It's not all instant gratification, P. Alternative medicine is more gradual and subtle than conventional medicine, remember?"

"I've only gotten pricked this once, and I feel peppy! Shouldn't your numerous treatments have perked you up by now?"

"I'm perking gradually . . . I think. I feel a bit less sluggish every time I come!"

"Wait, there's the bus, could you step on it, Alex, so we make it, please—cause by the time we walk home, you'd be so wiped out you'll need another treatment."

The slower Alex is, the faster Paula's fantasies speed forward. Fearful fantasies. Worst-case-scenario absurdities.

What a curious sight; there is a wheelchair rolling along the bicycle paths of beautiful Chautauqua, and in it sits the beauty queen who used to be the site's number one attraction. How quaint, how queer, to see her stationary, and queerer still to see this curiously enthroned invalid lashing backwards at her pusher, *faster faster,* not sadistic quite as much as desperate, with more vigor than one would guess an invalid could lash. It seems she wants adventure, ladies and gents, the thrill of old, but can't supply it except through the ministrations of her beast of burden. Up the ever-steepening paths they go with the stroller jogging. The pusher is climbing the cliffs despite the impossible obstacle of nearly sheer verticality: hoisting the cripple with the pickax and she supplying all the push until down they go *splat;* she is as flat as a shadow under the fallen chair, tipped back like a busted beach-lounger. Worse than being merely flat-chested (as Paula seems to think she is) is to be flattened to the form of an old-fashioned colorforms sticker that needs to be peeled from the ground! As if she were a vanquished Wile E. Coyote under an anvil. She feels insubstantial and bludgeoned: a stick figure that sticks to the ground until peeled off.

"Sure, I'll step on it," says Alex, rolling her eyes. How could she possibly explain to the partner who had been her twin St. Sebastian that running was out of the question because her muscles couldn't get it up; that they simply refused to perform. The signal from the brain that said: *move, increase speed,* fizzled out, never quite registered. Meanwhile the reply from the brain was a perverse idiomatic distortion that went something like this: RUN *that by me again!* Over and over, their frenetic but blundering dialogue raced. Brain: *Run!* Body: *Run that by me again!* Brain: *Run!* Body: *Run that by me again, wouldja please!* Brain: *Run* Bod: *Give it a rest. Let me rest. You're a nag. You're exhausting!*

And the yield? A trickle for a gush, a whisper for a shout, an inch for a mile. Ditto for every lesser command from the pain-in-the-neck brain, such as think, speak, cohere; or feel good, kiss, don't cry; or read, focus, no, *change;* Jesus Christ, for a change, just feel good!

The bus driver sees them, and for a minute Paula thinks he's speeding up instead of slowing down, but it's her paranoia, she realizes. He does decrease speed, does stop. He regards them matter-of-factly. Paula supports Alex's ascent from the curb to the front door of the bus, a bit less gently than she had intended.

"Hey, you're shoving me."

"No, I'm not. I'm just trying to make sure you don't fall down."

"If you push me, I *will* fall down."

"Alex, please, let's just get on and get a seat."

They cross the handicapped front section, Paula not allowing Alex's hesitation to take root. She considers it negative reinforcement to let Alex occupy the handicapped section, not to mention the embarrassment of explaining to the already puzzled driver. They find seats adjacent, smack in the middle.

"But listen, Paula, you've got to understand one thing: I can't become exactly what I was."

"I'm not looking for *exactly,* just something closer to it than *exactly opposite.*"

"It isn't that extreme, is it?"

"Well, you tell me. Who was boasting when we first met, 'I ain't afraid of no mountain lion, I'll outrun him?' Now instead it's, 'Leave me on the mountainside to die—I'll at least be food for some other creature! Tuck me under a bush!' Jesus Christ, I wanted you tucked under my bush—and it took a while to work up to that wish, you might recall."

"Of course I do. You were adorably tentative. It was charming. But it was even more of a thrill when you began to be the first-mover, the unprompted exhibitionist. After I liberated you."

"Or duped me!"

"What do you mean, duped you?"

"I mean that the flamboyant lifestyle you sold me on seemed to get reconstituted pretty quickly once I got involved with you. I feel like it's gone from larger than life to . . ."

"To what?" Alex waits at least two stops for Paula's uncharacteristically sluggish answer.

"I don't know. Everything was an adventure at first, even mundane things. Maybe especially them. Like it was one thing to go to Whole Foods when we felt strong and healthy, for alternatives, for abundance; now I feel we're going there in desperation."

"If I may correct you, that's the past tense—now we're on Whole Foods probation."

"Right, we're banned, I'm speaking generally. I just want to figure out, Alex, how did erotic turn pathetic in such a short time?"

"You're using that word a lot lately."

"The *e* word, you mean? Not to be confused with the *l* word!"

"No, the *p* word. Look Paula, there's no magic bullet to turn what you perceive as pathetic back to what it started out as, but the answer to the question is pretty damn simple. Everything changes. That's all there is to it. Something changed, and I hope it'll change back."

"Sounds like you have been sneaking sessions at Naropa."

"They have classes for degrees; I don't know if they do freelance sessions or not."

"Why not find out? Try to take a class?"

"You keep pushing with that. As if you're such a expert. First of all, I already have a degree, that one you mention every other minute. I don't need another one. Secondly, I've been outdoors more or less consistently since I arrived in Boulder years ago. Once I finished college, the idea of any indoor class was anathema to me."

"Well, you sure spend a lot of time indoors now. And if you're not planning to switch gears and study something that you can parlay into making a living, an indoor living, like . . . I don't know, feng shui, then you may as well absorb yourself in something self-helping. Maybe something like that would be good for you, Alex. Who knows, maybe they have some sessions outside. Isn't there something called walking mediation? It might be the perfect way to start the day: some hope, some focus."

"Be realistic, how could I take meditation classes when even reading makes me dizzy, when I can hardly get out of bed? Besides, I do my own version of meditating. And if I tried to meditate at eight in the morning, I'd fall asleep."

"You'd fall asleep at three in the afternoon too. There's no time of day you're not tired. Why get up at all?"

"Sometimes I ask myself the same question. I truly don't know why I bother."

They sit in sullen silence for some minutes.

Paula had intended provocation to be energizing, galvanizing: another form of acupuncture needle. Thus she walls out Alex's despair, hearing only self-pity, and is disgusted by it. Resorting, without even thinking, to her customary theatrics, Paula cups her hand to mimic some sportscaster's microphone, or as if she were the Boulder tour guide and the locals and commuters surrounding them were tourists and sports fans in town for this special mock event: "Ladies and gentlemen, Alexandra Davis is not conditioning herself for the triathlon this time but the T-R-Y-athlon. She'll *try* to get up, she'll *try* to make breakfast, she'll *try* to go out. She's trying to set the Guinness Book world record for futility." The bemused passengers register their various responses, a few yet more disgusted with this rambunctious stranger: Paula, than is Paula with her listless lover.

"You're a stitch! But do you ever think about the way our conversation has devolved into a million permutations of mocking my condition?"

"Do you ever think of how our relationship has devolved into a nonrelationship?"

"You know maybe you're the one who could use the meditation. This edge—it's not like you—you weren't like this before."

"Well, that makes two of us, cause you sure as hell weren't like this before either. And you're so busy seeking every bogus treatment that you never have the time to think of *why* you changed so drastically! What if this stuff is psychosomatic after all, Alex? In the midst of all those healing visualizations, did you ever stop to contemplate that possibility?"

"Mind over matter—open and shut case. It isn't so simple, Paula."

"But maybe it *is* simple, Alex; at least a lot less complicated than you've come to believe it is. For example, you might be punishing me, seducing me, then, through this vehicle of illness, spurning me. Or maybe you're so repelled you'd *rather* be sick than have sex with me."

"Time out! Your paranoia is out of control. Get a grip!"

"You're always telling me to get a grip. I've got a grip, a grip on bigotry, for starters."

"Well, if that's not the pot calling the kettle black!"

"So to speak."

The bus driver interrupts genially but volubly from the driver's seat, "Ma'am you requested a stop. We've stopped." All the passengers turn toward them. But Paula and Alex are too riled up, though the former summons the presence of mind, or courtesy, to say, "I guess we need a little more time," as if they are customers deliberating over a menu before dining.

"O.K., I'm getting out the megaphone this time!" Alex says defiantly. "Now are you listening? Earth to Paula: Everyone is *not* repulsed by you. Least of all am I not repulsed by you; quite the contrary—*attracted*—from our very first exchange, which you've immortalized for my chastisement. We're hanging out in this mellow town for a reason, remember? We're not in New York or L.A. or Chicago, not even San Francisco, we're supposed to be chillin' in Boulder to keep stress at bay. So no paranoia allowed, O.K.?"

"We're *having* chillin', if you have your way! And in the meantime, we need couples therapy—not to mention two crash courses in intensive meditation. Or at least that feng shui I suggested."

"You mean so I could have a positive environment to feel crappy in?"

"Yeah, sure, and so I could carry you on a palanquin from house to house while you design interiors."

"Like Frida Kahlo, eh? All dressed up and no place to limp."

"Guess you should have stuck some painting lessons in between those tennis, skiing, climbing, windsurfing, and kayaking ones."

"Guess I should have fucked a bus."

"Here's your chance."

"I'll pass. I've got enough physical problems already."

"I don't think Boulder traffic can compete with Mexico City's anyway."

"But come to think of it, Mexico might be a good place to convalesce in winter."

"Should we give Mexico a try then?"

"You couldn't handle the sun."

"You couldn't handle the trip, period."

"Then I guess we're stuck in Boulder. Bus-fucking isn't one of the regional specialties; but today's menu does include mountain-lion-mauling, if you're in a reckless mood."

"I think you're the one in a reckless mood today. You're definitely competing with me in the black humor department now. And hold the mayo."

"You mean the ketchup."

"Don't be gross."

"Who me? Oh, I'm just getting started."

A uniformed figure enters their purview. The bus driver looks suddenly less genial and more menacing, no longer tucked away up front, unrestrained by any steering wheel. "That may be ma'am, but I'm afraid the rest of us are finished." Alex and Paula look up, startled.

The passengers sitting closest to them are visibly relieved. "Yeah, we're in this mellow town for a reason too," one of them says. "Have a little respect for your neighbors." Her companion adds derisively, "We were born here."

The driver is emboldened by this expression of solidarity. His chest seems to inflate, his biceps gain mass. "I am asking you to officially vacate the vehicle. Or I'll have to call . . ."

"Is this déjà vu all over again?" Paula whispers to Alex, as she rises, tugging her dazed partner behind her, exiting expediently through the middle door. The conspiratorial moment almost absorbs their prior tension, but after one block, Alex's adrenaline has expired; her pace slackens, and they resume their vexed conversation, a world away from where they were emotionally when they lay in tandem like contented porcupines, less than an hour ago.

"Hey, forget the rope. Here's a more straightforward question: do you care about me, or are you just bummed out that your little homosexual adventure hit a snag—not as romantic and exhilarating as you thought it would be?"

"Yeah, more like hit a rock, or a major shoal! Hit the goddamn Rock of Gibraltar. And don't think I didn't notice that *your* gender preference shift is deemed officially legit but mine is just dismissed as 'a little adventure.' By the official lesbian standard-bearer."

"Black lesbian standard-bearer to you."

"You weren't always gay, so you're not a hundred-percent dyke either and you know it."

"Yeah, and I'm not 'really' black, either. In fact, everything about me is illegitimate. And apparently, on top of all that, I'm not *really* sick."

"Well, I can tell you one thing; I'm really, *really* white!" In spite of herself, Alex erupts not in anger, but laughter at Paula's mock minstrelsy, arms out wide, a little dance step, with the mountain backdrop as scenery.

"You can still make me laugh, P. I always loved the way you make me laugh."

"As long as I keep my corn off the crab, eh? And tell me, was that past tense there a Freudian slip?"

"Present tense. I'm laughing right now, right?" Paula doesn't answer, having gained the lead, and Alex pulls her back by the hem of her shirt. "Right?"

"Seems to me that you mostly don't care for my jokes these days."

"Well, if I don't always care for them, P., maybe it's because when couples have 'in' jokes, they're supposed to be things they share, their own private language; tender, funny things—maybe at worst, things that compromise someone *else* they know, but not things that diminish either of *them.*"

"Yeah, and couples are also supposed to share more than just sickness; remember that significant little coda: *and health,* to have and to hold, in sickness *and* health."

"We weren't quite at the vows stage, as I recall, but if you like, we can line up in front of that progressive mayor of New Paltz just in time for our anniversary!"

"Geez, can it be twelve months ago that I flew into Boulder and entered that sauna of destiny?"

"Yup. Just check out those numerous customized calendars as soon as we get home. Twelve months exactly tomorrow. That is, if you still feel like celebrating."

"Well, how do you feel about it?"

Alex hesitates. Her pensive frown makes Paula just a bit annoyed. "I guess we should do it. We made the reservations weeks ago. I mean, I think it's important to honor it. You got my special dress back from the cleaners and all."

"That's enthusiastic."

"No, I *am* . . . enthusiastic. I just want to make sure I feel up to it . . . physically. But I think we should make a commitment. To celebrating. To creating the positive energy we used to let happen spontaneously."

"o.k. If you're sure."

"I haven't tried a whole evening out in ages. It will be good for us. It will be healing."

"The restaurant, the hotel, the works?"

"The whole nine yards."

Paula, sitting by herself, surrounded by brightly colored depictions of the Mediterranean, expels a protracted sigh. As she sits staring through her bioptics at the menu, bored out of her mind, the myriad letters of the Italian-to-Spanish-to-English version of every dish swim before her, but if she puts the menu down, and returns the magnifying glass discreetly back into her purse, she'll be even more exposed, more obviously abandoned, more conspicuously solo. She keeps coming back to the paella for two. Available *only* for two, it says. How delicious it sounded: shellfish stew over saffron rice: fragrant and spicy and steamy—and appropriately romantic on an anniversary: one heaping platter with two serving spoons! Alex would be up for seafood, wouldn't she? She didn't have an allergy to that, miraculously. Paula felt confident that she could talk her into it, as soon as she got back from whatever bar was broadcasting the big Colorado Nuggets basketball game. Or Denver Broncos football game—she could never keep those teams straight, all balls interchangeable; she'd never even watched a game all the way through.

"Mind if I run across the street for just a minute?" Alex had asked, immediately after they were seated, "to check the score? Back in a jiffy, promise." Wasn't that what she had said? How many minutes had it been now? Half an hour, she'd guess. A rather inappropriate anniversary errand, in retrospect. What if some sleazy guy is coming on to her right now: "Buy you a drink?" And then another guy'll strike up a conversation with them, figuring why not, the more the merrier, and may the best man win: "Wow, a sports-fan chick—and gorgeous too, don't find *that* every day!" They'll be all over her, each vying for her favors, and then, if five *more* minutes pass without a sign of Alex, Paula will designate herself the official spoiler: coming in like some dorky, dickless Plain Jane, as if in bobby socks and Mary Janes instead of the sexy satin evening gown from Whole Nine Yards. Yes, Paula might as well be sucking her thumb; she, who unlike them can hardly wield a bat, can barely throw or catch, whether base- or foot- or basketball; she who would instead be batting, unconvincingly, her nearly lashless pink-rimmed eyes, while crooning, "Pardon me, any chance you'd care to be my pie-el-la—no, I mean pie-ay-a—partner?"

They, meanwhile, would hoot at her pronunciation and her tentativity, or more likely, would be so wrapped up in their revelry, eyes on the ball, that they would never even hear the party pooper's not-a-bang-but-a-whimper crash—as they pounded the bar with every goal or basket, whooping and cheering and slapping each other five, Alex more animated than Paula has ever seen her lover since the first few months, since the beginning—since the glory days, when Alex and Paula were the inseparable duo, the sexual sideshow of Colorado. How bold they had been, under Alexandra's tutelage: "We'd sell more tickets than the folks who run the rodeo, just strolling down the mall." The show, said Alex, each time she upped the ante on the risk of exhibitionism, *absolutely* must go on. "Helmut Newton, here we come," Paula would surely have added, had she realized they might be adding salient props like crutches, braces, wheelchairs, and the like. And what was that slogan they'd conjured for the speculative real estate office they'd start one day? *Be Bolder in Boulder.* Indeed. She remembered their little verbal game and the exchange that prompted it. Alex had urged she give credit where credit was due, insisting Paula would never have gone bi in Watchung, New Jersey. Initially Paula had felt slighted, insisted Alex's unique character—not Boulder's—had unleashed her eros. In any case, who knew whose eros was unleashing itself this very moment—and with what consequences?

While Alex and her newfound sports-fan friends focus on the televised game in the bar, the restaurant's genteel dining clientele focus on a wheelchair navigating through the restaurant. Seated in it is an elegant, gray-haired Caucasian man, not more than sixty, Paula guesses, steered by a considerably younger man, most likely a son or a nephew? With great difficulty and awkwardness, the enthroned man is carried across a set of steps by several waiters, to the sunken platform of tables below bar level. Diners must scoot their chairs in tight, their burgeoning bellies snug against the tables' wooden edges; one table must be moved over several inches, another completely relocated. Clients stare as discreetly as possible at all the commotion, some no doubt thinking, the hubris, the self-indulgence, of the handicapped man who didn't have the sense or decorum to cook or be cooked for at home. Paula, watching the spectacle unaccompanied, feeling nearly as conspicuous, wonders, what if in a year or two it comes to that? Everything consistently conspicuous and cumbersome; many large maneuvers required to accomplish even the most simple, insignificant task. She'd be surrounded by an arsenal of bedpans, catheters, syringes, and i.v. trolleys, when she herself might not see well enough to insert correctly said i.v.

She envisions her own future wheelchair charge; around whom would evolve a complex choreography: left hand pushing the wheelchair, right hand pushing a stroller whose sperm-donored, pint-sized passenger is some-how (despite being technically fruit of Paula's womb) miraculously the spit-ting image of Alex! And wrapped around the left handle of the wheelchair grasped in Paula's left hand is the leash for Malcom, the evicted, but still highly energetic and effusive, Irish setter who unfortunately refuses to mimic its master to the point of adopting any species of fatigue, chronic or otherwise. (He remains frisky and jovial, on loan for this fantasy from Alex's sister.) Paula can't keep control of all three, has to put one in front of the other like cars of a train or a car towing a U-haul; and the dog like a mascot on the prow of a ship, the beast of burden that helps from the front while Paula, the human beast, brings up the rear! Exhausted by the alternating or simultaneous pushing, Paula, in this ineluctably anti-erotic fantasy, finally collapses perspiring in a heap and weeps. But she can't indulge herself for long, as there is work to be done, care to be taken. Of whom? You know who: The elegant dark-haired once-Amazonian invalid, who is currently— if not quite consciously—channeling the famously fetishized, pain-ridden Mexican artist, dressed to the nines, borne aloft to her party on her own pri-vate bed, Paula pushing huffing and puffing while everyone says, *What a beauty* (to the chair-confined glamour girl) and *oh, what a cutie* (to the adorable toddler-in-stroller in front of her). *Beauty/Cutie, cootchie-cootchie-coo* and *hubba-hubba* and then looking past the chair candy to the ever-erect ghostly pale one supplying the manpower, they inquire, *Who's that hag at the helm? Is she the hired help? Who knew that Ichabod Crane had a twin sis-ter? Go back to Tarrytown, and do not tarry, Ichabodess!* chant the spectators. *Or should we say Icky-body?* Even the classically ignorant bigot's imperative, *Go back to Africa,* would have more dignity than the admittedly more orig-inal, albeit absurd, command that Paula swears she then hears: *Give back her nanny's puddleduck!* What could that mean? Whose nanny? Whose rubber ducky? Or was it *her majesty's puddleduck* they were shouting? Or worse yet, *your nasty puddleduck? Come again,* she says, and it repeats. They can't be saying what she thinks they're saying. She finally succeeds in interpreting the gibberish *Go back to Hermansky Pudlak!*

Paula's daydream more resembles a nightmare: all Alex's fault, in absen-tia; yes, her absentia is the fault line precisely. Don't go back to Africa, Alexandra, neither literally nor metaphorically; I couldn't follow you because you know they persecute albinos. Don't return to the dark conti-nent of animus and leave me stuck alone in anima; keep being my Beatrice, my Helen, my siren, my harpy—on our goddamn anniversary. My Alex,

Paula prays, come back to me, please; rescue me from this luckless puddle—
that is, pudlak—of humiliation you created in the first place. Having
exhausted her imagination—and exhausted by its entropy of darker mani-
festations—and yet unable to bear the safer boredom of reading the menu
for the seventh time, Paula stands, resolving that if she does so, looking pur-
poseful, she will not appear so obviously, passively, "stood up." She will
head to the ladies' room, out of both physiological and psychological desperation. But her timing—just her fucking luck—is wrong. There's competition. She must have been in fantasyland far longer than she thought.

Apparently the whole chaotic acrobatic episode is being repeated so that
the handicapped man may be wheeled down to use the men's room. Paula
could have sworn they'd just arrived. (He should have gone before he left the
house; what was he thinking?) The two of them, uncle and nephew, take up
what seems an inordinate amount of room, like cars in a pedestrian zone, like
bulls in a china shop; in fact, their collaborative navigation would seem a perverse inversion of the progressive, inventive, almost whimsically simple economy of design embodied in a Whole Foods handheld basket mounted on its
wheeled platform. And what of Paula's charges, vividly available in her imagination? If they, in tougher times yet to come, garnered their own high-fashion,
innovative apparatus, what would its contours be? Something contoured to
hold Alex's buoyant derriere snug in the baby seat, her long firm thighs jutting
from the cart, her shapely legs wrapped round her caretaker, making ambulation all the more encumbered. Jesus, thinks Paula, who would *dare* be handicapped in this mountainous, this overtly boastfully vertical town? It defeats the
whole purpose if you have to be horizontal. How mortifying for him, and for
the son/nephew/caretaker. What a burden. And just when she wants to go to
the ladies' room! After waiting for over forty minutes, just her fucking luck!

Paula cannot entirely distinguish between antipathy and empathy and
finds this fusion discombobulating—emotions do not meld as smoothly as
the ethnic flavors in her by-now-memorized trilingual menu; because first
of all, she feels for him and secondly, she feels *like* him, but thirdly, by some
canceling osmosis, she absorbs the other diners' collective consternation,
which were it to be verbalized in the basest way might form the following
question: should this man be entitled not only to eat, but to perform bodily functions as well? As if protecting him from this unexpressed but palpable opprobrium, the nephew stands sentry, holding firmly the rubber
handle-grips of the wheelchair, thus framed by the wide unwieldy contraption, which sits blocking the men's room door.

But Paula can't wait anymore; at least she can't sit anymore; she simply has to stand and walk. When she realizes she'll be waiting for an unobstructed pee (her own initial often used affectionately by Alex) instead of for her absent A., she smiles, until she further realizes that her instant wish to share the silly quip with Alex, hoping to amuse her, is tantamount to sleeping with the enemy. The very enemy she'd yearned to sleep with later in the evening: an evening in fact constructed entirely around that intention, complete with a fancy Boulderado suite, which they would reach escorted in the elevator by a gentlemanly concierge, after sipping wine on velvet couches, listening to live jazz: the package deal, the specially requested, extra-special occasion, the whole nine yards. This very plan ironically had precluded Paula's strapping to her wrist her trusty Timex watch, lest she in insecurity be tempted to retain it on said wrist into the wee hours, surreptitiously pushing the tiny knob that illuminated its face, to clock her own beleaguered orgasm, so as to see if Alex's farmers' market allegations were in fact correct. She must wean herself of this lust to share with Alex, because Alex was the problem in the first place, right? She'd find a clock after she peed. And then at least she'd gain some objectivity.

There is awkward eye contact; the seated man regards her in a way that makes her slightly uncomfortable, as if he also felt some bond with her: a bond she does not wish felt. But his eyes are somehow kind and interested and even . . . captivating. Upon closer scrutiny, they appear to Paula to be twinkling, actually twinkling. (Non-albino eyes can do their own tricks, after all, she scolds herself. Or titillates herself? Or both?) "Can I give you a lift?" Did he really just say that to her? Or has she started hallucinating in her anxiety over Alex's disappearance? No, but you can give me the time, she is trying to say, but still thinking, *a lift?* A lift to oblivion, more like it. Is she bigoted to think a man in a wheelchair wouldn't have a wacky sense of humor? And furthermore, a sense of humor not unlike her own? "I've been stood up, you see, and I'm not sure for how long." "Well, I envy you, I've been sat down!" Mister Nephew glares disapprovingly.

Paula sees herself pushing just such a contraption, perhaps in alternation with a stroller. Or perhaps simultaneously, one powered by each hand! It almost makes her lose her appetite, makes her want to burst into the ladies' room and wretch, a sense more urgent even than the need to pee. Wishes she hadn't drunk all that water and could forfeit urinating, because ironically, unjustly, not only is the men's room but the ladies' room too off-limits until this handicapped transaction is completed, since the chair is so wide, the restroom's corridor so narrow. She notices that this restaurant's bar has a TV too, which angers her anew, unless Alex didn't realize this before she headed off to wherever in tarnation she went in search of screened sports: down the block, across the street. But eventually the dog and pony show commences its migration back into the recesses of the restaurant, and everyone who has been delaying is suddenly lined up en masse outside the ladies' room. But of course Paula is already there, first in line, bursting with entitlement. Anybody else's body's urgency be damned! When she gains access to the toilet, she feels much more than just the relief of micturition. The change of scene is as profound as if she'd found safe harbor after weeks at sea. And doesn't she deserve this modest luxury, having waited eons for her lover, then a stranger?

It merits all-out celebration that this seat, at least, is not in public view and is custom-made for solo occupancy. Was it any more peculiar to sit musing, dreaming, fantasizing on the john than to sit reading there? Paula always hated when thoughtless, oafish people crudely—never gently— turned the knob in lieu of knocking, so presumptuous; even in a classy place it happens. Even in this very restaurant, whose food, she fears, she'll never come to taste. The knob is being manhandled out there—someone is obviously convinced the door is stuck with no one inside—which makes inevitable its giving way and guarantees the rude intruder's horror—not exclusively from confrontation with the awkward impropriety of Paula's posture as much as confrontation with the exaggerated whiteness of the face and knees and arms that are to greet her, i.e., the same-sexed intruder. Or so it seems to Paula, who feels her whiteness can trump any porcelain toilet, and who would love to throw her own politeness to the wind—refuse to abdicate the throne! *Do you have any idea how long I waited to get in here? I deserve some peace and quite on my goddamn anniversary, don't you think?! Besides which, you have some nerve forcing that knob without first knocking.* She would like to shout all this self-righteously with hands on hips and arms akimbo, though the toilet paper holder would undoubtedly be in the way. Enclosed solitude is far preferable to exposed solitude! She feels close to hallucinating in her desperation to entertain herself and to maintain this change of scene as long as possible.

She spools back to the bizarre Chautauqua scenario: a procession in which she herself is on most unflattering display, and privy to the thoughts and speech of gawkers. *Thank goodness the baby takes after the glamorous cripple! Rather than the able-bodied but distinctly unattractive homely nanny.* All the men line up to watch, like throngs at the Thanksgiving Day parade (with Paula as the float!), or spectators on the sidelines at the Tour de France. (This time, though, they aren't lined up for Lance, to cheer his tragedy-transcending testicles, but for Alex, with her as-yet-untranscended entire physiology.) They are no doubt wishing they could be the ones to wheel her: all those toned and muscled spectators and cyclists, the better still to shelter her in their collective burly arms, as they assumed that Paula, straw-haired weakling, obviously could never do. *What a blessing,* the spectators continue to whisper, *that the tyke inherited the kinky, nappy, nifty hair instead of that scarecrow's faux-bleached-blonde, limp, capellini-textured strands!* One accosts her directly, asking, *Couldn't you do something with your hair?*

I could leave, she thinks, I could go across the street and stage a sit-in at The Whole Nine Yards—holding myself hostage in that very dressing room, after taking all my clothes off and wrapping some absurd feather boa around my person, maybe even a boa constrictor like Nastasia Kinski in that photo Alex likes—better yet, a western rattlesnake—and thus attired, I'd hold a solo sit-in, letting Alex comb the Colorado countryside until she finally returns to town exhausted, checking every shop, and finds me. (Let her worry herself even sicker, thinking I got eaten by that mountain lion.) Then I wouldn't speak to her, wouldn't even look at her until she gets on her knees—this time at *my* behest—on the stained, crummy carpet, teary-eyed, begging for forgiveness, her regal head bowed down in shame, bowed lower, lower, until positioned reverently at my crotch, making an opportunity for that same ditzy, lusty, unsuspecting salesgirl to barge in, announcing, *Ladies, only three items at a time in the dressing—oh, excuse me!* When she stumbles upon our tender yet illicit melding.

But who am I kidding? Alex won't even notice that I'm gone until well after last call, she'll be so caught up in the game and in the good-old-fashioned male attention; my symbol will remain a symbol, the unheard tree in the forest. I'll be holding *myself* hostage, holding myself *period,* touching myself while at the bar she expends her single and miraculously ample ounce of energy on "the guys," while I pathetically masturbate without her watching, dedicating my handiwork to the memory of our vintage–boutique tryst, and finally come keening, screaming, then weeping, just as she sees, on some stupid monstrous plasma TV-screen, someone snag the winning touchdown or winning basket. Some damn ball or other.

The clueless twentysomething salesgirl would then reappear, inferring, in error, a more superficial, material disappointment:

What, didn't it fit right? None of them worked for you? I'm sure you'll find something else. You're so . . . striking. Paula's awkward silence would only spur her on; she'd continue to offer constructive suggestions.

Can't that friend of yours help you, she's some kind of model, right? Maybe an actress too? Haven't I seen her in Vogue?

Correction, young lady: my 'friend' is none of the above, nor just my friend. Not model not athlete not actress not goddess. She is—or was—my lover and she is—essentially—an invalid.

When finally the svelte shape of her lover appears, Paula thinks it may be a mirage. But then she understands the images preceding Alex's return were the mirage, and she reorients herself.

"Where the fuck were you? Do you know what time it is? I'm starving! I've eaten every breadstick in sight, every roll in the basket, drunk three-fourths of this humongous Pellegrino bottle."

"Could we maybe order another one?"

"Another one! They're eight bucks a bottle. Blue Cross doesn't cover Perrier, I'm afraid, anymore than it does homeopathic consultations."

"You just said it's Pelligrino."

"Whatever. Designer water."

"In fact maybe we could get an Evian? I prefer noncarbonated."

"Here's the waiter. Suit yourself."

"I see you found our establishment after all. Care for a cocktail?"

"Just some Evian, please, a large bottle."

"She just got here and already she's mixing drinks."

The waiter smiles uneasily and keeps his blue eyes focused on his pad.

"And if it's possible, a glass bottle; not plastic."

"Why glass?" Paula interrupts.

"Because otherwise there's that plastic taste. I have a slight reaction to it. Only glass is pure enough to be a vessel for the water without imparting its own taste."

"It's the water that's pure or not, right? Whether it sits in plastic or glass, or in a goddamn paper cup. It's the same H_2O, right? Doesn't that sound logical to you? Waiter?"

"Why don't I get your beverages, ladies?" He escapes, returns with the bottle—glass after all.

"Could you open it?" Alex asks of Paula. "I'm not quite strong enough to twist the cap."

"But that's the idea, isn't it? No pain no gain? One can't simply *open* the special trademarked mountain bottle? Too pedestrian. You've got to climb it. And appreciate it aesthetically. It is a custom Rocky Mountain bottle after all."

"Well, I assume those mountains molded in the plastic are the Alps and not the Rockies, right? It comes from France."

"Ah, of course. Ten points for the Ivy League graduate! But not important ultimately. We're concerned with grosser distinctions here. And look, wombs!" She then displays the ovals that sit opposite in the bottle's lower half. "Now, let me demonstrate the climbing that I had in mind." Paula rubs her finger up and over the raised edges of the embossed peak and mimics the approach of orgasm.

"Please let's not do the remake of *When Harry Met Sally* just now."

Paula carries on a little longer, just to be obnoxious, then relents. "O.K., fine. Open it yourself. Or go ask one of those hunks at the bar you got so chummy with."

"I'll have the waiter do it." Alex gestures toward the fair-haired, baby-faced young man whose awkward gallantry has gotten them this far, but he is busy serving entrées at a nearby table. She tries not to fixate on her suddenly extreme thirst, knowing it illogical since she was drinking at the bar ten minutes ago. "I think those oval shapes are meant to be the pristine pools from which the water is collected."

"But come on, it's obviously a ploy: the phallus and the vulva, right, subliminal eroticizing of product."

"Don't tarnish my favorite water."

"Tarnish! For you? Miss *Eros!* Miss Would You Like To Be On Top? Miss Blow Me in the Dressing Room."

"Let's be precise, O.K.? Blow is what you do to a guy, a much more vulgar term than the subtler blow *on* someone. I blew on you. The preposition makes a huge difference."

"Well, that sure sounds sexy."

"Is something wrong, Paula?"

"We're making a scene. The tea shrine episode and accusation at Whole Foods is child's play in comparison. Whoops, I shouldn't have mentioned the word *child!*"

"We make a scene before we even open our mouths."

"You used to not mind that."

"I used to not mind a lot of things. When I had the energy to deal with them."

"I was just about to *blow* this joint. Or blow it up maybe. Because if I'd known I was going out to dine solo, I might have chosen a more modest venue."

"I'm really sorry, Paula, I got caught up in the game, I lost track of time."

"If you wanted to watch the game, we should have saved money and stayed home. We could've ordered takeout."

"Look, I can see you're upset. It was thoughtless of me; I was completely oblivious, o.k.? I haven't known the luxury of being distracted from feeling shitty in so long, feeling stimulated by something I used to love watching, and it just took over me."

"Maybe you'd rather take your new friends to the Boulderado, since they had such powerful effects on you."

"The game had the effect. Watching the game. I never said anything about friends."

"Are you telling me you watched it by yourself?"

"Well, no. There were other people at the bar, obviously."

The waiter appears again with his pad, looking nervous. He is young, like the rest of the staff and, Paula surmises, gay. She wonders if he would be sympathetic to her situation after hearing her side of the story, and considering he saw her waiting here this whole time more or less stood up. She is tempted to narrate the whole tragic story as non sequitur reply to his recitation of the specials. Would he valiantly record her disclosures with his pencil until it became absurd?

"Are you ready to order, ladies? First I must apologize that we are out of the pollo con arroz. Also the paella."

Paula means to make a theatrical gesture of despair, slapping her palm to her forehead, but en route to her head, her hand topples over the Evian bottle. The diners at the nearby tables turn toward the commotion, some disconcerted, some amused.

The waiter flees, swiftly returning with more napkins, then a dustpan and whisk broom, even a fresh tablecloth, and another bottle of Evian—a plastic one, Paula notes, and tries not to gloat but feels yet more emboldened by this indirect triumph—and somehow amid these exigencies, has apparently performed a loaves-and-fishes variety of miracle. There is, it turns out, one more order of seafood paella, now specially reserved for Paula, because she has waited so long, because she clearly would appreciate it, because she deserves the special treatment of this classy, fancy, and yet homey, customer-is-always-right establishment. He is very happy to report this revised forecast, and Paula is, that moment, very happy to receive it.

(Two successes in a row, after such grimness.) He is sympathetic, she rejoices to herself; at least someone can be sympathetic.

"Let's make sure to leave him a substantial tip," says Alex, almost sheepishly. But Paula wants to take that adjective and put it in the conversation.

"Look, Alex, now that you're here, maybe we should accept the fact that celebration isn't all our anniversary is about, and use this occasion as an opportunity for perspective. On the relationship."

Alex regards her lover soberly, silently.

"We have to think things through carefully."

"All right."

"Great. I've obviously been sitting here a long time, and I've never been so keenly aware of the disparity between where we began and where we are now. As a couple."

"I guess we should begin at the beginning then."

"o.k., I'll go first: For once in my life, I was trying not to think things out, and just be spontaneous, and let's face it, I had a little prompting, more than a little. I have no idea why someone as beautiful as you would be attracted to me."

"I can't believe you just said that—that you still think that way."

"Let me finish, please. What I'm getting at is maybe you got tired of being so striking with your beautiful swishing braids and your royal head and your gorgeous swaying bod so you just wanted to shut down the show, or maybe your unconscious found a way to convert the energy of attraction to a different species of attention—as an experiment, a change of pace."

"I thought this was supposed to be a self-analysis. Not a judgment. Is there an official designation for a neurosis that compels someone to waste her time concocting speculative diagnoses for others? I think I just got tired. Period. No explanation."

"You know, the thing is, it's awfully hard to tackle something like this when you haven't even been together that long. I mean there's no positive history to support the challenge, the tension, the . . ."

"If you want to leave, just say so, you're free to go, obviously, no obligation. Saves us a trip to the mayor of New Paltz. Don't think I don't see how wistfully you look at the peaked white tents of Denver International when we take that shuttle . . ."

"White cures white?"

"No, seriously, Paula, I'm surprised you lasted this long. Whenever we go to the medical center in Denver, I fully expect you to push me out the shuttle, stay on till the airport stop, and vamoose!"

"Since you have so much faith in me anyway, well . . . look, I don't want to say something so crass as 'call me when you're better,' but I just wonder whether, in the interest of the relationship, how healthy it is—I mean for the relationship—to have you so—so unhealthy. Oh, forget it, I can't explain it very well."

"It's utterly clear. And yeah, it sure as fuck isn't ideal. I'm not exactly in control of those factors, as you see. Or maybe you *don't* see, since you're always claiming blindness. You prefer to be blind."

"There's a double standard plain and simple in that comment—not to mention cruelty—but I'm going to ignore it. I'm sticking to the point."

"Which is?"

"The point is that my heart isn't handicapped-accessible yet, I guess."

"Pardon while I barf! Who's in the greeting card biz now?"

"Fuck it, it's just too hard, Alexandra, I'm out of my element twice over here."

"You *never* use my whole name."

The waiter interrupts them briefly, seems in fact resolved to be as brief as possible in serving their entrees. Meanwhile Alex is aware that anger, pride, and sorrow roil within her; maybe some relief thrown in as well. No one has ever ended a relationship with her before. She has always been the one to make the exit.

And now Paula seems to be in first place for the finish line, the finished-with-relationship kind, that is. The only day in so many months Alex has felt alive, engaged, and this is the price she must pay.

"I never meant to be in Boulder, let alone stay in Boulder. It was just a fluke that I was ever here in the first place—to stay the weekend with my old friend Tim."

"Tim who?"

"Tim, agent of destiny, remember? Tim, whom I was visiting when we met?"

"Tim, who was after your ass, you mean?"

"No, Tim, my coworker, my buddy. Don't caricature him, please."

"So everyone is after *my* ass, but I can't even think one guy is after yours? A coworker who invited you out to Colorado just to pal around? Sure. If you hadn't come out of that sauna talking about my legs, I suspect the buddy status might have altered by evening's end."

"You can't project ulterior motives onto everyone, or every *man,* I should say."

"That's the pot calling the kettle black: remember the homeopath!"

"Remember the Alamo-path—or is it the allopath?"

"No, seriously, Paula; even now you're not convinced he wasn't out to screw me, that he *didn't* screw me. So you've got conspiracy theories yourself."

"O.K., touché already. But look, Tim is a very kind person. He brought me to the health spa because I had a headache from the altitude—or the flight, or whatever. Sitting in the sauna, I saw your glistening, muscular, café-au-lait calves dangling in my face."

"Like a climber on a rope?"

"And you gave me that come-on line."

"What come-on line? What are you talking about?"

"You don't even remember how we met!"

"Of course I remember, I just have a different . . . interpretation. I asked if you wanted to switch places because I was hogging the top bench, where the heat is always more intense. You obviously weren't a regular, and I wanted you to have the quintessential sauna experience. I was being thoughtful, not lustful. Not unlike kindly Tim."

"You said, quote, 'Would you like to be on top?'!"

"I don't have any control over your interpretation."

"Your tone of voice was playful, and you fucking know it. So don't scold me for being disingenuous."

"And don't scold me for innocent flirtation! You're always flaunting your passivity, Paula. As if I victimized you. As if somebody doesn't always make the first move. *You* assented; *you* joined. You weren't coerced—not to be with me or to be in the Mountain State. So ditch the Patty Hearst Stockholm Syndrome pose already. Passivity avoids responsibility. You have to be pretty naïve not to notice that even the guy at the bottom is playing the game."

"Was playing," Paula says under her breath.

"What did you say?"

"I said *was* playing. Past tense. Game over."

Suddenly the tension is more somber. Alex seems quite close to tears. Paula is gathering her purse, her fake-fur stole from The Whole Nine Yards, and her courage; fully intending to act on her impulse, yet conflicted, slightly inclined to call her own bluff. But as she pushes out her chair, she sees the waiter coming toward them, not with the check in a leather billfold, but with something bigger, more conspicuous. The dinner is apparently not finished yet. She had forgotten, Paula had, about the cake she'd ordered, the custom anniversary concoction, intended to be—for this first commemoration of their eros—a stunningly elaborate echo of their fantasy wedding cake. It didn't have the actual dark-and-light bride and groom figures that they had discussed in the bakery aisle at Whole Foods months ago, but it absorbed into its overall design the same essential principle. In fact as it approaches them, Paula realizes how remarkable a confection it actually is: not just a black-and-white divided rectangle, but chocolate and vanilla alternately cascading across its surface in intricate rhythms that approximate the patterning of wind on desert sand, its gradations scaled from white to beige to brown to black. It truly is a work of art. A utopian work of art. How could she go? It would be so rude, if not to Alex—who deserved it, really—then to the waiter, baker, chef—whoever presided over this astounding piece of craftsmanship. You cannot ask to have a cake like that to go. That would be beyond gauche.

So Paula waits. She smiles. She sees the tears in Alex's eyes, sees that she's moved to receive this tribute to their love, their perhaps-despite-all-still-intact eros. And this in turn moves Paula. The waiter cuts with something sterling silver, elegant and spade-like; he serves to each of them in turn, a gentle smile on his face. Paula would have saved room for it, had she only remembered having ordered it; the frustration and anger had obliterated everything else in her mind. With the cake placed right before her, it is now even more apparent that the special instructions she had given were lovingly followed and even exceeded. The richness of the seafood, wolfed down because by then she was ravenous, alas did not so easily accommodate a coda of dessert, but how could anyone resist? Alex extends her fork toward Paula tenderly, tearfully, and even in her most vituperative anger, how could she refuse this gesture? She parts her lips and takes the dense, delectable amalgam upon her tongue, swallows solemnly, contorts her mouth and eyes immediately in an expression of ecstasy. "With chocolate like this," she whispers, "who needs cheese?" Lost in the sensation of contentment and delight, neither woman notices the incipient commotion.

The man and his nephew are coming through; they have been far more efficient in their dining and are leaving, with no option but to exit the same way they came in, of course. The waiter is more matter-of-fact now, clearing a path for the wheelchair, asking the diners to scoot in once again to their tables. Paula obliges. Somehow the parade seems to cast a shadow over the celebratory moment. Alex looks at her plate, no doubt aware of what the image likely conjures up for Paula, let alone herself. Paula is meanwhile beginning to regret her over-indulgence, as she dutifully continues to press her belly against the covered table edge, captive to the sumptuous, nearly overwhelming chocolate aroma. She feels lodged in her gut the festering mountain of breadsticks and butter and sourdough rolls compulsively consumed while awaiting her mate: flour and dairy, rice and oil, spicy broth and seafood, fudge and cream. She feels distended as if pregnant, and incarcerated by this table and the at-long-last-arriving wheelchair, whose occupant and chauffeur she thoroughly resents. Once again they block her getting to the bathroom, which this time she seeks in honor of a far more urgent physiological sensation.

Will they ever pass? She feels increasingly unable to control the roiling in her belly. Instinctively, she pushes out the chair to alleviate the pressure of the table but she hits the chair against the wheel. Her torso turns. The nephew looks slightly alarmed.

Now whatever wreaks havoc in her stomach is retreating up her esophagus; a stinging acrid force that will no longer yield and clearly has no truck with etiquette. Contorted, nearly in the cripple's lap, almost grotesquely elegant in her gold lamé gown, Paula steals the show, the silverware goes clattering, the Evian-filled glass tips over once again; but bile rather than water pours from Paula's font; yes, all the bile of months ejects itself onto the man's officially handicapped lap.

"Are you all right, are you all right?" the man is being asked by his caretaker, by the waiter, by the other members of his party, by the diners who have risen to the occasion of this outrageously distasteful installation, this spontaneously visceral one-woman show, its star, for once, an inadvertent exhibitionist. They wait for him to speak, concerned that this discombobulation has somehow compromised his circulation, stopped his heart, robbed him of breath. He does appear in shock. When finally he arranges his features in such a way as to suggest forthcoming speech, their own expressions are of awe, as if he'd come out of a coma after twenty years. They bend their heads toward his, ignoring the disgusting bodily effluvia that Paula has indecorously ejected. But he ignores them all, looks straight at Paula, who without assistance from a single guest or staff member, has righted herself and begun to clean, with the sopping Evian-soaked napkin, the stains of vomit.

"We've got to stop meeting like this."

Paula knows this is the kindest cliché a human has ever uttered.

"You know, I've heard of women jumping out of cakes before, but this is really something."

And just to make sure no one is confused about his lack of offendedness at Paula's physiological faux pas, he throws another bone, more audibly than before, no longer merely offering a private joke to his assaulter, but proclaiming to the masses, hamming it up to the hilt: "I asked her to sit in my lap, and she thought I said *spit* in my lap! I have to practice my enunciation."

And everybody laughs. The nephew, the waiters, the busboys, the maître d', the other guests, and even Alex.

Suddenly he, Paula, and Alex are as jolly as the trio in the neurologist's waiting room. Come to think of it, Paula decides, why couldn't heaving onto someone's lap be every bit as humorous as playing hanky hide-and-seek on someone's head? And why should stand-up comedy not have its nascent sibling, sit-down comedy?

"She'll do anything for attention," Alex volunteers, and winks seductively in the direction of both her lover and her lover's newfound ally. "Like that whole albino get-up she puts on whenever we go out. The wig, the makeup, contact lenses. Whole nine yards."

He smiles and winks back.

And the other diners gradually resume their normal interactions, the restaurant resumes its previous configurations, and by the time Paula and Alex make their exit, heading toward the Boulderado and their special suite, barely a diner bothers to turn and stare.

A Daughter in Time

When we packed up our daughter in a car full of CDs and toiletries, clothing, and technology (gadgets of all sorts: laptop, answering machine, stereo, VCR, and cell phone, of course, to make contact completely accessible), we had the average anxieties of average parents, I would imagine. I'd like to think *less* than average, given that my job as assistant dean of a small college gives me an intimacy with the needs, opportunities, and hazards of a college student's existence. I work primarily with first-year students, and particularly with first-year women, so the transitional period is my expertise, you might say, and thus I felt myself well-educated concerning what to expect and consequently how to prepare—although for the same reason a physician does not typically treat her or his own children, I occasionally feared being less resourceful should I have to counsel my *own* daughter on the issues that were likely to arise on any campus, anywhere.

By last spring, the *any* fell away from *where,* and we knew our daughter would be attending school in New York City. Countless conversations between my husband (from whom I am congenially separated) and me, both with and without our daughter, involved assessing the wisdom in catapulting a young woman from a semirural environment into an urban college experience, with all its attendant chaos and peril. (And excitement, granted: that too.) Of all the lovely, bucolic, protected campuses where young men and women walking backwards cited memorized statistics and extolled the various virtues of their beloved libraries, facilities, faculties, amenities, etc., gesturing toward pristine green or lofty hill, impressive edifices or languid lake; there were none that seemed to our daughter the right combination of social, intellectual, and cultural opportunity, and so she chose (ironically, we felt) the university environment that required her to make the greatest number of adjustments at once. I consoled myself, and we each other, by citing various specious advantages: at least she won't get SAD (as in, seasonal affective disorder), as she might in some upstate college far to the north where the snow is more than half the year ubiquitous, or have as her only social outlet the downtown bars and fraternity parties with their notorious vulnerabilities for female students. Nor be dependent upon institutional food and its sole alternative, pizza, and thus nutritionally deprived, given the availability, within blocks, of every variety of ethnic cuisine; and certainly not culturally deprived, with Lincoln Center, SoHo, MOMA and the Met, etc. at her disposal.

In any case, both of us having been brought up with limited choices, in particular with regard to education, we had a pact with each other regarding Kara's options: we would support, not control, discuss rather than dictate, and so forth. And what decision, after all, was more crucial than college? Where one's career was shaped, where perhaps one's life partner was to be found, as had been our case. (Granted not our *entire*-life partners!) And en route to perfect career and soul mate, I knew quite well from my profession, would be a thousand emotional and intellectual excursions, regarding trust and desire and disappointment and achievement: which major, which extracurricular activities, which gender, which sexual preference, which political allegiance, and I also knew that substance abuse, date rape, and DWI loomed over the troubling *enough* issues of being ostracized by this or that clique in the cafeteria, or failing important exams, or dropping a class after a deadline, or discovering dormant learning disabilities, or overcoming stage fright, or dealing graciously with messy, noisy, selfish, oftentimes unstable roommates, not to mention being initiated into credit card debt. I prided myself on my enlightened status, that unlike certain of my friends, I would (though disappointed and upset) not be shocked and hostile if my daughter came home pregnant, depressive, bisexual, bipolar, Republican, alcoholic, suspended, a dropout! I knew the drill. It was my job, after all. I was intimate with this sector of the population demographically assigned to find themselves, take risks, reach out, explore, expand horizons, every other platitude; I knew they could not do so without some casualties.

How casually I used that very term, *collateral damage* resounding, later, in my brain, its vowels collapsing: clattering, cluttering. How fortunate I felt to have the preparation my vocation afforded me, and to have a bond with my daughter that allowed me to speak openly, if not always easily, about such matters as might be relevant. For this was the u.s. of a., the apex of indulgence, of opportunity, of luxury, where it was appropriate that students have an education construed not exclusively from books. This four-year slot was not set aside for them to learn a trade, nor to pursue, through an aptitude assessment conducted in youth, some predetermined track that they had little say in changing. In other countries, it would be incomprehensible that thirty thousand dollars a year be spent to provide a context in which a young adult might easily do everything *but* study, an activity that could perhaps *more* easily be done at home! How many times had I imagined the phone call in which she would confide her initial homesickness, her apprehension about a first social event or about which class to drop or add, her distress about a menstrual cycle gone haywire, her confusion about (cliché of clichés) the meaning of life! And I, "empty nester," would offer strength, and *only over my dead body* project my loneliness upon my daughter; nor would I under any circumstances judge her for decisions made in haste that seemed to me unsound or unsavory. I would be her pillar, both of us would be, never other than supportive.

We dropped her off in August on a day so hot that it seemed impossibly premature, for it seemed preposterous to expect a student to function in the capacity of student. We attended countless orientation meetings not markedly different than those I organized myself (but this year, obviously, did not attend) at the school I knew my daughter would not—despite the potential for considerable tuition savings—choose (nor would I urge her to) despite our bond, lest she forfeit the experience of complete autonomy. (*Pretty cushy autonomy, eh?* my husband would say, on his less indulgent days.) Labor Day, I remembered, had been, for all my youth, the boundary between leisure and routine, freedom and oppression. But nowadays routine was already established by September 4th or 5th or 6th—whatever Monday signaled *back to business, party's over.* The party was, it turned out, definitively over—for there was nothing festive in the atmosphere less than a week later as a hundred panicked students streamed into the administrative offices, keeping the phone occupied the entire day and the next several as well, while we, the consoling-by-rote and yet uncomprehending staff, somehow organized activities, counseling, nondenominational chapel services, geopolitical lectures, etc. (the campus green blanketed not with snow but fabric: a dozen cotton-polyester sheets ripe for Magic Marker graffiti, the quad transformed into one vast trauma journal).

When the logjam of "all circuits busy" finally broke, and I made cell phone contact with my daughter, I was overjoyed to hear her voice, to know she was alive and safe, thank God, alive and safe. *I'll come and get you right now,* I blurted out, realizing even before she said, *You can't get here,* the absurdity of my proposition: the exponential chaos that would result if each student in my office were to be removed one by one by an endless funeral-like procession of parental vehicles. *(Your hubris is that you thought you could protect her,* an astute but insensitive acquaintance said at just the wrong moment.) But other than this, I could offer no solutions, for of course she offered no queries (on behalf of some putative friend) regarding plagiarism, contraception, bulimia, abortion clinics, not even measly time management skills. Even so, from the time we said good-bye, I mourned for her robbed indulgence. *(No, what you truly mourn,* the chorus of colleagues chanted behind the scenes, *is your disempowerment.)* Let me break it down for you. My husband, when I carried on for days and weeks said, *Jesus, Elaine, at least she's not in ROTC, get a grip, she isn't going off to war,* whereas the chair of the economics department added, *At least neither you nor your husband were above the 100th floor there, trading stocks into rubble, and now Kara an orphan, think of that. At least she's not a ten-year-old,* said the director of the teacher certification program, *whose whole class saw the horror live across the street instead of from a dorm room via CNN! Imagine those kids' dreams for the next fifty years!* And my worldly friend on the political science faculty said, *Listen, Elaine, imagine the poor mothers in Afghanistan, what kind of adolescence can their children ever have, and now? I mean, if she were an international student,* said my staff associate, *and had to confront real threats of bigotry because of race or creed, you'd have some substance to your worries. And you mourn her being robbed of idle pleasures, pedestrian traumas, "normal" rites of passage? Welcome to the real world!*

All right, I thought, I'll face facts: Ecstasy-induced dehydration, vandalism, racial confrontations, Rohypnol slipped in a drink, participation in unspecified illicit activities, unscrupulous teachers' sexual overtures, etc. instantly transmuted to frivolity. What then, I would like to ask, is the status of cutting class, computer crashes, disk erasure *lost all but the first draft, didn't realize the difference between plagiarize and paraphrase, had to pick up my friend at the airport, my roommate produced an identical paper—no shit?, alarm didn't go off, my dog ate it!* These are spurious sorrows, admittedly, and I say guilty as charged, *mea culpa.* I feel for the world, for the world's children, for the dead and wounded and bereaved, but am I not allowed in the margins of my mourning, this shameful ancillary grief, for a daughter whose false start in higher education underwent a vicious interruption on 9/11—the very number I had thought, besides my own, would offer her protection in a city full of arson, robbery, rape, and homicide (as well as, yes, I know, of entertainment, art, and cultural exchange)—so early in her journey as a member of the Class of 2005?

O shaken, tainted Class of 2005, each member of whose dorm rooms contained more sophisticated technology than that which was employed to make the glorious gravity-defying tower implode like a sand castle yielding to an inexorable wave, your September will not entail innocent flirting with classmates or casually borrowing a roommate's sweater, for all that should have been casual will henceforth sprout a tail: the suffix *-ties.* You will not come to class hung over after carousing nor will you oversleep after staying up all night talking about life and love and dreams. You will not play hooky watching soap operas or sitcoms but rather sit glued to a tube emitting a single unraveling image night and day, participating in a communal nightmare. You will make pilgrimages to the street shrines, perhaps create them, and then stand over the white sheets taped to walls or laid on greens and inscribe, on the first day, a prayer, then the next day, a haiku, and finally, some stab at assimilation, such as *This is our JFK,* which, when I confide to my husband, will garner censure. *What is that supposed to mean?*

I'll interpret for him as follows: this date will be emblazoned in memory, when you are middle-aged each of you will be asked, during barbeques or cocktail parties, *Where were you when the towers fell;* and our daughter will say, *I was there, in the very city, not right there, of course, because I probably wouldn't be here now, but close enough,* and yet no closer than any other viewer glued to a screen on which a gravity-defying tower toppled without resistance like a sand castle submitting to an inexorable wave, and my husband will say, *These teenagers, it's all about them, already it's co-opted like the capitalist machine that turns real tragedy into TV docudrama with a soundtrack: Generation XYZ yearning for a tragedy to legitimate their existence, to finally give substance to their superficial lives.*

For goodness' sake, they have to process it somehow, I'll say. *They're just trying to own it. Oh, stop with the dean-speak, would you,* he'll say, because everyone, everywhere, is tense. I am too, I admit, tense enough to resume the therapy I had halted months prior—knowing that he, at least (the professional whose advanced degree requires him to listen), will not bestow judgments on my bourgeois regrets. He will hear me out, listening sympathetically, and offer, in the final five of fifty minutes, only this: *Do you think you might finally be ready, Elaine, to surrender control?*

Junior Achievement

Held by the small, doughy fingers of a not terribly dexterous hand, the outer surface of the tweezers more often make contact with the sides of the cavity than they do with the diminutive objects they are intended to grasp: the Wrenched Ankle or Funny Bone, the Charley Horse or Wishbone, the Broken Heart or Adam's Apple, the sequence of slices nestled in the Bread Basket. Every time this slip occurs, a red bulb lights up and a buzzer sounds. The younger ones giggle as their older brother grimaces.

> It's *my* turn now.
> No, Robbie, let Kaylie try again.
> Why does *she* get to go again? *Not fair!*
> Cause she's the youngest. And because this isn't just playing a game, Rob, it's building skills.
> Building *boring* skills. School was more fun.
> Well, we're doing homeschooling now.

The red bulb that signals imprecision, once located between eyes and mouth, is now situated between the thighs of the game-board figure. A small tool kit lies beside the box and its cover.

> Hey, you changed the board around—the nose is gone. Why'd you put it—?

Oh yeah, I meant to tell you, it's the *south* nose now. I want us to get used to concentrating in that . . . zone.

Sheeez! I'm sick of Operation, we play it every day. Why can't we play Boggle or Clue or Pictionary—or go to the mall?

Well, guess what? We're too young to drive, it's too far too walk, and oh yeah, no money to spend. That's three good reasons to stay here, Robbie, and there are lots better ones I won't scare you with. Get used to it—we aren't going out for a long time.

You're so bossy since Mom and Dad died.

You think it's fun being the oldest? You're just all irritable from being cooped up. Let's get it out of our system with jumping jacks and the four-instruments cheer. Stand up, Kaylie, Repeat after me. One and two and three and four: *Vacurette Cannula, Dilator Tentaculum!* Come on, give it more oomph: *Vacurette . . .*

Two sets of chains, each set joined at the bottom by a curve of plastic, descend from the ceiling over a pool table whose felt is covered by linens patterned with cartoon characters. A boy sits beside a disassembled canister vacuum cleaner, gazing intently at its parts, fastening and removing the hose, attaching it to other tubing, testing its suction. Strewn across the linoleum floor are a population of stuffed animals; hard plastic men with animal appendages; and plastic play-food items: hot dogs and burgers in buns, diminutive plates and teacups, halves of fruit with painted seeds, corn cobs, ketchup bottles, and ice-cream cones. The boy steps over the numerous obstacles, carrying the tubing to the stairwell. The younger boy suddenly bounds down the stairs. His older brother glances up.

Hey, Robbie, wanna give me a hand here? The younger boy surveys the wreckage.

But I don't get what to do.

Look, you're the one who built that megazord there from the instructions when you couldn't even read them. It must've had a hundred parts.

Oh, did I tell you, Shea? I renamed my wild force glowing gorilla megazord RHOGAM.

I'm proud of you, Rob.

A young girl whose legs are less in length than the riser's height hovers at the top of the basement stairs. Every time her foot slaps a step, a smaller body whose pudgy calf she clasps in her hand thuds gently behind her.

What you got there, Sis?
I'm bringing Bitty Baby down.
Dollies stay upstairs, you know the rule. Did you eat breakfast yet, it's getting late. Some Captain Crunch or Fruit Loops?
I want Am-fraks with banana and milk.
Kaylie, I explained that anthrax isn't a cereal, it's a poison, and we can't eat it or even go near it. How about a bowl of Count Chocula instead?
Can I watch *Blue's Clues*, Shea?
After you've practiced giving the orange a shot. Remember how I showed you, right in the belly button. Plunger in, plunger out, a piece of cake, and if you do it right, I'll even let you *have* some cake, the chocolate cupcake with the white squiggles you like so much, and we can skip the cereal. It's all stale anyway.

The young children make shadows on the wall with two long-billed creatures of stainless steel.

See my ducky?
See *my* ducky?
Hey, why doesn't his beak open?
Don't *pull* the jaws apart, O.K.? Just move his head up and down. NO, the whole thing, up and down.

They boy and girl bump the two bills together lightly.

See, Shea, the duckies are kissing. Look at our duckies!

Then they slide one inside the other, meshing shadows.

Guys, now I have to sterilize the speculums all over again! And don't forget to wash your hands before we start. Can you tell me what kind of soap you need to use? Do you remember? Little Mermaid!

No, SpongeBob.

Not what brand, what kind! Don't you remember our little song? *When the ant is sad his back eye tears!*

And it feels like an eel, the children chime in.

So what kind of soap do we always use?

ANT-EYE-BACK-TEAR-EEL

Great, now one chorus of the blood alphabet together. How about it?

O.K., Shea.

A,B,R h, one two three, now I do my D & C. If she's Rh neg-a-tive, one more shot to go home with.

Can I have a Fruit Roll-Up now?

And a Go-gurt for me!

Two action figures are poised for battle. One's costume is red, the other pink. They wield long steel rods with curved ends; both their forearms and the arms they bear are simultaneously gripped within the fist of a child. The two children act as puppeteers, urging their Power Ranger dolls to battle to the death. Their striking ceases only to allow each to procure a second weapon in the opposite hand, but finally pink is vanquished by red.

Ninja Storm, watch out!

Mine is the fattest sword, so I win!

Their older brother intervenes. O.K., we don't want to scratch the nice, clean instruments. And they aren't swords, they're dilators, so stop banging them against each other and lay them out from thinnest to thickest in the order I showed you. Everything'll be ruined if they get mixed up before the procedure.

We won't mix up the pa-seizure, Shea, don't worry.

I have to worry when you can't even say it right. She could *have* a seizure if you *do* the *procedure* wrong, understand?

You mean, like with our Power Rangers, if the sword, I mean the dilator, dies him cause he bleeds too much?

Yeah, something like that. And remember our memory game, to tell the hard words apart: two girls, one young, one old. We clean with the old woman, we numb with the young girl.

That's kinda dumb.

No, it's smart. First Auntie Septic pays a visit to the lady pocket.

Then, her daughter Anna-sthetic puts the needle in so the lady has no pain.

I like the Powerpuff Girls better. Can't you make me a story with them instead?

Not right now—it's time to get ready for work.

The older boy lifts a pile of computer-generated signs from a table. He flips through them slowly. He lays them down, leaves the room, returns with Scotch tape. He puts the first one against the door: *Even a Child, Inc.* He tapes it, then obscures it with the second, tapes that, and stands back to survey it. *Docs on Trikes.* He yanks it off, replacing it with the last: OB-GYN-*Kenobie, Inc.* Finally he peels this too off the door, crumples each of the sheets, and takes them to the trash can.

She was sposed to come when the commercial's on!

The downstairs TV's on for you, K., don't whine.

You promised only during commercials.

I said *mostly,* I said we *start* in commercials, but you can't do the procedure in pieces. Besides, I can tape any program you want for later.

Well, I can't come down without my Lots to Luv Baby.

Kaylie, I told you, no dollies downstairs anymore, only up here.

Then I'll stay up here.

But I need you to help out. Remember?

It's not fair! Robbie gets to bring his action figures.

We need G.I. Joe to stand guard at the window.

But you put that black struction paper over the windows.

We still need protection.

I'll bring Happy Family Midge and Baby then.

Please, Kaylie, that's even worse.

O.K., then Baby Annabell. She's not even a doll! She's like a real baby. See, her mouth moves when I give her bottle or her button.

Look, K., you cry if you *don't* see the dolls, but the women cry if they *do* see the dolls. They get very, very sad. Rio Barbie is better. O.K.?

Shea, why don't Rugrats do pa-seizures?

Cause they have mommies and daddies, for one thing.

The older boy returns to the basement where, in front of a murky fish tank, a row of gleaming instruments lies upon a folded Barney towel. He

137

smoothes the sheets, then peers down at the space between the Lion King's paw and the white background, lifts the sheet.

Hey Robbie, there's a blood stain on the felt, weren't you supposed to clean that yesterday?

I did, I rubbed it hard with SpongeBob.

SpongeBob's not a real sponge, you dork; plastic doesn't soak up blood. You need a soft sponge, something from under the sink in the kitchen.

How am I sposed to know?

Just try to get it out before our patient comes.

O.K., but you promised I could do the seaweed this time. It's so cool to watch it get all fat just like the blob!

Robbie, it depends if the patient needs the seaweed. We don't do it for fun, and you won't see it where it's going. What's cool is that it helps open the lady pocket gently so we don't hurt when we operate. How about this? If she needs it and if you do it right, you can watch all of *Thornberrys*.

I guess so. Hey, Shea.

What now?

How come we never get to take Siamese twins apart or something cool like that?

Because doctors get medals for that instead of get shot, and there are plenty of mommies and daddies left to do that stuff.

The young girl appears at the stairway.

If Robbie gets to do seaweed *and* see his po-gram, I get Baby Annabelle.

Kaylie, you just gave me an idea; you're absolutely right. But don't you think Baby Annabelle is too old for a pacifier or bottle now? Take her upstairs and practice feeding her real mouth a straw—then another straw—one at a time, to get it to open wider and wider.

Why am I getting punished?

It's not punishment, it's practice. Just like when we play Operation, try not to touch the sides, just stay in the center of the hole. Now, pretend the dolly has a light-up nose too, and that she'll cry till her nose gets red every time the straw scrapes the inside of her mouth by mistake. Here, I'll watch you the first few times. Keep space on both sides as you go in. Pretty good, pretty good. Whoops!

The sun goes down, the doorbell rings, and the center of gravity of the raised ranch on Cherry Street drops too, the lower level suddenly full of activity. Four hands reach up to unlatch the door, grasp, and pull. A woman walks in tentatively, greeting her hosts and hostesses, bearing flowers and a large brown paper bag. She squats down to pat one's head, touch another's cheek.

> My, how you've grown. The spitting image of your dad, and you . . . so like your mom.
> Be right with you, Mrs. Kapreski.
> Mrs. Preski, I have to take your vitamins.
> No, Kaylie, vital signs. You take *your* vita*mins*, you take *her* vital *signs*.
> I'm not sure how many vitamins are in fast food. But you may as well eat while it's hot.
> Oh boy. What've we got?
> One chicken nuggets, that's for Kaylie. Medium fries, that's me. One burger, no pickle, no ketchup. Gotta be Shea. A Sprite and a Coke and a shake.
> No, the Sprite's here, sweetheart; that one's the urine sample, couldn't remember if you needed it—it's harder to remember things when you're older, just ask your . . . Oh sorry, love, how could I have for—
> That's o.k., Mrs. Kapreski, no problem, get relaxed now, lie back, hope the pool table's not too hard. Kaylie, take the sample to the back. Careful, don't spill it on the fries. We'll chow down and then get started right away.

Three children devour their Happy Meals while they sit entranced before a glowing screen.

> Gimme a fry.
> You took a bunch already.
> Where's the extra ketchup, Shea?

Never mind the ketchup. Time's up. And now that *we* ate, let's
list the other three *ates* that come out of *operate*.

Sedate, dilate, aspirate!

Exactly! Let's get to it.

He leads them over to the pool table, where the woman smiles uneasily.

Now, Kaylie, hold her hand, and if she has pain, you soothe her.
And Robbie, remember you can't force the curette like jamming a
megazord antler onto its ear-knob.

O.K., Shea. I'll do it right. You always do the hard part anyway.

Don't worry, Mrs Kapreski, Shea's a pro, he won't poke you.

That's right, but she might feel a slight pinch.

Shea's a pro, he won't po, the young girl echoes, and begins to
sing tunelessly a nonsense version of jingle bells. *Pro wont po, pro
wont po—*

Hush, Kay. How's our patient doing?

Pro-po-po, pro-po-po, pro-po-po-pro-po.

Kaylie, you're bothering Mrs. K.; she doesn't want to hear your
silly jingle bells, she's trying to relax.

That's all right, dear.

The woman strokes the young child's soft, fine hair.

Do you suppose a general anesthetic would be better under the
circumstances, Shea?

I'm really sorry, Mrs. K., the kids over on Sycamore are training [other place]
now, but it's a lot more complicated. No videos showed that.

Does Mrs. Presti want another shot?

No, Kay, she's just nervous.

The girl picks up the four-seps with two hands.

If she's nervous, we can take the butterflies in the stomach out
with the four-seps.

No, Kay, that's only in the Operation game.

But you said playing it was practice for pa-seizure.

140

Again she sings *pro-po-po, pro-po-po,* this time while sucking her thumb.

Kaylie, how many times have I told you only ring pops in the O.R. No thumbs. Go back upstairs until I call you. We'll manage without you. Robbie, tell me which diameter cannula you think is right for Mrs. Kapreski.

Upstairs, the young girl sits before a disembodied head the size of her own. She combs and styles and gathers and clips with an array of pink utensils and ornaments. She converses with the head—and it too speaks, though its replies are non sequiturs—as she attempts, unsuccessfully, to make a braid.

I could play with you all day, Make Me Pretty, the girl confides. It's so easy to make you byootiful. You don't have a south nose or south mouth or an ugly beard. I want all the ladies to have only heads, just like you. See how pretty you are already?

The girl holds a small pink mirror in front of the head, then puts her palm on top of it and pushes gently back and forth to fashion a nod of assent. Eventually she loses interest and finds her way to another, smaller doll, who is more than head, but whose lower half is fish. She waves the mermaid's movable arm at the nearby oversized head, and strokes her soft, luxurious, rubbery tail, until her oldest brother's call interrupts her reverie.

It must be time for vitamins, she says to the exotic creature. I'll bring you with me. I'm bringing Mermaid Fancy down, she yells, as she navigates the steps.

It's *Fantasy,* her brother corrects. Whatever, just come give us a hand.

If I was a wizard, I would change *all* the ladies into mermaids— then there'd be no legs to open up on the table. Cause I don't like the lady legs, or lady pockets.

We don't have that power, Kaylie.

We can sew a tail onto Mrs. Preski so she won't need to have a pa-seizure.

Hush, Kaylie, or you'll go right back upstairs. Never scare the patient. Maybe some other doctor in another hundred years can figure out how to do that, but it won't be with needle and thread, that's for sure. Now chill out. And take the flowers in where Mrs. K. can look at them.

The boy realizes he has raised his voice and modulates it appropriately to speak to the woman.

denial

I'm sorry about my sister, he says softly. She didn't get her nap today, and she's a little out of sorts. She's still—I looked up what they call it on the internet—oh, yeah, I think she's *in denial.* I hope you don't mind if we put on *Scooby-Doo* in the recovery room. It always does the trick.

The younger boy, after helping the woman down from the pool table and escorting her to the back room, races up the stairs, and back again, holding a box, the contents of which he proceeds to place on the linoleum floor: a board, a spinner, a plastic man in a plastic bed.

You promised we could take a break after we finished Mrs. K. I did my job and Kaylie's too.

O.K., O.K., his brother says, what do you want to play?

This. Look. I brought down Don't Wake Daddy.

Me too, me too, his sister runs in from the back room. I wanna play too.

cries

Look, you guys, why does it have to be *this* game? One of you always cries. What's wrong with Operation?

If we hafta play that thing one more time, I'm gonna throw up. That's what.

And we don't have all the pieces anymore.

Yeah, Kaylie vacuumed up the Wishbone.

Liar! Robbie did it!

It doesn't matter who did it. You both know the pieces should never be anywhere near the aspirator. Oh, what's the use? Look, if you hold out for just a few more procedures, we can take the flowers and visit the graves.

It's too scary to go at night.

safer

No, Rob, it's much safer for us at night. You're not a Power Ranger. Just spin, somebody.

Five!

The girl pumps the button in the board's center the designated number of times.

Three!

The boy does the same, but before completing the move, the pajama-clad plastic man jackknifes in bed, his sleeping cap flies off his head, his startled eyes snap open to attention, and just as suddenly, the children's eyes fill up with tears.

What's the matter with you two? It's supposed to be funny when he pops up. You're not supposed to cry!

The older boy presses the plastic man's torso back down roughly with his palm.

Why can't our daddy and mommy pop up from their graves like that and send their stupid tombstones flying? Why can't they, Shea?
Why can't you leave the stupid game in the closet where it belongs?
Why are you yelling at us? You're always yelling!
Why can't you ask me something easy, like why is the sky blue? I'm not so much older than you, you know! I'm freakin' twelve-years-old!

He kicks the board into the wall, and the plastic man is once again resurrected, his cap catapulted like a champagne bottle's cork. The younger children are hysterical.

Don't kick Daddy! Don't kick Daddy!
It isn't Daddy! Don't you get it, idiots? Daddy's in the ground!
Just like Mommy!

The older boy stomps up the basement stairs, sobbing. A woman's voice calls from the back room.

Is everything all right out there? Is there anything I can do?
Sorry to bother you, Mrs. Kapreski. Everything's fine. Don't worry.
I'll take your vitamins in a minute, Mrs. Preski, so you can go home.

The younger children walk up the stairs cautiously and position themselves on the steps, one below and one beside their brother, who sits on the landing with his head in his hands, still sobbing.

We're sorry, Shea. Please don't cry. We didn't mean to make you sad.

Thanks for takin' care of us, Shea.

They hold out their arms and their brother enfolds them in his, and all three rock gently together as his sobbing gradually diminishes.

Thanks, guys. I guess we just need to chill. Sorry I snapped. At least we're all together, right? And if we play our cards right, we can stay together.

Oh boy, cards! I'll go get Uno!

No, Kaylie, I didn't mean . . . It's just an expression.

Oh. Well, if we can't play a game, can we take a nap? A quick one?

That'd be great. We could all use one.

We'll sing your favorite lullaby, Shea.

They begin to serenade him softly, and soon he joins his voice to theirs.

A,B, Rh, one two three, now I've done my D & C . . .

The Translator

As certain as color
Passes from the petal,
Irrevocable as flesh,
The gazing eye falls through the world
*Hana no iro wa / Utsuri ni keri na / Itazura ni / Waga mi yoni furu / nagame
seshi ma ni*
—Ono No Komachi, from *One Hundred Poems from the Japanese,*
    translated by Kenneth Rexroth

A monk asked Master Haryo, "What is the way?"
Haryo said, "An open-eyed man falling into the well."
—*The Little Zen Companion,* by David Schiller

The way up and down is one and the same.
—Heraclitus, fragment 60, *Ancilla to the Pre-Socratic Philosophers,*
    by Kathleen Freeman

This ordered universe (cosmos), which is the same for all, was not created
by any one of the gods or of mankind, but it was ever and is and shall be:
everliving Fire, kindled in measure and quenched in measure.
—Heraclitus, fragment 30, *Ancilla to the Pre-Socratic Philosophers,*
    by Kathleen Freeman

The statue had all the appearance of a real girl, so that it seemed to be alive, to want to move, did not modesty forbid.
—Ovid, *Metamorphoses* Book x, Pygmalion and Galatea,
    translated by Mary Innes

 Alas, how I fear lest you trip and fall, lest briars scratch your innocent legs, and I be the cause of your hurting yourself. These are rough places through which you are running—go less swiftly, I beg of you, slow your flight, and I in turn shall pursue less swiftly.
—Ovid, *Metamorphoses* Book i, Daphne and Apollo,
    translated by Mary Innes

Otherwise this stone would not be so complete,
from its shoulder showering body into absent feet,
or seen as sleek and ripe as the pelt of a beast;
nor would that gaze be gathered up by every surface
to burst out blazing like a star, for there's no place
that does not see you. You must change your life.
—Rainer Maria Rilke, "Torso of An Archaic Apollo,"
    translated by William H. Gass

Liza Liza everyone eyes ya.
—Bard College, wall, circa 1977

I ———

Words are slippery—as treacherous on the tongue as ice under one's feet, and as wondrous as the latter's vitreous texture to the gazing eye. German is a solid language, all agree; Italian, French: more liquid. But what language would be flattered to be designated flatulent? Considering the coexistence of these varied states of language-matter, one could hardly expect the Tower of Babel to be as charming as the Leaning Tower of Pisa. It is therefore a foregone conclusion that language is to blame for almost any complication one encounters in one's daily interactions. And when you spend your hours gallivanting among languages, I assure you, the likelihood of complication becomes exponential. For we rely so heavily on the fiction of translation.

Ironically, a translator, who strives so valiantly to be, as the expression goes, part of the solution, may inadvertently compound the problem. According to this less-than-subtle mathematics, I am by default a perpetrator. Legend, even harsher in its verdict, targets me specifically. Legend sees my practice as insidious. This cursed prejudice derives from an Italian (or Sicilian?) uttering the famous epigram: *traduttore traditore;* the translator is a traitor! Please note my dutiful formation of a fist, its somber placement on my chest's left quadrant, the standard Latin recitation of the penitent: yes, I'll say it, *mea culpa*. And then, because I am a pedant to the core, I'll follow penance with a lesson.

When matter changes state, we learn in elementary chemistry, energy is neither gained nor lost. But in the case of verbal matter, the rule reverses; the rule itself perhaps evaporates. Call it perversity or unpredictability, or merely instability, that an hour of haste, American style, transforms into a Mediterranean hour of punctuation, of stasis. *Ora:* hour/time; *punta:* point, tip, end, peak; *di* is obviously of. Thus the term *rush hour* is freeze-framed to *top hour,* or in effect *stop hour*—by the time it moves from U.S. or British to Italian soil—or more precisely, asphalt. (Shift *punta*'s final vowel from *a* to *o* and you have full stop in Italian anyway.) At peak, one ceases, by default, to rush, as one can go no farther than the top. Thus rushing, a process, becomes its antithesis: stasis.

Do you regard me skeptically? Accuse me of tautology? (As if I needed more incrimination!) Rushing to one's job is bad enough; must you also rush to judgment?

I, on the other hand, am not provincial. I am aware it's narrow-minded, and clichéd, to say Americans are always in a rush, or uniformly crude, or fat. (The third assertion contradicts the first, in any case, for those who are obese more likely saunter.) But in all earnestness, I've embraced Italian attitudes more than I'd care to admit, and haste is sacrilegious in this nation, never mind counterproductive.

I do not arrive at such conclusions lightly. I am no armchair traveler (though I am, apparently, an armchair traitor). I know that that which vibrates when one culture rubs against another is as complexly interactive as an elementary particle is in physics. Cross-cultural dynamics, as they're called in the academy, must be examined closely and dismantled expertly, in the manner of explosives. Among the English-speaking academics of my acquaintance (that vocation which I myself might have entered were I more enamored of stability, more practical, or more—all right, yes, Liza, even more—pretentious), the idiom favored in the analysis of complex ideas, is to *unpack*. But how glib this infelicitous expression sounds to one whose ears have been attuned—through years of gallivanting among languages—to nuance.

Might we then amend the charming Mediterranean epigram to *professore traditore* (sacrificing the alliteration); for isn't it betrayal of both language and idea when some incisive, masterfully elaborated argument is greeted by the cavalier proposal, "Let's unpack that"—particularly now when our entire global culture is obsessed with such mundane associations as the size of so-called *carry-ons,* the quest for toiletries sufficiently diminutive to be permitted in them, the advances of x-ray technology (the indignity of which we suffer, each in turn, in stocking feet, albeit herded like some throng of hoofed creatures)? Yes, you know as well as I do that the mascot of our millennial era is that uniformed Cerberus, male or female, who stands at every airport security checkpoint: that stern, earnest individual who grills you to insure that you *yourself* performed the act of packing your valise, without assistance or intrusion, thus insuring all personal effects therein to be your own, completely your responsibility.

This may explain the prevalence of obesity. Indeed, why exercise, if one can easily increase one's heart rate through mere interrogation on security queues, perhaps disrobing partially, displaying this or that suspicious item in one's luggage or on one's laptop? I must admit I need some camouflage atop my lap when flying from Da Vinci or Malpensa, if some authoritative, dark-haired beauty asks if I and I alone have packed my bags *(Ha fatto i valigi lei—soltanto lei? Sicuro?),* for in such instances, it is not exclusively my pulse which quickens. Were she to follow me and monitor removal of my shirts, my shaving cream, etc., it might transform quite radically the drudgery of unpacking. Yet soon enough she would discover that I am guilty of collaboration regarding my American friend Liza's unpacking, and need to issue me a summons on the spot.

Who is Liza, you inquire, as if there could be some analogously simple three-word answer, in the manner of a grade-school catechism recitation. Who indeed is Liza? I formulate this strenuous equation daily. I'll start abstractly, as I often do. Consider Bernini's *Apollo and Daphne* at The Museo Borghese—a museum that, for the record, once did not require these elaborate advance reservations; so much for spontaneity. Is not Bernini's majestic sculpture, which transforms (via marble) Daphne's hands and feet to bark and leaf, the quintessential artistic embodiment of haste turned to stasis? And in my own subjective version of the myth, starring as the stopped-in-her-tracks sylvan nymph, is my Liza, passively enacting the hypostasis by which moment turns memory, flight as it were taking root. (Pedant that I am, I must here recite Ovid: *Mollia cinguntur tenui praaecordia libro, in frondem crines, in ramos bracchia crescunt . . .*) If it is the case that Daphne was ingeniously protecting her virginity, sensibly avoiding any congress that divested her of what my academic friends call (please insert inverted commas) 'agency'—or in so-called plain English, "I'd rather be a tree than have a man in me"—my Liza has inverted this scenario: she too has made stasis of haste, but in her own contemporary manner, by eschewing *agency,* though she wants so desperately to be unburdened of her version of—insert again inverted commas, please—'virginity.'

If you'll excuse my mixing mythemes, let's return to Cerberus, and the layered repercussions of one's packing. I'd like you to consider whether customs officers and security personnel, as they forage for controlled substances or box-cutters or over-quota measurements of liquid, or blighted foreign produce bearing vermin or bacteria, whether they censor the more nuanced, subtler—one might call it metaphysical—contraband that is the bread and butter, if you will, of cultural translation. I'd posit that only a security officer possessed of some exotic, paranormal, psychic x-ray vision would discern that Liza brought the rushing (and its paradoxical fruit, paralysis) with her, that she packed it unassisted and unconsciously, just as people say, colloquially, "you brought the weather with you" (as a compliment or an accusation, depending whether what's been brought is rain or shine: *scuro* or *azzuro),* and she is thus either the casualty or the beneficiary (depending on one's view) of the capriciousness of cultural translation.

Standing in inverse relation, Italy, for its part, is either blighted or boosted (depending also on one's view), engaged as it has always been in this perpetual tourist sweepstakes—recipient of yet another awestruck, culture-shellshocked tourist, in this case the winner of the Liza Prize. Italy has cut a deal, one might say, and Italy itself might say the following: you ogle the Berninis, Caravaggios, and Michelangelos, and we in turn will ogle you, *bionda bella*. But my Liza doesn't realize she has already signed on the dotted line—with Italy that is. With me she is not so much oblivious as tentative. Let me supply the background.

The bargain that we struck was this: if she were bold enough to remain in Rome indefinitely without the required *permesso di soggiorno*, then in exchange for her temerity, she would acquire indefinite *permesso* to reside with me. This permission will, I've told her, have no expiration date. Do you think me perverse for putting Liza at risk? I do not think myself perverse (though as I mentioned earlier, my vocation is perceived as such). Would you like to hear a sampling of the risks that I take on a daily basis? For example, if one translates clumsily, one is accused of lacking nuance and not doing justice; if too elegantly, one gives undue credit, as in an inflated grade; in each case, one misrepresents the author. Meanwhile, if one tries to be, as they say, 'fair and square,' one is accused of being pedestrian, middling, workaday, nothing more. When I goad Liza to be brazen, it is toward much milder risk-taking than I have just enumerated. I merely want to teach her to express herself, *fully* express herself—directly. A so-called crash course in boldness, you might say.

She, on the other hand, thinks her insufficiencies will be cured through one or two so-called 'immersion' courses in the Italian language, taken locally at one of the innumerable Italian programs customized for foreigners. She yearns to fully comprehend Italian idioms; her battered brain swoons with confusion before the *congiuntivo*. But what she needs more fundamentally, in my opinion, is an entry-level course in taking chances. She thinks she can cut a *bella figura* in speech if she masters the subjunctive and its nuanced applications. She is *bella*, both in *viso* and *figura*, *molta bella*, but I have also made a bargain with myself that I will not exploit her unless I can equip her with the means to seduce me, i.e., any man or woman, anyone—of any nationality. Because I will not overpower; that's too easy, not a level playing field, so to speak, so easy it's . . . immoral.

You're still not satisfied. You want to know how I arrived at Liza? (Patience, reader, dear, answer in-transit.) Why does she intrigue me? Were

I a photographer, I could answer more expediently, more succinctly: present her as a figure in the foreground of the landscape, that is, cityscape, of Roman rush hour, though she appears at first unfettered by this urban frenzy: a slender blonde, a striking one, at times seeming to float above the pavement in her romantic, empire-waisted, sweeping-skirted linen sundress, its fabric tinted the most perfect shade of pale mint green. She is somewhat ill at ease with the inevitable attention paid her. It unnerves her; looking closer one can observe the line of her lovely mouth harden, her elegant jaw tense, the incipient panic in her intriguingly unstable aquamarine eyes *(les yeux bleu, die blaue Augen, gli occhi azzuri)*, whose own tint shifts as if a polarized lens, when she moves from inside to outside, under saturated blue sky. Just wear the attention, I often advise her, just wear it like a cape thrown about your shoulders, casually yet elegantly. The secret, my dear, is this: do not let it trip you—drape it about you. At my elaborate extended metaphor, she rolls those gorgeous eyes, as if to say, how quaint you are, how useless is your silly simile. Does it not encapsulate contemporary culture: that the grandeur of a sweeping cape devolves into the coyness of a shrug?

You've likely seen that famous black-and-white Italian photograph, often reproduced on postcards, depicting a gauntlet of idle Roman men on some *strada* or other. They are hamming it up for the camera (hamming, I suspect, whether camera trained on them or not), admiring, i.e., harassing, an attractive brunette, whose disconcerted expression makes clear she had not expected the transaction of an errand to be quite so fraught with complication—that brunette's anxiousness as emblematic in Italian culture as the *Mona Lisa*'s smile. God help her had she been a blonde! Or better still, you surely remember the analogously anxious faux-blonde Monica Vitti in Antonioni's *L'Avventura,* surrounded by the mesmerized, vulture-like Sicilian men as she awaited her lover; the man through whose amorous 'agency' she had metamorphosed from her friend, the non-blonde and mysteriously missing Anna. Blonde from brunette, stasis from haste. As my Liza would say, with a shrug, *Go figure!*

Yes, back to Liza, upon whose heart-shaped face we can reliably place the postcard brunette's anxious look, trading the olive skin of the latter for the peaches-and-cream complexion of the former; trading as well their not dissimilar figures, such that Liza's long-limbed, shapely svelteness is now thrust into the foreground of the picture. Let me begin again. Initially to me she was only a slender blonde woman in a stylish and yet modest summer dress walking briskly during rush hour to the *fermata* at Piazza Venezia carrying a small satchel over her shoulder and a book clasped in her hand. (Although admittedly a woman in Italy is always a noteworthy commodity; yes, to respond to an attractive woman is compulsory: a national pastime if not a patriotic duty, for a male, and if a blonde attractive woman, up the ante, double the alacrity.)

I watched her walking thus on a number of occasions but only when we found ourselves haphazardly together, stationary, did I initiate a conversation. "What is that you're reading?" I inquired, not as a ploy, but with genuine interest, and I found it intriguing that in response she merely placed the book, faceup and open-paged, in my lap, such that I had to put my hands where hers had been, holding its edges down, lest it close. The expression 'spread-eagled' came to mind at the time, perhaps because I knew *my* question could, alas, so easily be construed as a come-on line; but it was a descriptor unworthy of the combination of mysteriousness and directness in her gesture—a gesture which, I must admit, compelled me so thoroughly that I neglected to absorb the words she'd placed before me, though I recall the sight of large type on a square page: the former sparse, the latter bright white.

Liza's provocative response was far too elegant to rhyme with crudely adjectival open thighs—although she was indeed, for all to see, an eagle spread, sublimely, one delicious August afternoon, during an outing to the Hotel Ergife's sumptuous pool, so many sweltering kilometers from Centro or Testaccio or Trastevere. It is an image I will retain for many years: how unself-consciously she stretched her limbs, wearing that simple, elegant, black maillot while leaning against the cabana wall, neither proud nor ashamed of her long, Berniniesque legs or her broad majestic shoulders or her strong but seemingly elongated arms, which she raised and spread before her like some beautiful, vertical bird about to take unharried, one might even say balletic, flight.

Quite the inverse of the pesky swarms of importunate starlings that gathered afternoons and at twilight to blacken the skies over Termini, or individually suicide-bomb themselves against the thankfully closed windows of the numerous villas that line the contrastively verdant Gianicolo. (A bloody nuisance are those starlings, though some find them ominous as well, an evil omen. Ancient cities harbor ancient superstitions, I suppose.) Meanwhile Liza was as natural and regal, as at home in her body in that moment as an ambassador's daughter; and indeed there are a cluster of such families in these parts, residing in posh residences upon the aforementioned Edenic hill, on streets such as the Via Garibaldi or Via Angelo Messina and the like. Was not Daphne King Peleus' daughter after all?

Who knows, perhaps the splendid verdant Doria Pamphili Park is full of girls turned tree. Not laurels but umbrella pines and cypresses, of course, for even metamorphosis must honor the indigenous. And after dusk *(tramonto)*, when the vast park is officially *chiuso*, imagine how transcendent it would be if that resplendent arboreal cathedral figuratively—no, literally— let down its/her/their sylvan hair and expelled a sweet collective girlish giggle at the effectiveness of their ruse, while all of il Gianicolo's citizens heard in the distance the delicate shivery timbre of silver bells. For even nature, even children of the gods, even magical creatures require some privacy: a bit of shelter from our prying eyes. Tell that to an Italian, though.

An Italian man, it is said, has fire in the blood; he is easily ignited, and to honor female beauty is as elemental as to cry out at the sight of conflagration, "fire!" That calls to mind my Liza's favorite line in one of her most cherished films: *The English Patient*. When Ralph Fiennes as the laconic Count Almásy, with such singular inflection, utters "fire," it makes his leading lady roll her eyes celestially, just as Liza often does with me. (The thrust of his anecdote was to prove himself comparatively verbose against a man who offered only one word during days of travel.) But Liza does not mimic Katharine's gesture of forbearance when the handsome count delivers this incendiary punch line. On the contrary, fire on *his* tongue would appear to make my Liza swoon. Whereas for me, it is Kristin Scott Thomas's recitation of Herodotus that (here, inverted commas) 'sends' me. And when, in order to chastise her leading man for slouching far too sluggishly toward adultery, Kristin, playing Katharine, slaps him, you bet your britches that my pickled pecker perked up straight away, even prior to the kissing and the bodice-ripping. Why does the tight-lipped fellow always get the girl, eh? Though one should not discount Phoebus Apollo on fire for Daphne in *The Metamorphosis*.

Pardon me, I would be derelict of duty were I to withhold attribution, for I neglected to mention not only ancient author Ovid, modern author Ondaatje, and Minghella as director, but also an anonymous Roman sage— the one who offered Liza the aforementioned charming metaphor regarding that which circulates in Mediterranean male veins. Folk wisdom, might one categorize it? The culture that condemns the translator sees its own men fueled by hearts that pump not iron but fire!—transmuting physiology to alchemy.

She met him at the bustling Largo Argentina while they waited for some notoriously tardy autobus; he explained calmly and matter-of-factly (rather than lasciviously or condescendingly) why it was inevitable that she be pestered constantly in his country. She was attentive to this native, more so,

I would wager, than she ever is to me, given that she reported the exchange verbatim. In one sense he merely stated the obvious, but in another he had uncanny prescience, for her adventure commenced the moment they parted ways, and he became in retrospect her fortune-teller.

What more quintessential anthropological encounter for a non-Italian woman is there than that with the Italian masher: fixture on any Roman autobus—where one has no opportunity to be, despite the moving vehicle, a moving target, in the manner of our agile, mythic Daphne? Thinking herself resourceful, even pragmatic, Liza, to insure against unwanted admirers while standing pressed against so many other bodies, had rotated her body to face away from an unsavory Italian businessman, as a prophylactic gesture of rejection. (You know that physics divides motion into three broad categories: rotational, vibrational, translational; by story's end I promise all three will have been miscegenated.) Nonetheless the latter exploited the bus's sardine-like density to purge himself at her expense.

Only after the fact had it occurred to poor Liza that she had actually made matters worse by turning her back to him, thus denying him access to her frown, her wrinkled brow, that signature locked jaw, thereby allowing him to be even more surreptitious, while unwittingly providing— turned as she was about-face—an even cozier harbor in which he could nest his unsanctioned erection, which was at this point furtively ensconced against the contours of her subtle, fetchingly proportioned derriere. (She meant to turn herself into a tree, like Daphne did, but turned instead into a fleshly sea, that beckoned rather than rebuked.) Any warm-blooded male, Italian or not, could infer that beneath the lightweight linen fabric of her mint-green dress resided ripe flesh such as a finger might sumptuously indent in the manner of Bernini's miraculously tactile *Pluto and Persephone*. It is said that a man yearns all his life to return to the womb or to suck again at his mother's breast, but when all is said and done, is there any texture more *gemütlich* than the flesh of a woman's pliant backside?

You know, I'm glad the impudent Italian letch didn't make contact by hand, only importuned with his arrogant cock through two layers of cloth; for the press of fingers, once you see Bernini's masterpiece, becomes more intimate than that considerably thicker—and ultimately far more clumsy—digit.

Signore, she scolded at raised volume (which takes courage for the girl— she's shy), but the terminal vowel emerged from her lips with the inflection of a feminine ending and thus confounded matters even further, considerably diluting the force of censure, though perhaps it was the most effective insult possible despite its inadvertence—though it was at the same time an obtusely counterfactual interpretation of the craven aggressor's identity! That's my Liza—ever bollixed, ever inadvertently theatrical—her florid cheeks betraying her resistance to an attention she did not quite mean to engineer. The Italian custom of cramming into each day no less than four *ore di punta* presumably gave Signore Masher the chance to return to his *casa* for *pranzo* (prepared no doubt by his mother or wife) and change his trousers before resuming work, but Liza was already halfway to the Vatican (its only free admission day), an excursion she had planned for weeks; thus she elected to retain the soon-enough sun-dried stain in lieu of forfeiting. The trip, I mean, not the dress, which she washed later, twice, I saw it hanging on the wooden rack inside my flat for several days! The coincidence of her parading semen at St. Peter's, she realized even then, was so patently paradoxical, so potently sociological, as to be absurd. A first-prize paradox indeed. Therein lie the contradictions of Italian culture in a nutshell.

Let us (inverted commas, if you will, again) rewind a moment, and then—*virgule, virgule*—zoom in, so as to scrutinize and analyze more deeply. Though she was a victim, she is mortified, and she has raised her arm more awkwardly than elegantly, near frantically, not like a soaring eagle this time but a caged canary, to press the oversized oval button for *uscita* and angle her way through the press of people to the middle doors so as to exit the bus. Heading toward the Eternal City she now walks. Observe, jury: this peripatetic exhibit A: a semen-stained dress: not blue, hence not newsworthy, stained not by presidential but civilian semen, no saliva there commingled, not in Washington but Rome, here in the capitol not of First World politics but of Old World Catholics, where nonetheless (paradoxically) such antics would not cause a citizen to bat an eye. Such circumstances are taken in stride, given that prostitutes and senators here can collide at times within a single Italianate identity. You can be sure that those colorful court jesters referred to as Vatican soldiers were not staring at the stain when Liza glided by to purchase several *francobolli* as colorful as their own preposterous costumes to affix to the postcard she would mail from Italy's only efficient, reliable postbox, but at her attributes *in toto,* shall we say. (Its destination will in a future passage be addressed—double entendre, reader!)

Roman buses—any tourist, any native, any worldly person knows—constitute ecosystems all their own. *(Un bel casino* is the idiom that best describes this charming chaos.) For if you could peer into the myriad covert activity masked by sheer human volume you would find a clearinghouse of petty crime: robbery and sexual harassment: pockets being ever so subtly picked, furtive cocks unloading against random hips, incoherent maledictions, heated political arguments, desperate inquiries, boisterous explanations of directions (their specificity and intensity often inversely proportionate to their accuracy), frenetic hugging and kissing (cheek one to cheek two), halfhearted translations, copious bustling and shoving, crowds leaning in like lemmings toward the red stamping machine with the same dogged yet mindless persistence with which they might dip their finger's tip into a marble basin of officially designated holy water (that lackluster sequence of morphemes cannot ever match its musical translation: *acqua sacra)*, all the while muttering the requisite *scusa* and *prego*. Heavens, once I swear I saw a man bowing toward Mecca even as the bus kept turning corners (a considerable directional challenge to one's internal compass, I should think)—or so I assume, some form of prostration in any case; uniformed officials boarding when least expected, albeit infrequently, so as to check for any scurrilous infidels riding black.

And long about half-July, when the tourist volume has tripled and the heat itself is, from Liza's stubbornly nonmetric Fahrenheit perspective, triple digits, and both natives and tourists are discernibly sweat-drenched and restless, one senses there is in Rome something about to explode. Fire in the city's circulatory system, would that sagacious bus-stop fortune-teller say? What is it about Americans and their intransigence; they are so inexplicably resistant to conversion—unless the Holy Roller Fundamentalist variety. But when it comes to the mundane, the elemental: kilometers or liters or Celsius or military time, and for that matter syntax, parts of speech, moods, tenses, etc., the raw material of translation, they are bloody hopeless! Or helpless? They cannot do, as the expression goes, the math. And thus must have it performed for them.

Forgive my outburst. I am opposed to muddleheadedness and superstition. Liza feels the *tessera* to be some kind of talisman, thinks that the colorful paper rectangle equips her with an instantly Italianate identity and thus immunity, whereas were she to purchase daily tickets she would be perpetually and immutably a tourist. I must debunk this sort of nonsense. I have explained to her time and again that the advantage of the *tessera* is considerable but strictly practical: one is spared the tedium and annoyance of having to go through the requisite motions; one is allowed to cut certain corners, one avoids having to enter from the bus's front and fight (adopting as one's demeanor that specifically Italian mass transit fusion of polite and pugilistic) one's way to the thoughtlessly, if not sadistically, placed stamping machine at the back. The pricey monthly *tessera* is a bargain not only for the infinite number of rides it offers in any direction (that is, if one were certain to use public transport copiously rather than sparingly) but for its power to reduce wasted motion on the bus itself, as those who wield it earn the privilege of entering through the back doors—illogical as that is, given there is for them no stamping necessary.

Isn't it so often the way, the privileged are granted further privilege, such as the infamous disparity in her country, four percent of the population with a quarter of the wealth, isn't that the statistic? But please don't quote me—I'm a word man, not a number man. (Although in comparison to Liza's grasp of the latter, I'm a mathematical wizard.) In any case, she purchases her *tessera* religiously—I use this adverb literally as much as metaphorically, for she regards the bureaucratic card as some apotropaion that can ward off evil. She always buys it on the day before the new month starts, as if this prudence were some function of the Sabbath. She strides resolutely up to the *tabaccaio*, looking with those otherworldly eyes past those ubiquitous magazines designed for neither word nor number men but so-called leg men, breast, etc. men, and also past the newspapers and allegedly news-bearing periodicals: *La Repubblica, Il Messaggero, La Panorama* and *L'Espresso*, even past *Mirabella* and *Italian Vogue*, and points to the desired artifact with a reverent index finger, her euros counted out far in advance.

When I first explained to her there was of *tessere* a limited quantity available, given that once the month's initial days have expired they become each day another fraction (approximately one-thirtieth) less valuable, I did not offer any specific advice, for in truth I hoped she might experiment with boldness; try on for size the bright red outlaw cape, engage in that nefarious hoax the Germans label *schwarz fahren*. Admittedly there is a risk (though very low) in this uncitizenly gamble; on rare occasions one is apprehended. I should not have shared with Liza my anecdote about a certain savvy but unlucky couple who were half-caught (half haste, half stasis); in other words, the wife evacuated, allowing her husband to take the rap, thus she turned him metaphorically to bark, if not to stone. A transgendered Daphne, as it were. Declare the verdict, Liza, I demanded after finishing my anecdote; was she an admirably pragmatic spouse, evading the doubled fine that would doubly deplete their conjugal coffers, or a fickle miscreant, who failed to stand by her man? Liza only rolled her eyes, providing incentive for me to play the devil's advocate, to explain to her that riding black was, after all, less complicated on a Roman bus than on a German metro car, where men in uniforms might be accompanied by German shepherds, or an Italian gondola, from which one could hardly, without peril, jump off!

I made no progress; Liza was insulted that I would dare augment her jeopardy by urging her to forego another bureaucratic document, even hypothetically. Besides, she said, she'd come to view the *tessera* with some affection. Within its Roman context and with all its Roman rituals, it stood for Italy *in toto*—no less symbolic than an Italian flag—insistently bureaucratic, exceptionally inefficient, erumpently erotic. Once I gave up fantasizing Liza as the Bonnie to some phantom Clyde, we were in harmony again, agreeing that in Italy convenience was ever rationed, charm ever abundant, and logic ever elusive. Just right for you, the logic part, I teased—call me incorrigible—and then I made a slogan just for her: *In logic's badlands Liza thrives,* continuing through the evening to exhibit the affectionate blend of playfulness and censoriousness that tends to drive her mad, yet keeps her— of her own volition, mind you—tethered.

Oh, did I mention, when she actually got to the Vatican, she bought a postcard of St. Peter's Square, then several more cards of the Sistine ceiling's images from Genesis: God creating Adam, the expulsion from the Garden, Satan tempting Eve. Nearly generic images, gorgeous of course, but chosen, I would wager, almost mindlessly. She passed right by the Delphic Sybil, for example—not to mention God creating Eve from Adam's rib. As an afterthought she did add two—let's call them secular—images: Hadrian's Castle and the Knights of Malta keyhole. (Do they sell everyday Roman postcards at the Vatican post office?—I can't recall; perhaps she purchased those at one of the innumerable tourist kiosks adjacent to San Pietro.) In any case, when she completed her transactions and affixed one of her lovely, sumptuous papal stamps, then placed into the bright red box her chosen *cartolina,* she did not send it to the States, or any other country for that matter, but right here, to Rome. To me. A local call, as you would say. All that supererogatory efficiency for what could easily have been hand-delivered. She's my private little paradox is Liza. (Also my palindrome, as she tends to go around in circles when deciding anything, perpetually directionally challenged.) Always clinging, somewhat awkwardly, to an element of mystery or ambiguity.

How can I capture the inflection of her enigmatic, though ostensibly straightforward, explanation? "It isn't healthy doing nothing but translating day and night. Besides, my intuition told me you were craving lighter reading."

II ———

Rewind, once again, if you'll bear with me, to the young, long-blonde-haired woman, obviously American, obviously attractive, not yet obviously anxious. What is her destination? As she walks purposefully in her pristine, at this point still well-pressed summer dress (as pure and classic as that simple—and yet elegant—cotton frock in which Kristin, playing Katharine, shows up at Almásy's door moments before the slap, the rip, the kiss). Forgive me, where was I? Oh yes—Liza walking, satchel over shoulder, book in hand. Her destination is, you have been told and shown, the Vatican, but subsequently, where then? At the long day's end—when she's reeling from the farrago of baroque details that comprise the interior of St. Peter's (the bronze *baldacchino* in its twisting immensity was in itself overwhelming to her) and felt compassion via Michelangelo for the grieving Virgin bearing in her arms her tortured, not-yet-resurrected son? Will you indulge me for one moment: Tell me if you would, which individual has greater *agency?* An altruistic, perhaps masochistic man nailed to a perpendicular pair of planks, or the grieving woman who enfolds him in her arms: she whose *raison d'être* was to deliver him literally and metaphorically to that very fate which is his universal *raison d'être?*

You can't help coming up with moral irrelevancies, living, and for some years working, in the shadow of the Vatican, believe me. In any case, when she's cleared her mind's eye of these details by fleeing back to the piazza and breathing in the cleansing symmetry of the splendid, awe-inspiring colonnade, and boarded yet another bus to bridge the considerable distance between San Pietro and the Vatican Museum, and then traversed the seemingly infinite rooms of the latter, casting her eye over its statues, maps, and tapestries, its overwhelming surfeit of trinkets and accessories, its glorious but perhaps ultimately tedious trove of treasures, she is definitively exhausted. By the time the Raphael room and then the stunning Sistine ceiling (its controversial cleaning now a moot point) is delivered to the eye, a straining neck now added to her aching calves and feet, where then will poor, fatigued, nearly expiring Liza orient herself?

What destination possibly could follow all of this? Only one, in fact—the same as the Vatican postcard's. It is—yes, even traitors should not lie—I; *my* flat, the spare décor of which is the antithesis of baroque surfeit! I am her motivation for enduring every evening the final *ora di punta* of the day—boarding, even on an ordinary, non-excursion day, not one but two successive buses, so as to arrive after approximately an hour at the flat of this alas-no-longer-young foreign man, who lifts his watery blue eyes by way of greeting, not even bothering to remove his reading glasses when she appears, despite her teasing him each time, "I think you put them on, low on your nose like that, for me, the minute that you hear me at the door, to play the role of the professor." (I suppose the sight of low-slung spectacles upon an aging nose seems as preposterous to the young as the spectacle of so-called low-rise jeans upon an adolescent female's hips seems to the middle-aged, though there is no precise rhinal equivalent to the inevitable corollary of bunched hip flesh—irrelevant in any case, since Liza with her svelte anatomy would never sport such bunching, nor would she ever be so trendy as to fall for such a style.) Point being, to regard corrective lenses as an affectation is the naïve luxury of those whose eyes have only started their fall through the world, eyes obviously not yet ravaged by the change in pressure. For it is only logical, applying laws of physics, that an eye would lose some corneal contour, deteriorate a bit in exchange for all that it assimilates—perhaps eventually accommodate such density of imagery as to be rendered blind.

Hana no iro wa / Utsuri ni keri na / Itazura ni
As certain as color / Passes from the petal / Irrevocable as flesh / The gazing eye . . .

I doubt that I, even with both eyes, night and day, wide open, could ever fully assimilate Liza, yet neither can I keep my eyes off her, and it seems that I have captured her fancy as well. Perhaps more accurate to say *attention;* I have captured her—and she my—attention. Not in the overt and sometimes vulgar manner of the attentions she garners on the street. Something far subtler, almost subliminal, ultimately inscrutable, whether insidious or ingenuous or in between, who can judge? Liza certainly cannot; nor is she inclined to. Ergo the relation of this five-and-twenty-year-old woman and this—let's just round it off to fiftyish—man is difficult to define, as it is not precisely amorous, though it is replete with the tension often correlated with the sexual. Simply put, there has been a bond between us since the day we met.

And where was that, you'll soon be asking, how did you meet, please? For this is *de rigueur* in romantic tales, is it not? (I should know, as I've translated my share.) But isn't what remains of romance conducted, as they say, "online" at this point, especially in the u.s.? (Just like those instant internet translations that one hears of! There's a perfect verbal one-night stand—the crudest possible betrayal, once over lightly, sloppy; slam bam thank you ma'am, let's cram one language in another's cavity, no intimacy there!) Such a personal country, the United States. A stranger enters any shop, is greeted warmly; minutes later told in parting, take good care. Only such a casual, off-the-cuff, personalizing country would boast of stores called Sam's Club, of legislation labeled Timothy's or Megan's Law—such chummy nomenclature for its permissions and restrictions. Where else but nonchalant, sophisticated San Francisco could one have ever dreamt up something as informally encyclopedic as that lifestyle soup-to-nuts compendium, Craigslist? Democracy demands a clearinghouse for every imaginable species of exchange. And why not, I suppose. I understand the lust to overload each moment with a million possibilities, coupled with the nostalgia that insists each new experience is original and spontaneous—not engineered. I understand the lust to furnish every bland coincidence with magical transcendence. But in the end, the only *bona fide* coincidence is that two individuals were both online, like all their peers.

It's really quite predictable our means of meeting, mine and Liza's; unremarkable, if one employs the rhetoric of the internist—though surely more exalted than some tryst derived from Craigslist! Tell me, please, what becomes in modern times, of destiny, of the whole concept of destiny? (Snuffed out with the apostrophe that should give Craig possession of his list?) Where goes romance writ large? For destiny, if scripted, becomes meretricious, relinquishes its grandeur—except in the traditional, old-fashioned, ancient sense, when scripted by the gods, the fates. In any case, fate surely can't be bartered every minute like the Footsie or the Nikkei or the Dow. Or can it?

All right, all tangents hereby—temporarily—terminated. If you insist on knowing, we met first in an English-language bookstore. Any English speaker soon enough learns where they are—one scouts them out soon after arrival, almost instantly betraying one's fervent promise to 'immerse' oneself in native culture, visits them within the first week, am I right? Either on the Via del Moro, or on the Via dei Bianchi Vecchi, or in Campo De' Fiori, or near Piazza di Spagna (the bookshop is an oasis of intellectuality within that fashion-saturated, capitalist utopia). They feel magical, of course, these *librerie,* whether the seeker be extremely literate or a halfwit, because you're seeking out the sustenance that at home you take for granted. How much more exotic one's native tongue becomes when one must hunt for every iteration of it, acting the verbal pilgrim on the labyrinthine cobblestone *viales* of Trastevere. As I mentioned earlier, she held a book when we first met (some novelty item, *The Little Zen Companion,* I believe: compiled quotations); she had just purchased it; and I, not empty-handed either, had been lured by something subtitled *Reflections on the Problems of Translation,* as well as a volume of one hundred Japanese poems, with English *en face.* Both were by Americans, and I applaud any American who seriously invests in 'foreign' languages, for so few do; so few, in fact, invest in English! I have told you long ago the word-for-word particulars of our initial exchange. What I may not have admitted is that she and I care for each other sincerely, if inscrutably—perhaps a bit peculiarly—and from a hypothetical outsider's view, so esoterically as to seem at times bizarre.

There are times when in my midlife-crisis, narcissistic mode I can delude myself into believing she is incomplete without me! Or is she, on the contrary, most fully herself before I've had a chance to mess with her, to mix her up, put words into her mouth? And yet the night we met, I felt that it was she who put the words to me, incessantly and fluidly (if not always coherently), but her alacrity was—how shall I say it—glowing. She was on fire.

Standing at the bookstore's entryway, we spoke animatedly of the Eternal City's splendorous beauty—I was not so crass as to cite hers on first acquaintance, lest I seem too forward, lest she feel too awkward; also of books (quite logical, given the meeting place); of words, of ideas, of images, of art—in short, luxurious topics. She was trying to make an analogy between the nightly shuttering of the storefronts of Trastevere (customary everywhere in Italy) such that this shop's entire book display evaporated— and the panoply of *trompe l'oeil* effects that animated baroque Italian art. It didn't quite cohere, but I could follow her intention—and appreciated her enthusiasm. She was still under the spell of Borromini's illusionistic corridor at Palazzo Spada, which I dismissed as so much gimmickry but she wanted me to see with a fresh eye. Her conflation of intriguing if inchoate intellect and charmingly overripe sentiment—and yes, I will confess, rapturous appearance—I found fetching, very fetching.

Alas such rapture I cannot reciprocate. Call me a vessel that reflects her beauty back at her and out into the world. This is not to say that I'm an ogre either; my appearance is not altogether unbecoming. I am a fair-haired, delicate-featured man, perhaps tending toward feminine in the refinement of my facial structure, with the exception of a nose that would appear to have fallen—splat—from some great height onto the center of my face, and also in my slender-fingered hands, but I am tall. Height is as essential a sexual component for a man as testicles, yes?—and not an attribute one takes for granted in Italian men. I believe that even Italian women respond to it. But to continue my self-portrait, I am slender; some might call me rangy, even gangly, and I stand out here among the thicker, swarthy, dark-haired, hirsute males, whose dark eyes would disappear under their forest brows were they not so very large. (I stood out in the land where I was raised as well, but that's another story.) She too stands out, as fair-haired females cannot help but do in the Mediterranean regions (as I mentioned prior) and I surmise that she feels linked to me because of this subtle commonality, though beyond that aspect of coloring we resemble one another rather little.

So if you accuse me of having engineered Liza's interest in me, you would have to scrutinize each causal element and claim that I manipulated my own genes to make for fair eyes, fair hair, fair skin. (Ah, soon such a statement may be far from absurd in our culture.) And furthermore you would have to claim my unpremeditated, nearly whimsical residency in this ancient city was inspired by foreknowledge of the eventual arrival of this happenstance attractive tourist from the u.s., of whom during my own sojourn in that grotesquely coveted country some years ago, I had no knowledge. (Thus you'll have to be 'on hold' if you are lusting for another *mea culpa.*) Our shared distinction elicits radically different responses: for her, as has already been demonstrated, advances, verbal, gestural, tactile (as on the bus), all manner of solicitations, cumulatively overwhelming for my darling; while for myself, cool stares, curiosity, more often tacit than articulated, and on the part of the dark beauties of the region, the curiosity is as often as not erotically tinged, there is a frank assessment in the stare, a kind of challenge, and I am admirably circumspect in my reciprocation. For my gaze, Liza knows, is incisive—perhaps she believes that masquerading as my blood, in lieu of fire, is that which extinguishes fire: its elemental opposite; not raging but streaming, cool, voluminous, a rushing waterfall controlled by hydroelectric engineering. (It is sobering, even chastening, to remember that the primal principle was, is, and ever shall be, living fire, as Heraclitus kindly would remind us, *kindled in measure and quenched in measure* αλλ' ην αει και εστιν και εσται πυρ αειζωον, απτομενον μετρα και αποσβεννυμενον μετρα.)

To each other we initially spoke smatterings of various tongues, predominantly Italian, naturally. (Our very first meeting must be exempt, since in an English-language bookstore one of course speaks English.) One must find

one's footing in a new relationship, and in that trial-and-error nature of communication (according to that paradigm of matter's changing states), one
must have the versatility to slip on ice, or boldly walk on water, even in
euphoric moments walk on air—at worst be told right to one's face, *you're full
of hot air!* It would seem falsely modest to suppress the fact that I possess command of several languages, that I am superficially acquainted with far more;
that my reading knowledge boasts a not unimpressive number; whereas Liza
knows only the most generic—and, inverted commas, 'hegemonic'—of them
fluently, much as she is wedded notionally to the concept of Italian immersion. She can also summon garnishes of others. To put it technically, she is at
approximately an elementary to intermediate level of Italian and has a mas-
tery of U.S. high school French essentially; no formal study of the classical languages, i.e., neither Greek nor Latin, certainly no Arabic, Chinese, or
Japanese, not even elementary German. Need I say more? In short, linguistic
ammunition of an essentially decorative—not substantive—persuasion.

   And yet these smatterings were vigorously plundered, and our communication, as a result, was as intense as incomplete, scattered and sputter-
ing—shards of verbal matter hurled back and forth, a combination of
chaotic and languorous, yielding at best an haphazard kinesis, and not
infrequently eliciting mild irritation. (All right, here it comes then. Fist to
chest and *sotto voce: mea culpa.*) A kind of babble really. At a certain point,
however, in a temper—I'm not proud of that now—I made clear that I was
doing her the favor of suffering *her* smatterings out of gallantry, duty, and
we scaled back by default into English. More expediently it seems, each
conversation, we traverse this universal path of least resistance.

I confess to having seen a postcard sent to her from Paris—I read it thinking
it a note related to one of my current projects, which is as it happens based
in France. I swear I was not snooping—and heavens, isn't verbiage on the
back of a postcard fair game—more or less in the public domain? An oversized postcard at that, bearing the hardly private image of the Eiffel Tower,
calling to mind (at least to mine) Barthes's famous essay of that name, with
its charming anecdote about the man who ate lunch in its revolving restaurant daily just so as to eliminate it from his purview. The clearly printed
block letters were almost impossible *not* to read. And in my own defense,
there was no salutation. Dear Liza was implicit but not written. (The name
itself, with surname, was of course penned clearly in the address portion of
the card.) The writer/sender, to use a popular American idiom, cut to the

chase, as follows: *So let me get this straight, it sounds like you've signed on for the female lead in a remake of Bertolucci's* Last Tango in Paris—*minus the sex! And minus Paris. Am I right?* Followed by the salutation/close.

She'd spoken of this Serena woman, they'd set out for Europe in tandem, then gone separate ways, i.e., Serena had continued 'exploring.' Though abroad the same amount of time, Serena had, it seems, bedded a score of men to Liza's naught. (And perhaps she now functioned as the Heraclitean Sybil with *raving mouth* and *unadorned, unincensed words.* Had Liza been the slightest bit adventurous and bought the Delphic Sybil postcard from the Vatican Museum, she could certainly have sent her friend that one with a reply.) How wistfully upon seeing the card must Liza have imagined the cool, chic City of Lights in all its enviable, functional modernity, momentarily superimposed upon this one: the sweltering, ancient, eternal city: every piece of tufa under constant scrutiny, one vast excavation site whose present was perpetually immured within its past.

And I was not so indiscreet as to inquire of Liza, after she received the piece of mail, whether she'd been shamed into renouncing our . . . what to call it? Shall we say cohabitation? Her friend would call it something else: compulsive posturings of masochism, unsavory entrapment in a May–December mock-relationship—well, to be fair, April–October—in which Serena assumed her stuck. But I would like to send my own card to Serena, asking, would a slave feel safe and confident enough to tease her master with the line, "I sensed you craved some lighter reading"? And then to add, "I gathered you weren't getting enough personal mail of your own"!

But I have no time for idle correspondence. Nor is it my duty to enter into dialogue with Liza's friends, as Liza is herself a full-time job. Eliciting her thoughts and feelings demands the full range of engagement from solicitous to agonistic. You can imagine how the postcard incident advanced our interactions, upped the ante, as the saying goes, and thus demanded of me even greater creativity. I asked if she would tell me more about herself, her feelings and so forth. And she said, "Why this sudden curiosity?" And I said, "It's not sudden really; I've been curious since the night we met. Isn't that obvious?" And on we bantered, neither of us saying anything about the postcard—elephant in the room—as if we played a prior century's parlor game. But then I gave the game a new dimension. From that day on, I foraged for her memories, perceptions, and sensations even more voraciously than usual, and over time unearthed a lovely little truffle. I think you'll find it as delectable as I did.

Apparently from time to time the almost nonsensical mantra pops into her head: *Liza Liza everyone eyes ya*—which is not her own original lyric but a remembered item of graffiti that reportedly stopped her college boyfriend in his tracks (a boy with whom she claims she seldom spoke of books or culture or the like) when he saw it on a dormitory wall, and he reported it to her—soberly, warily, perhaps even suspiciously; then, when it was repeated in a bathroom stall, in yet a different hand—accusatorily. He had apparently become uncontrollably jealous, possessive, behaved as if Liza herself had commissioned it; when the fact is she was—and I believe her—as surprised as he, and even more disconcerted. Was he Italian, I joked, so possessive? "Uh-uh," she shook her head no. "He was an all-American." His increasing agitation, and its no longer merely implicit accusation, caused her to feel guilty for her thick blonde tresses, her streamlined, long-limbed body, her lean but shapely model's legs.

How to translate such a phrase, she wants to know. I answer, stalling, *"Non lo so,"* and scold myself: a tiny five-word phrase, how hard is it? But I cannot 'come up with,' 'off the cuff'—one wants to ask sometimes, what isn't idiom?—some colloquial equivalent, although I am pleased that through osmosis Liza has become more attuned to the recalcitrance of idioms smuggled across borders. The challenge is the slang, primarily. It either stiffens or slackens, depending. *Lizabetta, gli occhi degli tutti? Un sguardo dal'ogni uomo? Tutti ti vedono?* Perhaps one might impose a Neopolitan dialect! Or any dialect: Berlin slang, for that matter: *Kuk mal. Dar ist Liza, es gibt Liza.* Oh, how should I know? I lack the proper sensibility to translate graffiti, I who primarily translate works of literature. I who in my Roman years have spent whole days shunning the elemental sun in poorly heated, ill-lit rooms, wrestling with a literary tense so remote it is not even used in common speech. *(Dappertutto, ognuno vede tu!)* Or if you want to find exalted literary echoes of the idiomatic phrase, indeed you should revert to German, not to dialect but high—indeed the highest— German, an elegiac Rilkean Deutsch. *Denn da ist keine Stelle, die dich nicht sieht. For there's no place that does not see you.*

Of course in your country, I say, the literature and the graffiti come closer together each year, yes? You'll allow me a barb now and then, won't you? I need diversion. It is an arduous and definitely not a lucrative vocation, freelance translation, performed by a man on the move among numerous locations, these environments that despite this inexorable global agglutination, continue to be called nations. I who carry words across also carry a cross. (You must excuse this verbal slut whom homophones seduce at every turn!) I'll take a crucifixion complex any day, here in the shadow of St. Peter's where I had my first, as they say, gig, translating for the Vatican Radio, handling only a handful of its twenty languages! And if I'm a traitor from the start with this vocationally, inverted commas, please, 'overdetermined' original sin, then what the fuck? I may as well say I'm a member of the *Cosa Nostra?* (Or would it be adapted to *La Lingua Vostra?*)

The journalists, meanwhile, get off scot-free, unless of course embedded or made hostage or shot. But I of all workers deserve a diplomat's privileges of travel, don't you think? Here in Italy a *giornalista* has a badge to wear that secures free entry to all and sundry cultural events: opera, theater, chamber music, art exhibits, installations, even fashion shows, which if you've ever visited Milan, you know are the equivalent of theater in any case. Why, you probably once consoled yourself with window-shopping on the Via della Spiga after failing to view the sold-out *L'ultima Cena,* learning too late that advance reservations for that exclusive two-dimensional dining engagement are now required. Perhaps one day Jesus will rise from his seat at the center of Da Vinci's painted table and proclaim to all the tourists feasting their eyes on him (a la Roland Barthes's delightful Eiffel Tower anecdote), "I let Leonardo paint me facing you because it's the only point of view from which I don't have to observe this damn thing. Where were all you people when I needed you, for Christ's sake? Go home, you give me indigestion!"

And where was I, just now? Was I perchance kvetching about the unrewarding life of a translator? Ha! He is not useful, as the journalist is; he is not functional, and even though he might at times be equally imperiled, speaking life and death instructions in a war zone, for example, he is considered largely decorative, ancillary, second-thought, supporting cast. My I.D. card and my badge of honor signal that I am insubstantial, ever in between: *zwischen, entre, fra, tra.* I live on borders, over mountains, across oceans. I breed words of other words; I live between the lines, inside consonants and vowels and across paradigms, in adjectives and expletives, in predicates and nominatives; for languages, like lovers, are differently inflected and variously proportioned, possessing ever-shifting moods and tenses, agreement not arrived at without constant vigilance and effort. Some languages, as you know, are more laden with one part of speech than another; consequently I must make a language of x words the equivalent of another with far fewer, etc. But on the scales they must weigh equally; else must I forfeit pounds, or lire, kronen, Deutsche Mark—pardon—euros, heavens, anything but dollars! The scorned wartime translators forfeit far worse: pounds of Venetian, Shakespearian, flesh! (But even I, with far less dire consequences, am compromised, for each one cost me pounds of sweat!)

And after navigating all this complication, someone has the ignorance, the gall to ask where I am from? The answer is no less complex than my response to your insistent query, who is Liza? The answer is no simpler than if I were burned beyond your recognition, than if I were an Eastern European count inside a hospital, labeled by default the *English* Patient. I am for and from the text, *amico, Freund, ami, amigo,* buddy, pal, I'm text-direct! And never the same linguistic river twice. Do not dare to either pity or to envy me! (Yes, I get the girls, it's true; I get all the girls, but guess what—I'm too circumspect to fuck them. It's a code of honor, so you see that in effect I'm bloody impotent!)

Forgive the outburst—it's a tense time, globally. And as a translator I'm essentially a beast of burden, though I wouldn't go so far as to say I'm driven to pasture with a blow (strike one) nor, mind you, by the prospect of a blow job (strike two) nor by the festering desire to blow up buildings (strike three) as I carry faithfully my treasonous accretion of *bon mots* across one border to another. But despite heroic efforts, I cannot make portable the clever rhyme invoking Liza on her dormitory wall. I would entertain a Faustian bargain if I could only make that slogan, currently as streamlined as a television advertisement, worthy of the far more noble Aurelian Wall! *Non c'e un posto cieco dove Liza e non visto?* No, too cumbersome. Inelegant. It must be nimble; the original is nothing if not nimble. But you have better things to do than watch the futile struggles of a beast of burden.

And that, my friend, my gentle, patient, possibly by-now frustrated if not altogether absent reader, is what we call the bridge, or when in Rome, *il ponte*—one of many, for here the plot may finally thicken. Let's not even broach the broader metaphor that I'm myself the bridge; yes I'm the bloody bridge—bearing you who can be bothered across the ever-longer Lungotevere—my suspension possibly in need of massive renovation. For I have barely managed to transport you, after all this time, to our initial slumber party.

III ———

Stay here for the night if you like, I announced casually; in response to which she, in a tone far more tentative than apposite for a young woman with such strong desires, asked if she might borrow something in which to sleep, and after considering this request, I approached the wooden drying rack in the corner of the bedroom—such humble devices are ubiquitous in Italian flats and I am sure Liza thought it a poor substitute for a monstrous American appliance—removed from it a freshly washed white cotton T-shirt, and laid it upon her lap. (I meant my gesture to mimic hers upon our first meeting, how she chastely laid the book, faceup, its vulnerable seams exposed, on the podium of my thigh.) On the contrary, she no doubt found my manner brusque: in the manner of some civil servant dispensing a form. But quite honestly, when I realized her intention was to wear my garment over her own slip, I was bemused; it seemed gratuitous to me: a second layer of fabric only doubles obfuscation. And yet I was entranced anew as Liza raised her long, slender arms, the very ones that had seemed to possess the elegance and grandeur of wings, worthy, in my view, of Canova, Michelangelo, Bernini (even on occasion Parmigianino) when she had spread them against that cabana wall. But here my proprietary proximity seemed to take the natural away—erase the very thing I wish to foster. (*Liza Liza I paralyze ya,* is what in retrospect I should have said, with fist to chest, acknowledging an element of *mea culpa.*) But twenty-twenty hindsight does not apply along the falling eye's trajectory, does it? Here then the unrevised exchange.

"But you already had something," I said, a trifle irritably, referring to the chemise previously under her sundress, now autonomous, providing ample if diaphanous coverage from approximately bust line to above the knee. It was a tad translucent, granted, although not transparent, not completely sheer. It was certainly far from obscene. I will not cultivate an American prima donna after all. (Given my profession, I am understandably an advocate of translucence.) "This is enough to sleep in. Why do you need more?" I scolded. By her puzzled expression, it was clear to me that this was not a circumstance in which she had anticipated anyone accusing her of being overdressed. She appeared as alarmed as if I'd accused her of some egregious tourist faux pas—though her particular excess was actually the inverse of the stereotypical American female's blunder of sauntering bare-shouldered or bare-legged into some historic church; for Liza, paradoxically (as far as I could see), was never bare enough. That is, unless I were the one to bare her;

were I to do so she would, I assure you, lie inert and eager, pent-up passion ready to explode if only I would activate it, abandon nuance, forgo foreplay, simply flip the switch.

But I will not. I won't. I will at most elicit, but I refuse to flip a switch. It would to me be the equivalent of instant internet translation. I who treasonously 'unpack' sentences the day long, dismantling clause after clause until I am able to reconfigure with integrity and accuracy, dare I say even transfiguratively, with just the right inflection, always with sufficient delicacy and yet fidelity to the author's original and its intention, do you think I find mere switch-flipping rewarding, even ethical? That would be vulgar—let alone, moronic. Sex is not a Pavlovian affair, no matter what you think a male is 'geared' to feel. I am patient; I can bear the tedium. In any case, Liza bore upon her heart-shaped face the tentative expression of the novice speaker of Italian unable to enunciate vowels with sufficient nuance. Such a speaker might easily, albeit inadvertently, solicit of a handsome waiter at a *trattoria* one or more male members when she means to say, "a platter of crustaceans, please" (the cocky little phrase is custom-made for trouble on or off the bus), or likewise inadvertently, transgender, verbally, a pervert—or in any foreign country mistake one gender's restroom for the other's, even though in many cases, stylized icons reinforce the foreign words for ladies, gents; *messieurs, mesdames; Damen, Herren; donne, uomini,* although in Italy of course, sometimes the unisex alternative is all that is available: a dingy, seatless, porcelain bowl beside a second dingy, soapless bowl, both circumscribed within some small subterranean cubicle, invariably located down some dark, steep, narrow set of steps.

Liza, have you guessed, is actually this very speaker; Liza did exactly blunder thus when ordering dinner at the *trattoria,* the very one above which my humble apartment lies! Liza found the handsome waiter's spirited *"voluntieri"* puzzling until she finally understood he took her—in his *spiritoso* manner—literally to be ordering his cock, and I admittedly *(mea culpa)* made no effort to assist her, amused rather than insulted. And after all, why should I feel cuckolded by the waiter's playful, mildly ribald offer, as might a *bona fide* Italian *inamorata*—for I am neither native nor her lover. Thus there was no actual competition.

"The man's alacrity is not an insult but a compliment," I said, attempting to console her, and to absolve myself. "His saying 'gladly' with that devilish grin comprised the perfect verbal garnish to the *mussels al diavolo* that he placed before you on the table. If on a menu's column, that smile would be labeled *sorriso di davolo*. In fact the entire incident is a quintessential instance of the oyster-textured slipperiness of cultural translation."

"Is that supposed to make me feel less idiotic?"

"Don't let the awkwardness put you in an ill humor, darling. Use it as a learning opportunity. Enjoy it. No reason that a conversation shouldn't be from time to time *un po piccante.*" I must confess I did enjoy watching the waiter watch her pry the first soft sea-meat of its shell and ask her with a sly solicitousness, *"Lei piace?"* By then he may as well have moved from formal *lei* to more familiar *tu. E vero?*

Liza is, for all her shame and *Sturm und Drang,* becoming more resourceful. Liza soon will be astute enough to gather that at my—if you will—church, a communicant is required—or should I say, beseeched—to boldly bare the shoulder, unabashedly request the member, announce with pride, through every door one enters, one's so-called (if I may, inverted commas) 'gender'; in short, surrender all superfluous etiquette and timidity. For here arrives a paradox of cultural translation. The coquette is not, within my private code of etiquette, the flirty girl, but the shy one who looks away, embarrassed. Call me unfair, call me provocateur, but I see immaturity enshrined in that averted gaze. For we have work to do in these our all-too-brief lives, and we must stay on task, eyes open, focused.

She must be at least subliminally aware of this—given the quote she had inscribed upon the verso of the Knights of Malta postcard that she sent me from the Vatican. *What is the way?* was written in block letters. *An open-eyed man falling into a well.* Now what is a faux-profound Zen koan doing scribbled on the verso of the keyhole of the Knights of Malta? How is a man expected to reply to such a missive?—with a message both evasive and sophisticated, cryptic yet somehow delicious, seductive but impenetrable— from one vantage, substantive, from another, preposterous. There seems to be in our increasingly global culture an irresponsible syncretism that defies cognitive assimilation.

And yet in all fairness, I too can be accused of using inappropriate tactics, and achieving undesired results. *Liza Liza I paralyze ya*—the mouth beneath my own transfixed gaze might as well repeat, perhaps even adopt as its mantra—when all I wanted was to liberate you, to send you out into the world more clear, more free, more open to the planet you inhabit. The most uninhibited gesture the poor bollixed creature could make was to sing in my none-too-luxurious shower, as the paltry supply of hot water swiftly expended itself, tracing its customary trajectory from tepid to frigid in ever-reduced increments (courtesy of Italian utilities). I heard the tail end of that folksy Irish tune, *singing cockles and mussels alive a-live-o.* "Why were you singing those particular words?" I asked when she emerged—I asked in Italian—for it seemed unconscious wit that she would choose to mutate in that moment into the infamous fishmonger Molly Malone, but she replied merely, *"Quale parole?"* Whether earnestly oblivious or dissembling I could not discern; thus I did not pursue it.

But more revealing still was a colloquial lament penned on the backside of another postcard (for no sooner had the Eiffel Tower card been dispatched to its intended recipient than this new one, *volte face,* took its place upon my bureau). *I seem to be putting my foot in my mouth every chance I get,* began the message to the infamous Serena, who from Liza seemed to elicit a frankness and succinctness frankly out of character, that is, more in keeping with Serena's character. The missive continued as follows: *told the pervert on the bus he was a fag. Then told the stranger serving food, "Give me a cock."* Why do I bother trying? Given that the author had made no attempt to cover up her words—perhaps deliberately displayed her words?—it hardly seemed transgressive to flip the card over and eavesdrop on its image. Thus I discovered that the bluntly worded *cartolina* bore upon its recto a photographic reproduction of Carlo Rainaldi's ingenious twin churches flanking the Egyptian obelisk at Piazza del Popolo. This seemed to me, just like the shower lyrics, unconscious—or deliberate?—wit—for what more phallic and testicular arrangement can be found in architecture than these two sumptuous *palle* guarding side by side this noble vertical projection? The wit does not stop there. Far more esoteric than this elemental—if you will, corporeal—aspect is the fact that Carlo had to be as clever as his rival Borromini, and fool the viewer's eye into believing the beguiling symmetry that disguised the fact that the left church's site was narrower than the right's. Rainaldi's resourceful squeezing of one circle to an oval made both domes appear equivalent though each space was disproportionate. Such resourcefulness is instructive to the translator, needless to say.

I must confess these plaintive words of Liza's, fused with this covertly *trompe l'oeil* image, nearly brought a tear to my eye. Was it a cry for help? I found it strangely—disproportionately—poignant. I felt my bureau had somehow become the direct descendant of that tongueless marble torso, the *Pasquino,* who, eloquent and silent both, bore courageously to the authorities of ancient Rome all desperate pleas, invectives, verses, whines, demands, etc. of its citizens, affixed upon his stony person! How ironic that a mute man be a vehicle for protest. But is it any more peculiar than the legend of the Emperor Trajan, whose live tongue died and was resuscitated just to tell a tale—all because Pope Gregory inferred his goodness from an image sculpted in relief upon a marble column?—a tale that I'll tell in a bit more detail later. I told it once to Liza but she merely yawned, though the *Pasquino* story roused her, if only because *Pasquino* is the clever title of the theater in Trastevere that shows English-language films, where she seeks refuge when Italian overwhelms her, and where we have gone together, I believe, thrice.

Ah Liza, my fair-haired girl, my charming, still-maturing woman, my incomparably fair lady. You're feeling overwhelmed. Defeated. Do let me be your life's midwife—for, à la Rilke's dictum, you *must* change it. There is always that juncture at which one feels immersion into foreign life and culture and especially foreign language study is equivalent to futility. It's challenging to try to burst forth into speech when you have yet to crack the code. It's hard to transmute unadulterated meaning into sonorous sound. But do persist, dear Liza, I implore you. Do persist, so as eventually to burst forth like a star.

I should be more inventive. I should be far more patient. I should find more effective means to share the benefits of my experience. But she'd roll her eyes and censoriously wag her index were I to bully her with pedagogical drill, and in fact does when I commence reciting nonsense such as: *The rain / in Rome / falls mainly on the domes!* Rolls her eyes and then inquires, "Why didn't you rhyme *Rome* with *home*? You've never told me anything about your life, your home!" I stall for time. "You've been there, darling. Don't you recall the Villa Adriana?" (I will explain this later.) My playful evasiveness appears to frustrate her; she becomes quite emotional, almost violently so. She calls me *schifo,* a traitor, claims she has given me secrets and I offer none in return. She is now genuinely distraught, irrationally conflating my so-called betrayal with the waiter's teasing; then excoriates herself for betraying her own intention to articulate the proper thing, and not the offbeat, inadvertently off-color, zany thing. It was embarrassing, she continues to berate herself.

Though sympathetic to her turmoil, I cannot help but find childish these dramatics. She had a perfect opportunity for womanly behavior, but chose to be girlish. And it makes me despite my best intentions churlish, when she habitually makes a mountain of a molehill, for distortions of this sort are much less interesting than Rainaldi's of a circle to an oval. Yet the lamenting will not end, no matter what I interject or how much I cajole. I have to keep myself from shouting, "Liza, dear, is this about the waiter or the translator?" I maintain levity somehow. "Heavens, no, it was amusing, Liza. Perhaps he found it titillating. What's the harm in that? Why, perhaps this very moment Paolo has removed his waiter's garb of white shirt and black pants, and is wanking off in honor of you as we speak." Her eyes are suddenly cast down at that remark, the color rushing to her petal-textured, heart-shaped face. But I persist. "No harm done. Except temporary damage to your own, alas perpetually frail, ego." I do not verbalize the most important part: *Were I simply to burst forth into you, it would detract from helping you to burst forth like a star! When will you understand that?* (Or should I ask my*self*: when will *you* understand that all your lucubrations cannot *ever* substitute for lubrications of a much more elemental sort, which she desires, perhaps fully deserves?)

She is, my Liza, awfully complicated, and yet from certain vantages, as the expression goes, *an open book*. Her shame anent the mispronounced shellfish and the waiter's bold flirtation is intrinsically related to her faux-virginal desire to don my suffocating cotton T-shirt as a supplement to her chemise. It seemed absurd to state what she considered obvious, for already she inferred the scorn I would likely display if she enunciated *modesty*, even if her inflection created of it a question. For I had been the one to roll my eyes when, far below the Via Nomentana in the catacombs of Sant' Agnese, we once heard a brown-robed friar tell the legend of the famous female martyr being stripped of her garments as a test of faith. (This anecdote was, as I recall, the warm-up act for his enthusiastically enumerating her evisceration.) It is said that St. Agnes received from God miraculously lengthened hair to protect her modesty. (I also recall the friar disapproved of Liza's sandals, given that they exposed the flesh of her shapely feet. Imagine that—a friar censorious of sandals!) As further counter to his absurd impromptu homily, I arranged, the following day, a trip to St. Apostoli. I pointed out the marble figures dubbed *Humility* and *Modesty* on Canova's monument to Pope Clement XIV. "Is *Modesty* compelling?" I had asked tendentiously. "All slumped in her chair? Is she the least bit erotic?" I was not through. "Even the grandeur of marble cannot make her less pitiable: she is intact, granted, but sorely lacking in comparison to a headless, eyeless, glowing Apollonian bust. Glowing, I'll remind you, *like a beast's fur*."

"You're raving, Hendrian," she'd told me then, employing her beloved sobriquet; "you're raving again." And no doubt in dubbing me part emperor, part professorial prig, she meant to underscore that I was being even more than usually didactic, and that she missed the spontaneous playfulness I had evinced during our more elaborate and yet comparatively frivolous excursion south to Tivoli and Villa Adriana, an expedition whose origin was as much whimsical as cultural.

In that period of our tryst (I use the term obviously metaphorically) she'd taken to calling me Nero. But I considered this nickname too generic. If I were to be decreed an emperor, I should not be just any emperor. During our repartee, I'd asked, "Are you implying that with all the shutters drawn, my apartment turns into the Cryptoporticus?" When she merely rolled her eyes, I tried again, "So, Liza, is my golden hair to be mistaken for a golden house?" "When golden goes to gray," she said, more lyrically—and mysteriously—than is her wont, "it more resembles ash."

I feigned insultedness, and then became, as is my wont, imperious, and so she found, as cannily as dutifully, another emperor's name for me. And I did ham it up, admittedly, as if I were some cocky Roman fellow in that famous postcard, when I retorted, "But how can I be emperor, Liza? I have no column, no triumphal arch, no coin. Nor for that matter, a beard, as did Herr Hadrian, to enshrine the affectation of the Greek philosophers—though I am, in my way, Liza, philosophical." "If philosophical equals pretentious, yes," she'd interjected. I'd feigned offense again, on cue, but only momentarily, for I was, as the expression goes, on a roll. I carried on.

"But if I truly practice what I preach, eschewing modesty, then how can I without hypocrisy refuse an imperial identity? In fact I'd be delighted to claim credit for the Pantheon, whose perfectly proportioned oculus is custom-made to snag an eye as it falls through the world." After blowing some enormous metric measurement of hot air, I caught her by surprise and said, "Let's go visit my grand estate then, shall we?" I felt chastened by the excitement she exhibited, at just the mention of an extracurricular excursion—I then became defensive—inexcusably—at her outsized jubilation, for it made me feel as if I normally kept her under lock and key, as if my imaginary beard were blue, as if my second sobriquet H. H. were not the Shavian but Nabokovian doubled initials. (Who is, when everything has been 'unpacked,' the more egregious traitor, after all? Henry Higgins? Humbert Humbert? Are you certain?) For is it not a mutual, collaborative endeavor, our cohabitation? I rattled off vocabulary to prove my point, or to console myself, or both. The words in Romance languages for *let/permit: lasciare, laisser, dejar, lasa, leicim,* then those for *force/compel: forzare, forcer, forzar, sili, comeicnigim.*

Nonetheless, she thoroughly enjoyed the outing, I believe, and indeed I could have been accused of fulsomeness when I told her that the noble caryatids of the *Canopus* at the Villa were as elegant as she, but I was earnest: their sculpted folds of drapery, their grandly erect posture, alluringly standing sentry by that opulent, rectangular body of water. And I even suspended my compulsive pedantry by not disclosing that they were cement copies rather than original marble, for even I could see that this was irrelevant. For a moment I imagined Liza diving in and gliding with smooth strokes across the length of that imperial canal, filled to the horizon with ancient waters, in her stately black maillot. I was poignantly aware that at this very spot, our absent host imagined, daily, his beloved Antinous. Hence this elaborate grandeur, this entire shrine to Egypt and its lovely sacrificial boy—a boy perhaps as lovely as my Liza. Liza too deserves to be enshrined, at least to shine, to glow. This is exactly what I have in mind, but there are times I feel I'm merely stifling her—times I feel she would be better served by *modest* goals, pragmatic ones—less grand, less fraught than total transformation. A little solitude perhaps. I wished that I could grant her these.

If the *Canopus,* for example, were her private pool, she would suffer no confusions over etiquette, such as she did one day at the *Ergife,* when an Italian man sharing her lane innocently bumped into her and was profusely apologetic, though he eventually became nearly apoplectic that she would not accept his blame, but instead ignorantly substituted her own. Over and over she courteously parroted back his attempts at apology, *dispiace, scusa mi,* and so forth. He had integrity, that bloke, not like the bus masher. He wanted only to have blame acknowledged: his own! When Italian words failed to clarify for my bemused darling, he apparently turned desperately to schoolboy English. "I bump-ed you. *Capito? La culpa e mia!*" He was a different sort of Apollo, I suppose, offering his vernacular translation of *"ne prona cadas indignave laedi crura notent sentes et sim tibi causa doloris!"* *Lest briars scratch your legs . . .* But still she kept compulsively apologizing, having at her disposal no other means of politeness, I suppose.

It startled me, the urgency with which I wished to give her something noninstructive, nontransforming. Just a simple pleasure. Incremental boost of quality of life—how much more *modest* than my customary full-blown change-of-life agenda. But it was an outlandish simple pleasure all the same, and obviously I lacked the means—for as far as I could see, the *Canopus* and the grounds were now essentially the property of Philip Morris, not for lease to a mere mortal, least of all a humble translator—therefore I substituted a yet-simpler pleasure. I added a more frivolous Part II to our excursion, supplementing Hadrian's grounds with the Villa D'Este, where we achieved a playful parity, for she had accrued some imperiousness of her own, and whenever she wanted to cut me down to size, she performed the same sort of vowel mutation that she did upon her bus masher by feminizing my pet name, while I teased her about the myriad grand fountains of the Villa D'Este. I claimed that every gargoyle creature on the Viale Cento Fontana was aiming its font directly at her in phallic homage, an aquatic tropism, modeled on the bus masher's. "Not every American is the recipient of a semen-fest in her honor," I bloviated. "Think of each of these one hundred fountains as a cruder—yes, an almost burlesque version—of a haiku." "*Sì, Professore* Hendrian," she said, rolling her eyes, yet continuing to hold my hand, which pleased me. In any case, it was an altogether effervescent day for both of us. Perhaps we had indeed become too insular, she and I, our discourse healthier, more leavened when aerated by the outside world.

IV ———

From a so-called 'objective' perspective, the texture of our time is sometimes frictive to no purpose, no concrete purpose in any case, or should I say, no resolution.

Much as I would like to claim that Villa D'Este effervescence as our signature modality, I must admit such levity is balanced by sobriety, and tension, resulting in a more beleaguered back and forth. She says one thing, I think she's meant another; when prodded she repeats like an automaton or lapses into silence. I interpret one way, then another, while she more often than not stares vacantly or shrugs—and vice versa, I suppose. On an exceptionally trying day she'll say I'm too demanding, too controlling, too much "in her face." "Did you perhaps mean in your heart, dear Liza, too much in your mind?" "You're out of yours," is her response, and she addresses me in sequence as My Emperor, then Hadrian, then Henry Higgins, and finally the amalgam Hendrian, which has, as you know, long ago become our special private sobriquet.

And yet we are—sparring aside—quite intimate, bonded by something almost innocent, although perhaps not altogether savory. What other adjective but intimate befits the universal, elemental, and admittedly delicious kiss we once spontaneously shared for nearly a full hour at the pinnacle of the Aventine, among lush Cypresses in the garden opposite the Priory of the Knights of Malta?—after taking turns peering through the celebrated bronze keyhole (a rather precious aperture in my opinion) in the famous doorway of the *Cavallieri,* when she was likely least expecting I might amorously approach her. Nor was I expecting it, though I was instigator; it was not planned, I swear to you. Wouldn't that be an absurd endeavor: scouring the gardens, the hills and parks, the labyrinthine streets of the Eternal City while musing, scheming, hmmm, where is the most romantic spot to stage seduction? Here, where nearly every random site oozes romance. (Not semen, mind you, romance—lest the verb mislead you.)

And what more ironic catalyst for an infinite French kiss than the ocular bauble of a diminutive San Pietro far below, as if shrunken through the looking glass and manufactured for a precious snow globe? She was quite charmed by it, of course. Not I. But believe me, I felt Liza's being, Liza's essence, deeply through that mingling of tongues. Come live with me and be my *tongue,* I wish to substitute for that first line's final word in Marlowe's "The Passionate Shepherd to His Love," with title modified of course: "Dispassionate Translator to His . . . (inverted commas) 'Roommate.'"

Do you know how many sense receptors the human tongue possesses? Ten thousand taste buds populate the mouth; that much I know. I translated a physiology text once when I was rather short of cash and learned a good deal. Kissing is a form of drowning, really. (That wasn't in the textbook—it's my own metaphor, tainted no doubt by associations with that u.s. waterboarding torture scandal.) I ask you, where is intimacy in a global economy, with its promiscuous, allegedly diverse communication? A single currency, unstable; a single language, Babeled; a single ideology, turned inside out a thousand ways; it takes all the frisson out of exchange. Excuse my outburst.

An ocean of saliva is a less than pretty image, granted, but I assure you I felt Liza's life vicariously pass before her eyes just as one does in drowning. (Admittedly, it is presumably one's own life in those cases.) Tongues, as a literary translator knows, can sometimes be most eloquent when silent. And my tongue, in that moment no less miraculous than Trajan's, told me Liza rode the kiss as if it were some marvelous, nostalgic contraption, sleek but obsolete, a time machine that sent her back to dizzying schoolgirl sensations, and well beyond—an ancient past perhaps, even preincarnation. Or do I, as they say, 'project'? Do I speak for myself?—a man whose formal education happened half a life ago; for graying here and there and more, I am no longer anyone's idea of schoolboy. Thus I am all the more equipped to ask the following question: when in one's mature adult life is there the luxury to invest so heavily, so thoroughly, in the press of lips, in melded tongues, without anticipation of progression? In such a case, perforce, the kiss's status shifts. No longer merely prelude or prologue—or should I say, 'prodrome'—to the seizure we mere mortals, neither Dionysian nor Apollonian, call a sexual connection, it metamorphoses. It becomes the whole, as one says in American slang, 'shebang.'

"A tongue is all one needs," she said, and I as well felt it to be, in those sensually protracted moments, the sleekest of vehicles, for it communicated everything. All other sectors of anatomy were merely its inferior appendages. This is amply demonstrated in the legend, to which I previously referred, of the Emperor Trajan's liberation from hell: when Trajan's ashes were exhumed (courtesy of Pope Gregory's intercessions), his tongue—fully intact within his skull—told everyone the tale of his release. (Of course he left out of his narrative that God warned Gregory, "No more pagans; that's your quota; don't ask me to save another pagan!") The posthumously chatty tongue: there's a gimmick if there ever was one—not unlike those chattering, plastic windup teeth one used to find in joke shops. (And guaranteed to keep your column standing—something to which every male—not just Italian males—aspires.) Coincidentally enough, as I've confessed, a gimmick was the catalyst for our romantic evening, since Liza was enchanted by the peep show at the Knights of Malta, courtesy of Piranesi—that tiny perfect sight of Michelangelo's grand column-kissed church, just like a rabbit from a hat, or from a box of Cracker Jacks! Rome is a perpetual festival of preciousness, of fetishized perspective, with its brilliant dialectic of colossal against diminutive, of chaotic against, shall we say, 'anal-retentive.' Such as the looking glass distortions engineered by our friend Borromini at Palazzo Spada, about whom Liza babbled when we first met.

"What do we need but a tongue," is the more elegant version of the sentence she attempted to articulate in several different tongues in the interstices of our drowning sessions. Indeed *my* tongue became my dowsing rod for that hour: that blissful slice of eternity. (Is that organ not a more sturdy surrogate for the mercurial, albeit more mythologized, male column?) She said it every which way actually: *we need nothing but tongue, a tongue is all one needs, is there any other organ than the tongue, would that there were nothing but tongue.* It was challenging to express it precisely, given shifts in tense, agreement, mood, etc.; I was scarcely bothered by the fumbling that surrounded this profound sentiment, this—in that moment for myself as well as her—universal truth. Far be it from me, pedant though I allegedly be, to have said, during such a tender moment, *Liza Liza let me revise ya*—even as she endearingly butchered every romance language she could summon. Perhaps her own tongue had been loosened by the *Valpolicella* we had shared just prior at our favorite *Enoteca* in Trastevere—we had gone there frequently before becoming essentially housebound—a place known by locals, not by tourists, near a popular bar which on Valentine's Day had featured an unadvertised and ultimately rather wholesome male stripper. It was perhaps piacular that I insisted Liza stay for his entire act, but it seemed the serendipity of the occasion should be honored.

The charming shards grew more fragmented as the evening advanced: *Besoin de la langue, bisogno della lingua, della niente, di rien, nulla, pero, mais,* etc. *"Basta, cara,"* I was close to saying, but instead restrained myself, and finally said, ever so gently, with the inflection of suggestion rather than injunction: "Don't speak just now." Even so I fear she found it patronizing. Emboldened by the intimacy, she challenged me, "Is that your diplomatic euphemism for don't wreck it?" Ah, Liza. I had wanted to fully inhabit the moment, to savor it eternally. Earlier that evening, I had also held my tongue; even as she gushed over the Knights of Malta bauble; I had only muttered to myself, "How can an eye responsibly fall through the world if every stop along the way is packaged with a pretty pink bow?" (She would have trotted out our favorite sobriquet and said, "You're raving, Hendrian.") Meanwhile, each time a viewer reenacts this little magic trick, the separate state that is the Roman Church is given more ubiquitousness, reminding us that that which stands in for the allegedly all-seeing Deity is not in any place unseen.

You claim we separate the church and state in modern culture, even here in Italy? Consider please that Roman traffic tickets can be issued days after an infraction with no interaction between officer and perpetrator—just a ticket in the mail delivered by a voyeur. Omniscience is everywhere—in all spheres of life, secular and sacred, mundane and exalted. *Liza Liza everyone eyes ya*— only in part because everyone eyes everyone nowadays. Everyone wishes to claim you, to mark you. And how easy it is to be stung without warning. That reminds me of Liza's encounter with a real live *vespa*—nasty, black-and-gold striped wasp, even more disgruntled to be trapped upon a Roman bus than a Roman human is. That wasp stung Liza when it could easily have stung another. But it chose her one sultry, urban summer evening when the windows sat wide open so the various commuters, tourists, students, gypsies, clergy wouldn't suffocate. And she cried out, the dear girl, startled at the treachery of nature, taken once again off guard by this simple conflation of insidious and innocent, this potent albeit diminutive phallic mimicry.

Liza understandably resents my tendency to be so rigorous, punctilious, unsparingly precise—to seem to test her words at every turn. She fancies me a martinet. All right I am demanding, I admit that. Tutored by my trade, I have the wherewithal to tutor others, although Liza, tongue in cheek, would say, "don't you mean *torture?*" ("I'll leave that practice to your country, darling," I'd counter-retort, and carry on.) "You must focus when you are on the bus surrounded by god knows what riffraff. Keep both eyes open." ("Whereas you'll make do with one?" she parries, and it catches me off guard.) "Be alert—that's all I'm asking—when you're crossing the parlous, lawless Roman streets, not to mention when you are trying to achieve something, anything. You are too scattered, too distracted. Don't you understand that eventually you may be seen by anyone and everyone, conspicuous as you are, and thus cannot afford to be oblivious. Get on with it already, Liza; change your bloody life!"

V ——

Three months later, the feast of French kissing has reprised itself neither in pastoral nor domestic setting. On the contrary, those very tongues that had been gloriously one appear to have recused themselves, and given an American's habitual resistance to the long view. I suspect my Liza translates this as pure rejection. Nonetheless, the organ is, for each of us, quite fully present, no less invested in producing speech (an activity at least as worthy, I would wager). The difference is only this; we have resumed our pre-Aventine postures: we now kiss merely as all Italians, i.e., Europeans, do, cheek one, cheek two, in greeting, parting, and in our case, also before sleeping. Perhaps I do dissemble slightly, for although there has occurred no escalation, i.e., no inexorable progression, from the kiss, the possibility seems to hover and thus our interaction is suffused in immanence, which has of course its own deliciousness and for neither of us does the memory of that briefly realized potential ever dissipate.

Nothing of these sentiments is articulated, of course; why need it be? Liza understands now all too well that she must adapt to her environment, but she has yet to accept that Italy, particularly, is a culture of contradiction, and that each citizen and visitor brings yet more contradiction to the mix, and that in a country whose custom is to make one stand in queue four separate times in a single day in order to obtain a ticket to an ordinary chamber music concert, that almost any activity one endeavors to undertake must become folded into long-term membership, each with its official *tessera* as proof, that rituals of patience must be endured before one earns one's prize.

But it is not all extra hurdles I insert into her life. I do endeavor to alleviate stress, when nothing can be learned from it. I am keenly (*nota bene,* sympathetically) aware that Liza, though she has no job *per se* in Rome, is as much in motion as a *bona fide* commuter, since it has now become our habit to sleep nightly beside each other, and my apartment lies outside the center of the city. Thus there is so much of *pendulare* (charming idiom here for commuting) for the poor girl. Were I unsympathetic, I might say, colloquially, "see how it feels to walk a mile in my shoes?"—or some such hackneyed phrase; for *pendulare* is exactly what *Il Traduttore* does with words: goes back and forth in sometimes sluggish, sometimes frantic, even schizophrenic fashion. Residing so much in between the lines that either side could justifiably ask, which is he *really* on? Hence traitorous? But I am *not* in truth a traitor;

I am not unsympathetic. I would quite sincerely like to spare her; so one Saturday morning, I lend her my trusty *motorino*, a.k.a. Vespa, the automotive homage to the buzzing, stinging wasp, i.e., one of those vehicles that serve as supernumerary testicles for your average Italian man.

All right, my sympathy is not uncomplicated. My gesture might be slightly irresponsible. But genuinely treasonous? Piacular? I know she will likely have a bit of trouble, as does any novice, particularly because within her curious grace is a component of endearing if at times supremely irritating clumsiness, particularly when she's unsure of herself; but I also know she will not harm herself substantially, and will possibly learn from the experience something of value regarding both acculturation and autonomy.

And in fulfillment of this destiny of course there is a mishap; gravity asserts itself to Liza's disadvantage, and some gallant Italian hunk abandons his own precious Vespa to play the hero to this damsel in distress, scrutinize the lovely leg's incongruous bruise, caress the shapely wounded calf with all the sedulous concern of Phoebus Apollo. (Concern that should have been, you'll say censoriously, my duty; I should have taken as my mantra his divine anxiety, calling out distraught to Daphne, *Ne prona cadas indignave laedi crura notent sentes et sim tibi causa doloris! Lest briars scratch your innocent legs and I be cause*—though not, I bid you to recall, offsetting his divine erection.)

Where was I? Yes, caress the calf and carry her gallantly (as if she were King Kong's Fay Wray) to *Pronto Soccorso* with its comforting, anachronistic red cross. If Liza was not embellishing when she conveyed the anecdote, the lad was even speculating where the queue of wounded might be shorter—thus the better to ensure her comfort and convenience—in Trastevere, or at Piazza di Spagna, or off the beaten track on Tiber Island (that charmingly sequestered little leper colony). Such shining knight solicitousness does he display; how quaint, how thoroughly romantic—as romantic and old-fashioned as *The English Patient*, with prewar hospital ambience included, free of charge.

My condolences, dear Liza, for the well-intentioned bluntness with which the doctor in his pidgin English barked, *Pants down!* What, did you imagine he could scrutinize the knee with x-ray vision, darling? Of course he had to see the flesh itself when bending its supporting structures this way and that, the various highly skilled manipulations performed to ascertain if the poor banged-up *ginocchio* were compromised. And I know you wore those fetching trousers because you thought a skirted girl astride a Vespa would be indiscreet! Italian women seem to manage with no awkwardness, a managed care if you will, just observe them; they would never give up skirts! *Italia senza gonne—impossibile!* What kind of urban landscape would it be without their legs, despite the fact that larger-than-life T and A are plastered across every advertisement on every major thoroughfare, and every bus stop, every street corner. What your so-called *cultural studies* academic calls 'objectification.' What Italian government and business term natural, not to mention profitable.

It's funny, I just thought of this. A Frenchman on the bus—some years ago—once said this very phrase *(pants down)* to me, not as a command or a seduction; he was not a homosexual. He wished to converse with whom he initially assumed an American—should I be flattered or insulted?—regarding Mr. Clinton's end-of-century sexual escapades. He meant to be both ironic and direct, making the most of his limited English grammar and vocabulary. We might have had a more nuanced discussion had he spoken French, as I can wield the accent rather deftly and have translated a variety of French texts (from Flaubert and Balzac to Bataille and Blanchot), but I did not wish to take the air out of his sporting gesture. (The French, as we know, are generally reluctant to recuse their native tongue.) We were actually passing by a hospital near the Vatican when he made his overture; that's why I think of it now—the pediatrics one: Bambino Jesu. From there the bus continues to ascend the steep Janiculum Hill, functioning as a 3-D version of the stripe rotating on a quaint, old-fashioned barber pole. (Liza would appreciate this primitive *trompe l'oeil* effect.)

I was going that day as it happens toward the Bramante *Tempietto,* at San Pietro in Montorio. (Better to take the bus part of the way, or all of the way and then walk down, because by the time one walks up the dauntingly steep hill to the site at the Spanish Academy, one is winded enough to sit passively—stands in handily for piously—in a pew for an hour.) Montorio is the church that we diverse expatriates refer to as the wedding factory, as it derives much revenue from that sacrament due to its picturesque setting. Years ago I failed to see the *Tempietto* due to bomb scares and the like, and having finally gained access, I feasted on its sixteen Doric columns with the stately frieze above, its diminutive scale fully equipped with classical proportions: an harmonious, quintessentially Renaissance whole. So perfect, so inspiringly, maddeningly perfect. Thus does the insatiable Italian lust for miniaturism produce, as if an oyster's pearl, a perfect perspectival opiate to snag the eye as it falls unmoored through the world—but in this instance a mature rather than precious gesture: elegant, not fatuous. So much of baroque architecture winks at one, coy and smug, almost impish, but Bramante's is more likely to elicit awe than to elicit cloying compliments like "it's so cute," or in Italian, *"che carino!"*

You could almost sympathize with someone's nihilistic wish to be incendiary, to light each stately column like the candles of a sweet sixteen girl's birthday cake, while uttering some mantra like, it's time to make a mess of this! Such is the volatility of a poor global citizen caught ever in between. (One hospital reminding me of another—that's the chain of association.) She had sat beside me on the *motorino* several times, behind me more precisely, clutching my waist as if her life depended on it, exuding an emotion somewhere between overstimulated and panic-stricken, perhaps even enjoying that surrender of control. And had she scraped herself under my care, she would have found my affect lacking in comparison to the heroics of her native stranger (because as mentioned earlier, my perorations are pedantic as opposed to sentimental; I do not fashion the contemporary equivalent—in neither English nor Italian—of the Ovidian sentiment *if briars brushed and I the cause)*. I'd have foregone gallantry, applied some ice *(giaccia)* to her knee *(ginocchio)* and clinically applied mercurochrome and bandage. *Basta.*

It sounds so crude in isolation, out of context, doesn't it? *Pants down!* But one day I would love to hear Liza enunciate this command with the authority of a harried casualty physician at *Pronto Soccorso,* enunciate those words to me, to *me*. For I would like the luxury of being ravished, in lieu of the responsibility of ravishing. Yet I am but a humble translator, whose task is to enhance others' intentions, others' desires, and to suppress his own.

Thus we, Liza and I, are on the whole much more domestic than dramatic. Our drama is supplied primarily by rented films, which we watch after—sometimes even during—dinner. (As she has traveled far to get here, we in general do not expend the energy to go back out.) I have always felt it pedagogically appropriate that we select films with some Italian theme or aspect, no matter how subtle or overt, such as the aforementioned Minghella's *English Patient* (her choice) or *The Belly of an Architect,* by Peter Greenaway (mine), she crying at the tragic, romantic end of the former and I, at the enigmatic middle of the latter, during—please don't ask me why—the scene in which a boy squints through a keyhole and cries himself. Afterwards, each of us inquires of the other regarding our respective selections, "but really, don't you find it . . . *un po troppo,* " meaning that her film from my vantage is too sentimental, too romanticized, too free in reapportioning the novel; whereas my film from her vantage is too self-indulgent, too hermetic, not to mention much too mannered.

But the activity we most often share is a simple culinary task: we make pasta (for which I will have started the pot boiling and done preliminary preparations for the *sugo* if the bus is particularly late—for example on Domenica it is inevitably off-schedule). I am allegedly quite particular about the mechanics of the meal. (Though not a native chef, I have acquired prejudices, healthy ones, I'd say, for I think it only proper to observe the culinary traditions of one's—even temporary—place of residence.) I believe she finds me courteous enough, and is never disappointed in the fruit of my fastidiousness, i.e., the meal itself, but claims that during cooking I can be even more punctilious, remote, and overbearing; thus at the time when one ought to be most relaxed, our conversation and behavior may be strained. But I assure you I am in many ways demonstrative.

What are our nights if not demonstrations of affection, as we lie together far from Centro's charm, here in the purlieus of Testaccio, lie together listlessly: docile, content, spent from the heat, spooned in my bed? And this is when one can be sympathetic to the bus brute—while not, of course, excusing his impertinent behavior—for it is irresistibly lovely to be nestled thus. I do not mind the heat, because I love the warmth that radiates from her skin. I hold her dampness against me fervently through the silken fabric of the chemise, under the cool cotton of the so-called marriage sheet—for this country assigns its bed linens not a regal but a conjugal nomenclature—over which even the thinnest of blankets would be unbearable. To me this contact is, albeit not luxurious, sweetest solace. Unlike my American friend Liza, I do not lust for luxury, or should I say I do not require comfort for fulfillment—which is the reason I do not dream of some sweet weekend cottage in Chiantishire among the olive trees, as do the native Brits, or some bucolic villa up in Monteverde, or some grand apartment in Parioli or on Piazza Farnese overlooking the Campo.

The ocher walls and terra cotta roof tiles that one conjures when one thinks of Italy are not in evidence in my environment. It is a neighborhood whose name derives from shards of stone. Here there are no fountains, no statues, no marble entryways, no balconies. The blue sky is occluded by the brick façade of someone else's building. But one can substitute a square of blue light radiating from the television through a neighbor's window. Superimposed over the blue square is the silhouette of someone watering basil on a windowsill, then lighting a gas stove under a *macchinetta;* while through the only window that gives out onto the street, elderly tenants with exquisitely lined faces stagger home in the heat with their *panne, mortadella,* and *formaggio* before the shops shutter their entryways for *pranzo* and obligatory *siesta.* I try to ration my relations with that window. I face a white wall and a white page—that is to say, a blank screen—beside a burgeoning bound page. But Liza does not see it from my side.

To put it bluntly, Liza blames me for the heat. Not rational, of course; am I a god? Am I a cosmic force? As if I, a mere translator, had the power to shape a climate, warm a globe. Furthermore she thinks me daft when I insist that if she focuses, she will not be hot. (I am of course well-versed in focusing, given the work I do.) The most amusing part is that the more formal my impeccable—albeit non-native—English becomes, the more reactively idiomatic her 'American,' as it were, responds. (You know the famous quote: two countries separated by a common language. And in this instance, obviously, further separated: more countries thrown into the mix.) I must admit it shows a kind of chutzpah when she gets to the end of her rope and finally comes out with something spunky like, "Good luck, Houdini. You do hypnosis, I'll do physics. I'm buying a fan, whether you like it or not."

"Come?" I respond, reverting momentarily to Italian, taking for myself in this case the role of the proverbial dumb blonde. I am more bemused than offended at her outburst. Were I a more ignoble gentleman, I would say, "You'll do physics, will you, Liza, you who are defeated by conjugation? That's a lark!" But I restrain myself: wisely, for immediately she softens, compromises. "I'll point it at me," she offers—"the swirling blades, I mean." But then she accuses me of micromanaging the purchase, and rolls her eyes when I proclaim, "This isn't the United States; there need not be an air-conditioner in every home," although I am begrudgingly impressed with her initiative in this matter. "Just wake me when the lecture's over," is her comeback.

"We're talking modest plug-in fan here," she concludes in a more conciliatory tone, "nothing extravagant." And yet to me it seems that something requiring an outlet is already too elaborate. Am I too frugal then—as costive in my spending as my Liza tends to be in action? Am I a mere contrarian? I do not care for fussy bourgeois gadgets, on the whole, and thus I make—not out of character—an executive decision. It should be battery powered, ideally, also bargain-basement budget—though if for some reason it has to be electric, there'll be at least no need for an adapter, obviously, as it shall be purchased here in Italy.

Thus an excursion to the infamous Porta Portese Flea Market is arranged. The option of the Vespa is not even debated; once stung, twice shy, etc. Early Sunday morning, we set out, stopping at the bar around the corner for a shot of espresso (me) and cappuccino (her), then lumber, groggily, to the bus stop, where of course we wait—it being Sunday—longer even than is customary; and when, a full twenty minutes later, it finally arrives, we are surprised to find how crowded on a sleepy Sunday morning such a bus can be, and count ourselves fortunate to find two seats together. Several stops later, when no one expects, it is *controllato;* the uniformed men always board after all the sardines are assembled, thus making it impossible to flee inconspicuously. I listen dispassionately while Liza explains to them that her *tessera* is in the *borsa.* But of course she must produce it; does she expect them to believe her without evidence, to give her special treatment, just because she is *una bella ragazza bionda,* an ignorant *straniera* with thick, silky, golden tresses and shapely, slender legs and lovely, perfect, cantilevered breasts? She must, they insist in Italian, unearth it before the next stop.

She gets to work, emptying everything from her satchel. I roll my eyes—borrowing her gesture—at the men. I do it affectionately; imagine the accompaniment of smiling mouth beneath my heaven-turned eyes, amused, but unperturbed; my gesture means to say to them, "Ah, women, who can manage them? Such care they take, such fuss they make." But the uniformed controllers are quite uninterested in having solidarity with me. They seem at first receptive to her earnest thoroughness, but gradually grow disgusted. *"Un disastro!"* they exclaim as they witness the incredible Rube Goldberg–like expansion of the purse, to no avail. Every piece of paper from the past six months is inspected hastily by her frightened lapis lazuleyes: receipts, scribbled phone numbers, movie tickets, crumpled xerox of her passport folded into quarters, Italian men's business cards ("When did you acquire those?" I ask. "Don't distract me now, and don't be nosy"), pamphlets on art exhibits, programs, discreet feminine items in pink plastic pouches, the tube of moisture for her lips, whose subtle citrus taste I do delectably recall, pocket hairbrush, travel toothbrush, change purse, loose coins both Italian and American, band-aids, an open pack of *fazzoletti,* at least one of which she will soon, I suspect, require to dry her eyes. Thank goodness they do not request the *permesso di soggiorno*—not yet—for Liza would be cross with me indeed! I'd never hear the end; in fact, it might comprise *our* end. Already she will blame me for encouraging her to think that riding black would have no consequences. They have written up the elaborate ticket, levied the fine, in exchange for which, at the final moment, before the middle doors reopen at the bus's largest designated stop, she excavates the crumpled *tessera*. It had been sandwiched between agenda and address book inside a flyer for some worthless art exhibit on the Via Nazionale.

They are even more irritated that now they must invalidate the ticket, exonerate her after all the bother of administering penalty. She has emasculated them through the most cartooned stereotypical aspects of her femininity instead of through its empowering authority (had she, for example, become authoritative Katharine rising Venus-like from the bath to deliver her apodictic, aphrodisiac slap). I am cross with her as well; I cannot help but scold, "These are not the tactics to employ to earn the status of the outlaw. You must convey both femininity and authority; you must not be sloppy, scattered, frightened, nervous! Just for once do not be *scervellato, hai capito?* You must virtually *seduce* them with your failure to comply." She screws up her eyes. "Every Italian girl knows this from adolescence onward, even earlier." (Such contradictory instructions; Liza strives to synthesize them.) "And as for the *tessera!* It is of no value if you cannot produce it for inspection when required. It is not an amulet, the *tessera.* "

Eventually we make it to our destination, having lost much time. Given our run-in with the authorities, we are a bit frayed. She wants to find a quiet place in which to recuperate, but as fate would have it, we've arrived at what is on a Sunday the most crowded spot in Rome—barring, I suppose, mass at St. Peter's. The market stalls, already jammed, will be much more so by afternoon. It is in our interest to be efficient. I take her by the arm and lead her toward the zone where we will most likely find some battery-powered fan. She is reluctant; her body resists my momentum. Childishly she has made herself a dead weight. Not solely out of stubbornness, apparently; she's become distracted by a row of votive figures, their silver surfaces glinting in the full sun. I become furious, for this tendency toward superstition is precisely what impeded us earlier; she didn't have the sense to put the *tessera* in a wallet sleeve or such, thought it would radiate protection magically. "Today we'll purchase no *ex-votos* please—we do have an agenda!" Forgive the irritation of a practitioner whose altar is not votive nor voluptuary but principally alphabetic. But Liza won't forgive me. She tells me I should not berate her. Her voice breaks in the process. In fact, how dare I berate her?—given that it was I who made her vulnerable, who robbed her of necessary documentation, etc. The *fazzoletti* emerge from the purse, a single tissue is plucked from the plastic packet. I can't stand to see her blue eyes redden. I am heartbroken and guilty, for every accusation she makes is justified.

I am reminded of the time I took her to the pharmacy when Roman automotive fumes had pinked her true blue eyes—except this time, I, rather than traffic, am the pollutant. That time, I went along to supervise, as Roman pharmacists can be absurdly supercilious, this imperiousness perhaps a compensation for their having jurisdiction over principally vitamins and homeopathic remedies and cellulite reduction creams—which my Liza of course hardly needs, for she is all unpuckered curve and line incisively defined by the stately seams of her black maillot—with the occasional antibiotic thrown in to insure legitimacy. This pharmacist—who was in fact (atypically) a kindly fellow—explained, that day, to Liza, that she must apply the drops to both eyes even if only one were irritated, since the eyes are, so to speak, twins, but when he said, *"Gli occhi sono piu o meno gimelli,"* she thought he said we were twins, she and I, so I became her translator for the remainder of the exchange. What she thought the *farmacista* said that day is in fact not far from what the flea market purveyors think today— unless of course they think us lovers.

Surely they at least assume we hail from the same region, given our blondeness. I get this feeling especially when we cruise the zone of Via Ippolito Nievo and Liza stands mesmerized before some dubious Russian icon until I drag her away. Despite whatever solidarity *i Russi* may assume, Liza and I are definitely out of synch today. We cannot, as they say, bounce back; we don't recover from the incident on the *autobus.* With my guard down, fraught with guilt, resentment, frazzledness, I—though the comparatively more assimilated Roman citizen—am uncharacteristically vulnerable. It chafes me to report that I am summarily robbed, by a duo of petty thieves with a well-practiced routine, as crude as a vaudeville act: man #1 steps on victim's foot, man #2 takes wallet from same victim's back pocket. ("They took lessons from the gypsies," I say drolly, avoiding histrionics, as is customary for me, and that is the extent of my commentary.) Thus the cheap fan excursion is officially terminated, and the foreign man—assumed by all to be the gorgeous blonde's *fratello* or *marito,* at least her *ragazzo,* when technically I'm no more than psuedoroommate—is hereby emasculated in his own and others' eyes.

Our hazy plan to take the *rapido* to Naples next week is likewise aborted, an excursion to which Liza had been looking forward but which I now see is hopelessly ambitious. If I am robbed in Rome, Lord knows what mischief would befall the two of us in even more chaotic Napoli. Liza and I, it seems, have made a scene with no resemblance to the one that took place in the Cairo flea market between Almásy and his Katharine in *The English Patient*, when the former offered gallantly to haggle with the vendor on the latter's behalf. Nor can our scene, alas, be excised from the script or edited or reshot. But we are, as they say colloquially, 'shot.' Disappointed and exhausted. It is, in short, the kind of day one wishes one had not gotten out of bed. I imagine going to the nearest *carabinieri* station to fill out a report, and running into our uniformed bus patrollers from this morning, who would roll their eyes, rip up the form theatrically, i.e., castratingly, and make some classic Italian hand gestures in my direction. Only after this debacle, do I, chagrined, permit her to pursue the nonbargain route, and find herself a fan by any means necessary. The consequences of this decision are far richer than I could have dreamed. Though she lacks the discipline to master proper articles and paradigms, and seems to be perpetually indecisive, I discover she can be persistent when she puts her mind to it.

She finds a grand appliance shop in the Jewish Ghetto, is thrilled with her discovery, perhaps because the vastness of the place in comparison to the myriad little 'mom-and-pop' shops seems American to her (though there are many cheaper markets, I suspect). She is prouder still of her exchange with the salesman, who even at the check-out register was saying, if she interpreted—and reported—correctly, that he would spare her the expense and personally, manually (chastely also, she assumed) fan her through the night. Oh, she is quite giddy to report this to me—though I suspect his boss would fire him on the spot were he to overhear. "Are you telling me the truth," I asked her, "or is this some private urban legend?" whereupon she puts her hand upon her heart (much as we'd once put ours together, solemnly, in the *Bocca della Verità),* and said, "Hendrian, I give you my word." In any case, I assume she took a rain check on the offer, because a fan came with her to my flat that very day, a monumental standing fan, much larger than the one we had agreed upon, at least much larger than the one I had envisioned.

Because I still feel guilty and do truly wish to make it up to her, I am initially quite diplomatic about the extravagance. She is delighted by the perceived benefits of the manufactured breeze, though I am underwhelmed; in fact, if I were not so dismissive of superstition I would swear that the enhancement of her comfort is at the direct expense of mine. On the third morning of using this miraculous artificial ventilation, the diagnosis becomes clear; I have no choice but to veto the behemoth of a contraption because it is bothersome to my sinuses. I cannot countenance a luxury that provides temporary comfort, when its true price is to wake with a sore throat. One needs one's voice. The woman can go home if she prefers cool, bourgeois comfort to my company; I can hardly be accused of keeping her here against her will. She's not chained to the bed, after all. If necessary, I can review for her the glossaries of force against those of permission: *compellere, constringere, contraindre,* etc. What's more, would any *Homo sapiens* male with a pulse, in finding himself recipient of a woman tethered to his bed, especially a fetching blonde like Liza, choose to have her costumed in a shapeless T-shirt rather than a camisole? A *no-brainer* is the U.S. idiom, isn't it?

This calls to mind—I am not quite sure why—a former lover—she was a linguist actually—with whom all words became irrelevant. We had burned through them, you might say, and yet long after the official dissolution of our romance, our passion would rekindle at the slightest opportunity. We avoided each other scrupulously for an entire year, and half of another, until we fell into the fortnightly habit of tacit sexual relations. One or the other of us would happen by, theoretically with some benign intention: a question regarding some literary reference, a just-found sentimental object that had been forgotten in the breakup, the restitution of a loan, or some mundane request to borrow cream or sugar; who knows what random catalyst it was that instantly mutated into reconnected flesh? Many nights thereafter, her tacit permission encouraged me to arrive at her door unannounced yet expected, and to be ushered in wordlessly. (Even more exciting were those times when *she* arrived at *my* door.) Always I was inside in minutes, and out the door not long after; and this celerity, believe me, was not perfunctory but incendiary (a kind of Heraclitean sex, if you will, although neither kindled nor quenched in measure but rather, immeasurably, immoderately). We could not help ourselves, as if the ghost of our relationship continued after we reneged: passion's highly active shadow—midnight masquerading as high noon.

Were I to narrate this to Liza, she would likely not forgive me. (I was in fact too craven to disclose it.) When she guilelessly revealed to me her little *Liza Liza* ditty, complete with its historical context, it's true that I milked her dry and offered nothing in return. A secret should not be a one-way street, it should be offered in exchange. On this occasion I was the one paralyzed—damned if I did, damned if I didn't; a traitor to disclose and to keep silent both. It is not on moral grounds precisely that Liza would hold me accountable; she'd harbor jealousy perhaps, not of the woman, but the mode, *la moda,* which would appear to be (I suddenly perceive) our own inverted! The fuckless talk in contrast to the wordless fuck, my fucklorn Liza ever in suspension as both *tu et vous,* both *Sie und du,* both *tu e lei,* unlaid. "Have you ever noticed," Liza had said to me the first night of the three in which we used the fan, "how the blades sometimes turn so rapidly you can't tell if they are stationary or moving? Is that officially an optical illusion?" "Mild-mannered stuff compared to Borromini, Piranesi, Brunelleschi, and Bramante, eh?" was my reply.

The fourth night the blades remain indubitably stationary; the stringently rationed Italian electricity is not expended, but preserved. The fan sits like some displaced, absurdly sited contemporary sculpture; on loan from The Belvedere or The Museo Borghese and we, the two nonlovers, supine and indolent, glisten with this sweat engendered by passivity rather than activity, which in her irritation no doubt seems to her a travesty of sexuality, as if the environmental heat were a parodic surrogate for what was not produced internally, through frictive bodies. She is disappointed, perhaps even angry that no *fuoco* rages in her motley foreigner on whose behalf she must endure the unmoved air; but if pressed she might cite something which shares certain properties of fire: lambent, hypnotic—or is that too much a stretch?—and *not* others—since she considers me controlling *and* controlled, and all too orderly.

To cheer her up, I ask her to review the story of the salesman's gallant offer: his wish to guarantee the purchase in such a charmingly idiosyncratic way, by the sweat of his brow as we used to say, and with this prodding Liza quite vividly succeeds in conjuring a dark, wiry, kinetic fellow; he must be a veritable perpetual motion machine, and jovial, of course, all smiles, winking at her. "Keep going, please," I say, "carry on, what happens next?" Were she to take him up on his offer, for instance, what would happen? She mimes his flicking open a pleated paper fan to manufacture a breeze, exclusively for her, through the entire sweltering night. Ah, so chaste. The part she has omitted, of course, is that in such a case, the other—blond—man's (i.e., my own) unattended body would all the while continue to perspire unknowingly nearby.

How clever she would feel to bring the repackaged appliance back the following morning, wittily requesting the exchange of his promised manual services for the appliance itself. But I am hoping—once he had made good upon his offer—that she would encourage him to lay down his pleated Japanese fan, thereby to lay himself beside her. "Is the fan made in Japan?" I ask her. "I guess so, sure, why not?" she says. "Is there some decoration on it?" "Well, I suppose so; do you have something in mind?" "I'd think there should be some sort of calligraphy. Painted on silk, perhaps glued onto wood." "Sure, that sounds good." "Then tell me what the calligraphic letters say." "I should have known this was a test. You know I can't read Japanese." "But Liza, you're in charge; you're making up the story. If you wished, you could create a fan so ample as to hold a poem of Ono No Komachi, for example. Imagine on the splay of its expanse, as if a parchment peacock's tail, the words, *As certain as color / Passes from the petal / Irrevocable as flesh / The gazing eye falls through the world.*"

"Imagine it yourself; it's always *you* who's making up the story. That is, when you're not taking station breaks for pedantry."

Another pause for pedantry; that's all it is to her. I meant only to be playful; I have strayed. But if it is, in essence, all a play, then why not play *puttana*, Liza. *Perche no?* (Pope Sixtus cannot resurrect himself to tax once more the Roman prostitutes and build anew the *Ponte Sisto.*) If not for me—which due to circumstances cannot be—then for Giorgio, or the waiter, or some man in a shop, any vendor, selling *oglio, aglio, arancia, nutella, qualsiasi cosa: whatever,* as one would say in the States with a shrug, while chewing gum. (I wish to release you into your full self, my dear. And thus I cannot merely make you mine!)

But Liza (despite my facility for vicarious fantasy) does not do my bidding; she does yet procure this Giorgio's services and does not get her money back. On the contrary, she spends more (though in all fairness, she does spend it in the right spirit). Feeling cheated by the fan debacle, pumped up with the adrenaline and frustration which in tandem fuels consumerism—that ingenious capitalist amalgam of dissatisfaction and desire—she purchases a rather sexy, lipstick-colored, cotton-lycra minidress from the street vendor, its form-fitting style more European in its femininity than any of her sweeping-skirted, classic summer dresses. This new one was likely available in myriad colors, for I believe I have seen them (or some version of them) stacked up every spring for some ever-fluctuating but not exorbitant amount of euros, and years before that, for something like 10,000 lire, at the various Saturday morning outdoor markets, and I suspect, given her tendencies, she vacillated quite some time before selecting.

Siren-red was not quite right for her coloring, I thought initially, designed perhaps with the dark, mysterious, and effortlessly stylish Italian women in mind, voluptuous and unselfconscious—style in their blood—but bloody hell, Liza, why not? Become a different person when in Rome! Especially when the vendor is so likely to be complimentary. He may even settle for a slightly reduced price. *Che bella, che bella, vestita perfetta, va bene. Eccetera. Liza Liza who satisfies ya?* (No, red in general does not necessarily suit blondes, in my opinion.) Go on, Liza, if not for me then for the appliance vendor, probably the owner's son, not likely an especially ambitious sort of fellow.

And on the evening of her purchase, she is—until arriving here, that is—emboldened, one might even say emblazoned; let us call her *Liza rosso fuoco.* She no doubt strides, with all the unself-consciousness she can muster, to the bus's front and speeds it forward, as if indeed she were a siren in her tight, red, slutty dress of fiery—they could market it as Heraclitean—fabric. If she could, she'd perch herself upon the bus's hood, a nearly phallic taslismanic woman such as those upon a ship's prow. (But she would never be fool enough to wear that dress on the number forty-six; that would be asking for trouble.) Please do not be misled—I do heartily approve of the new dress. I say as much. In fact, the color is considerably more becoming than I first thought. It is perhaps too predictable to think the blue-eyed should wear the shades that rhyme tonally with only that feature of their appearance, their soul's portals, enhancing the mysterious intensity, you know, the blues and greens and violets, ceruleans and such.

But I suspect that Liza thinks the spontaneity of her purchase will itself be sufficient, as if the stretchy redness of the cotton blend will ignite into passion, will effect an analogously spontaneous combustion of cloth—setting this poor surrogate for Phoebus Apollo on fire. She thinks, in other words, that she has bought sex—she who would be horrified to be called *puttana* in the street. The Americans tend to think of sex as a consumer product. This is not irrelevant to their current global vulnerability, given that there are cultures for whom this assumption constitutes a cardinal sin. Catholicism, such as it is practiced in this country, is precisely practical; your average practitioner here is perfectly content to lead a parallel and highly compartmentalized life, and every lingerie shop's seasonal display is as salient as the high-flying Vatican flag! If these Italian men were truly bold enough to gaze into their ladies' keyholes, prior to inserting tongue, then column, would they there behold an itty bitty San Pietro?

When I compliment her on it, the dress, I mean to cite both its frugality and sexuality. Uncharacteristically strategic, she strives to use the compliment as a segue, for no sooner has our dinner been digested than she lurches toward me, nervous but determined, blurting, "We could make love." Clearly she has mustered all her forwardness to suggest it, as close to *puttana* as her personality can manage—I could almost be proud of her, of this phrase that seems in her mouth a non sequitur. Even in English the inflection is tentative, constrained: a merely neutral, hypothetical proposition, backed by insufficient conviction, and when I pause before responding, she translates it, as if she fears I hadn't understood, as if she'd quite forgotten who I was. If only she had substituted *must* or *should* for flimsy *could,* and furthermore had said it cunningly, seductively, not woodenly, as if some phrase a teacher made her memorize. It might rain, the trains may strike, one day we'll die, that sort of thing.

Dovere is the infinitive you need, I want to shout: *must, should!* I could create a playful customized verb drill, *in times of lust you must use must!* Clearly *dovere* must be used to buttress that already heavily fettered infinitive, *fare amore*—for love, Italian-style, alas, has become something of a cliché. Besides which, it would have taken all evening had she extrapolated in Italian. Determining how forceful, how playful, how suggestive to be, and then matching that inexpertly to grammar, tense, voice, mood? Even Liza's standard presentation sometimes makes one want to say, now listen, Liza dear, I haven't got all day. Get to the point, *per piacere.* And so often, with Liza, by the time she arrives at the moment, the moment is memory.

"I believe that we should wait," I tell her, utterly sincerely and no less affectionate in demeanor or in sentiment, my eyes as always fixed on hers— they mesmerize one—and her response. But my American girl appears derailed by this instruction neither approval nor refusal; too nonplussed to retreat, too tentative to embellish her sincerity: the classic deer-in-head-lights paradigm, she the vulnerable, frozen-in-position doe and I the merciless beam. (Yet there is parity, for we are, after all, eye to eye.) The poor thing has no instinct for flirtatiousness—which should present itself more in the manner of a grace note, an *appoggiatura,* than a Mack truck with a flat tire. Unwavering conviction presented with a deft, light touch. All a matter of style. She does not persist, having prepared no tactics of persuasion. This is her error. Like the animated Italians who are nonetheless supple enough to grind to a halt indefinitely—for the sake of any number of bureaucratic exigencies—she now far too readily practices patience and suspends the very animation that in the spirit of their culture she had at last, albeit insufficiently, expressed.

The trouble is, I'm not a civil servant, and she is not on line to pay this month's utility bill. There is a different protocol required here. Like that man in the Ergife pool, who bumped her and apologized incessantly until she finally stopped apologizing back, I want her to be less polite, I want her, simply said, to *want*. Not secretly—explicitly. Convincingly, resourcefully, artistically! I want Liza here and now to change my bloody life. And thus her festive, brazen gesture bites the dust. Was it perhaps my mistranslation that her glorious *ora di putta* congealed into prosaic *ora di punta*—or was this just another instance of linguistic matter's slippery slope?

I suppose I have been too abrupt, though I intended to make only constructive gestures, help her build some verbal—also mental—muscle, insert hurdles such that she could learn to jump. Instead I seem to have brought the conversation to an utter halt. At a certain point she, clearly feeling desperate, accuses me of gross manipulation: feigning sinus trouble, thereby sabotaging the fan endeavor so as to force her not to wear the T-shirt. She is grasping at straws. Ah, this is wearying—even more outlandish than her usual imaginings; I don't see why it's even still an issue! For more than ever it seems patently idiotic to observe this excess of propriety in the heat of August when clothing has become virtually irrelevant, as we are the only remaining residents in the city, for heaven's sake. By the fifteenth, any sensible native has vacated north to the mountains or south to the shore. After Ferragosto you're in no man's land, almost literally.

"That's what makes it interesting, I tell her, to lose the natives and the bulk of the tourists, have the city to ourselves." "Yes," she says, "all to ourselves as we die of heatstroke—with no doctors left." "Therefore it is inadvisable to induce heatstroke through the wearing of an extra layer of fabric! If you must be stubborn, however, there's always *Pronto Soccorso*, darling"—which for the record I have christened with the mischievous alias, *Saint Pants Down*—"open the year round, or as you North Americans say, 'twenty-four-seven!'" I don't mean my exigency to seem imperious, or arrogant, or Hendrianic, but let's be sensible, shall we? It's just exasperation in my voice; she shouldn't take it personally, although I can hear the tone of bullying, I must confess. It's the same voice that has all this while been urging, "Wear the *sottoveste* instead—it's too hot for this," to which she'd reply, "Had we a fan it wouldn't be." Well that was not her syntax, naturally; what she actually said was, "It wouldn't be if we had a fan," and the rest, as they say, is history.

Liza and I are now as far from Count Almásy and his Katharine as any couple could be, far also from their embodiments in Ralph Fiennes and

Kristin Scott Thomas—the latter all the more beguiling as a faux blonde—
I'll hereby christen her the thinking man's Anita Ekberg. Oh, how that slap
sounded a reveille to my poor, shriveled, pickled pecker. That lucky devil
Almásy, whose pecker was the lever holding Katharine against the wall as
they on five erect legs, still essentially fully dressed, nearly in public but
tucked away from view at a Christmas dinner, consummated passion. Nor
are we archetypal Latin lovers who tear off each other's clothes upon arrival
(such as the old flame of mine I mentioned), but some bizarre hybrid of an
ancient married couple, inured to one another, and two skittish, awkward
newly-mets, discreetly disrobing in our separate nooks of pseudoprivacy.

We are both of us hybrids anyway. "I'm one hundred percent mutt,"
is what I say when asked my genealogy, though Liza tires of euphemisms.
Predominantly British educated, I represent nearly every continent in
some part of my blood and memory, and have visited a good many of
them and can bluff my way through a slightly lesser number of their
native tongues. Call me Mister Always-In-Between, but I am spared that
hideous responsibility of having a fixed identity—for these days who takes
pride in citizenship anyway? With no hope of global morality, badly
served by a global economy, at the mercy of compulsive and pugnacious
territoriality, what refuge have we but to raise the pen against the sword?
A citizen in desperation is obliged to fashion anodyne versions of that
ominous acronym WMD. I hereby advocate retreat into a wholesome, healing—well at least innocuous—WMD: *Words of Much Distraction, Words of
Massive Delectation,* and customized just for the translator, *Words of My*—
did you hear *my?* Don't dare leave *my* name off the cover this time!—
Deduction.

If she had brought *me* to the outdoor market, I would have given her
advice about the dress. And even if I'd advocated other colors, I would have
favored its bold contrast to some *prêt-à-porter* number off the rack at a predictable, respectable, American-style department store like Rinascente—
though I recall she'd been resistant to my couture suggestions previously. It
was an afternoon in early spring, if I recall correctly. We'd made an excursion to the Piazza di Spagna to see the highly educational Keats/Shelley
House, following a lovely late morning stroll through the Protestant
Cemetery. Liza and I had sat nestled against each other upon a cemetery
bench, her head upon my shoulder, gazing at the poet's eloquently melan-
cholic tombstone, feeling both of us ensorcelled by the bucolic serenity that
permeated this oasis. I don't think it presumptuous to declare that we in

tandem felt the romance of the Aventine come flooding back, until in a vir-
tual seizure of spontaneous fervor, I vowed that I, just like the collegiate
graffiti artist who had first immortalized her, would do all within my power
to ensure that Liza's name never be writ in water. I fear it spooked her,
whether my devotion or the specter of mortality I couldn't say.

To atone for my distressing her, we followed up the tour of the
Keats/Shelley house with what is called colloquially, 'down time'—sat
together idle, with no agenda, upon the legendary Spanish Steps, our mood
much brightened by the laddered cornucopia of azaleas. We were not vexed
by the innumerable tourists and gypsies who shared our breathing space,
perhaps retaining in our very bodies the serenity of the Protestant
Cemetery, where our only company had been the dead. The deep magenta
of the flowers against saturated blue sky, through the even bluer filter of my
Liza's eyes, was such sweet solace that I felt myself about to cry. (Full fathom
five my Liza's eyes, or is it I who deepen them in my beholding?) That day
a television crew was doing a fashion shoot for Valentino, so the lovely floral
elements served as backdrop to a more contemporary sort of Roman theater: cameramen with pensive expressions and tarted-up women parading
themselves on command. Ridiculous though such theater is—and in keeping with my resolve to distract Liza from the residue of Keats's mortality—
what could one do in the wake of such a display but window-shop? In this
section of the city, it is surely the default activity.

We strolled along the major thoroughfares of course, with all the mil-
lion-dollar haute couture name-brands displayed inside the shops Italians
call *negozi da miliardi,* but on the innumerable side streets beyond Via
Condotti, farther in from the renowned steps, things are a bit more reasonable both in terms of price and ostentation—though still far from
understated. As is usual in this vernal season for *le donne* in Italia,
midrange fashion's flag is all pastels and frills. In one window hung a
lovely flouncy-skirted, empire-waisted dress that somehow suited her, the
same way she thought Babington's and Caffè Greco with their golden old-
world charm and British tea suited me. I was directive and expansive in
my compliments.

"This one is very feminine; this would look well on you." And when
she raised her eyebrows skeptically, I said, "I have an eye, you know." "A
little fussy though, isn't it?" she asked. "Too . . . you know, overtly feminine?" I pondered silently, playing her game. Finally, to garner a reply, she
formulated it in Italian, *"Un po troppo, secondo me."* And she winked, to

prove that she remembered we had tossed about this phrase before. *"Troppo femminile?"* I countered, arguing as if we were some animated married couple, possibly some well-heeled, nouveau-riche Milanese couple, strolling through the ancient city on a southern jaunt: *"Come possibile?* How can there be such a thing as *troppo femminile?*—especially in a dress! *Assurdo!"* I was playing the Italian man to the hilt that time, I admit it. Isn't that what your average Italian man would say? I shouldn't generalize. The gentle, gallant bloke who bore her like an orphan or a cripple onto the steps of Viale Trastevere's *Pronto Soccorso,* wouldn't he say something of that nature? Or no?

VI ———

Such flashbacks are distracting, and they may attempt unconsciously to place rose-colored glasses on the love affair, if we can call it that. (Inverted commas, obviously.) The truth, unvarnished: Liza is wearing down; I feel it. I see the evidence. Three months have passed in this fashion and during this period, she must—I hope, for her own sake—be seriously considering the advances of the cheerful, effervescent man in the appliance store, who has consistently pursued her in these daylight hours, asking if he could touch her golden hair. *"Ciao, bionda,"* he would always say (or so she told me) when she passed him as she strolled the haunting streets of Rome's compact but amply atmospheric Jewish Ghetto. She did so when she required otherworldly respite from the all-too-earthly bustle of Viale Trastevere, seeking a tranquility that was not quite the ordered Eden of the Aventine or the likewise pastoral splendor of the Janiculum, for the Ghetto one might designate more earthy in its hauntedness. (Revisiting the peaceful, Keatsian tomb was not a realistic option—though relatively close to my apartment—for one might be thought morbid to frequent the Protestant Cemetery, not to mention the impediment of the repeated entry fee.)

Perhaps she lingers at the Tartarughe Fountain before deciding on a whim to buy one of the freshly baked kosher confections that lure streams of locals through the tiny portal of the Jewish bakery, and then feels frustrated when unable to locate it since its Hebrew letters are not visible during the hours when it is shuttered. Of course she might be frustrated even after finding it, put off by the demeanor of the two cantankerous, thick-waisted women who argue with each other uninhibitedly as they bring the broad trays forward from the ovens, regarding dismissively their bemused customers as if the latter were essentially squatters in their private kitchen. But I would say to her, "Do not be put off, Liza; this is earthy tension, this is lively conversation, this is . . . life. Rome is always full of life, and thus its Ghetto is not ghostly, like its Jamesian, Venetian version. Your frustration will in any case dissolve when you bite into that delectably rich comestible called Jewish pizza, whose orgy of plump fruits and candies and slightly burnt bottom give one's teeth a workout as ten thousand taste buds simultaneously register delight."

The appliance fellow must get many cappuccino breaks because whenever she walks by it seems he's there—*"Come stai oggi, bionda bella?"*—perpetually offering to carry her single sack of groceries or her little bag of toiletries, never considering how far she might be going. She muses she might let him carry them tomorrow. Or the next day.

Can you imagine—a night spent with this ardent, dark-haired fellow, stroking her hair on the pillow, making her healthy pink scalp tingle unto climax as he whispers ardently, *"I capelli della sole,"* the contact sensual enough to make her shiver. Thus I try to urge her on toward risk, adventure; heavens, happiness, fulfillment! I do so in the simplest ways. For instance, if we dine out, which despite being bombarded with options, sleeping every night above a *trattoria,* we seldom do (my vocation I have told you is not a lucrative one), but on those rare occasions when we do dine out, this Emperor Hendrian has decreed it must be authentic Roman fare: *soltanto cucina Romana: guanciale, ossubuco, puntarelle, baccala, carciofi fritti, fiori di zucca,* even tripe.

She puts her foot down there. "No tripe." "You are absurdly squeamish," I scold. "Where is your spirit of adventure?" And then a lightning storm reconfigures the planes of her lovely, heart-shaped face; the celestial eyes flash with an electric charge that I have seldom witnessed. "My spirit of adventure is to be here in the first place. My spirit of adventure is to be a squatter on Italian soil, with less security than a gypsy, in a city that requires a *tessera* for every trivial activity. I have passes to use transportation, recreation, every educational and cultural facility, but technically I can't be here in the first place, because on your stupid dare, I have no *permesso di soggiorno!"*

Bravo, Liza! Gumption! More of that, please! (Congratulations of this sort must not be said aloud lest too much praise create complacency.) Liza, I have found, needs to be pushed, or else she'll never grow beyond a certain limit. Thus I continue prodding. "Even so, you are determined to remain utterly American, unchanged by your experience." Perhaps as a gesture of reprisal, she passes over not only the tripe, but every other local specialty, and puts her finger stubbornly on the menu's *pollo* line.

"Americans and their chicken! Be less predictable for once! What point to go to a new country and not eat their delicacies; whether cat or squid or dangerfish or even shepherd's pie. You need beef! You are too close in spirit to this chicken as it is."

"Cocka-doodle-do," Liza responds, much more theatrically than is her wont, rolling those extraordinary, almost aqua eyes, no less beguilingly than Katharine to Almásy when he uttered, fire. (Liza, I have always felt— regardless of the *tessera* or *permesso*—is an honorary Italian, because her eyes are metaphorically Mediterranean.) *"Esatto,"* I reply, a semismile. "You expressed a strong opinion; this is good." "Don't patronize me, Adriana." (*Liza Liza I'll patronize ya,* for how else can I ever elicit your fire?) You see, she won't do it unprompted. As compromise she finally agrees to change the order to a *baccalà* and *insalata puntarelle;* but after sampling it, I can tell by the combination of slight frown and squint that she finds the *puntarelle* disagreeable, the anchovies in the dressing too robust a taste, because I once prepared for her a *pasta alla sarde,* and she made exactly the same face.

But her distressed expression is the portal to a marvelous, almost miraculous, confession. She has decided to succumb to the advances of the man in the appliance shop. She divulges this perhaps to see if jealousy will flare, or even flicker, her own motives no less inscrutable than usual. But regardless of the motivation, this is cause for celebration. I call back the *cameriere* and explain that I have made an error with the *puntarelle.* What the lady really wanted was the *pasta puttanesca;* it was my mistake entirely. Could he take away the *insalata* and replace it with the *pasta,* and adjust the bill? Meanwhile I advise her carefully on how to be seduced, how to make the most of this excursion. I'm as serious as she has ever seen me. I can tell that she is flummoxed by the intensity of my commitment to this amorous mission. This time we do not deviate from Italian, as if only in this language can seduction be transacted properly. *"Senti, Liza; devi farlo essatamente cosi. Come Io dico, capito?"* "Write an advice column for *Cosmo,* why don't you, if it's simply a formula."

It had been months since we'd tried speaking in Italian only; I find it bracing, but she obviously disagrees. I think she needs caffeine to keep her courage up, and order an *espresso:* one for each of us. We return to my flat for the items she will need; she packs them languidly into her satchel. "Leave the *sottoveste* here," I tell her, a peremptory flavor to my voice, and she looks up puzzled, but dutifully removes the ivory camisole from the satchel, almost as if hypnotized, before exiting. I hand her the key, a gesture I have never previously made or had to make, and she takes it wordlessly, a passive player in some ritual. She holds it in her palm like a stage key, a skeleton key; cumbersome, it weighs in her pocket. Usually of flawless posture, she appears upon exiting ever so slightly asymmetrical. I have counseled her to go directly to the man's flat, not to get distracted, but she undoubtedly will maunder.

And in this case it is much easier to guess her motives. She believes the refreshing evening air will give her ballast, fortitude, that the joyous bustle of humanity will offer her perspective. She will probably be carried with the tourist tide toward Santa Maria in Trastevere, where the spectacle includes exotic fire-eaters (better here than at the Campo, for it would be in poor taste to parade the incendiary near the site of Giordano Bruno's immolation). Peruvian pan-pipes accompany the fire-eating, which must vicariously be quenched by overpriced *gelato* at the fancy bar/*gelateria* that for yet another several euros promises a ringside seat. (Liza, I can guarantee, will not buy, and thus not sit, because she fervently believes that *Tre Scalini* at Navona is superior.) She will eventually reach Piazza Navona in her travels, I suspect—that rapturously elongated ellipse—the architectural equivalent of a mirage, which suddenly opens up before one's unsuspecting eyes, and I can only hope the agile marble bodies and ebullient spray of the majestic fountain's *Quattro Fiume* will be influential.

She seeks out the door the young man has given as his address, but lingers idle, somewhat agitated, suspends her index tentatively. Three minutes pass. The finger levitates; it will not land. But the man behind the door whose bell is almost rung—I see him with his curly dark brown hair, as if his kinetic nature permeated every fiber of his physical appearance, as if he'd stuck his finger in a socket. With his shining warm brown eyes he seems far too spontaneous to be the husband of a wife or father of a child—a good sign, Liza deserves full attention, she should not be merely some man's mistress. (I admit I went into the shop myself to have a look, feigned need of some trivial piece of hardware, some adapter or other, and then to make it seem less spurious, added a coda of curiosity about a certain brand of *frigorifero.*) He seemed indeed a man married to the moment. I approved of his confident, but not arrogant, manner: singing, laughing, joking, flirting with a female customer or two, milking the most out of every moment, playing the fool for laughs without self-consciousness.

She probably again studies the names beneath the various bells, to be absolutely certain. It is the right name, the right buzzer. But only of these facts is she sure. Her feelings are a mystery to her. Nervous Nellie to the last, she is a frozen photographic image all this while, and does not ever leave her fingerprint as souvenir. The index retracts; the forearm descends. This mystery still unresolved, she walks as in a trance, toward Largo Argentina. She walks around the ancient center of the city, which she has not done in quite some time, spending it instead indoors, engaged in the mundane, with me—as if we were in Frankfurt or Bridgeport: some random, unromantic, unremarkable city, just an outpost for an airport or a train—as if we weren't surrounded by history's magnificent movie set, a twenty-four-seven, brought-to-you-live shrine to antiquity. It is almost overwhelming to her, seeing all of this again under the nearly full moon: bridges, fountains, monuments, and ruins. Finally, feet and eyes both spent, she chooses the most reliable *fermata* at which to wait for the rather less reliable night bus.

Liza, *per fortuna,* has managed to return from Centro unscathed. It is far less dangerous to travel in the middle of the night in Rome than in some comparable metropolis in her country, but still it's inadvisable anywhere to travel unaccompanied at three in the morning. She returns to my—though I suppose by now it has become our—flat in the middle of the night, enters quietly after turning the key that she regards as excessively large and cartoonish the requisite number of times in the lock, first from the outside, and then from the inside to relock it. Paradox abounds. A tiny keyhole on the Aventine yields through trickery a microscopic image of a larger-than-life majestic edifice; meanwhile this average door here in Testaccio requires what appears to her a larger-than-life key. She thought, given these inversions, she might meet the Red Queen or the March Hare. This custom of locking oneself in feels to her almost as unnerving as locking oneself out, as here it is accomplished via key rather than mere fastening of bolt. Because it is not second nature to her, she wonders how, in the frenzy of fleeing from fire or intruder or demon, one would manage the precise repetition of rotation.

Is this unlikely fate so different than more likely ones constructed for the immigrants in her country, in those big box u.s. stores, performing some undocumented labor profitable to capitalists, and yet no key do they possess?—as if the infamous New York Triangle Shirtwaist Factory's tragic lessons were unlearned in time for each new sea of immigrants. But here in Italy the emphasis is on securing possessions—given prevalence of theft—with doors that bolt securely into the floor below them. Thus, Roman apartments suggest the accouterments of America's Fort Knox, and in American cities—the crime statistics of which suggest they harbor ever-present threats far greater than mere theft—one could seemingly blow a house down. But I feel such a gentle breeze when Liza's body moves into position next to mine, under the marriage sheet. It is a lovely way to be awakened.

Eagerness erasing somnolence, I find myself compulsively plying her with questions. Was she satisfied? Was her suitor interesting in bed—a satisfactory lover? When she reports that she called it off, I am cross with her. "Only you," I say—as annoyed as had been the *carabinieri* on the bus— "only you could do this. Do you not even know how to have an affair? You are a foreigner in a city of worshipful, hungry men, and you bide your time. You make excuses. You have learned nothing from me."

"What are you, my pimp?" she asks, uncharacteristically feisty, as she walks into the hallway to undress—then adding, voice still raised, "or my tutor, in which case instruction, I must say, has been minimal." (Sir Henry Higgins at your service, I resist the urge to say.)

"I am not your pimp," I tell her sharply, "nor your tutor. I am your advisor."

"Well, I guess I didn't realize your advice was mandatory." Nevertheless, we return to routine, despite a certain chill, a certain distance—fortunately mitigated, the next night, by a perfectly *al dente* (she was paying attention this time) *tortiglioni* with a sublimely melded *sugo melanzane* (if I do say so myself). Seldom is our collaboration in the diminutive kitchen so successful.

Through the next two weeks she seems more distant, less forthcoming. I feel we're going through the motions of cohabitation without really— though I loathe this verb—*connecting*. Approximately two weeks later she returns quite late again, undresses quietly: the same ritual. I gently place my hand upon her silk-sheathed hip, though only half-awake. Later, I brush my fingers across her cheek and stroke her hair, foregoing interrogation. Toward dawn, each of us rises in sequence to void our respective bladders.

The instinctive act of warding off the sun reminds me of the opposite celestial body which was last night nearly full, and so I ask her groggily, "Was the city splendid under moonlight?" She does not answer. "Were there many people out in the cafés in those wee hours?" She had always been intrigued by all the well-heeled men and women drinking at the chichi bars lining the Navona. (Harry's Bar for us, as you might guess, was metamorphosed into Henry's Bar!) There were usually more foreigners than natives, but not tourists exactly, a concatenation of expatriates she had begun to recognize, and perhaps it was reciprocal; a few of the men— British men, she thought—seemed to acknowledge her ever so subtly with a slight nod or shift of expression, posture. I too have seen them, heard them slurring to each other in her presence, sometimes crudely: "There's that blonde bird, she's brilliant, eh?" or, "By all means ream us, Romulus," after they'd had one too many in the elegant, glittering bar at the edge of Navona. Then they would continue carping about the mail, about the strikes, about the crowds, dreaming themselves into Felliniesque scenes, where they too might cavort in fountains like Marcello Mastroianni in *La Dolce Vita*.

"I don't know," she finally replies, and then adds, "I was inside making love with Giorgio."

"Ah, I see," I say, without hesitation, evincing neither jealousy nor ruefulness. I am, if anything, galvanized.

In fact, having waited many months for such a moment and having essentially abandoned hope, I will not let the conversation terminate, and so continue jauntily, "And how was that experience?" For the first time in all these months, she senses a quickening—the fire in the loins as miraculous as Lazarus's resurrection. I hope she does not think it calculated; it is not calculated on my part, it is simply the first occasion on which I feel a fully-fashioned physical desire for her. And as puzzled as she is by my lack of jealousy, she is probably all the more so by this incongruous turgidity against her spine, here in the bedroom of this solitary flat where she has nightly longed for it, but now—inured to lack—was least expecting it, far from the crowded autobus crammed with humanity and all its stink. Why now, of all times? That's what she would ask if she had the so-called balls. The answer so much simpler than she'd ever dream: because you demonstrated will, my dear. To put it more poetically, you arrived at the moment before it was memory, thus stirring your companion's Rip van Winkle.

And here we prove the proverb that is as Heraclitean as it is Zen, for we arrive, long last, at peripeteia. Since etymology (from Greek) marks this above all other moments as *the falling round* (not *fooling*, prurient reader, *falling*) and Liza's unintended aphrodisiac of a confession played a piper to my thus far dormant pickled pecker, sending its compass needle north, then the way up and the way down are manifestly, metaphorically, metafictionally one and the same. She—and you, vicariously—have endured all my Hendrianic antics, which were employed exclusively to get a rise from her, because I thought it would empower her to feel her own force, even fury; finally a self, unmediated. And she, more literally, i.e., physiologically, wished to get a rise from me, which, for what it's worth, she finally received. And finally you, dear reader, you desire a rising action: Freitag's triangle inscribed into this mess at last, so that the peripeteia may proceed—a falling eye recording, or contriving, falling action.

Who knows? Perhaps she'd come to regard me as some delectable stretch of malleable dough, something practiced Italian artisanal hands could fashion into pastry, pasta, pizza. It is as if our peculiar relationship had suddenly gotten a second wind. No sex for six months and then twice in one night, wouldn't that be my luck? my sweet and charming, sometimes bumbling, beauty is undoubtedly now thinking; I know Liza's mind by now. But of course it wouldn't be; it ineluctably could not be Liza's luck. Your luck, my dear, will likely remain pedestrian, unostentatious, albeit maddeningly erratic. Until you choose it to be otherwise, it will continue to produce prosaic semen stains and secondhand searches, inadvertent and deliberate collisions both, inscrutable and ironic courtesies; it will insure a lifelong bond to a baroque panopticon which is perpetually drooling desire. Meanwhile, I listen attentively, every corpuscle attentive, as it were, to her romantic little narrative about the boy from the appliance store—for she is sincerely trying to answer my question.

"Quite nice," she says, "all told, nicer than I expected, though I think it would take another few . . . sessions for us to find just the right . . . rhythms." (Her choice of nouns seems curiously generic, somewhat antiseptic, more appropriate for instrumental practice or appointments with one's psychoanalyst, but perhaps I scrutinize her words excessively.) She wants to keep on narrating; she senses this is the first thing she has said since the beginning that engages me, and yet she feels obliged to answer truthfully, albeit euphemistically, regarding this Giorgio's ceaseless, unphrased energy. He is, I mentioned earlier, apparently a kinetic continuum, like a very young boy unable to sit still for a moment, in fact (if her narrative is to be believed) once literally jumping up and down clapping his hands in delight as commentary on her intention to remain the night. (*Bravo*, I too would be applauding, from behind the scenes, over her shoulder.) He is bustling, in fact nearly buzzing, like a fully charged battery, up and down and getting her a glass of wine (innocently assuming up to that point she had, at well past midnight, just stopped by for a chat) and showing her some special book of photographs, then demonstrating his juggling routine, which if she understood correctly might someday in the near future be featured in some avant-garde circus in Milan. He wants to show her a technique which he has not perfected but is proud of. Relinquishing his juggling *palle,* he entreats her until she allows him to brush her hair, which he does reverently and gently, as if hypnotized, marveling at its texture and color as if it were some anthropological wonder, insisting then that he must look at her from near and far, to see her as a painting, and then displaying at last the camera (presumably borrowed from the shop), a vintage rarity, asks if she would honor him by letting him record her beauty? And she does, she did: almost an entire roll, if she is not exaggerating. Young boy that he was of course, he shot too soon, in spite of himself, but that was a foregone conclusion; and in this context, perhaps she found his over-eagerness endearing, not an insult but a tribute. Oh, I could teach a young man a thing or two about forestalling. "Yes, rhythms, I said, I understand. But he was sensitive, to your needs?" "Yes," she said, reflecting, still assimilating her own experience, "he was passionate and enthusiastic. And appreciative."

"Well, this is good," I tell her, "this is very good for you," and we speak no more, drifting off until the sunlight is so strong we could no longer fend it off. By midday I resolve we must do something special. We have a festive lunch outside the house—my treat. We rarely ever take our *pranzo* in a restaurant if we are out together at that time of day, usually grabbing frugal *tremezzini* in a bar or such—but this afternoon the penny-pinching translator insists; we order *vino rosso,* vintage left to the *cameriere,* who of course remembers us, *bucatini all'amatriciana* (it was that day's specialty), *insalata, frutta, basta.* When the serving of melded beef, pork, and tomato over those unwieldy, tube-like noodles is set before her, it is obvious immediately that her unaccustomed, frankly rather spastic, handling requires a spoon. (You would think she wielded chopsticks so maladroit was her manipulation of the standard cutlery.) "They do use forks in the United States, am I correct?" Rolled eyes, on cue.

And then I raise my finger to solicit Paolo. (I have dubbed him Paolo; thankfully one is not chummy on a first name basis with one's waiters here, as in the u.s.; his true baptismal name is his affair, not mine; he is eternally the *cameriere.*) *"Un cucchiaio, per favore, cameriere,"* I request. He brings the spoon expeditiously, and asks, his eyes on her of course, not me, *"Soltanto un cucchiaio, e sicura, lei?"* ("No cocks today," I am tempted on her behalf to say; "the spoon will do," but that would only make her blush more deeply.) So instead, I grasp her right hand gently with my own and guide the twirling of the *bucatini,* now supported by the concave belly of the spoon. Paolo watches with a twinkle in his eye as he attends to the next table's order.

"Will you see him again?" I ask, out of the blue, as the expression goes, and into hers: her equally capacious azure. She looks up, perplexed, her golden eyebrows knitted, her blue pools churning and confused. "You mean Giorgio?" (She pronounces it as *Joorjo!*) "Yes, of course, Giorgio, your suitor, your new lover." "Possibly," she said, "I'm not sure. I hadn't gotten that far," her lapis lazuleyes suddenly all murky.

"It is not important, I said. What matters is this first time. That you acted—you . . . connected—that you didn't vacillate."

"You must have left the merit badge upstairs," she says, the sarcasm softened by a certain playfulness of tone, "though it's a funny thing to get a medal for, I have to say."

Sei spiritosa, Liza. That's the clever girl I want to see more of. "And you in turn appear to have left upstairs those photographs taken by your lover. The ones you mentioned in your little narrative." And don't ask me to explain how I persuade her to fetch them from upstairs and bring them to our table, but I manage it. She's back before I've had a chance to process her departure, handing me the envelope as dispassionately as some FedEx courier waiting for a signature, but I, when I behold the contents of her envelope, am not at all dispassionate. I suppress the urge to whistle. How many times have I conceived of her as a figure in a picture, and yet I find it startling to behold her gently curving silhouette through Giorgio's 'agency.' His artful use of black and white somehow ingeniously suggests the rosiness of flesh: that of the woman I have nearly nightly slept beside, but who is only now laid bare before me through the framing of a rectangle.

"He has good technique, this Giorgio."

Liza remains silent, not regarding her own image, but regarding me as I regard her, reproduced.

"Or perhaps it's his equipment. Fancy cameras tend to let even a novice shine. Convenient working in a shop where one can borrow any gear one takes a fancy to."

"The camera isn't from the shop. He got the camera at Via Ippolito Nievo." It is curiously unsettling to have Liza correcting me.

"From the Russians, you mean? At Porta Portese?"

"That's right." I feel slightly nauseated when she tells me this, aware that Giorgio found not just a bargain, but a gem. Moreover, he found it at the infamous flea market where I failed to find a measly battery-powered fan— and had my wallet stolen in the bargain. But memories like these are best not resurrected.

"He captures something of you."

"That's more or less a given with a nude photo, isn't it?" she counters irritably, annoyed at my obtuseness, clearly feeling my response inadequate—if not irrelevant.

"I do not mean exclusively in the physical sense," I tell her, keeping my tone noncombative, refusing to capitulate to condescension.

But she's no longer listening. She flags the waiter over, to my astonishment, and says, *"Per piacere, cameriere, Io vorrei una penna."*

"*Si, certo,*" he nods, smiling at how cleverly she has transformed the phallic symbol this time. But remembering her propensity to err in Italian, he thinks in asking for a pen she means the check—or so I infer—because he brings them both and sets them somewhat dolefully upon the table, asking in puzzlement, "*Perché non voi vorreste dolce oggi? Al meno un caffè, un cappuccino?*" Then Paolo glimpses the breathtaking image on my lap. "*Allora,*" he says with the most appreciative inflection, "*ho capito. Abbiamo qui invece dolce per gli occhi.*"

Sweets for the eye, indeed; the waiter is a poet. "*Bellissima,*" he adds, and gazes until someone else's finger bids him come. Meanwhile, Liza, far less flustered than I would have thought in such a circumstance, takes up the pen and begins sedulously doodling on the paper placemat. But now she has ceded herself entirely from the conversation, having adopted priorities greater than providing me an interlocutor, and begun doodling on a paper *serviette*.

"It is also a very nice body you have," I tell her, quite sincerely; for the photographs served to confirm what had long been evident to me through nearly sheer material. She stops drawing for a moment.

"Thank you," she says, after hesitating, but her mind is elsewhere.

Paolo returns to see if I have placed a credit card inside the leather billfold. I—unlike Liza—can recall a time in Italy when credit cards were used exiguously, but what I place in lieu of one today is surely all the rarer, for I have placed the next of Giorgio's homage face down, its edges extending dangerously beyond the leather billfold's rectangular corners, and as a ruse I have told Paolo there appears to be an error on the bill. "*Il conto e sbagliato force?*" I wink as I hand it to him, and once he catches on, he is delighted to participate, and we repeat this ritual several times, each time a different image for his delectation, each time a bogus adjustment to the bill, whether for *carne* or *contorni, non importa.*

Liza all the while continues doodling on the paper napkin, more concentrated than I've ever seen her, then abruptly flips it over, rises. I take the liberty of turning her modest drawing from verso to recto following her exit, for being practiced, I can estimate how long her preening takes when she visits the ladies' room; there is no danger of my being caught snooping. Her composition is hardly elaborate, though carefully composed and executed: a nearly perfect circle, inside of which she's shaped a crosswise oval bridging more than half the circle's width, and within which lies centered another circle—not filled in by any cross hatching, just blank. To the right

of the oval she has sketched the less-than-flattering lineaments of my decidedly non-Roman profile. It adds up to an outlined iris in an outlined eye,
punctuated by the aforementioned profile—and enclosed, the whole
ensemble, in a circle, like a crude version of some stylized portrait on an
ivory-carved cameo: or even more like some cartoon of an Imperial coin.
The little sketch is curiously mesmerizing, albeit disconcerting.

She's taking even longer in the ladies' room than usual, and I exhaust
myself in trying to imagine what might possibly be keeping her. I recall the
dated euphemism, 'powdering her nose,' which ingeniously allowed a
woman of another era not only to freshen her makeup but also to avoid having to refer explicitly to a bodily function in polite company, should she
need to excuse herself to take a piss. And through this serendipitous association, it suddenly occurs to me that I can powder mine. I'll powder my
nose—with a pen!

Yes, if I blacken out the background to obliterate my non-Imperial
nose—a profile I have never been enamored of, for obvious reasons—what
remains is a rudimentary open eye—no lids, no lashes—inside a darkened
circle. The larger circle could conceivably be a rudimentary keyhole
through which the eye peers. But such a static image does not seem to do
the drawing justice. I must concede that the thing more urgently suggests a
falling eye, wide open, captured as it plummets down the center of a dark
well. Suddenly it occurs to me to ask someone—Paolo perhaps—if this
inglorious aperture is really so much cruder than the architecturally exalted
Pantheon's—simply because the latter is looked up through instead of down
into, and because it bears the noble label, *oculus,* and charts the restive patterns of diurnal progress.

I have ample opportunity to ask, for Paolo has returned for his next
installment, but it is I who have now become distracted. It does have a
strange illusionistic depth, this two-dimensional black hole and floating
(i.e., falling) eye—as mesmerizing as a mirror. He is bemused, but tries
obligingly to peer in tandem with me, over my shoulder. And the more we
peer at it, the more it is vertiginous, and the more it makes me think of
Rainaldi's faux twin churches at Piazza del Popolo. Paolo would know, of
course, being a Roman citizen—well, presumably he's a Roman citizen—
the history of the fraternal twin churches. I find I cannot shake the fantasy
that an oval dome (the eye, according to this paradigm) placed cunningly
beside a round dome (in my analogy, the coin) somehow passed through
the borders of the latter, as if some living viral organism through cell walls.

But then before my very eyes it has become the Hadrianic *oculus* again. Whereas the Pantheon will chart the motion of celestial bodies, the well's ostensibly more prosaic hole will chart the motion of a *human* body falling through it, open-eyed. Perhaps *my* body, *my* eye.

I feel as if I'm looking through as well as into; as if she whom both Paolo and I have gazed at greedily, she whom according to legend, everyone eyes, has made for me—or us—some kind of Imax Theater experience. Upon a single scribbled page, she has placed this dangerous, seductive hoop for me to leap through, at a speed no parachute could ever moderate, a speed perhaps vertiginous enough to cause the loss of consciousness. I try to translate some of these impressions—and emotions—into speech, without considerable success, for Paolo raises his eyebrows in a different way than when he first observed her image. Not *oo la la!* but *ah, come on!*

If these were your direct perceptions, Paolo, you would likely not dismiss them; nor would you probably be alarmed; you are young and resilient. You know your place; you know your state. But a middle-aged man, already globally unmoored, should probably consider such sensations harbingers of crisis: detached retinas, partial strokes, or some such other blow of fate—somatically, not metaphysically, delivered. (It might be worse; it might not be subjective: some apocalyptic foreshadowing.)

Yet on the other hand, the skeptic may be right. Perhaps this eye of mine, which peers at text all day, assaulted—or enlightened—by her *trompe l'oeil* drawing, is still playing tricks on me; for when I finally look up, I think I see her in the distance for a moment, walking toward the bus top, satchel over shoulder, book in hand, possibly turning around once to wink at me.

To determine if this mirage is truly optical illusion, I stop yammering, which I've been doing all this while in English, out of habit, thanks to spending time with Liza. This must have been the catalyst for Paolo's bemusement—that, along with my addressing him by what may be far from his given name, i.e., a name given him only by myself. I settle the bill, almost forgetting to retrieve the other photographs from him, and race up the stairs.

The trophy key is in the door and the latter ajar. The apartment appears ransacked, if such an act can be performed in a meticulous, almost obsessive fashion—for rather eerily, the entire holdings of my library are placed in pairs, spooned each inside the other, French, Italian, English, German, Spanish, Japanese, etc., beasts with two backs—I mean flaps, I mean jackets—though some are placed faceup. The print, meanwhile, perceived without my reading glasses, is all ablur, swimming toward me (or away) as I try to gain more fruitful vantage. The floating lines of text seem truly to be propagating. I raise my eyes lest I become unsteady on my feet, and see the wooden laundry rack is folded up against the wall. The translucent ivory-hued *sottoveste* seems to have evaporated.

What's more, the Knights of Malta postcard is promiscuously dupli-cated. She must at some point have purchased multiples of that single card as they are propped against the ledge, dominoed to create a *mise-en-abime:* a million mirrored San Pietros through a million tiny holes, meant to have been pointing, I suppose, toward the burlesque protruding key, the door of which reminds me that I've been distracted from my mission—to reveal Liza. I check the bedroom, bathroom, kitchen, closet, to make sure she isn't playing hide-and-seek. And then I find her. Through the only window of my flat that gives onto the street, she is indeed visible—as if the very sky around her were defined by her contours—walking, satchel over shoulder, book in hand, about, it would appear, to board the bus.

COLOPHON

All Fall Down was designed at Coffee House Press,
in the historic Grain Belt Brewery's Bottling House near downtown Minneapolis.
The text is set in Garamond.

FUNDER ACKNOWLEDGMENTS

Coffee House Press is an independent nonprofit literary publisher. Our books are made possible through the generous support of grants and gifts from many foundations, corporate giving programs, state and federal support, and through donations from individuals who believe in the transformational power of literature. This book was made possible, in part, through a special project grant from the National Endowment for the Arts, a federal agency. Coffee House receives major general operating support from the McKnight Foundation, the Bush Foundation, from Target, and from the Minnesota State Arts Board, through an appropriation by the Minnesota State Legislature and from the National Endowment for the Arts. Coffee House also receives support from: three anonymous donors; the Elmer L. and Eleanor J. Andersen Foundation; Bill Berkson; the James L. and Nancy J. Bildner Foundation; the Patrick and Aimee Butler Family Foundation; the Buuck Family Foundation; the law firm of Fredrikson & Byron, PA.; Jennifer Haugh; Anselm Hollo and Jane Dalrymple-Hollo; Jeffrey Hom; Stephen and Isabel Keating; Robert and Margaret Kinney; the Kenneth Koch Literary Estate; Allan & Cinda Kornblum; Seymour Kornblum and Gerry Lauter; the Lenfestey Family Foundation; Ethan J. Litman; Mary McDermid; Rebecca Rand; the law firm of Schwegman, Lundberg, Woessner, PA.; Charles Steffey and Suzannah Martin; John Sjoberg; Jeffrey Sugerman; Stu Wilson and Mel Barker; the Archie D. & Bertha H. Walker Foundation; the Woessner Freeman Family Foundation; the Wood-Rill Foundation; and many other generous individual donors.

This activity is made possible
in part by a grant from the
Minnesota State Arts Board,
through an appropriation by the
Minnesota State Legislature
and a grant from the National
Endowment for the Arts.

NATIONAL
ENDOWMENT
FOR THE ARTS

MINNESOTA
STATE ARTS BOARD

TARGET.

To you and our many readers across the country,
we send our thanks for your continuing support.

Good books are brewing at coffeehousepress.org